This Life
by
Shakara Cannon

Publisher's Note

This is a work of fiction. Any resemblance to actual persons – living or dead – references to real people, events, songs, business establishments or locales is purely coincidental. All characters are fictional, all events are imaginative.

This is Life

* * * * *

Published by Infinite Source Publishing
www.infinitesourcepublishing.com

Visit Shakara Cannon at www.shakaracannon.com
Email questions to shakara@shakaracannon.com

Library of Congress Control Number: 2013907971
ISBN 978-0-9835748-6-6

Acknowledgments

First, I must always thank God for giving me this gift and an outlet to share it with you all. To my mother, Carolyn Sharp, I don't know what I'd do without you. I couldn't ask for a better mommy! To my grandparents Tiny and Slim, thank you for always having my back. To my beautiful sister, Deya, I'm so blessed to have you as a sister and a best friend. I love you! To my sister Stephanie Murray Thompson, thank you for spreading the word and supporting me. To my cousin Taaj Higgins, thanks for always being excited about reading what I write. Cousin Misty Ivory, I thank you for encouraging me and always being eager to read my work and tell me to start over. (haha) Your honesty means so much to me. To my aunts Wanda Sharp, Sheila Sharp-Daniels, Sonja Sharp, Yolanda Sharp-Smith and DeAnn Sharp, thanks for always supporting me and spreading the word about my books! I love you guys so much! To my uncle Ray Sharp; you spoke the loudest and sold lots of copies of This Can't be Life and I love you even more for that! Thank you! If I've missed anyone, please know without a doubt that I thank you, appreciate your support and love you as well!

I'd like to send a special thank you to Lisa Mahon, Queen Brown, Derek Jordan, Melody Vernor-Bartel, Tina Nance (thanks so much for being the great editor you are!), Apostle Heloise Sulyans Gibson, Shaun Baylor...I'm sure I've forgotten someone and if it's you, I'm so very sorry and know that I thank you as well!

Last, but never least, to the wonderful people who read my books; I couldn't do this without you. Your support of my first novel and now the second is truly humbling and such a blessing. Thank you to those of you who have reached out to me via email, Twitter, Facebook, Instagram and to those of you who have left reviews; I love reading your thoughts on the stories I put so much of myself into. I'm grateful that you enjoy what I write. I'm definitely looking forward to hearing what you think of my next novel, The Great Pretender!

Shakara

Prologue
Simone

I was sorry for the pain it caused, not sorry for taking my life, I remember thinking before warmth and familiarity overtook me as a bright beam of light shone down and enveloped me. As I wafted deeper and deeper into the luminescence that covered me like a warm, soft down comforter, I felt weightless and free, welcomed and loved. Time stood still as I floated peacefully in the glow of the light. I knew I was in the right place, and wanted to stay there forever. As if short circuiting, pictures flashed before my eyes. It was reminiscent of watching an old grainy flash film. It was my life; mostly my father and I playing while I was only a little girl, then Stacey streamed through clearly.

"Oh my Lord! Do you have a pressin' comb I can borrow? I test in an hour, and I left the three I have at home! Who does that?" My classmate, Stacey, rushed over and asked me in a panic. We were three weeks into our classes at The Paul Mitchell School, but this was our first time exchanging more than a hello.

"Of course I have a pressing comb. I have a few. I'll let you borrow them all if you can help me out too." His creamy peanut butter complexion, large puppy dog eyes, and most importantly, his beautiful black mane of thick curly hair that I noticed was always pulled back in a bun was just what I needed.

"I'll do just about anything except date your sister. Although I know she'd probably be pretty, 'cause you sure are, I just don't do women. Anything aside from that, I'm in. What do you need?" He asked in one breath.

Laughing, I replied, "My model just canceled on me at the last minute and I can't miss this test. You have all that pretty hair. Please be my model! I promise, I won't mess up your hair. I only have to do a trim, no real cutting." I held my breath awaiting his reply.

"Oh that's all? Girl, yes! Consider me your model. I know you won't mess my hair up because I'd make you suffer every day for the rest of the semester. No pressure." He chuckled before strutting off toward his station.

Flash after flash, memories of my best friend, Stacey, played before my eyes like a movie. Then, all went dark, and different memories began flooding in. Memories that I'd rather not have! I was powerless against these images that played over and over in my head, taunting and mocking me. I wondered where the warm bright light went. I wanted the good comforting memories back. I wanted to see my father again. I wanted to see Stacey's smile and hear his laugh, but all that played before my eyes was everything I wanted to forget. It was everything that caused me pain.

I could actually feel the cold marble floor under my knees as I crawled into my bathroom. I felt the cool tap water from the bathroom faucet trickle down my throat as I swallowed every Xanax pill in the full bottle. I felt the comfort of the fluffy down comforter and Egyptian cotton sheets against my skin as I waited for death to take me.

In a flash, all went dark again. This time, there were no memories; there were no pictures flashing before me, good or bad. I seemed to be stuck in some state of oblivion.

Am I dead? Time stood still, and nothingness surrounded me. All was quiet, aside from my thoughts, which were extremely muddled. I don't know how much time had passed before I began to hear a gradual beeping, but it seemed like an eternity. The beeping was becoming more and more pronounced as my head began to clear. Then I heard faint voices.

"Simone, open your eyes, baby. Please open your eyes."

I was slowly coming to, and began to feel my limbs. I first wiggled my toes, and then I moved my fingers, realizing that both of my hands were being held.

"She's waking up," I heard my mother say.

Am I dreaming? I tried to fight my way to consciousness. The beeping was becoming louder, and the voices clearer as I struggled to open my eyes.

"I'm going to get the doctor and let Talise know that she is waking up." I recognized Mommy Miles' voice and felt someone release my hand. I could hear footsteps clearly as I continued the struggle to open my eyes.

"Simone, wake up baby. It's your mom, honey. Open your eyes. You can do it, sweetie," she encouraged softly, rubbing my hand.

When I finally succeeded in opening my eyes, the first thing I noticed was the horribly bright incandescent lights above where I lay. The unnatural yellow rays burned my eyes the more I focused. I looked around at the pale green walls and the two large windows with the bright sun shining through. I looked down at my hands and to the side of my bed, noticing that I was hooked to a machine, and had an IV in my arm. It then became clear; I was in the hospital and my suicide attempt had obviously failed. I was immediately filled with dread, and felt tears flood my eyes.

Someone found me. Someone fucked up and saved my life! I closed my eyes and felt tears stream down my face.

"It's okay, baby. Everything is going to be okay." My mother, Darlene, wiped tears from my face. I had yet to look at her. I didn't want to see the disappointment on her face. I didn't want to see the worry in her eyes, so I closed mine.

The plan was to be free of this pain! No one crossed my mind as I swallowed pill after pill, knowing for sure, that after I got back in bed and went to sleep, I wouldn't be waking ever again. The pain was much too great to think of anything but *it*. Plus, I wasn't supposed to be here to deal with the consequences of my actions.

"I'm sorry," I said, finally looking into her puffy, red eyes.

"Here baby, have some water. Don't talk." She raised my bed slightly so that I would be upright. I took a sip of the cool, refreshing liquid when she lifted the cup to my mouth, but couldn't drink much more, because my throat was so raw it hurt to swallow.

"Thank you," I whispered and closed my eyes again. I couldn't bear to look at her. I knew she wanted to ask me why, but I wasn't ready to answer that question.

"Thank you, Jesus!" Mommy Miles said as she walked back into the hospital room followed by the doctor, Talise, and Daddy Miles.

"Oh Simone, baby, I'm so happy you are okay," Daddy Miles said. All, aside from Talise, were surrounding my bed wiping tears from their eyes as the doctor checked my vital signs. I could tell they'd been sick with worry.

"Can I talk to Simone alone, please?" Talise asked once the doctor had left the room. Her eyes were puffy and her face was swollen, along with her belly. She was eight months pregnant with my godchild. As soon as my eyes reached hers, I felt my first pang of guilt. Tears flooded my eyes and slid down my face.

"I can't believe you did that, Simone," she said after everyone had left the room. "I can't believe you'd do this shit! How could you want to kill yourself? After Stacey...after everything that has gone on! What in the hell was I supposed to do if you died, or lived and was unable to take care of yourself?"

Tears rushed down my face. I didn't know what to say because she was right. I didn't think about anyone but myself. At that moment, I didn't care. Now the enormity of what could have been, had my suicide attempt left me unable to care for myself, or if I had actually succeeded, was overwhelming.

"You aren't that weak, Simone! You've been through hell and back, and you are going to let *him* take away your will to live? What about us? What about the people who should matter? The people who love you and can't imagine life without you? What about us?" She sat down on the bed and began crying convulsively.

I scooted to her and wrapped my arms around her as much as I could without unhooking myself from the IV.

"Talise, I've never been in such a dark place in my life. With all that has gone on, I couldn't deal with it anymore. I still don't know if I can! It's not just Carlton, it's everything! How much more am I expected to take, Talise? I am only one person and I can't hold all this shit on my own. It's just too much! Every time I close my eyes, I see them. I see Stacey's face, Carlton, Tyron... Marie telling me that she never loved me. Every damn day there is something else! Just when I thought one part of my life was right, that shit crumbled alongside everything else. I just couldn't take it anymore. I'm not as strong as you think I am, Talise. I'm tired! I'm so damn tired!" I cried.

"You have to promise me that you won't do this again, Simone. I can't take any more! I can't lose another friend!" She said, looking at me intently, pleadingly.

"Talise, I'm sorry. I couldn't think of anything else but stopping the pain. It hurts too much. I just don't know what to do or how much more I can take. My whole life is a lie. The only truth is you and your family. I don't have shit. Everything I thought to be true was a lie. My family, the man I love..."

"You do have something, Simone," she began, cutting me off. "You have people who love you! You have your real mom now and she loves you to death. She has always loved you. You have so much to live for, but you can't see past all the bad. I can't pretend that I know what everything you've gone through feels like, but I do know what love feels like and you have so much of it, Simone. My parents and I love you no differently than if you were blood. They raised you as my sister, and never treated you any differently than they treated me. Dad and mom have been here since I called and told them what happened. Darlene has been here since I called her. None of us have left this hospital since you got here!" I couldn't do anything but cry because she was right. "*This* is unconditional love, Simone. *This* is the kind of love that matters. That other love may come and go, but *this* is what you hold on to. You do have family, and it doesn't matter if we have the same blood or not!"

"I don't know if I can deal with this, Talise! Why would he do this to me? Do you think it was all a game? He probably never even really loved me! I'm just *so* hurt. I don't know what to think. I'm so confused. Do you think he had something to do with Stacey's murder? What am I supposed to think after seeing that video? This is just too much!" The words seemed to fall out of my mouth uncontrollably.

"I truly believe he loved you, Simone. I'm sure he still does. Yes he... cheated, but I don't believe that means he doesn't love you. I just think he's... confused," she said, searching for the right words.

I couldn't do anything but shake my head to try to clear the images that I saw on that video from my mind. I don't think that I will ever be free of it. No one should ever have to see the person they love having sex with someone else.

"And no, I don't think he had anything to do with Stacey's death. I really feel that he didn't. He's been here, Simone," Talise said after a long pause. "You're going to have to talk to him, you know that, right?" She asked softly.

There was no way I could hear his voice, let alone see his face any time soon. "I can't, Talise. I don't want to see him ever again. He's not who I thought he was. He's a damn liar, a fraud!" No matter how much my mind hated Carlton, my heart was not getting the memo. It pained me to think of life without him.

"I know, Simone, but..."

"How did I get here? Who found me?" I asked, cutting her off.

"Carlton brought you here. He saved your life, Simone."

"Well, he's going to wish he would've let me die. I don't

want him here and I won't take any calls from him, Talise. He's going to regret the day he saved me."

~ ~ ~ ~ ~ ~

"Ma'am, do you have any idea who would want to do something like this, to you? This isn't a random break-in," the detective asked me as we stood in the dining room of my ransacked home while two uniformed cops walked around inspecting every inch of it.

"No, I don't," I lied.

"Can you tell if there is anything missing, Ms. Johnson?" The pretty detective inquired.

"No, there doesn't seem to be anything missing, Detective. I searched around after I called you guys. My paintings are here, my jewelry, expensive handbags, my house is just trashed." I sighed, looking around at all of the destruction.

"If there is nothing missing, they were looking for something specific, Ms. Johnson. Do you know what they were looking for?" she asked, looking at me suspiciously.

Yes, I know what they were looking for, but thankfully, they were too dumb to look in the damn DVD player. If they had, they would have found what I'm sure they'd come for.

"I don't know what they could have been looking for," I answered, apathetically.

"You're on the fifteenth floor, Simone. What would make someone bypass all fourteen other floors and come here? Something isn't right about this, Detective. You're right," my mother, Darlene, chimed in. Worry was painted all over her pretty face.

"Ms. Johnson, you have to know something. There has to be something you aren't telling us. There are no obvious signs of a break-in. Who has a key to your home?"

"No one does. I've been in the hospital. Maybe the paramedics left my door unlocked after they came and got me," I offered numbly. That could definitely be a possibility, but I knew that Carlton had a key and that it was most likely someone he and Tyron had sent to find that video. He was the only one who knew I wouldn't be right back home.

"You don't seem too bothered by any of this, Ms. Johnson."

"Detective, I'm just getting home after spending a week in the hospital, and three days in a psych ward. I'm heavily medicated," I admitted honestly. The strong antidepressants I was prescribed made me feel emotionless and numb. I knew I wouldn't continue taking them.

"So, no one has been here since you were hospitalized?"

"Well evidently, someone has," I said flippantly.

"Let me rephrase that. No one that you know of has been here since you were hospitalized a week ago?" she asked aloofly.

"No, Detective."

"Does this building have camera surveillance?"

"Only in the garage."

"To be honest with you, there really isn't much to investigate here, Ms. Johnson. Nothing is missing. There are no obvious signs of a break-in..."

"What about the property damage?" My mom broke in incredulously. "There's thousands of dollars' worth of damage to her personal property!"

"Do you have renters insurance?" she asked coolly. I could tell by the tone of her voice, and by the way she was looking at me, that she knew I was withholding information, and had ceased to care about my predicament.

"I have homeowners insurance..." I began before my mother cut me off.

"What does that have to do with catching the people who damaged her property, Detective?" My mother asked, her voice rising with each word.

"Ms. Johnson, once you get a damage report from your insurance company, send it to me and I'll be sure to list the damage amount on your report," she said, not answering my mother's question. "In the meantime, you shouldn't stay here until you are able to get your locks changed."

~ ~ ~ ~ ~ ~

"Simone, do you know who did this? What were they looking for?" My mother asked after the police had finished their investigation and left. They didn't bother to fingerprint, even though my house was completely trashed. My sofas were slashed; my bed, dresser and chest were turned over. My clothes, shoes and the paperwork in my office was scattered everywhere. All of my flat screens were torn off of the wall and lay on the floor with busted screens. I'd never seen anything like this.

"Yes, I know what they were looking for, but they didn't find it. Please don't ask what, Mom," I sighed, sitting down in one of the dining room chairs that was left untouched by the intruders.

"Then you don't need to stay here, Simone!" My mom said, pacing around the rectangular, glass six-seat table. "You can't stay here!" She repeated.

I got up, went to my mother, and hugged her, attempting to calm her nerves. My mind was so cloudy I could barely comprehend the extent of the damage that had been done to my home. I knew I'd have to get a professional crew in here to clean things up and replace my damaged belongings.

"Mom, they only came because they knew I wasn't here. I'll get the locks changed and have a security company come in and set up an alarm system. I'll leave until everything has been cleaned up and replaced, but I'm not moving from my home. They won't come back. Please try not to worry."

"How can I not worry? Look what someone did to your house, Simone! Look at what you tried to do to yourself! What in the world is going on here?" She asked, holding each of my arms above the elbow and looking me squarely in the eyes.

I couldn't tell her what was really going on. I knew that would only make her more concerned and sick with worry.

"I'm sorry, Mom. It's better that you don't know. Just know this. They didn't find what they were looking for. As long as I have what they want, I'm safe."

Chapter One
Deon

"You don't have to go home, but you can't stay here," I said to the beautiful woman lying next to me. She'd just finished riding me like a jockey on a race horse, but it wasn't enough for me to want her to spend the night in my bed. What could we possibly talk about in the morning?

"But why, Deon? Didn't I please you?" The long legged air head supermodel stretched her long limbs in my king sized bed, her skin glistening with the sweat we'd created. With the only light coming from the city view, and the full moon that shone through the floor to ceiling windows, which held no coverings, she looked flawless lying next to me nude.

"You would've been gone a long time ago if you didn't please me." I got up from the bed and walked across the soft Berber carpet, into the bathroom, closing the door behind me.

I turned on the shower jets that were placed at a height

that my six foot seven frame would have the powerful stream of water hitting every exposed part of my body, and stepped in. With the hot water pounding my skin, I closed my eyes and let my mind drift to when I met Ashia and decided to bring her home with me a few hours ago.

~ ~ ~ ~ ~ ~

When I walked into Katana on Sunset, the first face I saw was Simone Johnson's—the woman who could've had my heart, but chose a dumb ass rapper instead. Of course, all eyes were on me, so I pulled my baseball cap lower on my head—never caring for being the center of attention—and spotted who I was looking for.

"What's up, man?" I asked as I walked up to my seven-foot teammate, Armond Jackson. He was standing near the bar, flanked by two of his boys. I gave them all a pound before surveying the room. We blew out the Houston Rockets earlier that day and were out to celebrate.

"These fine ass women in here, that's what's up!" he replied, almost yelling.

No matter where Armond went, people stopped and stared. It was obvious that he was on someone's basketball team. Not only because he was so tall, but more so because of the way he carried himself. It was evident that he loved attention, which is why everything he says is always louder than necessary. With his caramel colored skin, crooked nose, and slanted teeth, he would have to be a million dollar man in any professional league to pull even the most average looking woman.

"What's up with the table, man?" I asked Armond.

"They're moving someone from MY table right now," he said loudly. "Or you know this would be my last time in this bitch," he finished even louder as I felt someone tap me on my back.

I turned around, expecting to see Simone, but instead, an angry woman whose name I couldn't remember stared up at me.

"Hey what's up?" I asked, feeling slightly embarrassed for taking the girl home and never calling or thinking about her again.

She was a petite woman who couldn't have been taller than 5'2". Her skin tone was a milky caramel, which complimented her light brown eyes and thick sandy brown hair that hung in tight curls down her back.

"What's up? You tell me what's up, Deon. You haven't called," she said with her hand on her hip, a slight roll to her neck and her girl giving me the evil eye at her side.

"Oh... did I say I was going to call?" I asked, not intending to sound like the asshole she'd already pegged me to be. This was a legitimate question.

"No, but damn, what's up with that?" I could tell she was getting angrier by the minute. I'm not into scenes, so if she wanted one, she was going to have to look elsewhere.

"What's up with what? I gave you what you wanted and you gave me what I wanted. Now I owe you something? I thought we were even," I said in an even tone as Armond and his crew laughed behind me, which was definitely not my intention.

"Even? You call that even? Or do you take that many women home that you can't remember what went down?" She had me there. I couldn't remember what went down, but I figured if I took her home, I'm sure I had sex with her.

"Yeah, I remember what went down." I was trying my hardest to remember, but it just wasn't coming back to me fast enough.

"Well, if you remember, you should know we have

unfinished business," she said, sassily putting her hand on her hip and batting her eyelashes, all traces of anger gone from her pretty face.

"No, I'm good," I said, remembering exactly at that moment the night I allowed her to come home with me.

Shauna was her name. I was enjoying myself at a private beach party with about twenty other people as we sat around a large bonfire on Zuma beach. The night air was a bit breezy for it to have been 103 a few hours before, so people were bundling up in hoodies and grabbing blankets from their cars. Music played in the background as everyone talked and sipped on drinks. The waves were loudly crashing against the shore as the tide began to come in.

Shauna caught my eye a few times. She was outgoing and smiled easily. When she finally made her way to where I was sitting, she kept my attention with her light conversation and cute laugh. As the night went on, we continued to sip and talk. I was enjoying her company and didn't want her to leave when her friend, who had driven them both there, was ready to leave. I offered her a ride home and she accepted. Before the night was over, we'd gotten close and shared a blanket. She seemed cool, and I was digging her style. She was sexy, confident, and beautiful.

On the ride home, she surprised me by wrapping her full, luscious, Meagan Good lips around my dick as I drove up Pacific Coast Highway. The plan was to take her home, but when things got a little heated, I suggested we finish the night at my place. I was definitely digging her, so as soon as I got her in my room, I immediately laid her across my bed to finish what she'd started in the car.

My dick was so hard that it could have snapped in two. I was ready to give it to her until she opened her legs and emitted an odor that would make a sanitation worker gag. I was surprised that I'd forgotten her. As soon as I smelled her, my dick went soft. The putrid smell hit my nose so fast that she had to have smelled it too. There was nothing I could do. My dick would not get hard again after that and I now see that she had no idea why.

"So, I suck your dick, and when it's time to fuck, you go limp. And you say we don't have unfinished business? What, are you gay?" She asked loudly, attempting to put all of our business out there for everyone in the area of the restaurant to hear. She really didn't have a clue, I thought, looking at her face twisted in anger.

"I'm not going there with you because I don't want to embarrass you in front of all of these people. I'll at least give you that courtesy. Now please, leave me to my night." I waved my hand, trying to shoo them off.

"No, tell me! I'm a grown ass woman. Tell me why your dick went limp with this pussy ready for it!" She practically yelled, tapping her rotten coochie with her right hand.

"Come here," I said through clenched teeth, trying to remain calm. I was losing the little bit of patience I had as she slowly took the few steps to get closer to me. I bent down and whispered in her ear, "Your pussy stinks. It smells really, really bad. You need to go see a doctor about that shit. A woman should never ever smell like that, Shauna. Now please, don't ever try to front on me again or I'll embarrass you." I turned around just in time to catch the tail end of whatever it was that Armond was talking about.

"Go on now. Ya'll can go!" Armond said to Shauna and her friend after it looked like they were in no hurry to leave, although a couple of minutes had passed.

I looked over my shoulder to see them still standing right

behind me. Shauna was in the same spot I'd left her in with tears in her eyes. They finally turned and quickly walked out of the restaurant.

"Hey, D, what you tell her?" One of Armond's friends asked.

"Man, that's why I whispered the shit; I don't want to put the girls business out there like that."

"She didn't care about putting your business out there like that," Armond's other boy said laughing.

"What she said means nothing to me." I dismissed Armond's flunky friend, and without any regard to who was watching, stared at Simone as she sat at the other end of the bar laughing with a dark skinned bald headed man.

"Sorry for the wait, gentlemen. Your table is ready," the hostess said.

We followed her to the outside patio where the weather was at least in the mid-seventies.

"Your waitress will be right with you," she said, attempting to leave after we had all sat down.

"Aye look, bring me two bottles of Cristal; I ain't waiting for no waitress. I already had to wait for my damn table," Armond said before shooing her off with a wave of his right hand.

As I sat there, my mind kept wondering back to Simone and the fact that she was sitting in the next room. I knew I had to speak to her. It had been almost a year since I'd seen her. I excused myself from the table and walked toward the bar.

"Excuse me," I interrupted after walking up to her from behind. "Simone, long time no see," I smiled as she got up and hugged me.

"Deon Bradford, it's good to see you. How are you?" she asked.

"I'm good. How are you, Simone? Still beautiful I see."

"Thanks. I've been okay. Taking it one day at a time," she said, smiling up at me. "Deon, this is my friend, Nicco. Nicco, this is Deon," she said, introducing me to the man she had been laughing with.

"Hey man, nice to meet you," I said shaking his limp hand.

"Same here, same here," he said with a smirk on his face.

"How's your family doing? I bet Tyson is getting big," Simone asked with a smile on her face that didn't quite reach her eyes. Looking into them, I could tell that she wasn't happy. I could sense it as I always could when I was around her. Something beyond me had me connected to this woman in ways that I've never felt connected to anyone before.

"Everyone is good. Tyson is definitely getting bigger every time I see him. He asks about you all the time. How's Talise and Stacey?" I said, asking about her best friends.

"Talise is married now and they have a baby girl and… and Stacey passed away some months ago," she said, looking away.

"Damn, Simone, I'm sorry to hear that." I didn't know what else to say and wouldn't be rude enough to ask her what happened in this setting. I knew how close she was to Stacey. I didn't have to imagine what she was going through. When my best friend was killed, Simone was there for me. I didn't know which way was up or down, but she stepped up and looked out for me and my best friends' son, Tyson, until my parents got in from Atlanta. Although I didn't deserve her kindness after what I'd done to her, she showed me that she was my friend aside from it all.

"I'll make it. Looks like there really is no other choice, you know?"

"Yeah, no matter what, we have to keep living. That's what he'd want you to do. So, Simone, what else has been up?" I asked, wanting to change the subject. "Did you ever re-open your salon?"

"No, no more doing hair for me. I'm just trying to make it day by day to be honest with you. A lot has gone on in my life. I'm sure you thought I was complicated before... it's only gotten worse." She laughed, but I could tell she wasn't joking.

"That's understandable. Losing a friend is a life changing thing. Plus, I'm sure you will always be complicated, Simone," I teased. "So what are you doing for work? What are you doing with your time?"

"Nothing more than just trying to pass it to be honest with you. I have no goals, no aspirations... I'm just floating," she said with an ironic laugh. I always loved her honesty; she never fronted for anyone.

"You should let me help you pass some of that time. Hang out with me for old time sake. It could be fun," I said, surprising myself. I don't know where that came from.

"Hang out and do what? You know your reputation precedes you, now don't you, Deon?" She laughed.

"I have no idea what you're talking about, Simone. You know I'm harmless." I feigned ignorance, but she was right. I was nothing like the man I was when we dated. I killed the old Deon out of necessity.

"Yeah okay," she laughed. "Let's just keep things how they are and I'll see you when I see you," she said without a second thought. The look in her eyes told me that she hadn't forgotten nor forgiven me for what I'd done to her.

"Damn, like that huh? Okay, I understand. Well take care, Simone, and again, sorry to hear about Stacey," I said and walked off. I was over chasing her. If that's how she feels, *then fuck it! I headed back to the table, feeling like I felt the night before my best friend was murdered—I needed a drink.*

I sat back down with Armond and his boys, but my mood was thrown off. Between my run in with Shauna and then talking to Simone, I really didn't feel like being there anymore and I sure as hell wasn't going home alone. I poured myself a glass of champagne and looked around at the people sitting near us—that's when I noticed her; I recognized her face from the most recent Sports Illustrated Swimsuit Edition. I remembered her being a bit thinner than I preferred, but still curvy with nice sized breasts. I wondered how easy it would be to get her home with me. I was always up for a challenge and figured it wouldn't be that difficult when less than ten minutes passed before she was standing at our table with her friend.

Her honey colored skin had a golden glow. It looked soft and smooth, without a blemish in sight. She had on a hot pink, silky, mid-thigh length summer dress that tied around her waist; I knew it would be easy to take off. Her hair was cut short and looked good with the shape of her face and her long neck. She was beautiful, but I was in L.A., the city where pretty women come a dime a dozen, so of course I wasn't pressed. I sat back and waited for her to let her intention be known, like they always do.

"Hey guys. Good game tonight. I'm Ashia. This is my friend, Blanca. Can we join you?" She asked, looking straight at me. She was bold, yet confident, which didn't surprise me. Models never seemed to lack confidence. They knew they were fine, and knew you knew it too.

"Hell yeah! You! Come sit right here!" Armond yelled, pointing at Ashia. She looked at me, pleading with her eyes

for a way out. "Come on, I won't bite... yet!" Armond hollered before laughing loudly and startling the ladies.

"I'll sit here," Blanca stated before sliding in next to me like that was what she wanted to do all along. I could tell Ashia was pissed as she sat next to Armond, looking rigid in her seat.

"Where ya'll from?" One of Armond's boys asked. He was pretty short for a man, and his girth didn't help elongate him one bit. He was as round as he was short and reminded me of a little Oompa Loompa from Willy Wonka & the Chocolate Factory. He and Armond were an odd pairing.

"I'm from Argentina," Blanca said with a slight accent. Her olive toned skin was complimented by her thick, black mane of hair that cascaded down her back and hung right above her low rise jeans. She had on an almost sheer, red, silk-like shirt with thin spaghetti straps that kept sliding down one shoulder or the other. She was sans a bra, but her breasts weren't completely on display. Only the shape and perkiness of them could be seen through her shirt, which did a good job of leaving a little something to the imagination.

Ashia and Blanca both stood about six feet and gave each other a run for their money in the looks department.

"And you? Where you from?" Armond asked Ashia.

"Somalia," she answered brusquely.

"Know any pirates?" Armond asked before he and his boys fell out laughing. "Them muhfuckas out there jackin' ships out the sea an' shit dawg! Holding niggas for ransom! That shit be all on the news! No, for real, you know any pirates?" He continued to laugh.

"No!" Ashia replied curtly. I could tell she was pissed off. Gone was the pleasant smile and demeanor that she had when they first approached our table.

"Where are you from?" Blanca asked me.

"Everywhere," I stated, completely unenthused. My mood was shot and it was going to take more than idle conversation to change it.

"Oh really? Let me guess. Are you from... California?" She whispered seductively in my ear, blowing hot shallow breaths that made the hair on my neck stand up.

"No, guess again," I said with a smirk on my face while I stared at Ashia. She was getting more and more agitated by the minute.

"I'd like a drink. Can you please pour me a drink?" Ashia said more than asked Armond.

I could tell he was digging her. Although he was a professional athlete
with millions, she was still out of his league and he knew it.

"Okay, how about... New York?" She whispered in my ear, this time her lip grazed my lobe slightly.

"Still no," I said, becoming amused; more so by her friend being pissed off, than by her whispering in my ear. They both wanted it. Ashia didn't want to share, but I had a feeling that Blanca wouldn't mind.

Ashia took a sip from her champagne flute and continued to watch Blanca scoot closer and closer to me while Armond and his boys held a conversation about something insignificant. They were oblivious to this tug of war I was in.

"Okay, well I'm going to keep guessing until I get it. Are you from... Washington?" She whispered in my ear, sliding her wet tongue against the lobe as she slowly pulled away. By this time, her hand was rubbing my thigh and the champagne was kicking in.

"He's from Georgia okay, Blanca?" Ashia stated exasperatedly, looking back and forth between the two of us.

"Stop with the games already!" She huffed, running her fingers through her short hair then down her long neck. She was sexy as hell, and this little jealousy shtick was surprisingly cute.

"Yes, exactly. I'm from Georgia. How do you know that?" I asked. I wasn't surprised that she knew, I was just surprised that she didn't pretend that she didn't know. There was no shame in Ashia's game.

"Because I know who you are, Deon Bradford. I've wanted to run into you for some time now," she said with a smile, looking at me seductively.

"Oh is that right? Well, here I am. You ran into me, now what?" I asked, finishing off the last of the liquid in my champagne flute while Blanca sat extremely close to me, still rubbing my leg, looking back and forth between Ashia and me.

Finally, Armond and his boys caught on to what was going on and were waiting to see what Ashia's response would be.

"I can show you better than I can tell you," she stated, finishing off
her half-filled glass of champagne in one swallow and rising from her seat. "Can I show you?" She asked, standing there ready for me to take her home.

"Well I'll be got damned!" Armond roared laughing. "This nigga here always pulls the baddest bitches!" He laughed as Ashia gave him the evil eye for calling her a bitch.

"I'll be that bitch as long as you are taking me home." Blanca slid out of the booth and I followed right behind her.

"I'm staying with the guys. You don't mind, do you?" Blanca asked Armond as she slid in next to him.

"Hell naw! You good right here!"

"Alright man, I'll catch up with you later." I gave Armond and his boys a pound and headed out of the restaurant with Ashia.

It was always too easy. I'm sure we were at my place and in my bed by the time Armond and his crew's dinner was served.

Chapter Two
C. Banks

Bossip: Blind Item
Which Hip Hop Music Mogul Has A GAY Sex Tape
With Someone Very Close In His Camp?
A source close to Bossip has revealed that a certain powerful
music exec isn't the heterosexual man we thought him to
be. We've heard from a very trusted source that this
powerful man was caught on video getting boinked by a
man... a very famous man that every woman would be
heartbroken to discover is gay. We wonder if his famous
crooning girlfriend knows he takes it up the wahzoo? Oh,
it's about to get ugly!
Stay tuned for more, because trust, there is more to come!

"Yo, what is this? Is there something you need to
tell me, Ty?" I whispered loudly as I paced back
in forth in front of my business partner, Tyron Marks' desk.
I had just busted into his office and handed him my iPhone
so he could read the latest blind item on a popular celebrity

blog site, bossip.com. Call me paranoid, but something about this shit rubbed me the wrong way.

"Banks, yo, calm down, man," Tyron said, sitting behind his desk. "I've already seen this. Nobody will figure that shit out."

"What?" *No denial?* "Nobody will figure this out? Are you serious right now, B? What in the *fuck* do you mean by that?" I asked as I stood rigid in front of his desk. "Just answer me this," I said before he could answer the first question. I was so close to losing it that I had to take a minute before I spoke. "Is there a video of us?" I asked slowly.

"Banks, I'm trying to tell..."

"Just answer the question, Tyron! Yes or fucking no?" I yelled.

"Yeah, but..."

My fist connected with his head before I could even think twice about knocking his ass out. Tyron jumped up like he was gully, but thought better of it and sat back down.

"Banks, just sit down man and let me explain this shit," he said, trying to remain calm.

"Explain? Why is there a video of us and who has it? That's all I need to know!" My world was crumbling right in front of my eyes and I had to find a way to stop it.

"Just sit down, Banks. Do you for fucking one minute think that I'm not trippin' off this too? Come on man, you know me better than that. We have to stay level headed and get this ironed out," he said, trying to be the voice of reason.

I wanted to murder him!

"How can we get shit ironed out when you are just now telling me this? The last time we fucked around was almost a year ago! *What the fuck!*" I whispered.

"I thought I had it under control. I was gone fix this man, but... shit just went... wrong," he said, searching for the right words.

"What do you mean shit went wrong, Tryon? You need to tell me exactly what happened because right now, I'm feeling very homicidal."

I sat down in a chair in front of his desk and put my elbows on my parted knees and covered my face with my hands. I heard Tyron get up, and hoped he knew better than to come near me.

"I was dealing with this cat, and he snuck into my house the last time we fucked around, and he taped us."

I looked up at Tryon in disbelief.

"You gotta be shittin' me! Get the *fuck* outta here!" I couldn't believe this! "Where is this cat?"

"He's dead, B."

"Then if he's dead, who has the video, Ty?" I jumped up in a panic.

"Wait, just back the fuck up, I'm not understanding this. You're leaving something out," I said, sitting back down. I felt like I was in a nightmare.

"The muthafucka died before I was able to get the shit from him, Banks!"

"How did he die? You aren't telling me something!" I knew this guy well and could tell that he was leaving something out.

"I don't know. All I know is he was found dead in Vegas."

"Hold up. Vegas? What's this cat's name, man?" This shit just couldn't be.

"What you mean what's his..."

I was out of the chair with my hands wrapped around his neck before he even finished the question. "Bitch, you know what I mean! Tell me what I already know. Let me hear you say that shit," I said through clenched teeth. I was so angry my body was involuntarily shaking. I'd never felt this way before in my life.

"His name is, Stacey," he managed to say through the vice grip I had on his neck.

"Simone's friend, Stacey?" I asked sharply. I already knew the answer, but I tightened my hands around his neck and waited for his reply anyway.

"Yeah, let me go Banks," he pleaded. I released him and he dropped to the office floor gasping for air.

It all made sense now, I thought as I walked out of his office and past his assistant. I was so pissed off, I didn't notice anyone as I walked past offices and cubicles on my way to my office. I slammed the door shut once I got inside and began pacing in front of the floor to ceiling window. I didn't even look out at the Hollywood Hills as I usually did.

When Tyron told me that Stacey had the video, I knew without a doubt that Simone had it now. Why else would she tell me to never call her again, attempt suicide, and still refuse to accept my calls or let me come see her in the hospital, even though I'm the one who saved her life? This was the only logical explanation and it made sense; she knows. She's pissed off and has something much more dangerous than a loaded gun. She could ruin my whole world, and I'm sure she'd feel vindicated.

Chapter Three
Simone

Nothing felt better than having Carlton inside of me. His body on top of mine, his lips kissing my lips, his breath on my neck, his touch drove me crazy. As he moved in and out of me slowly, I was getting wetter and wetter. Bringing me to the brink of orgasm, he'd withdraw and go down to lick me slowly, sucking softly, making me cum in his mouth before he would re-enter me.

"This dick feel good to you, Simone?" he asked as he moved in and out of me.

"Yes, Carlton, please don't stop," I moaned, wrapping my arms around his waist and pulling him deeper into me.

"Whose pussy is this, Simone?" he asked, knowing it drove me crazy when he talked like this to me.

"It's yours, baby," I whispered, on the verge of a beautiful orgasm. "I love you, Carlton." I heard myself saying before the vibrations from my cellphone jolted me away from my wet dream.

Tears sprang to my eyes when I realized that it was all

just a dream. I wasn't in bed with Carlton. I was alone! I missed him so much that I literally hurt. Every day I cried because I missed him. It didn't get better; it got worse with each day that passed. I knew tomorrow I'd miss him more than I did today, which didn't make next week look very promising at all.

I don't think I can ever get over seeing him have sex with a man. Sometimes I wonder if I'd seen him on video with a woman, if I'd feel differently. If it were a woman that he was cheating on me with, would I still be with him? I asked myself this over and over again, but it doesn't matter, because it wasn't a woman. It was my best friends' boyfriend; the man that murdered him.

This thought made me cry even harder. My heart was aching for the loss of my friend and the loss of the man who gradually brought my guard down by loving me completely. I didn't know how to feel or what to think, because I still loved him. I still craved his touch and dreamed about him in some way almost every night.

Aside from it all, he was my friend! I missed talking to him. I missed hearing the phone ring first thing in the morning, knowing it's him. I missed his smell; I missed every single thing about that man. Having to let go of someone that you love more than you've ever loved someone before in your life is hard. I cried daily, as if I was mourning his death. I literally hurt and had to learn to live with the ache that no painkiller could ease.

My cell, which sat on the night table next to my bed, began to vibrate again, but I still did not intend to answer it. I didn't care who was on the other end of the line. The last thing I wanted to do was get on the phone and pretend that I was okay, that I was happy, when I wasn't. If they knew how I really felt, they'd worry even more. They had no idea how badly I wanted to die, but was afraid of failing again and being stuck here unable to take care of myself. I know it sounds selfish, but when you can't find many reasons to live, waking up every morning is like a bad ass joke. I had to keep these feelings and thoughts to myself because if I told my mom or Talise, or more importantly, my psychiatrist, Dr. Marge, they'd have me committed.

When the phone began vibrating for a third time, I figured I should answer it. Seeing Talise's number, I knew I had made the right decision. I've put my best friend through too much. The last thing she needs right now, along with all the stresses of being a new mom, is to have to worry about me.

"Hey, Tali," I said, trying to sound like I hadn't been crying.

"I was about to call your mom and track you down, Simone. You have to answer the phone when I call. I was worried that you, *you know?*"

"Talise, just because I don't answer the phone doesn't mean I've killed myself," I said incredulously. I knew I'd never be able to live this down, but understood her worry.

"Simone, you have to give me some time. I worry about you, so when you don't answer the phone, it scares me."

"It's eight thirty in the morning!" I couldn't help but laugh. There was no way I could be mad at her for fearing that I might try to kill myself again. It was a legitimate concern. "My mom is in the other room, Talise. As many times as she checks on me throughout the night, I don't think I'd have the privacy to try to kill myself again," I said facetiously.

I don't think she knew that I could hear her every time

she peaked in my room, but I could. I'd only had her in my life for close to a year now, and was still adjusting to her kindness and unconditional love. It was a far cry from the treatment I received from Marie.

"Good. She can check on you throughout the night and I'll be calling to make sure that you wake up every morning, so you need to answer the phone." I heard my goddaughter, Anastasia, cry in the background.

"What's wrong with my niecey?"

"Who knows? I don't speak baby." She laughed. "All she does is eat, poop, cry and sleep. What are you doing today?"

"Going shopping with my mom. You want to come?"

"No thanks, girl. I'm relaxing today. We were out all day yesterday at a picnic for Cedars Sinai doctors. Stop by after, if you can."

"I'll definitely come by after, since I'm sure I'll find many things to drop off for little momma over there."

"Simone, don't buy this baby another thing. Between you and mom, she will be wearing something new every day for the next six months," Talise laughed.

Mommy Miles and I always had shopping in common. Between the both of us, baby Anastasia had more than what she needed.

After getting off of the phone with Talise, I got up from my bed, showered, and dressed. I had to keep moving, or else that black cloud called depression was bound to take hold of me. The more I kept moving and stayed busy, the less time I had for my mind to wonder and fester on all that was wrong in my life. Every day was a struggle, with some days being much harder than others, but I had to fight for the people who wanted me alive, who needed me in their lives.

After my suicide attempt and the break-in at my house, my mother moved back to California and into my guest room. For the first time in my life, I felt truly loved unconditionally. Yes, Mommy and Daddy Miles, love me and have always treated me like I was their own, but nothing compares to the love of a mother; someone who has the same blood flowing through their veins, someone who actually carried you around inside of them for damn near a year. I've never felt that connection before now. Having her around to look out for me and love me was more than I could have ever asked for.

~ ~ ~ ~ ~ ~

"You want to sit outside?" I asked my mother when we stepped inside La Sandia, a cute, quaint little restaurant that was housed on the second floor of Santa Monica Place, a fairly new outdoor mall that I loved.

"Sure, why not? It's such a beautiful day out. It makes no sense sitting inside," she said as the waitress picked up lunch menus and led us toward the patio and an empty table.

I was enjoying spending time with my mother and was ecstatic to have her living with me. The bond we were creating was becoming stronger every day. Not only was she a mother to me, she was also a best friend. I felt comfortable talking to her about any and everything—aside from the video. It felt good to have this kind of relationship with her. She never judged me or made me feel stupid for my actions, thoughts, or feelings.

"Did you dream about him again last night?" My mother asked after we'd sat down and placed our drink order.

"Yeah. I did this morning. It's so frustrating, Mom. It's been months. I thought time would heal me, but it seems to hurt worse every day."

"Time will make it easier to deal with, but you have to do the healing, Simone."

"Have you ever hurt like this over a man? My dad?" I asked. I knew that he'd hurt her so many times. I wondered how she got through it.

"Being hurt by love is a part of life, so yes, I hurt bad over love. First your dad, but I self-medicated to mute out the pain he caused. I wondered why I wasn't enough. I wondered if my skin was lighter and my hair was longer, like Marie's, if your dad would have chosen me over her. Then I was at an all-time low when Dean passed. That was another very dark time in my life."

"Did you ever think about killing yourself?" I asked.

"I was basically already dead, putting that crap in my body. Being strung out on dope is like walking dead, Simone. It's like you are trying to kill yourself, just in a different way. Then when Dean passed, I definitely wanted to go with him."

"Do you still crave drugs? I'm sorry. you don't have to answer that." I was embarrassed for asking such a question.

"Simone, you can ask me anything. Nothing is off limits, okay?" Looking at me intently, she began, "After Dean died, I was so lost and alone. I did want to die. I sat on the sofa with a pipe made of foil and an eight ball of crack in my hand, thinking about Dean and the past nine sober years that we had shared together. All I had been doing was crying. My heart was heavy with grief. I'd just cremated him the day before and his ashes sat in an urn on the coffee table in front of me as I prayed to God, begging him to take me. I remember mumbling over and over as I rocked back and forth, praying my heart out. I'm not sure why I didn't just break off a piece of that rock, stuff it in the pipe, light it, and let the addiction that took so many years of my life, begin again, but I just held it as I rocked back and forth, praying.

I'm sure one hit from that pipe would have muted my pain, but I sat there whispering prayers and crying. Then there was a knock at the door. I just sat there for a few moments, trying to decide if I wanted to answer it. I was in such a stupor that I did not want to move. My limbs were heavy, but my heart was heavier. When another knock sounded at the door, I placed the drugs and paraphernalia under the sofa, picked up Dean's ashes, and headed to see who was knocking. Can you guess who was at that door, Simone?" My mother asked me with a smile on her face and moisture in her eyes.

"No, who was it?" I was very curious.

"I didn't even bother to ask who it was, nor did I take the time to look through the peephole. I just opened the door, and there stood Rob Maynard, the Private Investigator that found me for you. Had that man arrived even thirty minutes later, I'm sure I would have been so high that answering that door would have been the furthest thing from my mind. After he left, I flushed the drugs down the toilet and threw away the homemade pipe. Simone, you literally saved my life."

"How come you never told me this before, Mom?" I asked, reaching over and hugging her tightly.

"There was no particular reason that I didn't tell you. It just felt appropriate at this time. So to answer your question, an addict will always crave drugs, Simone. Thankfully, my life is full now and I work hard to keep it that way, so the devil doesn't try to get in and feed on my vulnerabilities. I have God, you, that's all I need. I feel whole for the first time in my adult life, so drugs are the last thing on my mind.

"I wonder if I'll ever feel whole," I asked rhetorically. "I do feel better having you here, though. Thank you for moving here," I said for the hundredth time.

"Simone, I would have been here years ago if I'd had you in my life. I'm here making up for lost time with my beautiful daughter. You are worth it and more. I just want you to feel that you are worth it too," she said, reaching out and rubbing my hand. "I love you more than I can ever express to you, Simone. I love you so much that you have to be able to feel it." She chuckled.

"I do. I know you love me and it feels good. I love you too. I'm happy I have you in my life. I'm sorry for everything I've put you through, though. I hope you don't regret being in my life with, all of this drama surrounding me. I hate that you stress over me and worry so much."

"Simone, stop it! Don't you know I would die for you? I'd lie down right now and give my life for yours. If it were a guarantee that I could remove all the hurt and pain from your life, I'd happily go be with the Lord right this moment!" She stated sincerely.

"I don't want to be alive if you're dead," I said honestly.

"Simone, you are supposed to outlive me! I'm supposed to go before you! No parent should have to bury their child, so you get that out of your head right now, okay? I cannot outlive you, you hear me? I cannot live if you succeed in taking your life. I don't mean to put that on your shoulders along with everything else, but just know that if you kill yourself, you are killing me too," she said as a single tear escaped her right eye. "I love you too much to see you take your life. If God decided that it's your time to go, I'd have to deal with that, but if you had succeeded in taking your life, Simone..." She looked away as more tears cascaded down her cheeks.

"I'm sorry, Mom, don't cry. I'm so sorry," I said, grabbing her hand and squeezing it.

"You have to find your purpose, Simone. God placed you here for a reason. You can do anything you put your mind to. You are beautiful, you want for nothing, you have things that women would kill to have. You can be happy, baby. It's a choice."

"The closest I've ever come to what felt like true happiness was when I was with Carlton and found you. Yes, I can buy anything I want. I have a beautiful home and a nice car. I know I'm smart. I believe I'm pretty, but I'm empty inside. I feel so hollow sometimes. Like I'm just a walking, talking shell of a person."

"Well baby, God can take care of all of that if you ask him to come into your life. Ask him to heal you, ask him to fill you up, and I promise you he will. He will give you everything you ask for and more. You know I don't want to preach to you Simone, but you need to go to church. Have you been praying?"

"Of course, Mom, I pray all the time. I just don't feel that being in church every Sunday means that you are saved. Some of the biggest sinners are sitting in the front pew, if not the pulpit."

"That may be true, but you have to form your own relationship with God. With what is going on in your life right now, you have to fight for that relationship, Simone. Whether you believe it or not, you are in a battle. The closer you get to God, the easier this battle will be for you to fight."

"The closer I get to God, the more the devil is going to throw at me. I can't take much more. I think I'll just stay 'middle of the road'. I'm no holy roller. That's just not me."

"Simone, it's not about being a holy roller, it's about forming your own relationship with God and having faith in him, no matter what."

"I know, Mom. I have faith and I believe in God wholeheartedly, but I will not be sitting in anyone's church every Sunday, that's for sure. My relationship with God is just that, *my relationship.*"

"Understood," my mother said as the waitress came to take our lunch order.

Chapter Four
Tyron

"*I* need that video! If she has it and don't want to give that shit up, then she has to go," I stressed to my bodyguard, Curse, who was sitting on the black leather couch in my office watching me as I paced back and forth.

"We have to make sure the same thing that happened to homeboy won't happen again. We'll be two bodies deep and still not have shit to show for it. We have to be more deliberate this time around, boss man. We have to really plan this shit out. As much as I enjoyed killin' that snake, we can't take the chance of messin' up a second time and still not havin' what we need," Cursed finished in his deep raspy voice.

I continued to pace back and forth, trying hard not to lose my cool. I knew Curse was right, but I didn't have time to plan shit out. The bitch was probably plotting revenge as I paced; the thought had me increasing my speed.

"This shit can't get out. We need to do something fast. I get the 'plan shit out' idea, but we don't have time for planning. She's already talking to people. Yo, the bitch is plottin' I know it! We have to shut her up immediately!"

"Boss man, have I ever let you down before? Trust me, I'll get everything we need and more by the time I'm done with this chick."

"Yeah, you let me down when you killed Stacey. He wasn't supposed to fucking die until we got the video! Now I'm in this shit knee deep. I want you to tail her and never let her leave your sight. I need to know what the fuck she is doing at all times. If she ain't in her house, I should know where the fuck she is. I'm going at this blind right now, B, and that shit ain't okay." I said as my office line beeped, alerting me that my receptionist was trying to get through. I walked over to my large, mahogany desk and stabbed the release button on the high tech phone so she could speak through the intercom.

"What, Molly?" I asked irritably. I had just told her not to interrupt me for anything.

"I'm sorry, Mr. Marks, but there are two detectives here to see you, sir. What do you want me to do?" She whispered in a panic making me want to fire her on the spot.

"I want you to start doing what I tell you to do, but now it's too fucking late for that! Tell them I'm not here!"

"I can't do that. *They're cops!*" Molly whispered.

"I don't give a shit if it's President Obama! I pay you, they don't! Just tell them I'm not here!"

"It's too late! I already told them that you *are* here," she said under her breath.

"Escort them in, and in five minutes, buzz me and say it's time for me to leave. Do you think you can do that?"

"Yes! Yes sir, right away sir," she said before hanging up the phone.

"Fucking detectives are here!" I told Curse. I was so angry. I knew I had to calm down before they walked through the door.

"Here for what?" Curse asked, standing up quickly from the couch he had been sitting on.

"Hell if I know. Can't be nothing good," I said as a knock sounded at my door.

"Let them in on your way out. Stay close, I'll be calling you back in as soon as they leave, so we can get a game plan together. Starting today, she needs to be tailed."

"What can I do for you two?" I asked after the door had been closed and they were standing in front of me. I didn't offer my hand, a seat, or any other courtesies. I knew who they were; I remembered them from Vegas.

"I'm Detective Jenkins and this is my partner, Detective Marsh. Sir, we need to ask you a few more questions regarding Stacey Flenoy's murder."

"I said all I had to say the last time we spoke in Vegas," I replied, trying to keep my cool and look unaffected by these suits standing in my office questioning me on some murder shit. If they could see how shook their visit had me, they'd know I was guilty for sure.

"There have been a few more developments, and we'd like to hear your take on things. Maybe you can help us clear up a few... inconsistencies," Detective Jenkins said. I could tell he was the asshole of the two.

"How can I help you when I don't know anything?" I asked.

"We know damn well that you knew Stacey, Mr. Marks.

We know more than you think we know. Now..." he said, taking a long pause before finishing, "because you told us that you didn't know him when we last talked, and since then, we've had some very startling developments, we are just trying to get to the bottom of some really huge inconsistencies in your story." He was full of shit and a damn fool if he thought that what he was saying would make me talk to them and or confess. Plus, there was no way they could prove that I had a relationship with Stacey, and I knew that.

"Like I told you in Vegas, I don't have shit to say to either one of you without my attorney present."

"Well, Mr. Marks, you need to get that attorney present, because we won't stop making trips out here for the sole purpose of visiting you and shaking up your nice little life. Maybe we'll talk to the media a bit and let them know that you are dodging us and not wanting to talk to us about the murder of a gay man who seems to have ties to you. You know how the media does. They just run with stories like these. P.R. nightmare. Sheesh! I can't imagine it," he said shaking his head. His words sent a chill down my spine, but I kept my composure.

"I don't have time for this. I told you before; I didn't have anything to do with that mans' death."

"Did you know him?" Detective Marsh asked, speaking for the first time.

"Listen, I have to be heading out for an appointment and need to finish up some work. I'm going to have to ask you guys to leave," I said as my office line beeped with perfect timing. I walked over to the phone and picked it up.

"Yeah?" I asked into the phone. "I'll be ready. Tell my driver to be out front in ten minutes," I said then hung up the phone.

"We're here for two more days, Mr. Marks. Make all of our lives easier and have your attorney call us to schedule a time to sit down and clear things up. Don't make us have to come back out here, or better yet, have a press conference in front of your office building."

"You can see yourselves out," I said, walking over to the door and opening it.

"We'll be seeing you soon, Mr. Marks. One way or the other," Detective Jenkins said casually before walking out of my office behind his partner.

It took everything in me not to slam the door after they had walked. I sat down behind my desk and covered my face with my shaking hands. When my office line beeped, I knew it couldn't be anything good.

"What Molly?" I asked sternly.

"Ms. Jordan is on the line. She said it's very important. I tried to take a message, but she wouldn't allow it. I'm so sorry. What do you want me to do?" She whined in a panic.

"Molly, just send the call through," I replied resignedly.

"Hey, what's so important?" I asked after the call had been transferred. "I'm really busy right now," I said, trying to make my voice sound as normal as possible.

"Tyron, what is going on with you? What is all this I'm seeing on the blogs and hearing through the grapevine. What do you need to tell me?" Platinum hit after platinum hit, Tomi Jordan was one of the most powerful women in entertainment and she never had a problem exerting her power when needed. Being one of the top singers in the game, she never bowed down to anyone.

"What are you talking about, Tomi? Do you think I have time to sit around and read blogs or give a shit about gossip?" I lied.

"You know what I'm talking about, Tyron. I've been getting calls all morning, and why did detectives just leave your office?" She yelled uncharacteristically and then lowered her voice to a calm level. "I'm chartering a plane now. Meet me at the Malibu house tonight." She hung up the phone before I could say more.

"This shit is getting out of control!" I slammed the phone onto the receiver and covered my face with my hands. For the first time since I could remember, I didn't know what to do. I didn't have a 'fix it' plan when I needed one the most.

~ ~ ~ ~ ~ ~

I pulled onto the circular driveway of my Malibu estate and thought about Stacey. I can't count the times I'd come home and he'd be here waiting for me to pull up. The tiny pang of guilt that touched me every time I drove up to this house had me on the verge of selling it. Then I'd remember that he was a snake and deserved what he got for betraying me and the thought of selling the house would go straight out the window.

When I walked into the house, all was quiet. I was filled with so much anxiety that my neck was sore and my shoulders were stiff.

"Tomi! Where you at?" I yelled after walking through the front door. I knew she was here because her black on black SLR McClaren was parked in the driveway. I made my way past the kitchen, and then into the family room where the floor to ceiling windows that spanned throughout the entire room was empty of any blinds or curtains. The eerie darkness and silence in the house made the hair on the back of my neck rise.

"Yo..."

"Quit yelling, I'm right here," Tomi said, cutting me off mid shout. She pushed the button on the handheld remote and the lights dimly came on. I could now see that she was stretched across the white, lambskin chaise lounge that was closest to the large backyard window. The glass slider was open and the breeze and sounds from the ocean could be easily heard.

"Why you sittin' in the dark?" I asked as I walked up to her and kissed her on her forehead. I loosened then took off my tie and sat on the edge of the chair.

We sat in silence for a few minutes before she spoke, never answering my question.

"Ty, what is going on?" She asked calmly. "I'm hearing shit about a video. Is there a video of you? Who are you fucking around with?" Her calm even toned voice was unnerving.

"I'm not fucking around with nobody, Tomi! That's the problem with you. You just believe shit too easily. No, there isn't a video of me 'cause I'm not fucking around!" I lied, hoping she wouldn't be able to see through me as she always could. "This is bullshit! I don't know what would make you take this blog shit so seriously? They could be talking about a number of dudes and you know that, Tomi! Why the fuck are you wiggin' out on me over this shit?" Tomi got up and stood at the open window with her back facing me. I hoped I was convincing enough, although I knew that she was much smarter than that.

I didn't know what to do or say next, but I knew to give her time. Tomi was a contemplator. She's not your average woman. She never made an emotional decision in her life. Anything and everything was always mapped and planned out. She was too logical. I knew I was heading toward an uphill battle.

"Tyron, ninety percent of the time there's some truth to this gossip shit," she said before turning and walking up to me. She stood between my parted legs and looked down at me with her piercing hazel eyes. She placed her right palm gently against my left cheek. "I know you're lying; I can always tell. I don't know why you can't just tell me the truth." Tears welled in her eyes and then cascaded down her cheeks, landing on my knee. Tomi never cried. "Don't play me and make me out to be the fool. I can't... won't let you or anyone else embarrass me. You better get your shit together," she said before walking through the family room and out the front door without saying another word.

Chapter Five
Simone

"*H*e's supposed to be coming here to pick it up," the sales ladies whispered loudly to each other as my mother and I tried on shoes at the Luis Vuitton store.

"Who do you think they are talking about?" My mother leaned over and asked me in an excitedly hushed voice.

"It could be anyone. Remember, we are two steps from Hollywood," I smiled, standing up to take a walk in the high heeled mocha colored Corfu sandals to see how they felt on my feet. They were beautiful shoes, but if they were uncomfortable to walk in, they weren't worth having.

"These are too cute and so comfortable." My mother was standing in front of a full-length mirror admiring herself in navy, Elba ballerina slippers which looked cute on her small feet.

"What do you think of these? They are cute, huh?" I asked my mother before bending down to unzip the back of the sandal, preparing to take them off to try on another pair.

"Yes, they are gorgeous. They make your legs look even more..."

"Beautiful?" A male voice startled me upright. I looked up and saw Deon Bradford standing there watching my mother and me.

"Deon!" I huffed, walking over to him and swatting him on the arm. "You scared me. I didn't know what pervert was watching me," I laughed and gave him a hug.

"Why does it have to be a pervert admiring two beautiful women? Simone, you didn't tell me you have a sister," Deon said, looking toward my mother who stood there with her mouth hung open.

"Oh! Deon, this is my mother, Darlene. Mom, come here and meet Deon Bradford," I said before walking to her and pulling her toward Deon when she seemed like she wasn't going to move.

"I see where you get your beauty from, Simone. Wow, you guys look just alike. Ma'am, you look way too young to be Simone's mother." Deon reached out and grabbed my mother in a bear hug, causing her to turn the darkest shade of red possible for someone with her skin tone.

"Why thank you. Just call me Darlene, honey," my mother stated,
patting her hair and smiling. I had to stop myself from laughing. Seeing my mother flushed and acting this way tickled me.

"Okay, Ms. Darlene, it's a pleasure to meet you. What's up with you, Simone, you following me around now?" he joked.

"Following you around? We were here before you, Deon." I laughed, bending down to take off the shoes. "What are you doing over this way?" I asked.

"Mom's birthday is this weekend. I'm grabbing some luggage for her."

"You are such a sweet son," I smiled teasingly. "Be sure to tell your mom happy birthday for me."

"How about you do it yourself? I'm having a birthday dinner for her on Saturday. Will you come, Ms. Darlene, and bring Simone?" He asked, purposely bypassing me.

Before I could utter another word, she had already accepted.

"We'd love to. We have no plans for Saturday anyway."

"Mom, I have plans…" I spat out before she cut me off.

"Plans can be canceled. We'll be there Deon. Do you have Simone's information so you can let us know the time and location?" My mother asked Deon as if I wasn't standing there. I knew Deon didn't have my new number and was hoping that he didn't verify it. The last thing I wanted to do was sit around a dinner table with Deon Bradford!

"Yes, ma'am, I have it if her number is still the same. Is this it?" He asked after pulling out his phone, finding my contact information, and showing the phone to my mother.

"No, she's changed it since then." My mother gave him my new number while I stood there in utter disbelief.

"Great! My mom is going to be so happy to see you, Simone," Deon said, winking at me as my mom took a seat and began removing the shoes she was trying on. The smile on his face was priceless as I gave him the evil eye before a laugh escaped my mouth.

"Whatever, Deon, you think you're slick. Mom, now you have to help me find a gift for Mrs. Bradford."

"Well, we are already at the mall. That shouldn't be too hard," she said and winked at Deon.

"What? Are you guys in cahoots or something?" I laughed.

"I have no idea what you're talking about, Simone. I'm going to head out of here. It was nice to meet you, Ms. Darlene. I'll see you both on Saturday. I'll send you the info by tomorrow, Simone," he said before walking over to the counter and purchasing the luggage he had come for.

"Mom, why did you say we would go?" I asked her after Deon was out of ear shot.

"Were you going to tell him no?" She asked with a smirk on her face.

"Mom, you have no idea the history I have with him. I don't want to sit and have dinner with him and now you've already told him we will go!" I was kind of pissed that she accepted his invitation without making sure I was okay with it. She had no idea what went down between Deon and me.

"What harm will a dinner do, Simone? There is no bad blood between you two anyway. If there was, you wouldn't have hugged him and been smiling up in his face as much as he was smiling in yours. Now, I need to find myself a dress to wear to this here birthday dinner." She smiled.

Chapter Six
Deon

*E*verything was set as I walked into Mastro's Steakhouse in Beverly Hills with my mother, father, younger brother, and Tyson. I'd reserved the Chef's Room and was looking forward to a nice private dinner with my family and friends.

The rectangular table was elegantly set for fourteen in the middle of the private, thirties inspired Supper Club setting. My mother looked beautiful in all white as her chocolate skin glowed on her sixtieth birthday. My agent and his wife, who were closer in age to my parents, were already there when we arrived. My teammates, Vincent Waters and Darryl Withers, walked in at the same time. Vince, with his wife Marian and son Jack, who was 11, as was Tyson, and Darryl with a tall blonde on his arm. Simone and her mother walked in shortly after, looking like beautiful sisters.

Simone's burnt orange dress clung to her curves and hugged her hips and thighs, ending right above her knees.

The neckline of the dress plunged slightly, showing off a nice loose necklace filled with sparkling diamonds that complimented the diamond hoop earrings and diamond ring and bracelet she wore. She had on the heels she was trying on at the Louis Vuitton store and they really did make her legs look amazing. Her hair was pulled back in a tight bun, adding to her elegant and classy look. She was flat out stunning, and still the most beautiful woman I'd ever seen.

"Simone! What an awesome surprise!" My mother smiled, approaching Simone and her mother. I was glad that she'd actually came and was happy when I saw the look on my family's face when she walked in. Since meeting Simone after my best friend Nichelle was killed, my mother asked about her more often than I cared for.

"Simone!" Tyson said excitedly, running to her and hugging her around the waist before my mother had a chance to get to her. "Where have you been? I missed you! I have a phone now! I need your number so I can text you. Are you on Facebook? Instagram? Can I follow you on Twitter?" Tyson asked, making us all laugh.

"Hey Tyson," Simone laughed, squeezing him tightly. "I missed you too and no I'm not on Facebook, Twitter or Instagram, but you can text me anytime." She kissed his forehead and then hugged and kissed my parents wishing my mother a happy birthday.

"Mr. and Mrs. Bradford, Tyson, this is my mother, Darlene." They each greeted her with a hug and welcomed her as my family has always been known to do. I walked over with my younger brother, J.R., and introduced him to Simone and her mother. I then began to make sure everyone who hadn't met before got a proper introduction before we sat down for drinks and appetizers.

After dinner was served, we were on our third or fourth bottle of Armand de Brignac and were enjoying each other's company. Simone was sitting next to me at the head of one side of the table while my parents sat at the head of the other side. Ms. Darlene—who was seated next to my mother—and my parents were deep in conversation with my agent and his wife while our side of the table laughed and talked about sports and current events. Darryl seemed to pay Simone a lot of attention while his date was in airhead land. She didn't have much to add to the conversation, so after trying to include her more than once, I gave up.

"I'd like to make a toast," I said, holding my champagne glass in the air as I rose from my seat. The waiter began to make sure everyone had filled glasses.

"Unfortunately, we aren't all blessed to have our mothers in our lives. I honestly can say that I don't know what I'd do without mine. She's actually the type of mom that tucked me and my brother in every single night while we were growing up. She's the mom that always supported me in anything I've ever wanted to do. She's the mom who never missed any of my games in high school and said she was proud of me even when I wasn't proud of myself. She is the mom that loves me unconditionally no matter what I do or how I'm living my life." I began to get choked up, so I paused before continuing, refusing to cry. "Mom, I just want you to know that I love you with all of my heart. I'm thankful that God chose me to be your son. I pray that you have many more birthdays to come, and that you enjoy your time in Turks and Caicos. To my beautiful mother!" I said, as we all touched glasses in salute to my mother, who was wiping tears from her eyes.

After my father, brother, and agent gave a toast, the cake was brought in and we sang happy birthday and gave her our gifts.

"Are you okay?" I asked Simone as she ate crème brûlée and sipped champagne. I could tell she was enjoying herself. I loved to see her eyes sparkle and to hear her laugh.

"Yes, thank you for inviting us. I'm glad we came," she smiled.

"Not more than I am," I replied, trying not to stare at her full, glossy lips.

"We should go out. Let's go to a party or something," I suggested, knowing for sure that she was going to shoot me down again.

"I'm down. I definitely don't want to go home. It's only eleven."

"Wow, I thought you'd say no!" I laughed. "Darryl, what you gettin' into tonight? Let's go out," I said to my teammate who was known for partying all the time.

"Bynum's birthday party is tonight, remember? Let's get it in!" he said enthusiastically. "I'm gonna leave now so I can drop her off and then I'll meet you guys at Drai's. I'll let them know we're coming."

I put Ms. Darlene in the car with my family so the driver could take her home, and hopped in Simone's truck.

"I can't believe you said yes," I said as we drove up Santa Monica Boulevard heading toward Hollywood.

"I can't believe I said yes either," she laughed.

"I'm just glad you did. Tonight is gonna be a night to remember!" I joked. I had no way of knowing how true that joke was going to turn out to be.

Chapter Seven
Simone

When we pulled up to the valet at Drai's, which was located at the W Hotel in Hollywood, I wasn't expecting to see paparazzi with their cameras at the ready.

"Don't worry, it's cool," Deon said when he saw the look on my face. "My security team will come let us out of the car. Just stay close to me and smile, so the cameras can get a good shot of that pretty face."

The door opened before I could object. I was whisked out of the car and surrounded by four men that looked like off duty cops. Deon grabbed my hand as we walked toward the entrance of the hotel with his security clearing the path. I could barely see through the blinding camera flashes as photographers called out his name, asking question after question.

"Hey Deon, who's the lady you're with?"

"Deon, stop and let us get a photo," a woman said.

"Deon, are the Lakers going to bring it home this year?"

"Smile for the camera, pretty lady," another said, speaking to me.

Once we made it through all of the mayhem, Deon's security team led us to the back of the hotel where we took a private elevator that deposited us in a twelfth floor office that had to be inside of the club because the music was so loud. The ceilings were high, sculpted in carved dark wood, and the walls were all a deep crimson velvet fabric. One of them held two large flat screens that displayed live footage of the club and the bar. A sitting area was staged in the middle of the room where tufted leather sofas and chaise lounges of beautifully complimentary hues rested on the polished dark oak wood floors.

A handsome man wearing an expertly tailored suit with thick, shiny, black hair that complimented his olive toned skin and deep green eyes greeted us.

"Deon, my man! As always, thank you for coming!" They shook hands and hugged before Deon introduced him to me as Kostas, the owner of the club.

"Darryl and his guys got here not too long ago," he said after kissing me on both cheeks. "I'll escort you to their table." He led us out of his office and through the crowded club filled with women and men of all ethnicities.

The club's ambiance had a similar feel to the office, but was much brighter with all of the sofas made of white soft leather and the booths of silver metallic leather. Red, silk pleated drapes hung from some of the windows while white sheer curtains hung from the others, allowing the city lights of Hollywood to twinkle through. All of the walls were silver metallic and complimented the shiny black pedestals that held Go-Go Dancers who gyrated on stripper poles in tiny outfits. Every woman we passed gawked at Deon. I could see the excitement in their faces and the dollar signs in their eyes.

When we finally reached the large booth, Darryl was

pouring a glass of champagne for a brunette who was smiling up at him. When he saw me, he handed me the glass of champagne, kissed me on the cheek, gave Deon a pound, and then introduced me to his boys as the girl stood there, forgotten in an instant.

Darryl and his boys were covered in diamonds that sparkled along with the huge chandelier that surrounded the interior of the bar. Elim, one of Darryl's boys, wore his hair cut low while a thick beard covered the bottom half of his face. Large diamonds sparkled in his ears, around his neck, and on his watch and pinky finger. Two teardrops were tattooed under the corner of his right eye and tattoos covered his neck and arms. He looked threatening until he smiled, showing a set of beautiful white teeth. Later, when I asked if his name was Muslim, he told me Elim was short for Eliminator, and got a good laugh from the surprised look on my face. Darryl's other friends didn't look less threatening, but they were all cool and welcomed me.

Women in tiny dresses, skin tight jeans and barely there tops began to gradually flock toward our booth as the club got more and more crowded. We were all enjoying ourselves and getting tipsy. I had yet to see Andrew Bynum, Deon's teammate whose birthday party was being held there, but the club was so packed, I'm sure there were plenty of people in there that I had yet to spot.

Deon popped a second bottle of Ace of Spade—probably the fifth or sixth if I was to include the bottles from dinner—as Rick Ross' "John Doe" spewed from the speakers. There were bottles of Ciroc, Don Julio, and red and white wines on the table with plenty of ice and glasses. The ladies were loving the free drinks and letting it be known that they wanted to be chosen.

I'm not sure how many glasses of champagne I'd had throughout the night, but I was feeling nice. I hadn't felt this good in a long time, and at that moment, I didn't have a care in the world. I was happy that I'd decided to hang out.

I was sitting on top of the booth with my feet resting in the seat where my butt should have been. Deon was next to me standing right outside of the booth with his back resting against my side. Darryl was posted up against the railing directly parallel to our booth as a pretty Latina in an extremely small, tight fitting dress and platform high heels danced seductively in front of him. Elim was not too far from the table, surrounded by a flock of girls. His smile and diamonds could be seen from across the club. Darryl's other boys were all standing near doing their own thing; talking to girls, pouring drinks, dancing, and having a good time. I could tell that this was something that they all did regularly. They knew most of the girls that approached the table and seemed to have a pretty big following when it came to the ladies.

Deon was pretty much reserved; he was the watcher and was taking everything in while periodically checking with me to make sure I was okay. Women continuously approached him and he was polite, but never showed any interest, although I wouldn't have cared if he did.

From my seat, I had a good view of the rest of the club, but hadn't paid much attention to the people in the booths around us. When I noticed the group that had gathered at the table directly next to ours, my heart seemed to freeze and my body got hot. I prayed that my eyes were deceiving me, but in my gut, I knew that they weren't. A large entourage and a couple of men standing near that had to be his security; Tyron Marks was partying at the booth next to ours.

A large lump formed in my throat as I watched his murdering ass raise his bottle of Voss water in the air when Jay Z and Kanye West's, "Niggas in Paris" pumped through the speakers. Everyone's head was rocking back and forth to the hot track, but everything seemed to go in slow motion for me. I stared at him, unable to remove my eyes from his face. I was so angry that my hands shook as it sunk in that this fucker was out partying and popping bottles like he didn't have a care in the world; like he hadn't murdered my friend; like I didn't have a video of him being fucked by a guy!

"You okay?" Deon asked, pulling me out of my trance like he could sense the shift in my energy.

"I'm okay. Help me down, please." I could no longer sit in my seat while this murderer was so close to me laughing and singing along to the song.

Ball so hard since we here
It's only right that we be fair
I'm Psycho, I'm liable, to go Michael, take your pick
Jackson, Tyson, Jordan, game six
Ball so hard...

I took in everyone and everything around me then continued to watch him. I got angrier and took bigger gulps of my champagne as I watched him.

I leaned against the seat of the booth as I stood next to Deon, clinching my fists hard enough to break the champagne flute that was in my hand. I was trying hard to calm down, but it wasn't working. I don't know if it was Tyron alone or the combination of the liquor and Tyron, but

I'd never felt so angry and hostile in my life. I think I was literally seeing red.

I noticed him moving from his position inside the booth and walking in my direction, probably heading toward the bathroom. I didn't think twice when I sat my glass down, grabbed the neck of the gold champagne bottle, and lifted it off of the table and waited. I could tell that it was empty because of its weight and was thankful for that; it would be much easier for me to handle. In my peripheral view, I could see Elim watching me and looking to see where I was staring, but I was in such a zone that it didn't register that he had moved and was almost next to me when I raised the bottle quickly and swung it at Tyron's head once he was within arm's reach. I felt the bottle hit my target, but it didn't break which meant I didn't hit him hard enough. I raised the bottle, preparing to swing again, but all hell broke loose.

Deon grabbed me from behind, lifting me off of the floor as I fought to get out of his arms. Elim was the first one to swing at one of the guys in Tyron's entourage, connecting his fist to the unlucky man's face. The music cut off and all you could hear was the commotion of the guys yelling and fighting. Tyron's security team had him surrounded, and was looking around, trying to find me, but I was covered by Deon, Darryl and their security as they tried to get me back toward the office through the thick crowd of party goers.

"You murderer!" I yelled. "You're at the club poppin' bottles while my best friend is in a fucking coffin?" I was livid as Tyron's eyes met mine. I could see blood oozing from between his fingers. He was holding the spot where the bottle must have connected. His eyes were wild. I would have bet money that those were the same eyes that Stacey looked into the last days of his life. I knew he'd kill me if he had the chance, and I was ready for the show down. "It's me, Stacey's best friend, you gay son of a bitch!" Was the last thing I yelled before they whisked me into the office and onto the elevator.

"What the hell Simone? What the fuck was that all about?" Deon asked as we descended with Darryl and Deon's security guards. They were amped up and in protect mode.

I was so angry that I could barely speak. Tears were pouring down my face as I stood there wishing I could just disappear.

"He killed Stacey, Deon," I managed to say as I tried to catch my breath. "He's out partying and jet setting around the world, and my friend is dead!" I cried. When Deon wrapped his arms around me, I cried harder. I was a mess and didn't care what any of them thought.

"We're going to the first garage level," I heard Darryl tell Deon. "From there, we can walk through and connect to the residences in the next building over. I have a place here. Let's take her there and let this shit die down."

Those were the last words I remember hearing before waking up the next morning in a strange bed lying next to Deon.

Chapter Eight
C. Banks

I sat in my car smoking cigarettes all night until Simone finally pulled into her garage close to eight in the morning. I wondered where the hell she'd slept, and couldn't stop my mind from picturing her laid up with some lame. I hopped out of my car as inconspicuous as I could, and slid through the gate right before it closed. Once she pulled into her parking space, hopped out of her truck, and closed the door, I walked up on her.

"Simone," I said, causing her to holler and jump back toward her car, almost dropping the high heels that were in her hands. She frantically pushed the button trying to unlock her doors so she could get back in her truck. "Simone, it's just me, Carlton," I said, trying to relieve her fear.

"What do you want? Don't try to hurt me! There are cameras down here so don't try to do anything to me!" Her words, together with the scared look on her face, made my stomach drop. I'm not sure if there was anything else that she could have said to me that would've hurt more.

"Simone? You think I would hurt you? I would never fucking hurt you, Monie!" I pleaded, trying to keep the tears that had just formed in my eyes from falling. I was a wreck and I knew it, but I had to see her. I had to talk to her.

"What do you want?" She practically yelled in a shaky voice. Her eyes and face were puffy like she'd been up all night crying. I wanted to grab her and hold her. I just wanted to make everything right, the way it was before.

"I can't believe you think I'd hurt you." I said as the moisture that I was trying to hold in fell from my eyes. I'd never in my life felt this way. Even when I was hauled out of court heading toward a thirteen-year bid, I felt less humiliated. "I love you, Simone. I would never fucking hurt you! I would *never* harm you!"

"Why are you here? What more do you want from me, Carlton? You've messed me up enough already! Just leave me alone!" Tears poured from her eyes as she tried to walk past me toward the elevator.

"I'm sorry, Simone. It's not what you think. That shit ain't what you think! I swear to God, yo, it's not what you think!" I grabbed her arm, trying to prevent her from leaving.

I knew I wasn't making sense. I couldn't stop repeating myself, but while I had her here and had her ear, I was not letting her go before I was able to get out what I had to say.

"What are you sorry for, Carlton?" She ripped her arm from my grip and tried to wipe the tears from her eyes, while more fell in their place. "Tell me why you're sorry!" She stood in front of me with her hand on her hip and her face wet from the steady stream of tears. I could tell she was trying to keep her composure; so was I.

"I know you saw that shit, Simone. I know you have it.

It's not at all what you think!"

"Saw what, Carlton?" She asked as we stood in the empty parking space next to her car. "Fucking just say it!" She yelled and backed up against her Range and leaned on it. It hurt me a damn lot to see her in pain, but it hurt even more to know that I was the sole cause of the shit.

"Simone, you know. You already know! Why do I have to say that shit?"

She probably thought of me as some punk the way I was standing here in front of her crying like a woman.

"Just say it Carlton. What did I see?" Simone asked with her eyes closed. She was shaking her head as if she was trying to clear something from her mind.

"The video, Monie, I know you saw that shit. I know you have it." I couldn't have been filled with more shame than I was at that moment. When she opened her eyes and looked at me, my heart should've stopped. I'd never felt lower.

"You're gay. This isn't a damn E. Lynn Harris book, Carlton! This is my life! Why couldn't you just tell me? Why didn't you just let me go? Why file for divorce? *Why did you fuck me up like this?* Why make me fall in love with you when you know you're gay?" I had no idea who the hell E. Lynn Harris was, but the emotion in her voice ripped through me like a sharp knife.

"I'm not fucking gay, Simone! Yes, I understand what you saw, but I'm not gay! Just call me a freak, but I'm not gay! I have no desire to be with men. I'm not attracted to men. You have to believe me! I love you more than I've ever loved anyone before in my life, Simone! This shit is *real.* I did not game you. That video was in the beginning of us. I never lied to you. I never cheated on you. I don't know what to do to make you believe me. I don't know what to do to make this shit right, Monie! I'm a fucking wreck, yo," I pleaded with her.

"Did you have anything to do with Stacey's death? Just tell me that. Tell me the truth!"

"Hell no, Simone, come on! I would never do no shit like that to you or nobody else. You think I'm a fucking monster or something? I just found out about the video a few days ago, Simone! I've never even seen it and I don't want to. I didn't even know about this shit. *I swear to God!* Do you really think I had something to do with Stacey's murder? Do you really think I could be in your face and hold you as you cried for dude if I killed him?" I asked, walking closer to her. "You can't think that, Monie! You can't think that shit!"

The thought never crossed my mind that she would think that I had a hand in killing her best friend. That almost hurt worse than the scared look in her eyes when she thought I'd come to harm her.

"You guys came in my house and trashed my shit! If your dumb asses would have looked in the DVD player, you would have found the damn video, Carlton!" She spat as tears continued to spill down her cheeks.

"What are you talking about, Simone? I didn't trash your house! When did someone trash your house?" I was stunned. I didn't have shit to do with this, but knew who must have.

"Whatever, Carlton. I don't even know who you are," she whispered.

"Yes you do, Simone. You know me; you know my heart. Aside from all this other shit, you know me!"

"What do you want from me, Carlton?" She cried, covering her face with her hands.

"I want... need your forgiveness. I need you to know that

I never intentionally meant to hurt you. I need you to believe that I didn't have anything to do with what happened to Stacey. I swear to God, this is my worst nightmare! Loosing you is like a bad ass dream. I can barely sleep at night and when I do, I wake up and you are the first thing on my mind. I'm fucked up, Simone! I need you in my life, but I know I messed up." I walked up to her and removed her hands from her face by gently pulling on her wrists. "Open your eyes, Simone." I had to ask her twice before she opened them and looked at me through what had to be blurred vision. "I love you, but I understand I fucked up... that's an understatement, I know." I said when she rolled her eyes. "I need you to forgive me. I need you to talk to me. I need you to give me that video!" I said before she jerked her wrists from my grasp and stepped away from me.

"That's why you're here! You just want the fucking video, *Banks!* You don't give a shit about me!"

"Simone, that shit is like a fucking grenade; it's a ticking time bomb! Dude is looking for that shit heavy, Monie! He has to know that one of you has it. I think he killed Stacey over that shit. You think he won't try to do the same thing to you? And now you are leaking that shit to the blogs?"

"Leaking shit to the blogs? Carlton, I don't even read blogs. What I'll do with that video if shit doesn't go my way will be much worse than some blog shit. You better tell Tyron that if anything happens to me, if I even have reason to be scared, I'll sell that shit to Vivid Entertainment and make gay porn stars out of both you. Whatever blog shit you are talking about will be a drop in the bucket. Also, tell that motherfucker that if I *ever* see him out partying and popping bottles again like he doesn't have a care in the world, I promise, next time I *will* kill him!"

"Do you hate me Simone? Is that why you are doing this? Do you want to ruin me? My life is already fucked up right now because I don't have you, but please, please don't do this! What about my kids, my moms?" I pleaded.

"Yes, I hate you right now! I hate you, I hate Tyron, and I'm pissed off at Stacey because he recorded this shit and I know it got him killed! I fucking hate life right now, Carlton," she cried hysterically.

I walked up to her and wrapped my arms around her. I was surprised that she let me hold her as she cried in my arms. I missed her so much that having her so close that I could smell her scent made me cry with her. As we stood in her garage crying like two women, I held her and repeated that I was sorry and that I loved her over and over in her ear.

"I'll never let anything happen to you, Simone. I'll kill anyone who tries to harm you. I love you. Do you believe me?"

"I don't know what to believe. I just need some time. Please, just give me some time okay? I can't do this anymore. Just let me go; don't follow me," she said and rushed off toward the elevator. I stood there until I heard the elevator reach the garage and walked off when I was sure that she was safely on her way up to her place.

When I got back in my car, I sped away from Simone's building, but I couldn't stop thinking about what she'd said. At the time, I was so caught up in her saying that she would release the video that I completely overlooked the; *"I promise, next time I will kill him"* comment. That shit went completely over my head and didn't dawn on me until now. *What did she mean by next time?* I kept wondering as I sped through Downtown LA. I didn't know what she meant, but I was about to find out.

Less than ten minutes later, I was pulling up to the Ritz Carlton where Tyron owned a penthouse suite. I had to get a handle on this shit and make sure Simone didn't get hurt in the process. That video can *never* get out!

Chapter Nine
Tyron

Bossip Blind Item Part 2

Which high profile music mogul got cracked in the head with a champagne bottle by a girl at a Hollyweird club over the weekend?

"**W**hat in the fuck am I paying you shits for if a girl can get at me? All you mothafuckas are fired! Get outta here," I yelled and stormed to the bar and poured a drink. I hadn't ingested alcohol in over five years, but today was the day, and I didn't give a shit that it was only nine in the morning.

"Leave man," I said to Curse who was still standing there like he wasn't included in the firing.

"Boss man, come on. You know if I was there that shit wouldn't have went down like that," Curse pleaded.

"That's why you are fucking fired too! You should've been there, B. That's why I pay you what I pay you, so you can be there at *all* times." I wasn't trying to hear shit he had to say.

"Come on Mr. Marks, my son was being born. I had to be there."

"I have five fucking stitches above my eye because you weren't there to do your job. I'm not trying to hear shit you have to say right now." I took back the shot of liquor and enjoyed the burning sensation it made as it went down my throat. I poured another and immediately took it back, swallowing the dark, warm liquor in one gulp. "Look man, just stay near." I said, after giving it some rational thought. I needed Curse. He was my most loyal and skilled employee. Plus, he knows way too much for me to let him go like this. "You're on call. I'll let you know when I'm ready to head out. Congratulations on the baby," I said, then poured and swallowed my third shot.

I couldn't stop my mind from racing. Everything that I'd worked so hard for was crumbling right before my eyes, and all over a bitch ass snitch that got too emotional. I was so angry I couldn't compose myself. I knew that Tomi would be calling any minute. Thankfully, she was out of the country, so I didn't have to worry about seeing her face. She was the last person I felt like dealing with, but I knew it was inevitable.

When the distinctive ring from the phone alerted me that a call was coming in from the front desk, I was relieved that it wasn't Tomi calling. I at least had a little more time before I felt her wrath.

"Yeah?" I spat into the phone after picking it up.

"Mr. Marks, Mr. Carlton Banks is here in the lobby. Can I send him up?" The Maître D asked in his thick Indian accent that grated my nerves every time I had to talk to him. *Fuck!* I thought, trying to think quickly enough to figure out what to do.

"Yeah, send him up," I said resignedly.

I knew Banks from high school, but we didn't hang in the same circle. Years later, while I was finishing up Tomi Jordan's first album, I ran into him at a studio in Uptown and asked if he wanted to jump on one of her tracks. After listening to the mid tempo melodic joint, he was eager to lay down his vocals. He transformed the song into what people later deemed a classic. The song was fire, so I released the single and it shot to number one in spins in less than a week and had over a million iTunes Downloads.

Before I ran into Banks, he was already making a name for himself as one of the illest MC's in the game. Every label wanted to sign him, but he wasn't interested in signing his life away like so many other eager rappers who were anxious to have a deal. He'd studied the game. He knew the history of the music business and was dead set on doing things his way, which was why we clicked; we thought the same and had a lot of the same goals.

Banks was smart and more patient than any cat I'd ever known. He knew what he wanted and was calculated about getting it. He was gifted and knew the formula that would later bring us much fame, recognition, and most importantly, power and money.

We dropped mix tape after mix tape that was downloaded millions of times. Radio was spinning our original joints and everyone was going crazy over his flow and clever rhymes and the beats I created. The more music we made together, the more we understood the power we had as a team. We were business savvy, determined, and talented men. What one of us lacked, the other made up for in leaps and bounds. Plus, we had a secret that connected us together and made us closer.

*We were creating a huge buzz, so when it came time to
drop Tomi's first album, we were able to secure a forty
million dollar distribution deal with Sony BMG. The deal was
unprecedented; it allowed us to keep eighty percent of our
royalties, seventy percent of our publishing, and complete
ownership of all of our masters. A deal like that was unheard
of, but after many meetings with Howard Stringer, the
president of Sony BMG, he was able to outbid Universal
Music Group, EMI and Warner Music Group by a long shot.
He believed in us and knew that we would bring a lot of money
Sony's way, and that we did.*

*Tomi's first album went diamond, selling ten million in
the first year. With the subsequent release of Banks' official
first album, which sold eight million copies—a million of that
selling in the first week—our label was a force to be reckoned
with. We signed several singers and rappers and had a crew
of the hottest producers. QP Records was the label to be
signed to.*

The knocking on the door brought me back to the
present, making me wonder why Banks was here at this
time of morning. I figured he must have heard about what
happened last night at the club. I opened the door and
walked away. I figured I might as well get this shit over with.
No need in hiding when everyone was going to know that a
chick busted my head open.

"What's up? You want a drink?" I slurred, walking back
to the bar to pour another shot.

"You tell me what's up, B. Who's here?"

"You're looking at him." I poured two glasses of whiskey
and handed him one.

"Yo! What the fuck happened to your head?" His face

contorted like he was looking at the Elephant Man when he finally saw the puffy, red stitched gash above my left eye.

The shit didn't look that bad!

"Banks, this shit is getting out of control, man. I'm going to fucking kill somebody!"

"You already did that," he said coolly.

"I'm going to kill that bitch, Simone," I said heatedly.

"That's why we're in this shit now, and you talking about killing somebody else? You fucked up doing what you did to dude, now look at the situation we're in. This shit is beyond out of control. This doesn't only affect you, Tyron. I'm on that fucking video too! My career, my family, my life is hanging off a cliff right now, B! One more wrong move and it's all over. She'll release that shit, dummy! I talked to Simone, man, and you not handling this shit right. I need to be involved from this point forward."

"Did the bitch tell you she hit me with a fucking bottle last night? An Ace of Spade bottle? I'm going to kill that bitch, Banks! I swear to God she's done!" I said, banging my hand on the cold granite countertop of the bar.

"Why in the hell were you at a club, man? We got serious shit going on, and you at the club?"

"I'm supposed to hide from that bitch? I'm supposed to stop doing what I do because of that bitch?" I asked, stepping from around the bar and plopping down hard on the large, hunter green couch.

"We have serious shit going on and you're at a fucking party?" He asked again and continued before I answered. "Whatever. What's done is done. Do you understand that this shit is serious? This could ruin everything we've worked for," he said, sitting across from me on the arm of the love seat.

"Of course I know this shit is serious! You just got

involved. This shit has been hanging over my head for months now!"

"When you trashed her house, the fucking video was in the DVD player!" he said.

"What are you talking about, Banks? I didn't fucking trash that bitch's house. I want to fucking trash her!" I lied, feeling even angrier after what he'd just told me.

"Whatever man," he said. I could tell he didn't believe me, but I didn't' give a shit. I knew I'd be having another talk with Curse for fucking up yet again. I wouldn't even be having this conversation right now if the dumb ass had looked in the fucking DVD player! "No more keeping shit from me," he continued. "Tell me what went down with Stacey. How did this shit get so fucked up? I need to know everything that went down."

I knew Banks was right, so I told him everything that happened after I found out Stacey had recorded the video.

I was surprised that Stacey willingly came to Vegas. After what I knew he had witnessed, I figured he'd be done with me and move on, but he was all too eager to fly out to see me. I wanted to get him out of LA. I thought that Curse could persuade him to give us the video, but we messed up. I think he knew I wasn't going to let him live after what he'd done, so he was dead set on not giving in and telling us where to find the video.

I would periodically come in and sit with Stacey, watching him as he moaned in pain. It made me feel good. I felt vindicated knowing that I had him right where I wanted him. I'm sure that he regretted what he did—regretted the action that ultimately cost him his life. I had no pity for him, though.

This idiot ruined everything.

By day three, Curse still wasn't able to get anything out of him. I don't know if I would have been as strong or stubborn as he was, but this cat wasn't going to talk, so we went to the second stage of our plan; we drugged him. I thought that it would loosen him up and make him talk, but again, I was wrong. That bitch was better off than he was before the drug. He wasn't moaning anymore and I wondered if he was even still in pain or if the fucking narcotic had numbed him to what was going on. The shit probably made him comfortable, which was the exact opposite of what we intended.

I can't claim to be a killer. I'd never even thought about taking someone's life before this, but us trying to get info out of that dude was like a bad Laurel and Hardy film; a fucking joke! By the end of that day, he was dead. We went into the room after Banks' final show and he was cold as ice. He didn't even look like the same cat that I'd had a relationship with.

I instructed Curse to toss his body somewhere it could be found—I'm not that heartless—and flew Curse back to LA to inconspicuously search his house to see if he could find the video. The shit wasn't there!

Chapter Ten
C. Banks

"So you killed this cat and didn't even get the video?" I asked rhetorically after he'd finished his story. I just couldn't believe this shit. If Simone hadn't told me what had happened to Stacey, I wouldn't have believed him. The shit was Beavis and Butthead stupid. A smart person would have been sure to keep him alive. A smart person would have kept that dude close and gave him whatever dollar amount he wanted, to get the video back. I thought Tyron was smarter than that, but I was wrong. He was the biggest dimwit in my eyes, and deserved to lose his life for this shit more than Stacey did.

"I know, B. It is what it is. I fucked up."

"Did 5-0 ever get at you? Did they question you about his death? Who knew you were fucking with dude?" I asked and watched as the truth flickered in his eyes for the briefest second.

"Naw, no, I haven't talked to any detectives!" he said. I could easily tell he was lying. "No one knew about us." Even the inflection in his voice changed; the shit went up a couple of octaves. This guy was a fucking trip.

"So you're telling me you don't think Stacey told Simone and Talise that he was dealing with you?" I asked cynically. *Did this cat think I was stupid?*

"He probably did tell them, but they can't prove that shit! That's some he said she said shit, right? What they call that shit?" he asked, another few octaves above the last.

"They call that shit hearsay and I don't *fucking* know! I'm not trying to get involved in that shit!" The last thing I needed was to be tied to some murder shit. If Simone thought that shit, 5-0 could think the same. I've done time in the pen and I wasn't going back, especially for some shit I didn't have nothing to do with.

"We just need a game plan to get that shit from home chick. What do you think she'll do? Is she capable of putting that shit out there like that? Is that some shit she'd do?" he asked intensely.

"She saw a video of me fucking the dude who killed her best friend. *I'd* release that shit!" I spat disgustedly as I stood up and went to the bar to pour another drink. I had to clear my head. *This shit was like a damn soap opera. Shit, I wished it was 'cause then, Stacey could come back from the fucking dead!* I thought as I took back the strong shot of expensive whiskey. "First, we need to make sure someone is tailing her..." No matter how I felt about her, we had to at least know what she was up to.

"Done!" He exclaimed before I could finish.

"Who do you have tailing her?" I asked dumbfounded. If someone was tailing her, I would've noticed them when she pulled into her building this morning. I was always on the lookout like that, and no one was tailing her. I was sure of it.

"Curse is, but his girl had a baby so he's been off for a few days."

I couldn't believe my ears! How could someone as smart as Tyron be so fucking dumb? This idiot had no street smarts what so ever!

"Are you serious right now? Why in the fuck would you have Curse following her? She's probably seen Curse before! We need a professional, not a damn bodyguard! Let me handle this shit from this point forward. Don't make no moves without going through me when it comes to this video shit." I pulled my cell out of my pocket and redialed a number from my recent call list. "Char, I need you to fly out here. I got some important shit I need to talk to you about. Get on the next thing smoking. I'll be at the Brentwood house." I hung up the phone with my soon to be ex-wife Charletta—we had yet to finalize our divorce. I headed toward the door. "Remember, B, don't make another move without going through *me* first!" I said before walking out of Tyron's penthouse suite. My number one priority was getting that video!

Chapter Eleven
Deon

"Deon, why don't you ever invite me to any of your games?" Ashia purred after swallowing all that I had released and removing my semi erect penis from her mouth.

"I don't do that, Ashia. I told you that before. I don't invite girls to my games," I said for what had to be the tenth time. I hated when women asked me for tickets to my games. If I wanted them there, I'd invite them, but that wasn't how I got down. I wasn't one of those players that invited random chicks to my games and put them in 'the ho' section for every other player to know.

"I'm not just any girl, Deon. I want to be with you. Just us, me and you," Ashia said, rubbing her hand across my bare chest.

Here we go with this, I thought as she snuggled her naked body closer to me and draped one of her long, soft legs over mine. I was depleted as I rested on my back, waiting for my energy to return.

"We would be good together. We make such a beautiful couple. We should be together, Deon," she repeated.

She didn't want to be with me; she wanted to be with the NBA star, the multi-millionaire athlete with high paying endorsements. She didn't even know me to want to be with me like that. She should have chosen Armond. He'd be happy to have her on his arm and would be none the wiser.

"You are with me, Ashia. We're together right now," I said, feigning ignorance as I caressed her long bare leg, snaking my way up her body to her soft plump breasts.

I'd stopped to visit her at her single level contemporary home that sat on one of the bird streets in the Hollywood Hills. I hadn't been there longer than thirty minutes and she was getting on my nerves. Had I known she was going to be in a talkative mood, *again*, I wouldn't have come.

"Deon, you know what I mean. We've been seeing each other for a few months now. I love you."

"Ashia, you don't love me. You don't know me to love me," I said as nicely as I could. She was ruining the mood.

"I do love you! Just because your heart is cold doesn't mean mine is!" she said, her voice rising with emotion.

"Here we go with this," I said, rising from the oversized, round, plush bed that sat in the middle of her large red painted room. I grabbed my boxer briefs off of the floor and slid them up my legs. "How could you love someone with a cold heart? Why do you call me if I'm so cold hearted, Ashia?" I asked.

"So now you want to leave? When the conversation gets too heavy, you run?" she taunted. She was used to getting her way and getting what she wanted, but I wasn't about to put up with her bratty attitude.

What Ashia wanted was to be a professional athlete's wife. I knew her type. She'd be on *Basketball Wives* the first chance she got. She wanted fame, money, and power. If she thought she was going to get that through me, she was wrong. This was definitely going to be my last time seeing her; she was making this too complicated.

"Is it because of *her*?" She asked, rising from her leopard print sheets and slinging her red silk robe over her naked long limbed frame.

"Ashia, what are you talking about?" She was starting to piss me off. I didn't have her in my life so we could have deep conversations or to hear her nag all the damn time. That was never what I had in mind and I thought she was on board too. No pressure, no labels, just fun. Now she's talking love?

"The girl you took to Andrew Bynums' party, Deon! The girl you *obviously* didn't mind getting seen by the paparazzi with, even though you've been fucking me for months! Do you know how embarrassing that was for me, Deon? Do you?"

"Why would people seeing me out with another woman embarrass you, Ashia? We aren't a couple? Is that what you are going around telling people? If so, you shouldn't be doing that. You will only embarrass yourself, Ashia," I said, trying to keep calm.

"How would you feel if you saw me coupled up with some guy and the photos were plastered all over a magazine and the internet?"

"Ashia, I'm not even gonna answer that. You're tripping!"

"What are you doing? Why can't we just have a conversation, Deon?" She asked, now standing in front of me with her hands on her hips.

"I'm leaving, Ashia," I said, pulling on my jeans.

"Deon, don't. Stop!" She grabbed my wrists, trying to prevent me from pulling my jeans all the way up. "We can talk about this later," she purred, changing her tune and trying to get my pants back down my legs.

"There's nothing to talk about. I'm leaving and that's it. You killed the mood." I pulled away from her and was finally able to button my pants. As I began to buckle my belt, she snatched the buckle out of my hands and pulled the belt out of its loops and from around my waist. She swiftly grabbed my shirt and undershirt off the chair next to the large dresser, swooped up my Air Yeezy's, and ran out of the room.

"Ashia, what in the hell are you doing?" I yelled after her.

I'm not about to play chase with her ass, I thought as I sat on the bed and waited for her to come back.

Minutes later, she walked back into the room empty handed. I waited for her to say something, but she didn't so we were quiet as we stared each other down.

"So you're leaving?" she asked, finally breaking the silence.

She stood in front of me with her hands on her hips and her robe hung open, exposing her nakedness. Her chest heaved up and down and her nipples were at attention as she waited for my answer.

"Yes, as soon as you give me my stuff, I'm leaving, Ashia. I'm not with playing these silly games with you."

"Then you're going to be leaving without a shirt on your back, a belt around your waist, and shoes on your feet," she said smugly.

"Ashia, quit playing and give me my stuff." I rose from the bed and stepped around her, grabbing my phone off of the nightstand before she tried to hold that hostage too.

"You're not leaving, Deon," she said and lightly shoved me in the back.

"Go get my shit and keep your hands to yourself, Ashia," I said sternly.

"What are you going to do if I don't give you *your shit*, Deon?" She asked with a smirk on her face, shoving me yet again.

"Ashia, you better stop pushing me," I warned.

She tried to grab the phone out of my hand, but was unsuccessful. She stood in front of me with her chest heaving up and down and her flawless honey toned skin glistening with a light sheen of sweat as her chest rose and fell.

"Make me stop, Deon," she said seductively, letting her robe fall to her ankles. This chick was acting like Sybil with her ever changing personality.

She turned away from me, exposing her long slender back, and positioned herself on all fours on the bed. To my chagrin, the sight of her pretty, wet middle made my dick hard.

"Make me stop, Deon," she purred yet again.

"You're crazy, Ashia," I said before walking up behind her and slapping her hard on her ass. "Is this what you want?" I smacked her ass harder the second time. "Answer me!" I said, slapping her left, red cheek a third time when she didn't respond.

"Yes! I want you to fuck me, Deon. Make me pay for getting out of line," *Sybil* begged.

"I'll make your ass pay alright!"

I kneeled down and lapped my tongue across her wetness. When the tip of my tongue flitted across her clit, she moaned sounds of ecstasy.

I jabbed two of my large fingers inside of her and slid the thumb of my right hand roughly into her ass, causing her to yell out in pain. I continued to lick and suck on her clit as my fingers worked both of her openings. I licked, sucked and fingered her until I knew she was on the brink of orgasm then stopped and pulled away.

"Oh my God, what are you doing? Don't stop, I was about to cum, Deon! Don't stop, *please!*" She begged as her hips gyrated back and forth, trying to entice me to pleasure her more.

"I told you I was going to make you pay, didn't I?" I asked, smacking her yet again on her left ass cheek, making her yell out a moan of pain filled pleasure.

I took my time removing my jeans and grabbing one of the condoms I'd placed on the nightstand. I peeled off the gold wrapper, slid the rubber on my hard thickness, and forcefully slid my dick inside of her, making her yell and lose balance. I gripped her around her waist and continued to pound in and out of her. My right arm held her securely around the waist while my left hand squeezed her breast and pinched her nipples. I snaked my hand down her flat stomach and rapidly flicked my finger over her clit. When I felt the slightest tremble from her body and noticed her getting back into her zone on the verge of cumming again, I pulled out and slapped her hard on her ass.

"Deon! What are you doing? Quit playing with me!" She said in a high-pitched voice as she lay on the bed with her ass in the air.

"Oh, you can play, but I can't?" I asked, smacking her on her ass.

When I was sure that the orgasm had passed, I grabbed

her ass cheeks and spread them apart a few times, massaging her middle before entering her again. I moved in and out of her, giving her exactly what she wanted. I wrapped my hand around her neck and pulled her to me so that her back was to my chest. I held her in that position, gently squeezing her neck as I pounded in and out of her from behind.

As she got wetter, her moans grew louder and I went deeper inside of her.

"You don't cum until I say you can cum, you hear me?" I asked gruffly in her ear, taking her lobe in my mouth and biting it.

"Please, please let me cum, Deon. Please!" She begged as I moved in and out of her warm wetness. She felt so damn good I could have stayed inside of her all night.

"Please let me cum!" She moaned again as her body began to convulse.

I continued stroking her as her body went limp and her opening throbbed and clenched my dick as her body shook. I moved in and out of her as she continued to cum all over the Magnum condom that served as our protection. The way she repeatedly clenched and unclenched her vaginal muscles had me releasing only moments later.

"Now go get my stuff, Ashia," I said as we lay splayed across her bed.

"You're still going to leave? Didn't I please you?" She seemed to always want to know if she pleased me. As beautiful as she knew she was, she was still insecure.

"Yes, you pleased me, but your games earlier didn't. If you wanted it rough, all you had to do was ask."

Still refusing to return my things, I left her home beltless, shirtless, and shoeless, thankful that I at least had a pair of shoes in my truck. As much as I enjoyed being inside of her, this was definitely going to be my last time messing with her crazy ass. This lifestyle I was living was definitely getting old.

Chapter Twelve
Simone

As I sat on Talise's plush, slip covered sofa in her family room holding Anastasia as she slept, I felt the first bit of peace that I'd felt in a long while.

"I can't believe how big she's getting. She is so beautiful, Talise. She is the perfect mix of both of you."

"Yeah, she is looking more and more like her daddy by the day, though. It's so crazy that she came from me. I still can't believe that she's mine sometimes," she confessed, looking adoringly at Anastasia. "Let me go lay her down in her room so we can talk," Talise said, attempting to take Anastasia out of my arms.

"No," I whispered. "I'll take her," I said, rising from my seat and heading toward the nursery that was beautifully decorated in pale yellows and greens with giraffes, elephants, and monkeys painted on the wall. Talise and Malachi had outdone themselves decorating this nursery, it was beautiful.

I gently placed little Ana on her back inside of her crib,

patted her stomach gently to get her back into a fitful sleep, and kissed her fat cheek
before I left the room.

When I returned to the family room, Talise handed me a hot mug and began to sip from the one in her hand. Since becoming pregnant and now breastfeeding, she'd become a tea connoisseur and had an assortment of the tastiest teas.

We sat on the sofa next to each other both folding our feet beneath us.

"Anything new from the detectives?" Talise asked.

"Nothing since they handed everything over to the DA. Now we just wait and see what they decide to do," I sighed.

"I hope they indict him and put him on trial for the world to see. People have no idea who that man really is, and they worship him!" Talise said, sounding pissed off.

"One way or the other, he *will* be exposed!"

"Simone, what are you planning? You really need to be careful with this... *situation*," she tried to plead. "We both know Tyron killed Stacey. He had someone break into your house. He will hurt you if not kill you too, Simone!"

"Especially after what I did to him when I saw him..." I trailed off. I knew she was about to be pissed that I was just now telling her this, and even more pissed that I put myself in danger like that.

"What do you mean when you saw him, Simone? When did you *see* him? What in the hell happened?" She asked as if she was my mother instead of my best friend. We'd always had this kind of relationship, though. She was always the voice of reason and I was always the emotional one trying to pretend that nothing affected me.

"Remember when my mom and I went to Deon's mother's

birthday dinner?" She shook her head in affirmation. "I went with Deon to Andrew Bynum's birthday party after…"

"Yes I know, Simone. Malachi brought home a copy of US Weekly that had pictures of you and Deon in it. You already told me this! What did you *not* tell me, is what you need to get to!" she said impatiently.

After telling Talise how I busted Tyron's head open with a bottle, I took a long, slow sip of my tea, never taking my eyes off of her. She sat her cup of tea on the end table that sat to the right of the sofa and stared at me.

"What kind of tea is this? Fortnum and Mason?" I asked with a smirk on my face. I knew she wouldn't answer my question, which made me chuckle.

"OH MY GOD, SIMONE! I can't believe you did that shit! What in the hell is wrong with you?" She said as she jumped up from her sitting position and walked the distance between the sofa and the love seat then back to the sofa before sitting back down.

I was back to sipping my tea as I watched her, waiting for her tirade to end, even though she was just getting started; her tirades never lasted long though.

"You said he was bleeding, Simone?"

"Yup!" Again, I went back to sipping my tea and waiting for what was to come next. I knew it was going to have something to do with me going to jail, but to my surprise, she burst out in uncontrollable laughter that had her holding her stomach as the gut wrenching cackle spewed from her open mouth. I thought she would wake the baby she was laughing so loud.

"What if he presses charges, Simone? You can go to jail for stuff like this!" She scolded, wiping tears from her eyes after her laughing spell had ceased. I *knew* she'd bring up jail!

"That's not going to happen, Talise. I'm sure he feels like the bitch he is right now. Let him try to press charges on me and that damn video will go viral in less than ten minutes!"

Serious again, Talise asked, "Simone, what are you trying to do? This shit is dangerous!" She cursed again uncharacteristically. "Yes, I'm glad he got popped upside the head with that bottle, by you especially, but this isn't some petty stuff, Simone!" She was trying to convince me, but I already knew this. They started it and I was going to finish it.

"Talise, Tyron killed Stacey! Have you forgotten that shit?" I asked exasperated. "I'm getting revenge if it's the last thing I do! I'm sorry Tali, but I can't let this shit fly! Tyron and Banks both deserve what's about to come to them!"

"Simone, Simone, Simone. Mark my words, this isn't going to end well. I really wish you would reconsider and let the authorities handle this!"

"You know me better than that, Talise. I can't let this ride. I'll give the justice system a chance to work, but their time is running out. Vengeance will be mine one way or the other."

Chapter Thirteen
C. Banks

*C*harletta finally made it to the house close to midnight. I'd been chain-smoking all day and knew I looked like shit. Once she saw me, she knew something was wrong. We'd been together since we were teenagers, she was the mother of my kids; she knew me.

I'll never forget the day I told her that I wanted a divorce; that I was in love with another woman. I knew I'd be breaking her heart, but I wasn't willing to lose Simone. She was like a drug to me. I felt things that I never imagined I could feel while I was with her. She lifted me up and now she was letting me down.

"Are you fucking kidding me?" Charletta yelled in her strong New York accent. "I know EVERYTHING about you! I don't judge you, but I bet that bitch would! You are the only man I've ever loved! I was fucking there for you when this new trick wouldn't have paid your lame ass no mind! Divorcing me?" she asked her emotion raw and thick.

She always knew that I did my thing, but I never let emotions get involved. She knew men had needs and that I had even more needs than the average man. She always let me do me. She was my ace and my wife, but the crazy intense love that I experienced with Simone, I never felt with Charletta or with anyone else. Simone was everything.

"I'm sorry, Char! You know I will always love you. You know I will always have your back and take care of you, but I have to follow this shit that I'm feeling, yo! I know this is fucked up. I know that I'm the shittiest bum in your eyes right now, but there is no other way." I felt like scum of the earth.

"Why divorce me, Carlton? Have the bitch on the side!" she cried. "Don't break up our family!" She pleaded, walking up to me and grabbing my hands.

"I'm sorry Char! That's not fair to you. You deserve better. You deserve to be with a man who is crazy in love with you!" I tried convincing her. "I'm never around. I'm always on the road..."

"But you found time to fall in love with some other bitch, Carlton? You've always been on the go. You're always on the road. This shit ain't no different! It won't last!" She tried to reason with me. "She don't know you like I know you! She CAN'T understand you like I understand you! You know that!" She cried and dropped to her knees.

"I'm sorry!" was all I could tell her. My decision had already been made.

"What's up with you Carlton?" Charletta asked, walking over to the couch and sitting across from me. Her small five foot four frame, slim waist, and thick hips still looked as they did when we were teens. Child bearing had done nothing to disfigure her body. If anything, it had given her more ass and hips, putting many mothers of two to shame.

"Some real foul shit is going down, Char, and I don't know what to do," I confessed. She was the one person that knew me inside and out. There were no secrets between the two of us. She loved me unconditionally, and wasn't bitter toward me after she got over the shock of me filing for divorce.

"Wow. This must be some sticky shit if you don't know what to do. Talk to me." She said, placing her Hermes bag on the seat cushion next to her and crossing her thick legs. Her fair skinned face couldn't hide the rose color that started to spread across her cheeks as I began to tell her what was going on. I could read every emotion that crossed her face as I relayed every single detail, concluding with Stacey's murder. Tears were in her eyes as she sat there, for once, not having anything to say. It was rare for Charletta to be rendered speechless, but she had just gotten an earful.

~ ~ ~ ~ ~ ~

I met Charletta at the end of my last year of middle school. She was a freshman in high school and worked at her father's real estate company answering phones after school every day. I could easily pass for a junior in high school and had no reservations when it came to mackin' girls, no matter their age.

Her father was selling my parents a second home in Upstate New York, and they dragged me along with them— knowing I would get into some kind of trouble if left alone—to sign the final paperwork. I stayed in the lobby and talked to Charletta while my parents took care of their business. By the time they were done, I had her number and planned on calling her that night.

My pops was a smart Yale educated man. He was a successful Investment Banker on Wall Street and provided us with a good living, but he was never around. I barely knew him and from a young age, I resented that he never spent time with us, so I lashed out often. Because of my quick temper, I was kicked out of multiple private schools for fighting. I would get warnings from the head of school, then detention, suspension, and then ultimately expelled when there was nothing else they could do; no one could control me. It seemed the only time I got my pop's attention was when I fucked up, and still, there were no real consequences. My parent's wealth could always buy me into another school, but they were fed up, and they had decided to send me to boarding school, where they thought I could learn discipline. They hoped I'd begin to appreciate the advantages their money provided me. But, before I was shipped off to Connecticut to start high school, everything fell apart.

My pops was one of very few black men who managed multimillion-dollar hedge fund investment accounts. He was in charge of overseeing a lot of money for wealthy people. All was legit in the beginning, until he brought in two business partners that led him down the path to greed. According to the Securities & Exchange Commission, that's when the Ponzi scheme began and unraveled less than 5 years later.

My pops and his partners received multiple charges for the scheme that totaled over one hundred million dollars, and were set to be tried. Hundreds of investors went bankrupt, while hundreds of others lost half, if not all of their net worth. They were facing life in prison.

My pops was out on bail with a tracking bracelet around his ankle to ensure that he wouldn't flee before he could be tried. He could barely face my moms and me; he was ashamed. That shit broke my pops down, but it broke my mother down even further. She was humiliated. She wouldn't even leave the house. She was ashamed to show her face to the neighbors, let alone her friends.

She was the type that was all about appearances, looking neat, and having the best of everything. That scam shit was the end, and she was sure to make pops remember that he had ruined our lives; that while he rotted in jail for stealing all of those investor's money, we'd be standing on the county line applying for welfare. She badgered him so much that the shame she wouldn't let him hide from and the extra stress she was putting on him, coupled with the high probability that he would be spending the rest of his life in prison, drove him over the edge. He shot himself in the head in front of my mother while I was at school. I'm sure she was in mid bitch when he pulled the trigger, splattering her with his blood and brain matter, scarring her for life.

She wasn't the same woman after that. Hell, nothing was ever the same after that. The only constant in my life from that point forward was Charletta. She was the only person that I could talk to. She always listened to me and told me that everything was going to be all right.

After pops killed himself and the SEC confiscated and sold off all of our shit, we moved to a one-bedroom tenement in Harlem. We didn't have shit but our clothes. Moms got a job as a secretary at an insurance agency, not too far from where we lived. She worked for an Italian man who paid her pennies and worked her hard. I started my first public school venture, which didn't affect me at all. I finally felt like I was in my element.

I held my own in the public school environment and was

around a lot of other kids who had tempers just as bad as mine. I was young, hotheaded, and had a lot of built up aggression from trying to stay strong for my moms after all the shit we'd been through with my pops. When I got into my first fight at my new school, I blacked out and beat two cats pretty bad. I unleashed months of pent up anger on the guys, and wasn't even punished by the school because it was evident that they were trying to jump me. Thankfully, no one tried to test me after that; my moms had too much shit on her plate to be worried about me getting into trouble.

High school seemed to fly by. I had a cool crew of dudes that I hung with. We were all into rhyming and music. Hip-hop was everything to us. We used to wild out to the Rough Ryders and DMX. Reasonable Doubt by Jay Z was knocked over and over. Nas's Illmatic was the illest thing I'd ever heard! Biggie Smalls and 2pac were killing the game with the east coast, west coast beef. Music was everything to me. It was the only thing that really took me away. I could write away my aggression and ease my tension by battling one of the cats from around the way. No one could defeat me in a freestyle battle, and my writing skills weren't to be rivaled. I didn't need to use my hands to fight any more; I used my words and they were much more powerful.

As my freshman year progressed, I got tired of seeing my mother work her ass off, come home tired, and still not have enough money to pay the bills and keep food on the table. Moms would go without paying bills to make sure that she kept me looking presentable. I wasn't laced in the flyest gear, nor were my clothes designer, but I knew how to work with what I had and made it look cool. One pair of shell-toe Adidas could last me for months and still look like I'd just taken them out the box.

After noticing some of my boys getting money and hustling, I wasn't going to be the one left behind, so I jumped in headfirst. The game came easily to me. I had a good way with people and was fair in my dealings. I was trustworthy, so I moved up pretty quickly and got close with the main man who took me under his wing. I was now able to pay all the bills and take care of things at home like they should have been.

Moms knew what I was up to; I didn't hide it from her. That was never how I did things. She didn't like it of course, but she didn't protest. She was used to being taken care of, and tired of working her ass off for a check that didn't even cover all of our bills. She just told me to be smart about my business, watch my back, and not to trust anyone. That was the best advice she could have given a son who was going to be out in the streets hustling, whether she liked it or not.

By the time I was a senior, I still went to school, but not as often as I should have. I was getting money, and school wasn't where the money was. Charletta and I were still tight, but she was always on me about doing right and going to school so I could graduate. She was now working full time at her father's real estate business. She had gotten her sales license after she graduated high school and was doing pretty good for herself. We bought a co-op and I bought my moms a small condo in upper Manhattan to get her out of that shit hole we were living in. I paid her bills and made sure she had everything she needed. She had long since quit working at the insurance agency and spent her days shopping and doing whatever made her happy. She deserved that.

Charletta's dad was an old hustler who turned his illegal money into a legitimate business, so he schooled me and made sure my money went in the right places and was protected. He didn't have a son, so he took me in and loved me as his own. He was like a father to me and I went to him as a son would go to his pops.

All was well in my life. I managed to graduate high school. I was getting money, saving it, taking care of my family, and I was ready to get out the game and make my mark in the music industry; that's when my temper got the best of me.

Disrespect to a man who also happens to be a hustler was a very dangerous thing. A man can never allow even one person to disrespect him, or others will believe they can do the same. Weakness was never in me; the man who thought so, is now resting in peace.

To me, there isn't much worse than a liar and a thief, so when my money came up short from one of my most trusted workers, I couldn't give him a pass. I couldn't if I had wanted to, because I blacked out. The only thing I remember is being hauled off by four police officers and thrown in the back of an NYPD squad car with cuts on my knuckles and blood splatter on my clothes. I'd beat him to death with my bare hands and couldn't even remember it.

At eighteen, I was sentenced to thirteen years at Rikers for first-degree manslaughter. My moms was crushed. Charletta vowed to stay by my side and Mr. Carlyle, Charletta's father, handled my money and took care of my moms as I would have, while I was locked up.

Charletta kept her word to me and stood by me through my entire bid. She never once wavered. Even when I tried to break up with her, she wouldn't let me. I felt she deserved better than that shit. But like clockwork, she was there to see me every weekend with my moms, made sure I had money on my books, and looked after my moms like a daughter would. She was my rock, and held me down, when *most women her age would have bailed.*

I spent the majority of my time locked down writing rhymes and working out. I took every educational class that was offered and tried to keep my head down and stay out of trouble.

Prison was a horrible place for an eighteen year old. I experienced things that changed my life, things that would probably have me in a different situation this present day; things, that had they not happened, would make the possibility of that video existing impossible. I vowed to myself that I would never go back. It was either death or freedom for me.

True to his word, Mr. Carlyle doubled my money by the time I was released. He invested it in different real estate development projects, flipped houses, and made nice profits for both of us. He even bought a couple of rental properties and signed the deeds over to me when I was released. Shit like that is almost unheard of, but that man looked out for me as if I were his blood son.

~ ~ ~ ~ ~ ~

"So yeah, you're right. This *is* some very sticky shit. You know I don't even really get down like that, Char. That shit was the last time and that was over a damn year ago. I was drinking that damn Patron and on a fucking power trip, yo," I sighed to Charletta.

"I can't believe this! You don't have to explain that shit to me, Carlton. I know you inside and out. I just can't believe you wanted to leave me for that bitch! A bitch that would do some shit like this to you! What do we need to do to get that video from her, Carlton?" she asked, her voice rising with panic.

"I'll handle that. I just wanted you to know what's going

on and to make sure that you are still down with me. *Are you still down with me, Char?*"

"Carlton, come on! If you didn't already know that I'm down with you one hundred and fifty percent, you wouldn't have just told me all this shit!"

"I know, I know, just needed to hear you say it. Contact Rob Maynard and let him know that I need him to fly out here immediately. Tell him to bring his top investigators and be sure to tell him that time is of the essence. I need him here yesterday!

Chapter Fourteen
Tyron

The continuous ringing of both my cell phone and landline woke me from my drunken sleep. I'd been up all night drinking and partying with a few people and hadn't been asleep for more than two hours.

"Get up right now and go to TMZ.com. I'll be up in less than ten minutes. I'm pulling up to the valet at your building right now," Gretchen, my publicist said before hanging up the phone. By the tone of her voice, I knew something serious was going on.

I got out of the bed as fast as I could. I was still drunk and unsteady on my feet, but made it to my laptop and powered it on. I called the front desk to tell them that it was okay to let her up when she got there and then opened the Firefox browser, typed in the site, and waited impatiently for it to load. Once it did, my knees buckled at the sight of Stacey's smiling face.

Tyron Marks; a Person of Interest in the
Brutal Slaying of a Los Angeles Hair Stylist

Las Vegas Police Detectives are reaching out to the public and anyone else who may have information on the brutal murder of Stacey Flenoy, a Los Angeles hair stylist whose body was found dumped in a ravine off of I15 near the W. Sahara Avenue exit in Las Vegas, Nevada. According to detectives, Tyron Marks is a person of interest and has been less than forthcoming regarding his relationship with the victim.

"His refusal to speak with us and clear up a lot of inconsistencies has caused us to believe he is hiding something. Stacey Flenoy was a homosexual male who we believe was close to Tyron Marks, yet Mr. Marks denies ever knowing the victim. We are just trying to fill in the blanks and he isn't being cooperative. We've invited him to speak with us and bring his attorney, but Mr. Marks feels he is above the law," Lead Detective Jenkins with the Las Vegas homicide division said. They are asking anyone to come forward if they have any information.

After reading the statement over and over, I stared at Stacey's smiling face until I heard Gretchen's knock at the door. I quickly padded to the door and swung it open and walked back into the living area of the suite without waiting for her to walk in.

"Do you know anything about this, Tyron? You know I don't like being blindsided! What in the hell is going on? I need to know everything so I can try to fix this, pronto!" The petite, blonde Jewish bulldog of a publicist said as she paced in circles around the couch.

"Gretch, sit down. There is nothing to this shit," I lied. My nerves were shot, but I had to keep it together in front of her. "Listen, I need to talk to my attorney. I can't tell you how to respond to this shit yet."

"Tyron, we need to hop on this shit immediately! I'm already dodging calls, emails, and texts, and I can't for much longer," she said, finally taking a seat across from me.

"Gretchen, you can do what I tell you to do, and right now, I need you to quit buggin' out on me, yo!" I rubbed my hand across my face, feeling the stitches that were to be removed tomorrow under my hand. *This shit is getting worse by the day.*

"First the club shit and the stitches that you wouldn't let me say anything about, even though everyone knows that Banks' ex girl did that to you, and now this? Come on, Tyron, this is what I do! This doesn't look good for either of us," she complained as my cell vibrated.

I looked at the caller ID and saw Tomi's photo and name. She was the last person I wanted to talk to. I sent the call to voicemail and it immediately rang again. I looked down, expecting to see her face again, but it was Banks, the second to last person I wanted to talk to. I sent him to voicemail too.

"Gretchen, listen, this shit is *my* life and you work for *me.* You can advise me, but ultimately, it's up to me what statements will be released on my behalf. Let me meet with my attorney, and then I'll let you know what can be said, if anything."

"Did you know this guy?"

"Gretchen, I'll call you after I talk to my attorney. You can let yourself out." I left her sitting there as I walked through my room and into the bathroom. I turned on the shower and sent my attorney a text. I knew by the time I got out of the shower and dressed, he'd be here ready to make all of this shit go away.

Chapter Fifteen
Simone

"Hey, what's up?" I answered when I saw that Deon was calling my cell.

"Just got home from my game, we lost. What are you up to?" he asked, sounding like his dog died.

"Oh, I'm sorry to hear that. I'm not doing much, just relaxing." Deon and I had been talking at least once a day since the incident at Drai's. I usually left it up to him to reach out to me when he felt like talking. I didn't want to send him the wrong message by calling frequently because being with him in that way was the furthest thing from my mind.

"I'm hungry. Feel like grabbing something to eat?" he asked.

"Yeah, I can eat. What do you have in mind?"

"Something low key. I need to get out of this house, even though I just walked through the door."

"Why don't you just come over here and we can order delivery or something. I'd rather not go out in this weather anyway," I suggested. It was a rare rainy and cold day in

Los Angeles, and like most natives, I didn't care to be out in it. My mother was in Carson with Mommy Miles at some church revival, and would most likely not be coming home until morning.

"That's perfect. I'm on my way. Do you need me to bring anything?"

"No, just bring yourself. See you when you get here." After getting off of the phone with Deon, I didn't bother to change my clothes. I had on black leggings, a long sleeved, purple fitted v-neck, thermal t-shirt, and some comfortable fluffy striped yellow, blue and lavender socks. I was home relaxing and wasn't going to change just because he was coming over. It wasn't like that between us anyway.

I grabbed the folder labeled 'menus' out of the built-in desk in my office and started looking through them to narrow down the choices. I had over fifteen menus from delivery restaurants, so deciding could be challenging, and tonight wasn't one of those nights that I could tolerate my indecisiveness. I put aside Chinese, Thai, and Indian and knew we'd be good with either choice.

I sat the menus on the kitchen counter, poured myself a glass of Sauvignon Blanc, and sat on the sofa. I kicked my feet up as the rain pounded against my windows. The sounds soothed me. The shutters were cracked, allowing the scent of the fresh rain cleared air to sift in, but my home still remained warm and cozy from the heat emitting from the logs that burned in the fireplace. I had the lights on dim and there was no TV on or music playing.

As I sat in the quiet—save for the rain that splattered against the windowpanes, the crackling of the logs burning in the fireplace, and the occasional light traffic noise from the street fifteen stories below—memories of the times Deon and I shared together began to fill my mind.

I would never allow myself to think back on the months we spoke multiple times a day and spent intimate time together, but in the quiet of that moment, I let those thoughts flood in. Back then, I couldn't even admit that I had allowed myself to be hurt by him. The foul shit that he did to me; the way he cut me off and threw me away like I wasn't shit, was undeserved.

With each sip of wine, I became more and more agitated. The feelings I felt when he disappeared from my life with no explanation was starting to resurface, or surface I should say, because I had never allowed myself to feel these feelings. I did everything I could to distract myself and harden my heart so I wouldn't feel anything, so I wouldn't think about him.

But that night, when Deon stood me up, really hurt me. I didn't hear from him until close to a month later, but by the time he decided to call, it was *way* too late. The multiple messages he left on the salon answering machine—why he didn't call my cell or home numbers was beyond me— pleading with me to call him back so he could explain, fell on deaf ears. I wasn't trying to hear anything he had to say. I remained steadfast, even with Talise and Stacey in my ear, telling me I should at least hear the man out. At the time, I didn't want to hear what he had to say over the phone and I didn't want to hear what he had to say when I ran into him when I was on my first date with Carlton at a party for that video game, but tonight I wanted to know!

By the time Deon knocked on my door, my agitation had increased tenfold. I had let his ass off too easy. He'd hurt me! Yes, I tried to pretend that the shit he did didn't really bother me, but it did! I'd buried it so deep inside the crevices of my mind, that I allowed myself to hang out with him and talk to him like I didn't deserve at least some explanation for the shit he'd done to me.

When Nichelle was killed, I had to be there for him. What happened between us was a moot point at that time. We were all grieving. That wasn't the time or place to bring it up. I figured he'd hooked back up with his college girlfriend when he went back to his hometown, and that was the end of it. I was happy and enjoying my time with Carlton. I didn't need or want to hear his excuses. *Boy, times have surely changed.*

It took me three tries to turn off the alarm because I had worked myself up so much. I was pissed!

"Hey Mone," he said, hugging me after I'd opened the door and let him in.

"Hey," I replied, hugging him back halfheartedly. The apathetical embrace didn't go unnoticed by him. He was always able to easily read my mood.

"What's up with you?" He asked as he walked through the door, heading toward the living room. His eyebrows furled together in puzzlement as he sat his long frame on the sofa.

"I need to get something off of my chest, but first do you want a drink or something?" I asked dryly. I figured I should at least be hospitable.

"No, I'm good. What's up Simone? Tell me what's on your mind." He crossed his long legs at the ankles, sat back on my deep, plush LoveSac sofa and looked at me intently.

"I need to know what happened. I need to know why you just cut me off like I wasn't shit, like I didn't deserve at least an explanation or a goodbye or a 'I'm not into you anymore.' I'm starting to question if I should even be entertaining you as a friend after how you did me!" I said sincerely as I stood there, the emotion clearer in my voice than I would have preferred.

"Simone, come sit down," he said, patting the seat next to him.

I walked over and sat across from him on the love seat, not wanting to sit next to him. "I've been trying to tell you this for a long time," he continued once I was seated. "I know I handled that situation the wrong way. Hindsight is always twenty-twenty. I should've given you a chance to defend yourself, and I know that now. Hell, I knew that shortly after it all went down, but it was too late," he admitted.

"Defend myself against what, Deon?" I asked. I was truly puzzled.

"That day at the Mid-Summer Nights game after I got off the phone with you, I ran into Byron Boyd," he said.

"Okay, and? What did that asshole have to say?" I asked incredulously.

"Simone, he told me that you set him up. That you lied and told the police that he beat you when he didn't. He said you sued him and got a large settlement. He told me a lot of stuff that blew me away, to tell you the truth. I was really digging you and wanting to be with you, but after he told me all that stuff, it made me feel like I could be in a bad situation if I kept dealing with you. It made me question my judgment. I felt stupid..."

"If you were digging me so much, why didn't you come to me?" I asked, cutting him off. "Why didn't you just ask *me*? If anything, I thought we were cool, that we were friends. You don't and didn't owe me anything, but as a man, you should have gotten both sides of the story."

"When I asked you what went down with you two after we ran into him at the Cheesecake Factory, you completely shut down, Simone. I didn't know how you'd react to me questioning you and I wasn't sure it was my place anyway. What was I supposed to think when a dude that I've known since college tells me something like that, Simone?"

"If you allow one person to tell you their side of the story, you should at least give the other person a chance to tell their side as well," I stated, shaking my head. I wasn't surprised that Byron would tell lies like these, but I was a bit surprised that Deon believed what Byron told him, without at least checking with me to see what I had to say. I thought we were closer than that.

"You're right. I did the wrong thing and I tried to explain it to you. I called you at the salon multiple times and tried to talk to you at the PlayStation party, but you weren't trying to hear anything I had to say because you were with that rapper dude."

"True," I admitted.

"Nichelle told me that I had to live with the decision I made, and that's what I've been doing," he confessed. "Will you tell me your side of the story, Simone?"

I got up to pour myself another glass of wine before answering. "Only if you'll have a glass of wine with me. Should we order food now?"

"I can wait for food if you can," he answered when I returned with the bottle of wine and an extra glass for him. I filled his glass, handed it to him, and sat next to him on the sofa. Not close, but at least on the same piece of furniture this time.

"Byron was my first boyfriend," I began, not really wanting to revisit these memories, but needing to for the sake of clearing my name, if nothing else. "He was the first man I ever had sex with. Hell, he was the first boy I ever kissed," I remembered. "We went to high school together, we went to USC together before he transferred to Clark, and we lived together after he got drafted to the Chargers. Byron had, and probably still does have a lot of issues. He was abusive in a lot of ways. At first, it was just him controlling me, wanting to know where I was, who I was with and what I was doing every minute of the day. Then he would flip out when he couldn't get ahold of me. His temper was really over the top and got progressively worse as our relationship continued.

"I loved him and wanted to make it work because I thought he loved me, and at that point, he had never really hit me. He would push me around, but he had never actually put his hands on me. When he finally did, it was really bad. He broke three of my ribs, fractured my arm... he really messed me up," I said, trailing off. This shit was too painful to think about, which was why I hadn't in a very long time. "I loved him and I think he loved me the best way he knew how. He was just jealous. He crossed the line, though. I could never allow a man to kick me and beat me like I'm worthless!"

I took a long sip of my wine before continuing. "It took some coaxing from Talise and her parents, but I did press charges. I wanted him to pay for what he had done to me. That man scarred me for life, Deon," I said honestly. "You know what the sick thing is, though?" I asked rhetorically. "I didn't want to see him in jail. After everything that he had done to me, I still didn't want to see him locked up and lose everything. I just wanted him to get help, so I settled out of court and made it a requirement that he got extensive counseling. I don't know if that was the right thing, but it was the right thing for me at that time."

"Wow! Now I'm even sorrier for not talking to you about it beforehand, Simone. It's crazy because my ex girl is the one that put the seed in my ear that Byron could have been lying about what he told me. She was around when we were in school and she never really cared for him. I felt like shit once the realization hit me, and I knew you wouldn't let me back in after that. I knew it was too late, but I did try."

Oh, so he had talked to his ex about me. That admission didn't go unnoticed.

"I figured you were out there with her and just played me. It really did hurt my feelings though," I finally admitted.

"I'm sorry, Simone. That was never my intention. I went to have dinner with my ex, and we officially ended our relationship. She told me that she was seeing someone else, a woman," he said and smiled at my reaction, not knowing that I could one up him on that, if I told him about Carlton and Tyron.

"Damn! How did that make you feel?"

"To be honest, it made me feel relieved. There was always some disconnect between us that made me try harder and harder to please her, but even that never seemed to work. She's happy now. That's what matters."

"That's deep. Hey, why didn't you ever call my cell or home phone? You had those numbers," I asked curiously.

"I deleted them," he admitted abashedly and for some reason, we both found that funny and started laughing.

"You're a loser!" I joked.

"Seriously though, will you forgive me, Simone?" Deon asked sincerely.

"Yes, I forgive you, Deon. We can be friends, but don't

ever do anything like that to me again," I said and gave him a playful punch on the arm.

"So what happened with you and the rapper dude?" he asked, sipping his wine.

"If I told you, you wouldn't even believe me," I replied and looked away. His eyes always seemed to bore into me like he could read what I was thinking. Sometimes, Deon was so intense... too intense. "It seems like the craziest things happen to me when love is involved."

"Try me."

"It's sticky, Deon. With Carlton being who he is and with the other people involved, this is... dangerous." I admitted, shaking my head sadly because this shit *was* sad.

"Okay, so let me ask you this. Did what happen between you and the rapper have anything to do with what happened at Drai's?"

Why he always called Carlton the rapper was beyond me. I had yet to hear him call him by his name.

I contemplated my answer for a good while before speaking.

"Actually," I started, trying to find the right words. "What happened between Carlton and me had nothing to do with why I did what I did at Drai's, but had Carlton not done what he'd done, what happened at Drai's probably would have never happened. Mull that over. I know that was a bit confusing."

I got up, went to the kitchen, grabbed a fresh bottle of wine out of the wine cabinet, uncorked it, returned, and sat back next to him. I refilled both of our glasses, sat the bottle on the coffee table, but didn't continue as he probably thought I would.

"In the elevator at Drai's, you told me that dude killed

Stacey. Later, once we got to the room, you told me he would kill you. You said you had some stuff on him that he'd kill you for."

"I told you that?" I was shocked. I had no memory of telling him anything of the sort. I must have been drunk out of my damned mind to let that slip off my tongue!

"Yeah you did. You told me some shit," he admitted.

"What else did I tell you?" I took a sip of my wine and pulled my feet beneath me onto the sofa. He locked his piercing gaze on me and didn't answer until I began waving my hand in small circular motions, trying to encourage him to continue.

"I asked you what you had on him, but all you'd tell me was that Stacey recorded something and that Tryon Marks dude killed him to get it, but didn't get it and now you have it. You wouldn't tell me what Stacey recorded, if it was an audio or video recording; nothing else," he finished.

"I don't remember telling you that and I can't believe that I did. That was a crazy night for me. I just lost it when I saw him. I was thinking, 'this guy has a lot of fucking nerve!' and I lost it."

"So what you told me is true?" he asked, wanting it to be clear. I looked at him for a long time again, contemplating my answer.

"Yes, It's true," I decided to admit, as my eyes filled with tears that I refused to let fall.

"So what are you going to do, Simone? Is this worth you risking your life over?"

"If it was worth Stacey's life, it's worth my life. When everyone knows the truth, I will be at peace."

"I don't like this, Simone. I really don't. I didn't do anything for Nichelle when I knew I should have, and now you're in a situation that could cost you your life. I hope you know I'm not about to sit around and let that happen," he said, his voice rising slightly.

"Deon, I'll be alright. As long as I have what I have, they won't do anything to me."

"Stacey probably thought the same thing, Simone," Deon said, sounding like he'd talked to Talise. "I don't care what you say or how much you protest, I'm hiring security and they will be with you twenty-four-seven, whether you like it or not. This isn't up for discussion."

Chapter Sixteen
C. Banks

*A*fter meeting with Rob Maynard and telling him there was a "package" out there that would be very damaging to me if it got out, he immediately understood the urgency of the situation and knew what needed to be done.

Once Charletta called him, he was here the next morning just as I knew he would be. Rob and I go way back; he would drop anything to come see about me. I kept him on retainer, so he was paid a nice fee every month, even when there was little work to be done.

When I started hanging heavy with Simone, I had Rob send one of his guys to keep a watch on her just, so I could be sure she was who she said she was and was doing what she said she was doing. People will lie about a lot of shit, so to know for sure *for sure* that who you are dealing with is on the up and up is priceless, especially when you have the status and recognition that I have; shit popping out of the woodwork is a public relations nightmare. Even when the shit is about someone in your camp, your name is

plastered all across that shit: *"So and so part of C. Banks'
entourage was arrested for rape."* Shit like that will always
have my name attached to it if it's someone in my crew, so
I was always careful about who I let in.

I knew everything about Simone before she told me. So
when she did, it made me like her even more. She wasn't
the type of person that told all of her business, but when
she felt she could trust you and was comfortable with you,
she would let you in bit by bit, revealing more and more
about herself. She didn't try to sugar coat shit. Her past
was her past and what she had been through was what she
had been through. She was a take it or leave it type of chick,
and I liked that shit.

A lot of times, chicks are so concerned about what
you'd think about them, that they don't see how sexy that
shit is when they be themselves and are unapologetic
about it. That was Simone; she didn't try to pretend that
her guard wasn't up or that she was a perfect woman.
She'd look you dead in the eyes and not answer a question
if she thought it wasn't any of your business. Her tough-
ness was all a façade though. Once I got past that outer
tough shell, I saw that she was sensitive and emotion
driven; she was beautifully flawed.

One part of me wanted to protect her, and the other
wanted to hurt her for putting me through this shit when
she could easily give that damn video up and let this shit
ride! I loved and hated her at the same time, and that shit
was enough to drive me crazy if I let it.

Rob discussed my options and gave me his opinion on
what he thought would be the best way to go about this.
He was always straight forward and to the point. We talked
for over two hours when he came to me that morning over

two weeks ago. By the time he left my office, I felt confident that he would get the job done. 'Plan One' had already gone into effect and 'Plan Two' was in the works. This situation was too intricate and needed someone skilled in this type of work; Rob was the guy.

Ricky, one of my assistants, knocked on my office door. I could always tell it was him because of his single tap against the tinted glass. He walked in, carrying a note pad, smart phone, and a pen, ready to go over my schedule with me. I sat behind my large glass and oak wood desk and waited for him to sit down.

Ricky had been working with us for close to four months and was good at his job. He helped me and Tyron out tremendously. I was apprehensive about hiring him at first because he didn't come from a music background. He was previously an executive assistant at an advertising agency, but Tyron thought he would be good and the lady in HR highly recommended him. We needed someone fast, so I gave her my go ahead and hadn't regretted it once.

"What we got up today?" I asked, leaning back in the comfortable leather swivel chair.

"You are due in the studio with Drake in two hours. You have a radio interview in three hours, so you are going to have to duck out of your studio session for about thirty minutes," he said apologetically as he sat in the chair in front of my desk. "Cookie already has your complete schedule. She will make sure you get where you need to be on time." Cookie was my other assistant. She was always with me when I was out working. Ricky held things down here and let Cookie know what needed to be done each day and then Cookie made sure everything went according to plan.

"Ok, that's cool. Who is the interview with?"

"Angie Martinez, Hot97. You also have a photo shoot at eight with Annie Leibovitz for the cover of Rolling Stone tonight!" he said excitedly. I had forgotten all about it with all the shit that had been going on. This was big, and I couldn't even get excited. Too much was on my mind and on the line.

My career was skyrocketing more than I ever imagined. My music had crossed over without me ever compromising who I am as an artist. I was making more money than I ever could have dreamed. *Shit!* If that video gets out, nothing I've achieved in the past would matter. I'd be done.

"Tyron keeps asking me to see where you're at tour wise," Ricky said.

I couldn't believe this shit. The fact that this dummy is even contemplating leaving town and going on tour with everything we have going on has me wondering if he's already fucking checked out.

"Is he in his office?" I asked, reaching for the phone when Ricky said yes. "Yo, a tour? Are you serious, Tyron?" I asked when he picked up the line. This guy was definitely losing it. "Man, come to my office; we need to talk." I hung up the phone and asked Ricky if there was anything else.

"That's it for now. We do need to talk about local performances and shows though. Jimmy Fallon would like to have you on and so would Jay Leno. Maybe you could appease Tyron by doing a local concert or two. Maybe the Nokia Theatre or the Gibson; just a thought," he said, rising from his seat at the knock on the door.

"A great thought. I'll talk to Tyron about that. Let me know when it's time to go." He agreed as he let Tryon into my office and walked out, shutting the door behind him.

"What is wrong with you, Ty? Are you losing it, B?" I asked sincerely, getting up from my desk, walking to the front of it, and sitting on the wooden edge.

"Naw, Banks! I'm just saying, we need to get on the road! We have to stay active! We have to stay relevant!" He tried to explain way too excitedly.

Yeah, he was losing it. He was not acting like his usual calm and in charge self.

"Tyron, you need to chill the fuck out! We *don't* need to go on tour. We *don't* need to go nowhere. First off, you need to lay low, calm the fuck down, and do what you've been doing. You are acting out of sorts; that's my word!" Tyron paced the room a couple of times before stopping at the floor to ceiling window.

"This shit *is* getting to me, I can't even lie! First the blogs, then that TMZ shit! I don't know what the fuck to do!"

"You have to keep pushing, Ty. You can't let this shit run you down like this. What did your attorney say?"

"I'm meeting with the fucking detectives, Banks. This shit is just too much," he sighed, taking a seat in the small leather chair by the window. He covered his face with his hands and sat that way for a few moments.

"You can't make this shit go away, Tyron. You have to face this shit head on. You ducking and dodging 5-0 is only making you look more suspicious. Just knock that shit out and get it over with and keep pushing forward. You gotta focus man," I tried to convince him. This guy was falling apart before my eyes.

"Shit, it's hard to focus right now, Banks. That's why I think I need to go out on the road or something. I have to do something!"

"You have a lot of shit to do here, Ty! You can't run from

this shit. We got Wink's first shit being mastered right now. We got Sajaira in the studio with Glow and her video shoot is around the damn corner. There is a lot of stuff to be done here! You just need to focus and try to get back to your shit as much as you can. You having a fucking meltdown ain't gone help you... us." I was hoping he was getting what I was saying. I had never seen Tyron this broken. Thankfully, he still took the time to dress and make himself look presentable, but this shit was definitely cracking him. *I'm going to have to keep my eyes on him too*, I thought as Ricky's voice buzzed through the intercom, letting me know it was time to head to the studio.

Chapter Seventeen
Simone

I was beyond tired of dreaming about Carlton. I would erase him from my memory if it were possible. He was still heavy on my mind daily, and I just wanted a reprieve.

I wanted to stop loving him, I wanted to feel normal. I wished I could make the love, feelings, and all thoughts of him go away, but I couldn't. I'd be fine, then he'd cross my mind and my heart would take a dive from the pain and hurt every memory of him caused. I missed him like crazy and wanted to be with him, but that wasn't an option any more. I had to go on without him and I didn't want to.

I looked over at Anastasia sleeping peacefully next to me—Talise and Malachi were having a date night and I was happy to have her spend the night with me. I snuggled up next to her and kissed her cheek and watched her as she slept soundly without a care in the world. I ran my hand over her mass of dark curly hair, kissed her forehead, and rose from the bed. I hadn't had a full night's sleep since all of this mess began.

I walked to my large bedroom window and looked out at the clear morning skies. It was close to eight, and light morning traffic had already begun to fill the streets below. I could clearly see the black Mercedes S600 parked in front of my building where Ed and Marlo sat waiting on instruction from me. Even though I'd profusely protested, Deon still hired security to be with me every hour of the day.

For the past couple of weeks or so, I've been chauffeured and escorted by men who looked like they were in the Secret Service and could do serious damage to even the toughest man. Everywhere I went, they were by my side. I couldn't even get my mani and pedi without the Asian ladies asking me who the men standing outside were. I didn't like the attention they brought. No matter where we were, people stared at me and it made me very uncomfortable.

I'll admit; it did warm my heart to know that Deon cared about me enough to make sure that I was safe. I know that it bothered him a lot that he hadn't done more to protect Nichelle, although I would guarantee that she would have flat out refused to have bodyguards.

After dressing myself, little sleeping Ana, and having breakfast with my mom, I placed her in her car seat and made my way to the front of the building after texting Marlo to let them know I was on my way down. By the time I made it to the front of my building, they were standing at the door waiting for me. I handed Anastasia to Ed and began to follow them to the car when I heard my name being called from behind me. Before I could turn around, Marlo was already walking over to the unfamiliar woman.

"Do you know her?" Ed asked, placing the baby into the back seat of the car before closing and locking the door.

"No, I don't know her," I said under my breath in response to Ed's question. "Yes? I'm Simone," I looked the petite, fair skinned, shapely woman up and down wondering what she could want with me.

"Can I talk to you?"

"Who are you?" I asked, trying to step around Ed who was now standing partially in front of me.

"Can you step away from them so I can tell you who I am?" She asked as Marlo's 6'5" frame stood almost directly in front of her, preventing her from getting any closer to me, but she never once looked at him or Ed. It was overkill, but they were just doing their job, making sure I was safe.

"What do you want to talk to me about?" I had no idea who this woman was, but was very curious.

"How about the reason why you need security," she said with no trace of malice in her voice. "Please, can we take a few steps away and I will tell you who I am?" She asked pleadingly.

She was a beautiful woman, stylishly dressed in fitted camouflage jeans, Louboutin ankle boots, and a thin oversized black sweater that hung off her shoulder. I was stuck for a moment and didn't know how to answer her.

"I mean you no harm. I just really need to talk to you," she said sincerely, looking me intently in the eyes. "Will you please just step away for a moment?"

"It's okay guys," I said walking toward her.

When we stepped a few feet away from Marlo and Ed and were sure that our conversation couldn't be overheard, she finally told me who she was.

"What do you want from me?" I couldn't believe that Charletta Banks was standing in front of my building wanting to talk to me.

"Can we go somewhere and sit down and talk, Simone? It's very important," she said as we stared each other in the eyes. "I think I deserve at least that from the woman who took my husband."

"I'm not with your husband, Charletta. You can have him! We are over! There really is no reason for you to be here. I'll never be with Carlton again."

"Simone, woman to woman, *please,* can we go somewhere and talk privately?" She kept her eyes glued on mine pleading with me through them.

"I can't right now. I'm dropping my goddaughter off at home..."

"Can you meet me after? Beverly Hills Hotel Polo Lounge? Noon? Please, Simone, I really need to talk to you. Carlton doesn't even know I'm here. No one knows I'm here," she pleaded.

"Okay, I'll be there at noon," I said and walked back to Marlo and Ed.

I watched her get into her gold Jaguar XJ as we pulled away from my building. I was anxious to know what she wanted to talk to me about, but was glad that I had a couple of hours to get my mind right before sitting across the table from the wife of the man who helped turn my life upside down. I wondered how much she knew about her husband.

Chapter Eighteen
Deon

*B*asketball has always been my first love. When I first started playing the game, I fell in love with it. It was everything to me and it came to me naturally from an early age; I could play the game with my eyes closed. From basketball camps, leagues, and school teams, I played year round when I was younger, but during my years playing professional ball, I'd come to appreciate my time away from the sport.

While growing up, playing basketball was all that I wanted to do. There were always talks that I'd be playing on a professional level right out of high school if I wanted to, and I could have, but I decided to sit out the draft until I graduated college. Having my degree in business meant a lot to me and was something I was proud of and had put to good use.

I controlled my finances and had final say on how every dime was invested, and it was all invested well. I had ventures with Magic Johnson Enterprises—where my money was not only growing steadily, but rapidly—and many other small and large investment and holding firms across the country. It was important for me to not only leave a career legacy, but a financial legacy for my children and grandchildren. I live a very comfortable lifestyle, and pride myself on having the best of everything, but I donate my time and money handsomely and never spent frivolously.

When I walked into the luxury suite at the Four Seasons Hotel, I was greeted by a beautiful woman who introduced herself as Nadia Sanchez. I was here to do an 'Up Close & Personal' interview for a sports spread Marie Claire magazine was putting together on eligible bachelors in sports. This wasn't really something I'd usually do. I didn't like talking about my personal life, but hey, I didn't have to tell her anything I didn't want her or anyone else to know.

The photo shoot for the article had taken place earlier that morning, and wasn't much out of the norm; beautiful models flanking me as I posed in designer suits, jeans, shirtless, etc. They're all pretty much the same set up.

"Would you like something to drink, Mr. Bradford? Cognac?" She asked, walking toward the bar, her pencil skirt accentuating her small waist, round hips, and full ass.

"Sure, and please call me Deon," I said, impressed that she had done her homework. She knew what I liked to drink.

I walked over to the couch and sat down. This was definitely one of the more expensive rooms. It had a six-seat dinner table, expensive sofas, and expansive views. I was impressed with whoever put this together.

"I see Marie Claire set you up nicely," I said, more to get the conversation going than anything else.

"Yeah, they tend to hook us up when we interview the

big fish. It's more so to impress you than to make sure we are comfortable," she laughed, handing me the short thick glass filled with brown liquor. "Stand up for me," she said as she clipped a small microphone onto the front right collar of the black button up shirt I wore. She sat the receiver on the table next to the couch I was sitting on, instead of clipping it to my pants like they do when I speak on TV, and then told me I could sit back down.

She took a seat across from me and picked up a glass of wine that had been sitting on the small table next to her chair. She then clicked a button on the high tech recorder, which sat on the coffee table that rested on the carpeted floor between us.

"This way, nothing will be printed that you didn't really say. We'll have it all right here on tape," she winked, taking a sip of her wine.

She was getting sexier as each minute passed. It was as if she was emitting some type of pheromone that was drawing me in. Something animalistic in me wanted her *badly*. My senses were so heightened that I could smell her perfume, which I knew was Jo Malone Blackberry and Bay; she had my full attention.

"Tell me about your girlfriend," she said, getting right into it.

"I don't have one. Haven't in a while actually," I admitted.

"So you're the type that's commitment phobic?" She asked with a smile.

"No, not at all, actually. I was the type of man who was a one woman guy, but it's not easy to find the right woman, especially when you are a professional athlete who doesn't trust easily." I took a sip of my drink, "Hennessey?"

"Paradis," she smiled.

"Nice," I said, taking another sip of the rare cognac.

"Wish I could say it's from me, but it's a gift from Joanna Coles."

"I'll have to be sure to thank her," I said. Joanna Coles was the editor-in-chief of the magazine who had personally called and asked if I'd do the spread.

"When you say '*was* the type of man'," she began, catching the word "was" in my previous statement and jumping on it as any good journalists would, "are you saying that you *used* to be a one woman man. Why has that changed?" She took another sip of her wine and repositioned herself on the tan wingback chair. Her olive toned skin and dark almond shaped eyes twinkled at the question.

"I went through a really bad... experience," I said, searching for the right word. "in the last relationship I was in, so I just started to do me. Live like most people think all athletes live. You probably think we all just sleep around too, right?" She raised her eyebrows, surprised with my candor.

"Well, the shoe usually fits," she answered with a smile. "So, what did she do, cheat? Is that what made you say goodbye to Mr. Nice Guy?"

I wish it was just cheating. I wanted to say.

"No, monogamy has never been an issue in any of my relationships. I've made a few bad decisions, trusted the wrong people..." I thought about Shelly and Byron Boyd, which made me wonder what would have become of Simone and I had I not believed what Byron had told me about her. Maybe we would still be together and I would have never met Shelly.

"So how has that been for you? The sleeping around

thing?" She sipped from her glass of wine and looked at me with those dark sexy eyes. At that moment, I knew without a doubt that she wanted me.

"It's been both fun and unfulfilling," I admitted honestly.

"Wow, fun *and* unfulfilling," she asked incredulously with a cute smirk on her face.

"Exactly. Fun while I'm in the moment, very unfulfilling after."

"Then why do it? Just to get off?" she asked bluntly.

"At the time, yes," I laughed. "It's much better than masturbating," I said, instantly thinking about what my mother would think when she read this interview.

"You're a pretty straight forward guy," she said laughing. "Are you this straight forward with the women you take home?"

"I'm straight forward with everyone in my life. I don't lie or mislead. I'm a very honest man."

"Do you ever feel guilty doing what you do? You know, giving someone a piece of something they probably could never actually really have?" She asked, smiling seductively.

"I only deal with adults. Consenting adults who can make their own rational decisions. I'm not a bad guy, I'm just not monogamous right now and I don't have to be. I'm single, unmarried, and in the prime of my life."

"Do you think you will ever be monogamous?"

"Of course. I've been monogamous before and when I meet the right woman, I'll be happy to be monogamous again. Until then..."

"You're going to sow your royal NBA oats," she finished for me.

"Exactly," I smiled, taking a long swig of my drink.

"So your last girlfriend tainted you that much and made

you stop being the nice guy?" She asked with a seductive smile that spread across her face as I continuously shook my head no.

"I haven't stopped being the nice guy," I laughed. "I just stopped looking to be in a committed relationship."

"Do you ever see a woman more than once?"

"Of course I do. Listen, I'm still the man my parents raised. I'm just enjoying myself and having a good time. I don't lead anyone on. I don't make promises I can't keep. I'm good. My mind is right. I'm focused on making the playoffs and living my life the way I see fit.

"Do you want kids, Deon? Do you see yourself as a father?" She asked.

"Very much so. I've been ready for a while, but other things just haven't been aligned. I was raised by both of my parents who are still married and in love after thirty years. I want the same for myself and my children. I want to come home to my kids, not have visitation with them."

"Are you telling me you believe love like your parents' still exists?" She asked, toying with me.

"Actually I do. I really do. Whether or not I'll find it or if it's out there for me is another question, but I do believe it exists," I laughed.

We talked for over an hour about my childhood, college, and everything in between. I was open with her and answered just about every question she asked. I almost forgot that I was being interviewed, which may or may not be a good thing.

"Well that about does it, Deon. Thank you so much for this interview. It was definitely fun and interesting. I've learned a lot about you. I'm sure our readers will too. I'll send the final draft to your publicist before it goes to print as the contract states," she smiled, turning off the recorder and walking over to me to remove the microphone from my shirt. "Please don't rush. Take your time and finish up your drink. Have another, if you like. Either way, you are expected to take that bottle of cognac with you," she smiled as she knelt down in front of me and took her time removing the mic.

Her breath smelled sweet and her hand felt soft as it brushed against my chin when she finally unhooked the device from my shirt. The yellow silk blouse she wore buttoned down the middle revealed her black lace bra as she bent in front of me. The top 3 buttons of her shirt were undone and the small, gold and diamond cross that hung from her neck by a slim necklace dangled in my face. By the time she pulled away, I could see that her nipples had become erect.

"What are your plans for the rest of the night?" I asked, rising from my seat to pour another drink.

"No plans. I'll probably just get started on your piece," she replied, standing at the bar in front of me as I poured my drink.

"Is that what you *want* to do?" I asked, walking up to her and standing very close.

"No, it's not what I want to do, but..." I bent down and placed my mouth on top of hers, kissing her speechless.

"You can start tomorrow," I whispered as I kissed on her neck and rubbed her full ass with my hands.

"I've never done this before, Deon. I swear," she murmured between pants from me kissing her neck and rubbing her body through her clothing.

"Done what? Are you a virgin?" I joked as I unbuttoned

her shirt and let it fall to the floor.

"I don't just sleep with men I interview. I've never done this before! It's... unprofessional!"

Her breath caught when I licked her firm nipple through her bra. I pulled one strap off her shoulder, releasing one of her large full breasts from its harness, and put her nipple in my mouth and began to suckle lightly. I flitted my tongue gently across it, back and forth, up and down in choreographed movements, making a guttural moan escape from deep within her.

My mouth found hers again and we ravenously connected our tongues like we were in a friendly dual. I walked her backward toward the dinner table as I began unzipping her skirt.

"Seriously, Deon, I don't do this!" She said again as I slid her skirt down her legs.

"It doesn't even matter. I want you... right now. Let's just go with that. If you want me like I believe you do, let's just forget about everything else and enjoy each other."

I bent her over the dinner table, squishing her beautifully perky breasts against the dark cherry wood. Her jet-black hair splayed across the table as I placed kisses on the back of her neck and down her spine. I bit her ass cheek when I got to it and removed the black lace thong that covered her. As I slid it down her legs, I could see the moisture between her thighs began to drip toward her ankles.

I lowered myself to my knees so I could have a better vantage point, and then lightly rubbed the wetness between her legs with my fingers, causing Nadia's breath to sharply draw inward. She began to shudder as the middle finger of my left hand moved in and out of her slowly, stroking the soft, wet flesh as it enveloped my finger with each thrust. My right index finger played with her clit, causing it to swell without much effort.

"Oh my God, Deon!" She worked her hips round and round, assisting the entry and exit of my large appendage in her tight, dripping hole. My large finger probably felt like a small dick in her tightness. I couldn't wait to enter her and feel myself inside of her.

"Do you have a condom?" I asked, realizing that I'd used the last one in my wallet a couple of nights ago. Nadia continued to moan and twist her hips as if she were in a trance. I slapped her on her ass and asked her again when she didn't answer.

"Yes, I'll grab it. I have to use the restroom first. I'll be right back," she said and went into the room naked aside from her black lace bra that hung half way down her right shoulder.

When she came back into the room, she dropped to her knees and unzipped my jeans. She attempted to take all of me in her mouth, gagging with each attempt. I grabbed the back of her head and glided myself between her soft lips to the warm wetness beyond. I hadn't noticed that she'd expertly slid the condom onto my shaft with her mouth until she'd bent herself over the back of the couch ready to be taken.

When I entered her, it felt like pure bliss. I took my time moving in and out of her slowly, enjoying every stroke. She was sexy as hell and seemed to be getting wetter with each thrust. Her loud moans and full ass gyrating round and round taking all of me inside of her made me even harder.

I methodically lowered my speed and kept a steady movement as I eased in and out of her, kissing the back of her neck, and nibbling on her ear. The thick moan that released from deep within her as her thighs and legs began to shake uncontrollably was animalistic. It turned me on.

I continued to stroke her, increasing and decreasing my speed periodically. She felt so good; I wasn't ready to get out of it. I took my time as I made her cum, eventually allowing myself to explode inside of her.

I pumped a few more times before I slowly removed my slight erection from her still throbbing hole. I was expecting to see a full condom—I'd released a good one—but there was barely any semen in the rubber.

"Oh shit!" I rushed to the bathroom and turned on the light to inspect the condom. As I looked closely, I could see that it had tiny holes in it. "This shit didn't pop! It's been tampered with!" I said under my breath. *What in the hell was I thinking, having sex without my own condom? That's the first damn lesson in Professional Athlete 101!* "And I have some in the fucking truck! Stupid, stupid, stupid!" I said through gritted teeth as I paced back in forth inside the nice sized bathroom. I felt like a complete moron.

"The condom had holes in it, Nadia," I said, trying to keep my composure when I returned to the living room of the hotel suite. I hadn't wanted to hurt a woman like this since I found Valtrax in my ex-girlfriend, Shelly's bedroom drawer.

"No, it couldn't have," she said nonchalantly as she lay across the couch that I'd just had her bent over. "Are you sure?" she asked, looking up after what I had told her seemed to sink in.

"Hell yeah I'm sure! The fucking condom is almost empty! Are you on birth control?" I asked simultaneously, praying that she was.

"No, I'm not active like that. I told you, I don't usually do things like this." *Yeah, but you had a condom readily handy. Bullshit!* I thought as she continued to lie there like this wasn't a huge problem.

"Shit, shit, shit, Nadia!" I sat on the couch across from her and put my head in my hands. I couldn't believe that I had let her set me up like this!

I looked up to find Nadia on her knees in front of me.

"Deon, listen, the condom was old. I'm sorry; we shouldn't have used it. I was just so horny and wanted you so badly. Look, I don't want any kids any time soon if at all. It's not that easy to get pregnant, but if I do, God forbid, I will not be having this baby!" She stated almost believingly as she looked seriously into my eyes.

"Nadia, fuck!" I got up and straightened my clothes.

"Seriously, Deon! I'm not a groupie! I have a career that I love and a life that I love! This is not what I want. And as a matter of fact, I'll be going to get the morning after pill first thing tomorrow. You can come pick me up, take me to buy it, and watch me swallow it if that will make you feel better. I don't know you like that! I don't want your baby, Deon!" She said incredulously.

"I'll be here to get you at nine tomorrow morning. Be ready, Nadia. I'm not fucking joking," I said and then walked out of the door.

Chapter Nineteen
Tyron

"Did you know Stacey Flenoy?" Detective Jenkins asked as we sat in the living room of my penthouse with a small recorder laying on the table between us.

I looked at my attorney, who nodded his head, giving me the go ahead to answer the question.

"Like I told you before, I didn't know him," I said.

"Had you ever met him?"

"It's possible. I meet a lot of people in the business I'm in. I can't remember them all and you shouldn't expect me to."

"So you never had a personal relationship with Stacey Flenoy?" He asked again, looking at me sideways.

"My client has already answered that question, Detective," my attorney, Lem Boldlaw, interjected. He was the best defense attorney money could buy. Of course, I'd only have the best.

"Are you sure, Mr. Marks?" He asked again, looking at me intently.

"Detective, my client has already answered that question. You can continue on to your next question," Lem Boldlaw said again, more firmly this time.

"Can you explain why Mr. Flenoy was in Paris the same

time as you, in the same hotel, in the room directly next door to yours, and how you two just coincidentally ended up on the same return flight back into LAX, yet you don't know him?"

"I'm advising you not to answer that question," Lem instructed.

"Can you explain why he told his closest friends that he was in a relationship with you, Mr. Marks? Why would he tell his friends he was flying to Vegas to see you?"

"People tell stories about being in relationships with high powered millionaires such as my client every day, Detective. Don't you read the tabloids? That should come as no surprise to you."

"No Counselor, that's no surprise to me, but when they turn up brutally murdered, that's surprising," Detective Marsh said.

"Sadly to say, it's not an anomaly for someone to be murdered in Vegas. Was he a gambler, Detective? Did he owe anyone any money? Did he go out there to maybe make some extra cash? That's just something for you two to ponder. In the meantime, I'm going to go ahead and call an end to this interrogation," Lem Boldlaw stood, the detectives following suit with sour expressions on their faces.

"I believe we have enough anyway," Detective Marsh said, gathering the recorder and dropping it in his pocket. "We'll be in touch."

"You have my business card. Do not contact my client again," he said, seeing the two detectives out.

"Mr. Marks, I'm going to need you to be frank with me, if I am to help you. I'm your attorney and I'm on your side. My job is to get you off, no matter what. Attorney Client Privilege will keep everything that is discussed between the two of us private, it's the law. I need full disclosure if I'm going to be able to help you to the best of my ability," he said, sitting across from me. "Did you know Stacey Flenoy?"

"Yes, I knew who he was, but I didn't know him like that. I didn't kill him! I didn't have anything to do with his death, Lem," I lied, staring him square in the eye.

"How did you know him?"

"What do you mean?"

"In what capacity was your relationship with Mr. Flenoy?"

I took a moment before answering the question, debating on whether or not to tell the truth. Deciding against the truth I said, "He was in a relationship with my bodyguard, and I know *of* him because of that. I don't *know* him."
He was deep in thought and remained quiet for a moment before responding.

"Was he there to see him in Vegas?"

"I don't know. I was hardly around. I had a crew of security with me, as I usually do when we are on tour, so I'm not sure what my bodyguard was up to."

"So you didn't see Mr. Flenoy in Vegas?"

"No I didn't."

"What's your driver's name?"

"His name is Travis Davis, but we call him Curse. I doubt that he'll tell you the shit I just told you. He's married and has a new baby. I'm sure he doesn't want that shit getting back to his wife."

"I'm going to need to speak with him either way."

"Don't tell him what I've told you, Lem. He trusts me and is loyal to me. I don't want to jeopardize that." I also didn't want Curse to know that I was throwing him under the bus. Shit, it was either him or me and my life and freedom was much more important than his.

"No need. I'm just going to ask him what he knows, to which he will probably say nothing. If he sticks to that, I'm not worried about anything else."

Chapter Twenty
Simone

*T*he hostess led me through the old school swanky restaurant and to the outside garden patio where Charletta was seated under a bougainvillea topped canopy. She was sipping on a mimosa when I sat down across from her. She still wore a massive rock on her ring finger and had brilliantly cut, oversized diamond studs in her ear. There were diamonds in every piece of jewelry she wore. She looked like money... someone else's money.

"Thank you for coming," she said, sitting her champagne flute on the table and looking around.

"Curiosity got the best of me," I said honestly, as I crossed my legs and adjusted my crisp, white Phillip Lim Pintuck dress.

"Where're your bodyguards?"

"They're in front. Did you think I was going to have them sit at the table with us? I'm not scared of you or anyone else, Charletta, so let's get that straight. A good friend insisted on hiring security for me and I couldn't talk him out of it. It's not so bad being chauffeured through L.A. traffic," I said, feeling the need to clarify that as the waiter came to the table and asked if I wanted a drink.

We were silent for a while after I ordered my pomegranate martini and she another mimosa.

"Did you know that Carlton was married when you started seeing him?" she asked evenly.

"Do you know that Carlton is gay?" The words slipped off my tongue before I could even think to stop them. Shock didn't register on her face; there was no emotion there.

"I know everything about Carlton, and gay he is not. Do *you* know everything about him?"

"I know he sleeps with men, and that's all I need to know."

"So what he sleeps with men, Simone!" She began in a high-pitched whisper. "Because he likes to have sex, I'm supposed to hold that against him? You see, that's the thing with most women. Their man can have sex with other women and be forgiven, but if they have sex with men that's different? Sex is sex, Simone. Carlton has different needs, and I don't judge him for that, and that's why he doesn't hide anything from me. It doesn't diminish the love I have for him either. Him fucking a guy does not make him gay, no matter what you or anyone else may think."

I couldn't believe the words that were coming out of this woman's mouth. Did Carlton have her that brainwashed that she believed that this shit was normal?

"What does it make him, Charletta? It sure as hell doesn't make him a heterosexual man."

"Maybe it makes him bi-sexual, Simone! But you know what? I don't give a shit what it makes him! I have been with that man since the end of my freshman year of high school. He was my first... and the only man I've ever been with. Nothing can change the fact that he is my husband and the father of my kids. Nothing can change the fact that I can still get his dick hard, and evidently you can too. Most importantly, nothing can *ever* change the fact that I love him and I don't think less of him because of who he chooses to have sex with!" She huffed.

"Well, I guess you are perfect for him then because that's never something I'd be okay with."

"And that's the difference between you and me. Did you know that he was married when you started seeing him, Simone?" she asked again.

"Charletta, did you ask me here to grill me on my relationship with Carlton? I will never be with him again, so whatever went on between us in the past shouldn't matter. You two can get back together and live happily ever after," I said just before the waiter came into earshot.

As soon as he sat my drink down, I picked it up and took a long swallow. It was deliciously cold and mixed just right. I was going to need a few of these if this went on much longer.

She waited for the waiter to leave before responding.

"Simone, I'm going to get right to it. Fuck the small talk and the shit that doesn't really matter anyway..."

"Good, that's why I'm here. Let's get to it. I have somewhere to be," I lied, cutting her off.

"Was Carlton good to you?" she asked, slightly throwing me off. "Honestly, this isn't a trick question. *Was Carlton good to you,* Simone?" She stared intently in my eyes, willing me to answer her question.

I took a few sips of my drink, trying to swallow the lump that had formed in my throat. Carlton was damn good to me. Just the thought of it, of him, could easily bring me to tears, but I wasn't about to cry in front of his wife.

"Carlton was *damn* good to me, Charletta," I answered honestly as we held each other's gaze. I'm sure she could see the mist form in my eyes and the sincerity they held.

"I've been with him since we were teenagers. He's not only my husband and the father of my kids, he is my best friend. What you're doing to him isn't right, Simone..."

"What do you mean what I'm doing to him? Do you even know what's going on? What *he* did to *me* isn't right!" I said incredulously, staring her down.

What I'm doing to him? This woman had to be out of her damned mind.

"Like I said before, I know everything about Carlton. *Everything!* He told me about the video—I hope you believed him when he told you that he didn't know anything about it until after you tried to kill yourself. He also told me about your friend Stacey..." she said softly before I cut her off.

"What did he tell you about Stacey?" I sat my drink on the table and used every bit of will power I had to keep from jumping across the table and choking this woman out. *Until after I tried to kill myself? What in the hell is happening right now?* She was seriously throwing me off!

"He secretly recorded the video. Tyron killed him because of it and now you have the video." I was stunned.

"Why are you telling me this, Charletta? Why did you bring me here? What in the fuck am I supposed to say to that?" My voice rose slightly with each word that came out of my mouth, but still low enough for us not to be overheard by the other patrons.

"I want to help you and help my family at the same time, Simone!" Tears unexpectedly began to fill her eyes and she quickly grabbed the cloth napkin off her lap and dabbed at her eyes. "This is my family! My kids' father! *My husband!* If that video gets out, you ruin the only man that I've ever loved! You ruin my kids' legacy and their right to grow up with some semblance of normalcy! If that shit gets out, everything will be done, Simone! Carlton's and Tryon's life won't be the only lives ruined. My life would be ruined, his kids', his mother's, all of the people that work for them will be jobless when all the dominoes fall! This isn't a game! This shit is bigger than..."

"Nothing is bigger than my best friend being murdered!" I said through clenched teeth. "Nothing, Charletta!" I couldn't stop the tears that fell from my eyes.

We both sat there silently crying before either of us spoke again.

"I'll help you, but you have to leave Carlton out of it. He doesn't even know I'm here, and will more than likely be pissed off at me because I am. I know that man, and I know that he treated you good, because that is who he is. That's how he is with the people that he loves. So I wanted to talk to you woman to woman and look you in your eyes and ask, if he treated you damn good, Simone, is ruining all of these people's lives by doing something crazy with that video worth it? Does he really deserve that for fucking Tyron? I'll give you two hundred thousand, Simone. Please give up that video and focus on getting the man who killed your friend, not the man that you feel betrayed you!"

I slowly drained the remaining liquor from my glass, never once taking my eyes off hers. I got up and left her and her ridiculous offer sitting in the posh Polo Lounge of the Beverly Hills Hotel without another word.

Chapter Twenty-one
C. Banks

Spending time with my kids relaxed me and made me feel at ease. Charletta packed up and came to Cali to be here to support me. Her loyalty to me is extraordinary; she truly loves me unconditionally.

I sat on a lounge chair in the backyard of my house and watched my son and daughter splash around in the pool. *I missed this! This is what I should have been focusing on,* I thought as I watched them jump in and out of the pool and slide down the slide.

It was early October and eighty degrees, a perfect Southern California day in my opinion.

"Daddy, watch!" My eight year old daughter, Catera, yelled.

"I'm watching, baby girl," I replied as she dove off the diving board almost perfectly, once she made sure my attention was on her fully.

Catera was definitely a daddy's girl. Even when we weren't together, she was calling or texting me throughout the day. My son, my namesake, was only five, and more attached to his mom, his iPad, and his bike than me.

I love my kids more than life itself and would do whatever I had to do to protect them and their legacy.

"That was perfect, baby girl. Let me see you do it again. Carl, be careful, you might fall and split your head open," I laughed at my rough son. I loved to see them happy and enjoying themselves.

Charletta walked outside of the kitchen door, carrying a tray of small sandwiches and drinks. She placed it on the table that was between the two lounge chairs and sat down. She picked up a small rectangular sandwich, took a bite, and smiled at me.

"Turkey and Havarti, your fave."

"I know you didn't make these," I said and laughed. Charletta didn't cook and never had.

"Of course I didn't. Maribel did." She laughed. "You know me way better than that. Don't start acting brand new."

"Yeah, you right, I should've known better." I laughed, picking up a sandwich off the tray and popping the whole thing in my mouth.

"Yeah, you should've. You better act like you know! It hasn't been that long, *Carlton*," she said playfully, rolling her eyes.

"True, true. I know you can't even boil water, Char," I popped a second sandwich in my mouth.

"Yeah whateva! I'm gonna learn, watch."

"You've been saying that same shit for the longest!" I burst out laughing. She picked up a glass off of the table, plucked a piece of ice out of it, and threw it at me. "Why are you throwing stuff at me for telling the truth?" I asked, still laughing.

"I *am* gonna learn. I just don't have time. I'm raising your kids!" she said, pretending to be angry.

"You can get help and you know that, but I don't care if you ever learn how to cook, Char. You are perfect just the way you are," I stated honestly taking a sip of the sweet tea that she had just plucked the ice cube out of.

"I'm perfect, but you were ready to leave me for that bitch," she stated.

"Char, let's not even go there, alright?" She had been letting me have it over divorcing her for Simone since she'd been back in L.A. with the kids. Although it was driving me crazy, I couldn't blame her. I should have either stopped fucking with Tyron, which I didn't do frequently, or stayed with the woman who accepted everything about me.

"I'm just sayin," she rolled her eyes again and flung her hair over her shoulder.

"You always just sayin'," I mimicked, trying to lighten her up, which wasn't too hard to do.

"I don't know why I love your ass the way I do," she said, looking at me with a serious expression on her pretty face and her eyes full of emotion.

"Because I need your love, Char. I don't know what my life would be like without your love," I responded honestly. "I know I probably don't deserve you, but I thank God for you every day."

"Mom, Dad, watch me!" Carl yelled from the top of the slide. He went down headfirst, landing in the water with a mediocre splash.

"I can make a bigger splash, watch me!" Catera slid down feet first making a bigger splash, which caused the two to go back and forth a few times, trying to beat each other's splashes.

"Are you going to stop the divorce, Carlton?" Charletta asked, surprising me.

"Is that what you want?"

"Yeah, that's what I want, but I don't want you to be with me if you don't love me and really want to be with me. I understand your situation with home chick. I'm sure you are feeling a certain kinda way over that shit, but this is our family, Carlton. *This shit here is what matters!*" She got up and sat next to me on my lounge chair. "We can make this work, no matter what happens with that video. Although it's the last thing I want to happen, we have to be prepared if she leaks it."

"That video can't get out, Char. I will do whatever is in my power to make sure of that. I'm telling you now, Charletta, I don't think I can survive that humiliation," I confessed for the first time.

"Carlton, what are you saying? You can survive anything! We can ride it out! You are not alone in this, babe. I got your back like I've always had your back. I believe in you. I believe that this shit will get fixed. I have to believe that. *We* have to believe that!"

"Well, keep believing that, Char, and know that I'll do everything I can to protect our family."

"This is just another hurdle we have to jump. We've successfully jumped over many. You're a fighter, babe. You can get through this shit. *We* can get through this." This was classic Charletta. She was one in a million.

I sat up, pulled her into my arms, and kissed her.

"Ewwww!" The kids laughed from the pool.

"I love you, Char. I'm sorry for everything I've put you through. I promise, once all this shit is over, I will make it up to you."

"No divorce?" She asked.

"No divorce. I'll call the attorney and have her stop the shit," I replied, kissing her again as my phone buzzed. "Shit, I forgot. I have to do this interview with Angie Martinez. I already rescheduled once." Drake and I were vibing in the studio and I wasn't going to stop for anything aside from fire, death or some major catastrophe.

"No probs, babe, we'll probably still be out here."

"Okay, bet. I'll be right back out after I finish the call."

I walked into the house and went into my office. My assistant, Cookie, got me on the line with Angie and we went live no more than three minutes after I'd picked up the phone.

"Yoooo, what's up man? How you been?" Angie Martinez asked.

"I've been good for sure. What's good with you, Ang?" I asked. We'd always had a cool rapport.

"Everything is good, good! So the new album is burning up the charts, which isn't a surprise for a C. Banks record! You sold over a million in the first week. That's what's up!" she said, her voice hype and her New York accent strong, making me wish I was back home.

"Yeah it is. It's definitely a blessing that I'm able to continue to make music that the people like. I'm in this for the long haul. I put my everything into every record on that joint. My heart and soul is in every single bar!"

"That's what's up! You can tell, you can tell. You know one thing I've always respected about you is that you never watered down your music. You are loved across the world, but you're not one of those *switch up who I am* type of cats, and that's says a lot for dudes in this industry. A lot of them will do whatever it takes to reach mainstream like you have.

To have the following that you do, a lot of these rappers will start singing!" We laughed.

"Hey, if you can sing, sing. Drake does that well. We were just in the studio."

"Yeah, I know! That was the day you stood me up!" she joked. "I'll forgive you as long as you give me the exclusive when that record drops. I know ya'll were making a banger!"

"Everything Drake touches is a hit."

"Everything *you* touch is a hit!" She reminded me with a laugh.

"Yeah, thankfully that's true." I laughed.

"Alright now, we got some callers who wanna talk to the one and only C. Banks! You with that?"

"I'm always with that. Let's do it!"

"Hey, you're on with Angie Martinez and C. Banks! What's your question or comment?" she asked the caller.

"Hi, my name is Shanisha and I have a question for C. Banks," the young sounding girl said excitedly.

"Okay Shanisha, ask your question," Angie Martinez said to the caller.

"Hi, C. Banks!" She squealed loudly and giggled.

"Hi Shanisha, what's good?" I asked, making the young girl and her friends in the background squeal again.

"Are you going to be in Staten Island anytime soon?"

"I'm not sure sweetheart, but keep an eye on my website, www.cbanks.com. It's updated with all of my tour dates, so you can know when I'm coming to your city. I'd love for you to be there."

"Okay, thank you! I love you, C. Banks!" she yelled.

"I love you too," I laughed.

"Wow, could she have yelled that any louder?" Angie laughed. "Okay, let's get to one more caller before we take a short break. Hey, you're on with Angie Martinez and C. Banks. What's your question or comment?

"Oh hey Ang! This is Lisa Lips of Loose Lips Sink Ships dot com. How are ya, honey?" She asked in her nasally voice. I couldn't stand this chick. She was so damn messy. I hated that gossip blog shit, but found myself checking them every now and then. It's a good thing I did, otherwise, I might still be in the dark on this video shit.

"Wow! Lisa Lips! What's up, chica?"

"Oh you know, same ole same ole. Hey Banks, how are ya hon?"

"I'm feeling good, Lisa. I'd like it to stay that way," I said laughing, but not joking.

"Oh you know I'm all about feeling good. Hey, I have a question for ya," she began.

"And I may not have an answer for you, Lisa. Just be prepared for that," I said, making Angie and me laugh. The way she was beginning ever sentence with "oh" was already starting to annoy me.

"Oh I'm always prepared. Okay, so a little birdie told me that your partner, Tyron Marks," she started, making my stomach drop, "was involved in a little altercation at Drai's in Hollywood, and received a few stitches on his forehead from being hit in the head with a bottle..." she said, trailing off.

"Alright Lisa, just about everyone knows what happened with Marks and that incident in the club," Angie said butting in.

"Oh yes, but what hasn't been reported, and what I've learned from my very, very reliable source, is the fact that Banks' ex-girlfriend, Simone Johnson, was the one who wielded the champagne bottle that resulted in the five stitches, *and* this is the same woman whose best friend was murdered in Las Vegas. We all know that Tyron Marks is a person of interest in that murder case," she continued.

"I don't know what you are talking about, Lisa. Quit starting rumors." I couldn't believe this chick was calling in with this shit like I would comment on it anyway.

"Oh no, Banks, this is fact. A rumor is something like... a gay video floating around out there with Marks and some unknown man..."

"Come on now, Lisa, I don't even know how you got through or why we are even entertaining this. Thanks for your call anyway," Angie said before I heard the click of the line, confirming that we had been disconnected from the call. "Alright ya'll, we have to take a short break, but we *will* have more C. Banks when we return!

"I'm sorry man, even the crazies get past the screeners sometimes," she laughed after we'd gone off air.

"What type of nutso callers do you have, Ang?" I asked with a laugh that I hoped didn't reveal the tension that was coursing through my body.

"Yeah, and she is the nuttiest of them all, word!" She laughed. "She really on some bogus Sandra Rose, Media Takeout crap," she said, referring to a couple of blogs that always reported false rumors and malicious, hateful gossip.

"No worries. I run into a lot of crazy shit. None of it fazes me," I lied. This shit was definitely fazing me. If they were getting hot on Tyron and that video, it was only a matter of time before they tried to put my name in that shit! 'Plan two' had to go into effect immediately.

Chapter Twenty-two
Tyron

I was in a rage as I trashed my penthouse after calling Tomi over and over again, not able to reach her.

The morning began no different than every other morning as of late. Getting that video was always the first thing on my mind.

When I turned on my phone, I received text after text from people giving me their condolences and telling me how shocked they were. I thought someone had died! I didn't know what the fuck they were talking about until I read the text from Banks that simply read *check the net*.

I jumped out of bed and grabbed my laptop off the dresser. I couldn't power that shit on fast enough. I couldn't imagine what was going on as I impatiently waited for the *Bossip* site to upload onto my laptop screen. When it did, I choked on my spit and had a fucking coughing attack as I hacked like my lungs were about to give out. Even through the coughing fit, I was still able to read what was on the first page of the gossip/news site.

The first thing I saw was a photo of me and Tomi at the last American Music Awards. I remembered the photo. I happened to like it a lot, but this copy had a line that zigzagged right through the middle of me and Tomi. The headline read:

It's Splitsville After More Than 15 Years
for One of Music's Favorite Couples.

Tomi Jordan releases statement confirming the dissolution of her personal and business relationships with long time boyfriend and manager Tyron Marks

I am saddened to say that after many, many great years as a loving couple and devoted business partner, Tyron Marks and I have decided to part ways. We will always love each other and will never forget how we made history together. We both think it's time for a new chapter in our lives. It's time that we branch out and see what else is out there for us.

As I'm sure most of you know, I've had a personal and business relationship with Tyron Marks since I was a teen. I will always love him. I will always cherish the times we had together growing up and making music all night until we fell out from exhaustion. I will always cherish the guidance and unconditional love he bestowed upon me. He will always be in my heart and I will always care for him. This isn't the end for either of us; it is the beginning for bigger and better things.

We'd appreciate privacy during these times. Our aim is to move forward on the next journey that this thing called life has in store for us.

Thank you all for your prayers and well wishes.

Tomi Jordan

I couldn't believe she would do me like this! No warning, no heads up, no talk, no nothing?

"After all the shit we've been through together! After all the shit I've done for you! If it wasn't for fucking me, you wouldn't be you! I FUCKING MADE YOU, TOMI!" I yelled. The suite was empty. I was by myself and about to lose my mind! "YOU FUCKING BITCH!" I yelled as I threw a chair against the wall.

When the phone rang, alerting me that the concierge was calling, I knew it was Tomi. It had to be! There was no way she would do some shit like this to me. There is just no way she'd jump ship and do me dirty like this without coming to see me face to face.

"Yeah?" I spat into the phone.

"Mr. Marks, you have someone here from Ms. Tomi Jordan. Shall I send her up?" He asked.

"Yeah, send her up!" I replied, my voice rising. I *knew* it was her! I couldn't wait until she got her ass up here and explained herself.

I went and unlocked the door so she could let herself in. There had to be a perfectly good explanation for her pulling some shit like this on me. I shouldn't have found this shit out online.

When I heard a knock at the door, I didn't say shit. I figured she would eventually realize that the door was unlocked and just come in. *She wouldn't knock any other time. Why in the hell is she knocking now?* I thought as the knocking on the door began for the third time. I walked over to the door, slung it open, and was shocked to see a red headed woman holding out an envelope for me to take. I was prepared to see Tomi, so the sight of this woman at my door was a surprise. There had been no doubt in my mind that it was Tomi at the door. I could have sworn that's what he'd said in that damn accent of his.

I took the envelope from the lady, closed the door in her face, and never once uttered a single word to her. I sat on the sofa and opened the letter that I noticed was on letterhead from one of the best entertainment attorneys in the business and began to read. It was the official dissolution of our business relationship. She was firing me as her manager, and she planned to leave QP Records after the completion of the album she was currently working on. This was the last one she was contractually obligated to do as a QP Records artist, so she would have a clean break after this.

I picked up the phone and dialed my publicist, Gretchen, to get her working on a press release. I couldn't let anyone know or even think that I wasn't in agreement with the breakup, and that I didn't already know what was going on. Shit was looking real bleak, but I wasn't lying down without a fight! I'll *always* end up on top!

Chapter Twenty-three
Simone

When I heard the buzzer alerting me that someone was downstairs, I looked at my mother lying on the other side of the couch dozing off as we watched Top Chef.

"Are you expecting someone?" I asked her.

"No, I'm not expecting anyone," she replied.

I turned the channel so that I could see who was ringing my buzzer, and was surprised to see Bradley Dubois' face staring up at me as I looked at him on the TV screen.

"Who is that?" My mother asked with a puzzled look on her face.

"That's my... granddad," I said, looking at my mother in confusion. "I wonder what he's doing here. He's never come over here before," I said, more to myself than to my mother.

"Only one way to find out," my mother said, rising from her seat and kissing me on my forehead, before leaving the room. "I'll give you some privacy. Let me know once he leaves." As my mother left the room, I pressed the button to unlock the front gate, allowing him entrance into my building.

I sent Marlo a text, letting them know that my 'grandfather' was coming up, and then paced impatiently in front of the door waiting for his knock.

My granddad was the only one that was always genuinely nice to me and seemed to care about me as I was growing up. He was so controlled by that wife of his, that he could barely make a sound without her correcting him or having something to say. She was demanding like that with everyone, and wanted to control everything. That was why it was so easy for her to cut my mother off when she married my dad. Marie wouldn't let her control her. She wouldn't do what she wanted her to do any longer, and that was something Caroline Dubois couldn't and wouldn't accept from anyone, let alone one of her children. They went eleven years without talking, although Marie did continue to keep in contact with her father.

After my dad was killed, Caroline accepted my mother back into her life, but never seemed to warm to me. I don't know if she knew all along that I wasn't really her grandchild, if she didn't like me because I was my father's child, or if she was really just a mean cold hearted bitch. I truly thought the latter.

Whenever Marie and my mother would get together, I was never there. My mother usually went to their house to spend time with them, taking me along fewer times than I can count on one hand. Unless there was some type of family event going on, to which they always wanted me present looking like the consummate grandchild, I was left alone, and later with Talise and her family.

The soft knock on the door jolted me from my reverie

and made me jump back a few steps.

"Hi... Bradley," I said apprehensively after turning off my alarm and opening the door. I wasn't sure what to call him. After all, he wasn't really my grandfather.

"Bradley? Simóne, if you call me anything other than granddad or something like it again, I will fall out and die right here at your door," he said with a sad smile on his face.

"Hey Granddad," I said, giving him a hug as I let him inside my home. I led him to my living room and offered him a seat on the sofa and something to drink. He sat down, but declined the drink. As he took a moment to gaze around my living room, I sat next to him and waited for him to explain why he was there. This was his first time coming to my place; even Marie had never come to see my home.

"This is a very, very nice place you have here, Simone. I'm so proud of the way you've turned out. I know that your grandmother and I don't have much to do with this outcome, but it definitely gives me some happiness to know that you are doing well for yourself."

I told him thank you, when what I really wanted to say was that they had nothing at all to do with my outcome! He was the only one from the Dubois clan who ever gave me any words of encouragement, and those were done in hushed tones and on the sly like he was doing something wrong. He was always under Caroline's thumb, and that was something that I could never respect. No person should allow someone to control them so completely, and that is exactly what he allowed her to do.

"The last time you came to the house, Simone..." he began before I cut him off.

"I can't talk about that, I'm sorry," I said, my words

catching in my throat. I didn't want to revisit that day.

"We don't have to talk about it, Simone. I just want you to know that I'm sorry. I'm so sorry for everything you've been through, and I wish I could have been a better man for you, a better father for them. You will always be my granddaughter. I don't care whose blood you have running through your veins, you hear me?" His face was serious and as distinguished as it had always been, but I could tell that he had been through a lot since the blowout at their house. His face was more worn and his eyes held so much worry and sadness.

I couldn't stop the tears that flooded from my eyes when he said those words to me. He grabbed me in a hug, and I cried in his arms like he was the granddad I always wished he could be. I pretended for a moment that he was and let him hold me in his arms as I cried on his chest.

"Your mother is sick, Simone," he said after I'd gotten myself together a bit. "She doesn't have much longer to live." My granddad's voice cracked as the last few words escaped his mouth.

Tears filled my eyes—my emotions betraying me again. He rested his hand on mine as I sat next to him, having not yet responded to his statement.

"She wants to see you, Simone," he said gently. I continued to cry freely as I sat next to the man whom I really barely knew.

"What's wrong with her?" My emotions were so screwed up, I didn't know how to feel about this news.

"She has leukemia, honey, and she's withering away fast. I hope you will at least go see Marie and have some final moments with her. I know things could have, *should* have been much better between you two, but you, just as she does, need closure," he said intensely. "She keeps asking for you, Simone. That's why I'm here. *She keeps asking for you.*" The defeated look on his face softened my heart.

"How much longer do you think she has?" I asked.

"A few days, a week, a month. I don't think she will last much longer, though. She is ready to go, but she keeps asking for you.

I sat on what he said for a few minutes, searching the recesses of my mind and heart for the right thing to do. I'd built up such a deep hatred for Marie after what she had done to me, it was hard to pity her as she lay on her deathbed having lived a fairly short, selfish life. That thought made me feel ashamed, but this woman who left me with her brother, who molested me repeatedly, even though I begged her to take me with her. *This is the woman who called me a conniving lying bitch, a whore!* I thought as tears continued to spew down my face. This is the woman who blamed me for my father's death! She said so many hateful things that I couldn't even imagine saying to my enemy, let alone the child that I'd watched grow up from a baby. She was an evil lady, and I wasn't sure she deserved a chance to make amends. *Should everyone have that chance?*

My grandfather allowed me to sit there with my thoughts. He didn't say another word as we sat in silence, my periodic sniffles the only sound that filled the air. His hand still resting on my arm, I broke the silence.

"I'll go see her," I said, looking at him. "I'm doing this for me though, not for her." There were things that I wanted to ask her... things I needed to know, whether they were going to hurt me or not.

Chapter Twenty-four
Deon

If it ain't one thing, it's another, I thought as I sat in Dr. Wharton's office waiting for him to give me the results of the herpes and HIV test I'd taken a couple of weeks ago. I knew it wasn't good news when he called and asked for me to come into his office. The time before, we talked over the phone when he delivered the positive news. Now I held my breath as I sat in his office waiting to hear news that I knew would change my life.

It had been over a month since I'd picked Nadia up and took her to the local pharmacy to purchase the morning after pill. I stayed in the car and waited for her to come back—not wanting to be seen buying the pill. The way the paparazzi stalked these days, nothing was private anymore.

I watched Nadia pop the pill in her mouth and swallow it down with a drink from a bottle of water. She even stuck out her tongue and moved it around so she could show me that she had really swallowed the pill. I dropped her back at her hotel and didn't care if I ever saw her again. No matter how she tried to play it, I knew she was trying to be slick. I prayed that her plans were thwarted by the strong pill.

I was disgusted with myself, and I was seriously thinking of turning over a new leaf as I sat there awaiting the results of the blood tests. The lifestyle I was living was draining the life out of me. Something had to give.

"Deon," Dr. Wharton began when he walked into the room. I stood and gave him a handshake before he sat behind his desk in his worn, charcoal colored leather office chair. "I have good news, and some not so good news for you," he paused. I wanted him to just get to the damn test results so I could know. I was becoming light headed from holding my breath. "Which would you like to hear first? Good news, or not so good news?" he asked.

"I don't care, Doc. I just need to get this over with!" He looked at me, eyes filled with empathy, or maybe it was sympathy...

"The HIV test..." he began before I cut him off by swiftly rising out of my seàt.

"No! Don't tell me that it's positive! Don't tell me that!" I pleaded with him as my 6'7" frame stood over his desk in a non-threatening way. "Please don't tell me that!" I begged as my eyes misted with the realization of what he was about to tell me.

"Deon, sit down, please. The HIV test came back negative. It's the HSV2 that's come back positive," he said, looking at me through kind, non-judgmental eyes as I sat back down. I was speechless. *HSV2? That shit must mean herpes!* I think he saw the question in my eyes and answered it without me having to ask.

"Yes, HSV2 is herpes, Deon.

"Why didn't it come up last time? When I had the sore

it was negative!"

"Yes it was, but by the time you came to us, the sore was all but healed, and the culture we did came back negative. We didn't test your blood for the herpes simplex virus and we should have, I'm sorry."

"So you're saying that I've probably had this all this time?" I was floored by these test results. Yes, having HIV would be much worse, but I'm still going to have to live with a virus that has no cure; a virus that's infectious; a virus that I've been most likely walking around with for over a year.

"It's possible. Listen, Deon, herpes is more common than many people think. It is the most common STD in the US. Studies show that one out of nine men has Herpes Simplex 2, and one out of every five women carries the virus. Last I checked, forty eight percent of black women have the disease. I say all of this to say that you are not alone in this. It can be managed. You've never even had an outbreak since the first one. This isn't the end of the world for you," he said kindly. "There are many men living normal, healthy, happy, productive lives with this disease." Although I knew that's what it was, I wished he'd stop saying 'disease'! It just made it sound even dirtier.

I was numb. I felt filthy and embarrassed. I felt low and ashamed of myself. And to think that a woman I loved gave this shit to me! She knowingly had this shit and kept it from me. I had to snoop through her shit to find the damn Valtrax prescription and confront her with it before her lies would stop. I covered my face with my hands and shook my head, trying to clear my mind from all that was going through it.

"So what do I do? Will it be necessary for me to take a pill every day? How can I have sex without putting someone at risk? Can I have kids? Will this affect that? Could I have given this to someone else, even though I use condoms? I need to know everything Doc!" *How can I ever have a normal relationship with a woman? Who would accept this?*

"It's a possibility that you can pass on the disease, even if there is no present outbreak. It's called viral shedding, but the likely hood of that is slim. You don't have to take a daily pill. If, for some reason, you start having outbreaks, you may want to consider that, but at this time, the best thing you can do is keep caffeine out of your diet, stay away from as much sugar as possible, and take multi-vitamins daily. The ones high in Vitamin C and Lysine are optimal. Keep your stress levels low. It's very manageable, Deon. You're a healthy young man. You will be fine. You are not alone in this. When you get home, search the net. You will find a lot of people who are in the same boat as you are and living normal lives."

"Thanks for seeing me, Dr. Wharton," I said as we both rose out of our seats.

My mind was still numb as I left the Dr.'s office and headed toward my truck. I pulled out of the parking lot with no destination in mind and drove. I was thankful that I wasn't HIV positive, but having herpes was a hard blow to take. I felt so ashamed. I wasn't a promiscuous man when this shit was given to me. I was faithful, I was in love, I would have married that woman and she betrayed me in a way that has altered the rest of my life.

What woman would want a man who could possibly give her an incurable disease?

Chapter Twenty-five
Tyron

I wanted him. His dark, chiseled face looked like he could be an Abercrombie model, but his height was average, at maybe five nine and was perfect for his slender build. I couldn't tell offhand if he was on my team or not, but I was determined to find out.

I was spending more time with Ricky than usual. He was working with me on scheduling shows for Banks and our other artists. I wasn't the person that would usually handle this, but I found this the perfect opportunity to see what was really up with this cat and keep my mind on something aside from that Stacey shit.

He was very detail oriented and seemed to have a knack for taking care of things before you realized it needed to be done. Ricky was always one step ahead, like the perfect assistant should be. I knew he would be a good hire.

Dressed in dark denim jeans, a burgundy button up with a nice silk tie, a navy Tommy Hilfiger preppy sport coat, and black Kenneth Cole boots, he sat across from me at the small conference table in the corner of my office with his pad and pen in front of him, ready to get started.

"Give me the rundown on what's already booked," I said, staring at him intently.

"Well Mr. Marks..."

"Tyron, call me Tyron," I said, cutting him off, not once averting my stare.

"Okay, Tyron," he started. "We have both Jimmy Fallon and Jay Leno booked. I'm working on getting two performance slots on Jimmy Fallon. Maybe Banks and Wink can perform Wink's first single? That would be great publicity for him," he said, waiting on a response from me. "I'm talking with a few promoters so we can put something together at the Nokia Theatre or the Gibson, or both," he continued when I still hadn't said anything.

I couldn't stop staring at this dude as he talked. I don't know what the fuck came over me, but I literally had nothing to say. I wanted him to keep talking, so I nodded my head in agreement and continued to stare at him like a love struck bitch.

"I've also gotten started on Sajaira's promo tour. I've already set up a few radio interviews, Power 106, Amp Radio with Carson Daly, and On Air with Ryan Seacrest. All the top local ones are just about booked... is there something wrong Mr. Marks, I mean Tyron?" he asked.

"Why do you think there is something wrong?" I asked, staring him square in the eyes.

"Well..." he paused. "You haven't really said more than a couple of words to me this whole time. I feel like I've been talking on and on and you are just sitting there... watching me, to be frank." He answered, staring me back down.

From that look alone, I could tell he knew what was up, but I couldn't tell if he was for it or against it.

"You're doing good. I'm just letting you do you."

"Then why are you staring at me like that?" He asked, tilting his head to the side and giving me a sly smile.

He's on my team! I thought excitedly, so I took a chance with my answer.

"Because you're easy as fuck to look at," I replied honestly, making a big ass smile spread across his face. His perfect white teeth and full lips caused me to inadvertently run my tongue across my lips.

"Oh, is that right?" He laughed. "Well you're definitely pleasing to my eyes as well." He crossed his legs, placed his left elbow on the arm of the chair, and rested his chin on his fist as he stared at me like he was trying to figure me out.

"What in the fuck are you thinking right now?" I laughed. I had to ask. The look on his face was unreadable.

"I'm just surprised, that's all."

"What's surprising?" I asked, spreading my arms out to my sides.

"Are you flirting with me?" he asked.

"Yes."

"*That's* surprising."

"Why do you find that surprising?" I asked, laughing. I already knew what he was going to say. It's what every man says when they find out that I fuck with men.

"I wouldn't have pegged you for a down low brotha." he said and chuckled.

"Ah, that's cold as shit right there, Ricky." I had to laugh, though. This dude had balls. "I'm not a fucking *down low brotha!*" That word put a bad ass taste in my mouth. "I'm just a man who lives in the public eye and happens to be in a business where my lifestyle wouldn't be acceptable. You should already know how that shit goes down."

"Yeah, I know how it is. I'm an openly gay man, though. It may not seem like it outwardly because I'm not as... *feminine,"* he said, finally choosing the right word, "as some gay men are, but I don't hide who I am or what I do from anyone."

"That must be a nice life," I said honestly. I don't see there ever being a time when I'd be able to live an openly gay life. I've never imagined that image of me going public, and now it was a big chance that it could be plastered across the fucking net for the world to see.

"Yes it is. I understand where you are coming from, though. Trust me, I'm not judging you," he said, and for some reason it took some heaviness off my chest.

"I want you like a mutha fucka," I admitted, making his smile spread again.

"Is that right? How bad do you want me?" he teased.

"Fucking bad!" I said, adjusting my dick. It was growing in the slacks I was wearing, and I'm sure he could easily see it; I wasn't a small man.

"We'll see how badly," he smiled. He stood up and started gathering his shit as I sat there and watched him. *I haven't wanted anyone this bad in a long time,* I thought as I got up, went to my desk, sat on the edge of it, and watched him as he headed toward the door.

"You know where to find me if you need me," he said suggestively and walked out. A distraction like him was just what I needed.

Chapter Twenty-six
Simone

I walked into Marie's hospital room with the weight of the world on my shoulders. They literally ached because I was so full of tension from not knowing what to expect from this visit. When I saw Caroline and my grandfather sitting at her bedside, I moved forward before I noticed the look in Caroline's eyes; she didn't know I was coming.

"What are you doing here?" She growled, rising from her seat and heading in my direction, causing my granddad to get up and stop her.

"She is here because Marie wants her here, Caroline. That is why she is here. Now come on, let's give them some privacy." He attempted to pull her toward the door and past where I stood.

"I will *not* leave this, this liar alone with my daughter!"

Her words were like a slap to my face; it stung. She became dead weight in my grandfather's arms, making it harder for him to move her as she continued to protest.

Her body was as limp as a fresh corpse while my

grandfather tried to hold her up. It was almost comical how dramatic this lady was.

"It's going to be *all right*, Caroline," my grandfather sighed, still trying to get her limp frame out of the hospital room.

"She shouldn't be alone with *her*, Bradley! She is unstable! *She hit her last time!*" She said harshly, trying to shake herself free from his grasp. "I have a bad feeling about this, Bradley," she said through clenched teeth.

"My goodness, our daughter is dying, should you have a *good* feeling, woman? Let them speak! *Marie requested her, Caroline!* You cannot control every damned thing!"

"Mother, please stop it."

I turned toward the bed, knowing whose voice had spoken those weak words. I saw Marie for the first time since I tried to beat her down like she was a common stranger. To say this moment was awkward would be an understatement.

"I am not comfortable with this!" Caroline said in protest as she finally allowed my grandfather to pull her out of the room.

I walked to Marie and stood at her bedside, looking everywhere but into her eyes. She looked nothing at all like the beautiful woman she was before. Her face was gaunt, ashen, and the rest of her five foot ten inch frame looked as if she couldn't have weighed more than ninety pounds, and she was covered with hospital sheets and blankets.

When my eyes finally met hers, tears were spilling down her face. I grabbed a couple of tissues out of the box that sat on the small roller table next to her bed, placed it in her hand, and watched as she feebly wiped her face. It felt like I was in a room with a stranger, not the woman I thought to be my mother for damn near twenty-eight years.

"I'm glad that you came, Simone. Thank you," she said weakly and slowly. "I didn't think you would."

"Granddad came to my house," I said softly as I stood next to her bed.

"I'm glad he was able to convince you to come." I nodded and sat in the seat next to her bed that Caroline had been sitting in. "I know these words will probably mean nothing to you at this point in your life and after all that you've been through, but I'm *so* sorry, Simone," she said sincerely, her voice breaking with emotion. "I didn't know how to love you because I was so busy trying to love myself, and failing miserably. I was focusing on the love I felt I could never have, and not on what should have been important to me—raising you as my own, as your father entrusted me to do.

"After my baby died, I had really dark times where I felt like I couldn't go on. Times when I *knew* that death had to be better than life," she paused, giving herself time to catch her breath. She continued after less than a couple of minutes of silence. "I was a mess, Simone. As I'm sure you already can see, I didn't have the best role model as a mother," she said, attempting a smirk that caused her breath to catch. "But she is the mother I was given. The way I was distant with you, she smothered me. She controlled everything down to the color socks I wore each day." She paused again for a short while before she began again.

"We didn't have the perfect childhood they like to make people think we had. My mother's brother molested me from the time I was eight, until I turned thirteen." Her cries were barely audible as her eyes flooded with tears.

For some reason, I couldn't find it in myself to reach out to comfort her. I just sat there and waited until she got herself together and felt able to carry on.

"He molested both my brother and me—in front of each other! That's why I just couldn't believe what you were saying about my brother! He'd been molested. he'd been through it! I just lost it and all of the hatred that I'd held for you since you were a baby boiled over."

"But why? Why did you hate *me*? I was only a child!"

"Because I wanted *my* baby, Simone! My *own* flesh and blood!" she said, desperate for me to understand her. "But after losing my baby, I wasn't fit to mother anyone, and then I found out about you and your birth mother. Then he brought you home," she said and then began coughing. "I was completely blindsided by that," she finished once her coughing spell had concluded. "My mind couldn't get past the fact that you weren't my baby, and that your father had cheated on me for all of those years and had a whole other family! I couldn't connect. Maybe I didn't try! I didn't see that what I lost in my baby, I could have had in you! I don't know how I could have held so much jealously in my heart toward you, but I did! I could never once forget that you weren't mine and that our daughter was in a coffin, having only lived three weeks.

"Julius doted on you and loved you so much, and that just *ate me up* and that's something I have to die with. I'm sorry! I was a mess. I was depressed and always worried about him out there doing what he did, and worried about him seeing other women. My mother hadn't spoken to me in years! I felt alone! I was not right, but your father didn't see that because he was always gone!" I didn't know what to say, so I said nothing.

"Simone, I wanted to see you so I could speak to you from my heart for once. When I found out I had leukemia—and by then it was too late to do much—I started to look at my life and see all the wrong I'd done. I saw things so clearly that I cried and I cried. I was filled with so much shame. I still am ashamed, as I should be. As I lay here about to die any day now, I can't *believe* how selfish I was! I can't *believe* I missed the blessing that God had given me in you! You would have loved me unconditionally! You would have loved me as your mother. Instead, I failed you! I can't tell you how sorry I am for what my brother did to you! I'm sorry I wasn't the mother to you that you deserved. I'm so sorry for all those mean and evil things I said to you at mother's house! I'm sorry that I couldn't love you like a mother loves her daughter!" She sobbed.

Tears spilled down my cheeks as well.

"I never understood, but now I do. I did love you as my mother, because that's what kids do. They love their parents. All I wanted was your love, your attention, your approval, for you to be proud of me! I only wanted a mother! Now I see that you were never capable of loving me," I said as tears continued to cascade down my face.

"I'm only human, Simone, a very broken one at that. I made many, many mistakes that I wish I could go back and do differently, but we both know there's no changing the past. I just pray that you take what I've told you and at least understand that I wasn't right in here," she said, pointing her frail finger toward her head and then her heart. "I wasted my whole life masking pain and trying to be something that wasn't fulfilling my soul. *Heal!* Live your life and be happy, Simone," she said intensely. "Don't be the miserable, mean, narcissist that I was," she smiled, causing an unexpected chuckle to escape my mouth.

"I didn't come here to dwell on the past or throw my bad childhood in your face. I do forgive you, Marie." Her eyes flickered at her first name coming from my mouth instead of mom. "I'm glad we were able to talk," I said, smiling at her.

"Me too, Simone. Did you get my package with the letters and things from your birth mom?" she asked. I could tell she was losing steam.

"Yes I did, and actually, I found her."
Shock flashed across her tired face before she smiled genuinely.

"Simone, I'm really happy to hear that," she said, trailing off. Her eyes started to close as she spoke her last words to me. "The drip is taking effect," she said, her eyes motioning toward the IV bag. "Pain meds, they put me out pretty fast. I'm sorry for everything, Simone. Please heal and live a happy life. No one is guaranteed tomorrow," she said, and drifted off to sleep to never wake again.

Chapter Twenty-seven
C. Banks

I couldn't believe this was my life. Only a few months ago, everything was perfect. I had everything I wanted, and then I couldn't reach Simone. That was when all of this shit started. First, she wouldn't answer any of my calls, texts or emails, and by the next day, all of her numbers were disconnected. I was in San Antonio, Texas, touring and couldn't think straight from worrying about her. Something wouldn't allow me to let it go, so I had Cookie make sure the charter was ready so I could fly to L.A. directly after my show. I wouldn't make it to Cali until three or four in the morning, but I didn't care. I had to see what was up with Simone. I knew something was wrong.

Simone, open the fucking door!" I yelled as I continuously banged on her front door, pissed that I didn't have the key she'd given me. It was at the Brentwood house and I'd come here straight from the airport. I ran back to the front of the building where my driver was waiting, and told him to get in the passenger seat. I didn't have time to wait for this cat to maneuver and get directions on where to go. I hopped behind the wheel and got us to Brentwood and back in less than forty minutes.

"Simone?" I walked into her condo, looking around for any sign of her. Maybe she isn't here, I thought as I looked through each room. When I reached her bedroom door, I tried turning the knob, but it was locked. I banged on the door for a while, trying to decide what to do. I knew if she was in there, she would have come out by now if only to tell me to fuck off. Maybe she's with Talise. Yeah, Talise came and got her, that's why her truck is still downstairs, I told myslef as I started for the front door. There wasn't shit I could do if she didn't want to see me no more, but I at least needed to know why. My anger boiled over as I turned around and broke open her bedroom door with one strong kick.

When I saw the form of a body lying in the bed, still and not alarmed from the sound of the door breaking open, I panicked. I ran to the bed, praying it wasn't her; hoping that it was only covers that made it look as if a body were in the bed, but it wasn't. It was her!

"Simone! Wake up baby!" I yelled after pulling the covers off of her and taking her limp, lifeless body in my arms. I put my cheek so close to her mouth and nose that I was practically touching her, but I couldn't tell if she was breathing. I pressed my fingers to her neck and felt a faint pulse thumping against the index and middle fingers of my right hand. I laid her back on the bed, snatched my cell phone from my pants pocket, and dialed 911.

The operator instructed me to lay Simone on the floor and start CPR. She calmly took me through each step as I followed her instructions through the speaker on my phone, doing everything in my power to keep her alive. The operator continuously told me that an ambulance was on the way, but it seemed to take forever. Time was standing still as I alternated between chest compressions and giving her air.

"Come on, Simone! Come on! Don't do this to me!" I yelled as the paramedics pulled me away from her. I didn't hear them come in, I was so focused.

As the two paramedics knelt beside Simone, I stood there in shock.

"Sir, do you know what she took?" The female paramedic asked me.

"No! What do you mean what she took? What's wrong with her?"

"I'm not certain, but I need you to look around, check the bathrooms and everywhere you can. See if you find an empty pill bottle or something she could have ingested. I think she may have overdosed."

I began searching around as they quickly lifted her onto the gurney. I noticed her cell phone sitting on the night table next to her bed. I grabbed it, dropped it into my pocket and continued to search. As soon as I walked into the bathroom, I saw the empty prescription pill bottle lying in the sink. I grabbed it and rushed to hand it to the paramedic as they wheeled her out of the room.

As they pushed the gurney with Simone's lifeless body out of the door and onto the elevator, I slid in with them and watched them continue CPR as we descended the fifteen flights to the lobby.

When we arrived at the hospital, they quickly wheeled Simone into the emergency room and instructed me to have a seat in the waiting room. I pulled Simone's phone out of my pocket, powered it on, searched for Talise's number, and called her so she could get down there immediately.

"You need to leave!" Talise growled when her and her husband rushed into the ER waiting room.

"What? What? What are you talking about, Talise? Why?" I was shocked as I stood up and approached her.

"This is all your fault you son of a bitch!" She said through clenched teeth as tears streamed down her face. "You fucking did this to her!" Her husband held her back, her large protruding belly moving up and down with her heavy breathing. "If she dies, it's on you!" she said pointing her finger at me.

"Talise, what did I do? Tell me what happened! What did

I do?" I pleaded as her husband pulled her out of the room, telling me he'd come back to talk to me after he calmed her down.

"What happened? What did I do, Malachi?" I asked when he returned to the waiting room fifteen minutes later.

"That's not for me to talk to you about, man, but for now, I have to ask you to leave. Your being here is upsetting Talise even more than she already is. It's just best if you go now. I'll give you a call once we know what's going on," he said.

"I can't leave with her in there like that. I won't do that! That's my girl in there, man! Malachi, you know I love her!" I couldn't understand what was going on. I didn't know why they were treating me like this. I thought we were cool. I was at their wedding!

"Carlton, man, please leave. If you love Simone, just leave before Talise causes a scene. I just stopped her from calling the police. I doubt I'll be able to stop her again."

"Please call me, man," I conceded after thinking on it for minute. Shit was fucked up enough. The last thing I needed was 5-0 dragging me out of there. "Let me know what's going *on, Malachi. Don't leave me in the dark," I said as tears fell from my eyes. I handed him Simone's cell phone and stormed out of the hospital.*

The vibration from my phone alerting me of a new text message pulled me away from my thoughts and back to where I sat in my car in front of Simone's building. She wasn't home, but she was on her way. I knew exactly where she had been. I always knew where she was, which was why I had chosen this time to come. The text message gave me the heads up that Simone would be pulling up any minute, so I got out of my car so she could see me before she pulled into her garage.

Simone had been spending a lot of time with that square ass ball player, and that wasn't sitting well with me. The shit was killing me, as much as I hated to admit it. I know who she is spending her time with isn't my business anymore, but I needed to know what was up with them. Was this her new dude or some shit? Was it that damn easy for her to just move on and forget about me? I *needed* to know what was up with her.

I wanted to love Charletta the way I love Simone, to feel that deep passion inside of me for my wife, the mother of my kids! But from the first moment I saw Simone, something inside of me shifted. I had to know who she was. Then once I spent time with her and got to know her, I had to have her completely. It was different than anything I'd ever felt before. She had me faster than I ever thought I could be had. Having her in my life was never an option or a choice; I *had* to have her.

My eyes were on Simone before she noticed me standing there. I could clearly see the pain in her red-rimmed eyes.

The shit made my stomach drop like I was on a damn amusement park ride. I waved for her to pull her truck behind mine, and when she did, a black on black Benz pulled up behind her and two large men got out and approached me. I wasn't surprised.

Simone was out of her truck and standing next to the men in record time.

"Carlton, what are you doing here?" Her voice was deflated and resigned as she stood between the two men with her arms crossed over her chest.

"I miss you, Simone," I said simply. I hadn't planned on saying that, but it spilled from my mouth like a fucking unintentional fart. "Do you at least miss me?"

"Why are you doing this to me, Carlton?" Tears filled her eyes and I could tell that she was struggling to keep them from falling.

I cautiously and slowly walked closer to her, not wanting to alarm her, or her security. I never once took my eyes off of her beautiful dark, sad eyes.

"Why are you here, Carlton?" She asked again, raising her voice and losing the battle with her tears.

"I don't know. I just couldn't stay away—are you fucking that ball player now?"

A wave of shock crossed her face. "Are you seriously standing in front of my building asking me who I'm fucking, *Banks*?" She was pissed off. She hardly ever called me Banks, and whenever she did, it was always said like it tasted nasty coming out of her mouth.

"I just need to know what's going on with you, Simone! I see it's easy for you to just fucking forget about me and move on with your life, but this shit ain't easy for me!"

"You think this shit is easy for me?" She asked after

instructing her security to get back in their car, and walking over to me. "I can barely sleep at night without seeing your face! The majority of the time that I close my eyes, I see you fucking Tryon, and it hurts like it did the first time I saw that video! Nothing in my life has *ever* been easy, Carlton!" She was trying to regain her composure, as she stood in front of me, close enough to be touched if I were to reach my hand out. I wanted to touch her so bad. I wanted her in my arms.

"What am I supposed to do, Simone? I can't take that shit back! I'm not gay..."

"Then tell me why you were on a video getting your dick sucked and fucking a guy, Carlton?" she asked incredulously, cutting me off.

"Can I talk to you? Can we go somewhere and talk more privately? Please let me try to explain, Simone." I pleaded, looking intently into her eyes. "You can follow me, and your security can follow you. We can go sit down somewhere and have a drink and talk. I never got the chance to do that. *Please,* give me that chance!" I continued when I saw in her eyes that she was considering it.

"Explain what, Carlton? How in the world can you make me understand this? How can you ever make this better?"

"I don't know, Monie, but please let me try!"

"We can talk here. I'm not going anywhere with you, Carlton." This was definitely better than a no.

"Can we at least sit the car, Simone?" I asked.

After letting her security guys know what she was doing, she walked to the driver side of her truck and got in. This was my chance to lay it all on the table. It was all or nothing.

Chapter Twenty-eight
Tyron

*I*t didn't take long for me to get Ricky on my side and in my bed. I was happier than I'd been in a while. Before Banks, I'd never met a cat who got me to submit to him. I was always the dominant one, but there was something about Ricky that turned me on and excited me. I wanted to be inside of him *and* have him inside of me. He was exactly what I needed at this time in my life, and no one was the wiser. He eased my mind and took a lot of shit off of it by being around and doing him.

Ricky was my right hand now, because he was so efficient. Banks was a little heated that Ricky was doing more work for me and with me, than he was with him. But I think he was glad that I was keeping busy, so he ended up being cool with it. Plus, Ricky was juggling *everything* very well.

Freddy Jackson's, *Nice and Slow,* was flowing through the speakers as I rested on my bed face down. I was naked as Ricky mounted me, sitting on my ass. When his warm skin touched mine, my body relaxed. His hands began to knead warm oil into my back, giving me a firm massage that rivaled some Burke Williams shit. I was in heaven as the weight of the day released from my mind and the tension released from my body. He'd done this almost five nights a week since I started dealing with him, and I was definitely feeling this shit. He knew how to take care of me, and that is just what I needed.

As he made his way from my neck, down my back, and to my ass, I was dozing off. I felt him massaging my ass then moving down, ending at my feet where he took a lot of time pressing and rubbing every step out of the soles of each foot. I turned around when he asked me to, and was face up with my eyes closed as he crawled back up the California King-sized bed and began to massage the front of my body, starting with my head and moving down to my ears. I swear I wanted to pay his ass every time he did this shit. Every damn thing he did was on point, and I was feeling it, feeling him!

I was in a nice doze by the time he got to the front of my thighs, and almost in a deep sleep when I felt a warm wetness on my dick. I woke up and looked down to find it in Ricky's mouth. I inhaled when his beautiful mouth slid down my shaft again, rubbing his tongue against my hardness.

"Oh shit!" I said as he continued to take me in and out of his mouth expertly—like everything else he does.

Both hands wrapped around my dick, he twisted them in opposite directions as his mouth remained on the head, releasing plenty of spit. His mouth was so warm and soft, he could've been toothless because his movements, which began to increase in motion, were flawless.

"Oh shit, I'm about to cum!" I clenched the sheets as I

released into his mouth and felt him swallow every drop.

My toes curled as he continued to suck softly, making sure he got every last drop. "Fuuuck, Ricky!" I said, grabbing his head and pulling him up toward me.

We kissed as the Isley Brothers', *Atlantis,* began to play. I was really feeling this cat, and was definitely off my shit. I can't remember the last time anyone made me cum that quick.

Ricky rolled over and laid next me.

"Come here. Why you move?" I asked.

"It's getting late. We should both get some rest," he said, kissing me on my cheek.

"You sure?" I asked, wondering if he was serious, because rest was just what I needed.

"Very sure, now let's get some sleep. You have an early morning tomorrow. Sajaira's video shoot is at five in the morning."

"I won't be there that fucking early," I yawned. "I'll be through there around nine."

"Well, I have to be there early, so I need some sleep." He pulled the covers over us, snuggled up next to me, and kissed me on my neck.

"Good night," I think he said, but I was already in a deep sleep. I didn't hear him leave the house the next morning.

Chapter Twenty-nine
Simone

When I saw Carlton standing on the sidewalk next to his car, staring at me with his dark tight eyes, my heart took a quick leap. As much as I detested him, he was still so beautiful to me. His toffee hued skin and dark slanted eyes were so alluring. He always seemed to look through me, to understand my wants and needs before I could voice them. I truly thought he was the man that I would spend the rest of my life with, and then I saw that video.

I was feeling good, and hoping to keep this rare feeling a bit longer, but when I saw Carlton's face, my mood immediately changed. *What in the hell could he want now?* I thought, pulling behind his car and throwing my truck into park before hopping out.

I was returning home from one of the best sessions I'd ever had with Dr. Marge. After visiting Marie, a great weight had been lifted off of my shoulders. I didn't know that a lot of the heaviness I'd been carrying had to do with my relationship with her. I've had so much drama going on in my life, that there really was no way to know what issue held the heaviest weight, until it was lifted.

To my surprise, Marie's words seemed to heal all of the hurt she'd caused me. I will never forget what I went through growing up, but her apologies and regrets were antidotal, and my forgiveness was the remedy that helped mend some of my brokenness. I finally felt a bit of peace and was thankful that I was able to have last words with her before she passed. It was much needed closure, and I was thankful for it.

Her funeral was small and elegant, and surprisingly sad. Talise accompanied me and understood when I decided not to go to the burial ceremony at the cemetery. We went to the Miles' house after. Mother and Mommy Miles were waiting for us with lunch.

~ ~ ~ ~ ~ ~

It was a very awkward couple of minutes after Carlton hopped onto the passenger seat of my truck.

"I still love you, Simone," he said after we'd sat in silence for longer than either of us were comfortable with. "Do you at least still love me?"

I looked into his eyes, which seemed to plead for an affirmative response. I did still love him, but none of that mattered, so he didn't need to know that. Nothing can change what's already been done, what I've already seen.

"Carlton, just say what you have to say, please," I sighed, shaking my head, trying to clear the images of that video from my mind for the millionth time.

"This shit is unreal," he grumbled under his breath as he wiped his hand down his face from forehead to chin. "Doing eight years at eighteen on Rikers would change any

mans' life," he began bleakly. "It could've been worse, that's for fucking sure, but I was schooled from the jump; it was dominate or get dominated.

"I was serving time with Charletta's uncle. He was an old head lifer who had respect throughout our block and others. He looked out for me and showed me the ropes. He protected me. Thankfully, he never tried to violate me because of my ties with his niece and brother, but I saw how he got down. I saw how he controlled shit, dominated shit by making cats his bitch. No doubt, I was disgusted, but I didn't judge the man. He's in this shit hole for life, I'll be walking the streets again. I don't have to do the shit he's doin, I thought. Then these cats tried to get at me in the shower—I can't believe I'm telling you this shit," he said, pausing for a few beats before continuing. He hadn't looked at me once since his story began.

"Like I was saying, these cats tried to get at me in the shower. They were going to have to kill me to take me, but I've always been good with my hands, so it was never hard for me to come out of most battles on the winning end. I got with both of them. Knocked one out cold and submitted the other—then I made him my bitch as he intended to make me his. It was all about power and dominance, Simone. I had to take a stance. I had to show those muthafuckas and everyone else that I wasn't to be fucked with! I made a statement and that statement protected me! That's just how shit went down behind those walls, or at least the fucking block I was on. It was all about who's on top, who had the power. I was never, and will never be on bottom! It was never about no attraction shit or no love shit for me, Simone! It was dominate or be dominated—shit is looked at differently behind those walls, Simone," he said again with a sigh.

"Well why were you fucking Tyron then, Calrton?" I asked as calmly as I could. "By 'behind those walls,' do you mean behind any damn four walls?" I asked exasperatedly. "Hell, if you were so good with your hands, why did you have to fuck the guy? Why not just beat his ass and everyone else's ass who came at you?" My head was beginning to pound. I really didn't feel like hearing his shit any longer.

"That shit with Tyron just fucking happened—"

"How does your dick just end up in a man's mouth, and then in his ass, Banks? That shit just doesn't happen without forethought! Don't bullshit me!" I said, cutting him off.

"It wasn't like that, Simone! I don't know how to explain this shit!" He said, his voice full of frustration.

I looked at him and asked, "How long have you been fucking Tyron?" I figured I might as well get all of my questions answered while we were on the subject of his homosexuality.

"For years, but not often," he said after a long while of what I assumed was contemplation. He looked uncomfortable and embarrassed, but I didn't give a damn. This was his excuse? I could respect him more if he just came straight out and said that he's always been attracted to men, that he is bi, not this bullshit dominance, power crap!

"Look, Simone, I never thought I'd get out and continue that shit, but I did! If an opportunity came for me to secure a better position, I did. Not often, but I did. I hadn't fucked around with any cats before that night in a long time. I don't even expect you to believe that, but it's the truth. That night, on that video, that was in the beginning of us and the last time I even fucked around with that cat or anyone else."

"Has your wife always known this about you?" I asked,

wondering if he truly didn't know that she had come to see me.

"Char knows and accepts everything about me," he said, looking at me for the first time since he began to explain.

"She's a better woman than I am." *I was so done with this conversation and with him! I was disgusted!*

"I wouldn't say better, maybe more accepting. She loves me unconditionally, Simone. There's no limit to her love for me. We grew up together. She held me down for eight years while I did my bid..."

"And you divorced her for me? That's very loyal of you," *I muttered sarcastically.*

"The divorce isn't final..." *he began, but stopped when he saw the look on my face.*

"Do you know she came here to see me? Do you know that we went to the Polo Lounge and had a talk?" *I asked.*

"What do you mean she came to see you? My Charletta?" *He asked with a genuine surprised look on his face.* "What did you guys talk about? What did she say to you, Simone?"

"Yes, your Charletta. Ask her what she said. I'm done. Carlton, please get out of my car," *I sighed. I couldn't take any more of this.*

"You'll never let me back in will you?" *He asked, looking so damned sad. As much as I thought I loved him, at that moment, I felt nothing but anger and disgust. Who is this man? I thought as I stared at him, wondering why he asked me that a question.*

"Stop your divorce and get back with your wife, since she accepts everything about you, Carlton. Please, I've had enough. Get out!" *I started the engine and put the car in* drive as he sat there staring at me. "GET OUT!" I yelled when he didn't move immediately.

"I love you, don't forget that," He muttered as he got out of the car, closing the door behind him.

Chapter Thirty
Banks

"**W**hy in the hell did you go to Simone's, Charletta?" I asked, unable to keep my voice at a calm level. She was in the theatre room laid across the large custom-made couch watching a movie when I stormed in on her.

"What makes you think I went to Simone's, Carlton?" The tone of her voice was accusatory and the look on her face was hard. She got up and stood in front of me with her hands on her hips and her head tilted to the side.

"Just answer the damn question, Charletta! Why did you go to Simone's?" I asked again.

"Just answer *my* fucking question, Carlton!" She yelled, pushing me hard in the chest with both of her hands. "Did *you* go to Simone's? Did *you* see her?"

"Why in the fuck would you go to her, Charletta?" I asked, intentionally not answering her questions. "What is wrong with you? Do you think her seeing the wife of the man who she feels fucked her over is a good idea? All I need to know is what in the hell were you thinking doing some shit like that?"

"What makes you think I went over there, Carlton? Are you fucking her *again*? Do I need to be prepared to pack my shit, *again,* and have my heart stomped on, *again*? Just let me know!" I'd never seen Charletta like this before. I no longer needed her to answer my question. The jealousy written on her face spoke volumes, and Char was not a jealous woman. She'd definitely met Simone.

"Come on, Char. Quit being dramatic and tell me what you guys talked about. What did you say to her?" I asked, trying to take a calmer approach. I needed Charletta on my side, but what I didn't need was her getting involved in this shit.

"What did she say I told her?" The roll of her neck and the squint in her eyes was classic Charletta. She was fully pissed off right now.

"Why are you being so difficult right now, Charletta? Just tell me what was said. I need to know that shit. It's important." I was using every tactic to try to avoid answering her questions outright. She didn't need to know that I went to Simone's house. She didn't need to know that I'd leave her again in a heartbeat if Simone would take me back.

"I don't have shit to say to you right now, Carlton!" She said as she headed out of the room, pissed off. "You over there in that bitch face and you come running in here asking me what the fuck I said to her like she told you I hurt her feelings or some shit. You coming in here trying to protect her like that bitch isn't trying to bring you and everything you've worked so hard for down!" She finished as she walked out of the door with me right behind her.

I grabbed her arm and turned her to me, stopping her before she got any further down the long hallway that held my novice art collection.

"Charletta, don't do this. Yes, I did go see her," I finally admitted, causing tears to spill from her eyes. "It's not like that, though. I'm not trying to get her back, Char," I lied.

"You know I'm trying to do everything I can do to get that video from her and get this shit behind us so we can move forward. I'm not accusing you of anything, and I'm not mad at you. I'm sorry I came at you like I did. I just don't want you involved in this shit, Char! I don't want you or my kids anywhere near this shit!"

"But we are near it, Carlton! This shit affects us too! It affects me more than you even realize! I can barely sleep at night thinking about our future, the future of our kids, and what they may have to grow up knowing about their father! I don't judge you, but every other fucking person will, and this is heavy on my shoulders and heavy on my heart! My father can't find out about this shit! Your mom can't find out about this shit," she cried. I didn't know that she was this worried about the situation. I knew she was concerned, but had no idea that she was losing sleep over this shit like I was. "I offered her almost a quarter mil for that shit and she wouldn't take it, Carlton! She is not going to let this shit go, and I'm worried sick about it. I can't even front anymore!"

I pulled her in my arms and held her as she cried on my chest. "I'm going to do whatever it takes to get that shit, Charletta, I promise. I've hurt our family enough. I won't do it again."

I knew a quarter of a million dollars was nothing to Simone. Paying her off would be a crapshoot, but I never shied away from a bet.

Chapter Thirty-one
Simone

As soon as I walked into my house, sat my handbag on the kitchen counter, and began to take off my boots, someone rang my buzzer from the front of my building. I walked to the small flat screen that was mounted to the wall between my kitchen cabinets, and pushed the button on the remote. It automatically tuned in to the camera that was aimed at the front entrance.

A tall, slender, sandy haired white man stood staring into the camera. I noticed he wore an expertly tailored suit that I could tell cost a pretty penny.

"Yes?" I said through the speaker in the remote control device I held.

"I'm looking for Simone Johnson. Is she available?"

"This is Simone Johnson."

"Ms. Johnson, my name is Dan Snyderman with Snyderman, Murdock and Fitz. I'm an attorney. I have something very important to talk to you about. Something

I think you'd want to hear," he said with a heavy southern accent.

"What is this regarding?" I asked.

"I'd rather talk to you face to face. Can I come up and speak with you, Ms. Johnson?"

"Can you come back in a couple of hours or leave your card and I'll call you?" Marlo and Ed would be well on their way to finding some place to sit down and eat. I had no plans to leave the house for the rest of the day, and insisted that they go take a break—which I had done more than a few times since they'd been with me. If this man was up to no good, he picked a perfect time to come to my home.

"Ms. Johnson, can we please talk now? I promise, you will want to hear what I have to say," he said in his silky, sultry southern drawl.

"I'm not comfortable letting you inside my home. I don't know you."

"I understand your concern ma'am, but I'm not here to harm you. Call this number..." I picked up my cell phone off of the counter and dialed the number he had given me. "That's my law office. I'm one of the senior partners. Ask to speak to Sarah, my secretary. She'll tell you that I'm here and that I'm legit," he continued as the phone rang.

I asked for Sarah, who came on the line rather quickly and verified that he was indeed an attorney and that he did have it on his schedule to stop by my house to discuss a "business matter" with me. She wouldn't tell me who had hired him, no matter how many different ways I asked her the same question.

I hung up the phone with her and opened the browser on my phone. I Googled *Dan Snyderman, Attorney, Los Angeles, CA,* and a plethora of searches were returned, all belonging to him. Dan Snyderman, the high-powered entertainment attorney who has battled to the death and won all but one of his cases, was standing at my door wanting to speak to me. I knew who'd sent him.

Curiosity got the best of me so I let the man up. I offered him a seat in my living room and something to drink. He took the seat and said that he wouldn't mind some water. When I returned, he had his briefcase open on top of the coffee table. I handed him the bottle of water and sat across from him.

"Ms. Johnson, I understand that you are in possession of a *very* sensitive... item, and my clients are eager to get it back and make this... all go away," he said, taking long pauses between some of his words. "With that being said," he continued when I said nothing. "My clients are offering you five hundred thousand dollars for the return of said sensitive item.

I'm not sure how I was able to keep a straight face or prevent my eyes from betraying what was really going on inside of my mind, but I pulled it off. I stayed silent as I stared at the gangly man who vaguely reminded me of Ryan Gossling. He was handsome and sure of himself, successful at what he did, and loved the power it gave him. I knew his type.

"Okay, seven hundred thousand and that's it!"

"You can tell your clients to kiss my ass," I stated calmly. This shit was amusing. They were trying to buy me off, get rid of me, sweep this under the rug, just shit on Stacey! It took a lot of effort for me to keep my outward demeanor cool, because I was boiling on the inside.

"Simone, think about this. Think about what that amount of money can do for you!"

"It's Ms. Johnson," I said reminding him that we were not on a first name basis. "Look around you, Mr. Snyderman. Does it look like I need your clients' money?" I asked, cutting him off. "This place is worth twice what you're offering. I own it *and* it's paid for. No mortgage," I said proudly. "I'm financially well off so they… *your clients*, can't just pay me off for less than what one of… *your clients*, paid for that damn Bugatti Veyron he just purchased," I said, rising from my seat. "If they… *your clients,* want the video, it's going to cost two million, no negotiating," I bluffed. I tried not to laugh at the man as his mouth hung open in surprise. "I'm sure you have my information. Give me a call once you've had a chance to talk to… *your clients.*"

He gathered his things and I had him out the door in less than three minutes. I immediately picked up the phone and began speaking as soon as she said hello.

"You aren't going to believe this shit. An attorney just left my house offering me seven hundred thousand dollars for that damn video. Can you believe that?" I asked in one breath.

"You've got to be kidding me, Simone!" She said, her voice rising and then lowering quickly. I'm sure Anastasia was sleeping. She usually was around this time. "What did you tell him? What did you do? You should really get rid of that crap and just be done with it, Simone, seriously."

"First, I told him to tell his clients they could kiss my ass, and then I told him two million would get his clients what they want."

She didn't say anything for a while, so we both sat on the phone in silence for a few beats.

"What did he say?" She asked in astonishment.

"He said that he would get back to me. I was bluffing

anyway. I don't plan on selling them that video, Talise. They could pay two million without blinking, though. Between the two of them, that's nothing. Hell, either of them could pay that easily on their own," I sighed.

"Do you think they sent Charletta to offer you that other amount to see where your head is at?" Talise asked.

"Maybe they did, maybe they didn't. I really don't know, but I'm tired of all of this. I can't leave my house now without hoping someone isn't outside my building wanting to talk to me. I just need the damn justice system to work, and lock Tyron's ass up. It's like this shit is consuming me, Talise. I wake up, it's the first thing on my mind. I eat, it's on my mind, I shower, it's on my mind. I sleep, I'm dreaming of the mess! I can't escape this shit, Tali, and I just want it to be over... this ordeal, not my life, Talise." I clarified with a dry chuckle before she asked, because I knew she would.

"Well, I'll kill you if you ever kill yourself, so let that deter you," she snickered. "The justice system usually takes a very long time, Simone. It's a process. Give them time. It hasn't been nearly as long as some folks have had to wait to get justice for their loved ones. We just have to stay hopeful that it won't be much longer. In the meantime, I think you should just sell that video, Simone. Or better yet, give it to the police as evidence. We know that video is why Stacey was killed. That's motive right there," she suggested.

"Trust me, I've thought about every single angle, Talise. Think about it. How can that video prove that Tyron killed Stacey? They can't prove Stacey recorded it. They can't even prove he ever had it! Tyron being in a secret gay relationship with Stacey should be motive enough, you know?"

"I just want you to get rid of that video sooner rather than later, Simone. It's dangerous, and you having it worries the crap out of me!" Talise pleaded. "Thank God Deon talked you into having the bodyguards, but I still worry! Just let the justice system work, Simone."

"What if they never charge Tyron with Stacey's murder and we have to continue to watch as his career skyrocket and his net worth triple, while our friend is dead? I don't think I can get rid of the video right now Talise. I'm sorry."

"Well then promise me you won't do anything stupid with that video, Simone," she pleaded.

"I'm not going to do anything stupid with it, Talise," I partially lied. I didn't know what I was going to do with that damn video, but if the right opportunity arose for me to use it to my advantage, I wouldn't hesitate. "Don't worry about that. I'm not selling them the video, though. If I sell the video and Tyron doesn't get indicted, then he's scot-free, reputation and all. I won't allow that to happen," I said stubbornly.

"Just sell the video, Simone. Do something good with the money in Stacey's honor and move on with your life! You aren't safe having that damn video! Why don't you see that?"

"That video *is* keeping me safe, Talise."

"Yeah, just like it kept Stacey safe huh?"

She had me there...

Chapter Thirty-two
Tyron

I wasn't giving her shit, and couldn't believe that Banks was standing in my office telling me that we had to pay Simone off!

"That bitch don't deserve a damn dime for giving me something that wasn't hers in the first fucking place!" I was livid as I paced around my office.

"We have to do whatever we can to make this shit go away. You thinkin' about saving your fucking money while I'm thinkin' about saving our reputations, our careers, Tyron! I'm not asking your permission, B. We already see that you don't know how to handle this shit. The first thing you should've done was hit homeboy off with a mil and let his ass live," he said agitatedly. I never once thought about paying Stacey off and I wasn't about to give Simone a penny! "Sit down, Ty, and calm the fuck down, man! You aren't thinking clearly right now. You can't be."

I sat across from Banks at the conference table in the corner of my office and tried to calm myself.

"Do you really think she'll take a payoff?" I knew something needed to be done; I just hated for it to be this.

"I already know she will."

"How much Banks?"

"We went in low with half a mil," he started before I jumped out of my seat.

"Half a mil? Are you shittin' me, Yo? Half a mil? That is *not* fucking low! What are you thinking?" I lost all of my calm as soon as that amount came out of his mouth.

"Simone ain't stupid, Ty! She knows what she has, and she knows what she can do with it! Half a million ain't shit to you or me, and neither is two mil, which is what she's asking for!" He said angrily, rising out of his seat and approaching me. "You *will* give me half. *Motherfucker* you should be paying the whole fucking thing!" He hissed through clinched teeth as he stood in my face, his dark, tight, slanted eyes angry.

I walked away from him, sat back down, and covered my face with my hands, putting my elbows on the glass table. It was still hard for me to believe that this shit was my life.

"It's not about the money, it's the principle of the shit, but fuck it, I'll do it. When are we meeting with the attorney?" I said, relenting. What other choice did I have, aside from killing her and possibly still not having the damn video?

"I know you'll do it. Dan will be here any minute." He sat back down and looked at me from across the table. "Now you're fucking Ricky," he said, shaking his head. He was looking at me like a father would his son who had disappointed him. His statement caught me off guard and made my reply to him sound weak.

"What are you talkin' about? I'm not... fucking, Ricky."

I wouldn't have even believed myself.

"You're a dumb ass..." He was cut off by the knock on the door and Tina, one of our newer receptionists, escorting Dan Snyderman, one of the high-powered lawyers we kept on retainer, into the room.

He took a seat at the conference table after shaking both of our hands.

"Alright gentlemen, as I'm sure you already know, she wants two million," he said, pulling a yellow legal sized notepad out of his briefcase. He plucked a Montblanc pen out of the inside pocket of his suit jacket and sat it on top of the pad.

"What did she say? How in the hell did it get up to two mil, Dan?" Banks asked.

"First, she looked at me stone faced when I gave her your initial offer of half a mil. Then she rolled her eyes when I went up to seven hundred thou, and then she said to tell you to kiss her ass, but I think she was referring to you, Mr. Marks."

"Bitch!" I said under my breath.

"Okay, well, how did it get from seven hundred thousand to two million?" Banks asked incredulously. "I said don't go higher than a mil!"

"Mr. Banks, I think you know what type of woman this Simone Johnson is. I said seven hundred thousand and she said, and I quote," he turned a couple of pages on his legal pad then began to read. "This place is worth twice what you're offering. I own it *and* it's paid for, no mortgage. I'm financially well off, so they... *your clients*, can't just pay me off for less than what one of... *your clients*, paid for that damn Bugatti Veyron he just purchased. If they... *your clients*, want the video, it's going to cost two million, no negotiating.' End quote. That's what she said, and that's what I'm relaying to you."

Banks looked at me with disgust in his eyes at the mention of the Bugatti I'd picked up a few days ago. He called me after he heard that I bought it and bitched about me not laying low. Cars were my thing. *I could buy what the fuck I want!* I thought as I looked away from him. I don't know how he knew practically every damn thing I was doing lately, but I'm a grown ass man, and will do whatever the hell I want, when I want, and with who the fuck I want!

"Is there a way for us to make sure that she hasn't given copies of the item to anyone else? We *must* make sure that she doesn't sell us a copy of the shit and still leak it, Dan. This has to be it. It *has* to be over after this, after we pay her!" Banks said.

"Mr. Marks, I understand. The confidentiality agreement will cover all of what you mentioned and a copious amount more. I'll make it so if she even tweets, let alone speaks either of your names, she will have her ass sued off. As proud as she is, I'm sure she wouldn't want to go to the poor house, because I'd milk her dry."

"How soon can we get this done? The sooner the better," I added in. I was sick about giving this bitch two million dollars, but I needed this shit behind me once and for all.

"I'll give her a call and set up an appointment for her to come into my office, sign the paperwork, and give her a check as soon as you give me the go ahead."

Banks gave him the go ahead and then he left to get started on the confidentiality agreement.

"I can't believe this shit," he said when he sat back down across from me.

"Yeah, it's a fucking nightmare, for real," I sighed.

"What's up with you and Ricky, Ty?" I was hoping he wouldn't bring this shit back up. "Do you understand what you're doing? He fucking works for us. He could file a sexual harassment lawsuit against you... shit, us! He could fucking set you up like Stacey did, he could expose you like Simone can! What in the hell are you thinking right now, B?" he asked in an annoyed tone. "And don't fucking lie to me, Tyron!" He narrowed his tight eyes at me, making me rethink the lie that was about to come out of my mouth.

"He won't do that shit, Banks. I know this cat! He won't betray me."

"How in the *hell* do you know that? Tell me how you can think that in your mind and then say that to me like it's a guarantee? How can you be so sure of that shit? *How*?" His chest rose rapidly under his smoke grey V neck t-shirt. He was heated, but in all actuality, I didn't give two fucks. "You need to quit fucking with these dudes, Tyron! You need to find another girlfriend and leave that gay shit alone!"

"I'll do what the fuck I want to do! I have this shit under control! I know what I'm doing, Banks!" *Leave that gay shit alone?* His words had me boiling. My fists were balled as they sat on top of the table, clenched hard enough for the veins in them to pop out.

"You're a fucking numbskull! You better not ever say shit about me and you to him! I guarantee you this is gon' bite you on your ass!" He got up and stormed out of my office, bumping into Ricky on his way out. "Mark my word, Yo!" He turned and said as he passed Ricky.

Chapter Thirty-three
Deon

A familiar calm came over me as I suited up for the game that would determine if we were going to make the playoffs. The locker room was abuzz with energy as my teammates talked loudly with each other, joking and preparing to take home this win against the Clippers.

It had been over a month since I got the positive test results, and I was still in a haze. My only distraction was Simone and basketball. I hadn't had sex with anyone after finding this out and I didn't plan to. I'd made up my mind that I wasn't having sex again until I was with someone that I trusted enough to disclose this shit to. I'd already put a number of women in danger; there was no way I'd do it again. It was as if God was trying to tell me something or warn me. I had to get my life right.

I used to pride myself on not being *that* man, on being discerning and not just giving myself to women frivolously. I never wanted to be put in a situation like I had been with Nadia. I was not only disgusted with her, I was also disgusted with myself. I should have never been so careless and as hormone driven as a teenager.

When I walked onto the court, I noticed Simone and Talise sitting in the courtside seats I'd secured for her. She looked effortlessly beautiful as she sat there with her long legs covered in black skinny jeans and black lace up platform ankle boots. She looked at me and pointed toward the Laker purple blouse she was wearing and gave me the thumbs up and a smile.

Simone and I had gotten very close over the last few months, and I'd come to look forward to spending time with her. It didn't matter what we were doing, it just felt better having her with me. We were friends getting to know each other again and neither of us had our guard up. We were enjoying each other as friends and that was refreshing.

After a short warm-up, the lights dimmed and the large crowd that filled the arena began to scream. The announcer's deep baritone voice began to call off the names of our starting line-up, ending with mine.

"Small Forward, number 11, six foot seven, eighth season, out of Clark University... Deoonnnn Braaaadford!" I ran through the parted line that my teammates stood on each side of, slapping their hands as I passed each of them as the crowd cheered. This was always where the excitement started for me. The butterflies in my stomach began to flutter as they did before every game. I was ready to play!

We won tip off, and the game started out at a good pace. I didn't need time to get warmed up. As soon as I stepped on the court, I was in another zone, another place, in my element. We dominated the first half of the game and were up by 10 at halftime; I'd scored twenty of the fifty-seven points that were on the board, and was more than anxious to get back to the game by the time the third quarter started.

The fans were going crazy in the stands when Armond dunked on Blake Griffin. Chris Paul brought the ball back in and was heading down court when Kobe stole it and passed it off to me. I was open and went up for the easy layup, bringing the score to 61-52. I was heading back up court as Chris, again, brought the ball in and prepared to take it all the way to the hole. I beat him there and planted myself under the basket, ready to take the charge when he attempted to bypass me and failed. I took the hard charge and was on my back when he came down, landing on my knee, causing it to bend in a grossly unnatural way. The ref blew his whistle and fouled Chris as I laid there holding my knee, writhing in pain. I'd experienced small injuries, but nothing I wasn't able to play through. I knew this was serious.

As I lay on my back, it seemed like everything and everyone was moving in slow motion. I couldn't believe this was happening. As our team physician and trainers examined my knee, my coach, assistant coach, and Darryl Withers knelt beside me. Daryl was on one knee with his head down in prayer as his right hand rested on my shoulder. I looked around and noticed my teammates and players from the other team standing near. Some had their heads down; I could see the sadness and pity in the eyes of the ones who didn't.

"How does it feel when I do this, Deon?" The doctor asked squeezing my knee. The agony on my face was answer enough. "Get a stretcher, let's get him off the court."

I felt like I was in a dream, like I was having an out of body experience. *This was not happening to me!*

I was placed on the stretcher and wheeled off the court

as my teammates and a couple of players from the other team touched some part of my body in support. I could hear the fans chanting, "Bradford! Bradford!" as I lay on the gurney being pushed toward the tunnel that led to the locker room.

I heard heels clacking rapidly before I saw Simone's face once she caught up to the gurney. She grabbed my hand and walked briskly alongside the doctor and two trainers.

"It's going to be okay, Deon. Don't worry," she said, but I could tell that she was. She kept one hand tightly around mine and the other clasped around the laminated family access pass that hung around her neck.

~ ~ ~ ~ ~ ~

The MRI results were just as devastating as our loss to the Clippers. I was scheduled to have surgery the next morning to repair my patella, the grade 2 tear to my MCL, and the partial tear to my ACL. I knew this could be a career ending injury as soon as the doctor spoke those words.

I couldn't help the tears that formed in my eyes as Simone drove me home from the doctor. I rested my head on the leather headrest and just let them fall from my eyes. I didn't care what she thought; I didn't care what anyone thought. My basketball days could be over, and I wasn't even thirty! I had at minimum five more years in me. I wasn't ready to stop playing. I couldn't picture my life without basketball in it and I didn't want to.

"I'm sorry, Deon," Simone said softly.

"I just can't believe this shit, Simone. It's like a nightmare," I admitted.

"I know it feels that way, but like the doctor said, there is a chance that you will be able to play again."

"Yeah, a fucking small chance," I said bitterly.

"A small chance is better than no chance, Deon," she said gently.

"We fucking lost to the Clippers! We didn't make the playoffs! I have to have surgery! I won't be able to walk and get around like normal! I can't even fucking drive! What if I can't play anymore, Simone? What in the hell would I do then?" I asked as tears continued to spill down my face faster than I could wipe them away.

"You *will* be able to play again, Deon!" She said sternly as she stopped at the red light and looked at me, her eyes blazing. "Even if the doctor said there was no chance that you'd ever play again, you could *still* beat those odds. It's up to you and God, Deon. You can and will play again if that is what you really want," she finished as the light turned green and we continued down Wilshire Boulevard toward my house.

"I want to not be hurt! I want this shit to be a dream! That's what I want!" I spat out angrily.

"Well, that's not realistic, Deon. I understand that you are pissed right now. I get that you are worried as shit about having surgery tomorrow, the physical therapy, whatever is going to come after that. I get it! But there is nothing you can do about it. It's done! The sooner you deal with it head on the sooner you will heal and get that fire in you blazing. You're going to need that fire to make it back. You made it to the NBA, Deon. Those odds are very slim. You did that, you can do this," she said, glancing at me before switching lanes.

Simone was a confident driver. She knew how to maneuver in and out of traffic effortlessly and smoothly. I tried to relax as I mulled over what she'd just said. I knew she was right. I had to quit sulking and just do what I have to do to get back on the court.

"Yeah, you're right," I admitted as she pulled up to the valet in front of my building. "I just have to take this one day at a time. That's all I can do." I wiped my hand across my face and sighed as I looked down at the brace strapped around my right knee, preventing it from moving. The throbbing seemed to increase as I looked down at it, shaking my head in disbelief. I couldn't believe this was my knee. I couldn't believe this was my life! I was determined to get back on the court and play even better than I had before.

This wasn't the end. This *couldn't* be the end!

Chapter Thirty-four
Tyron

"What's under your skin?" Ricky asked after he came into my office and closed the door behind him. He walked directly over to me and began to massage the tension out of my shoulders.

"Business shit. Nothing for you to worry about."

"Try to relax. You are so tense." Ricky said, moving his hands up to my neck.

"Do I get next?" Both Ricky and I turned to find Tomi Jordan standing in the open door, watching us.

Ricky's body stiffened at the sound of Tomi's voice. I looked up and couldn't believe that she was standing there like someone should be happy to see her. Heat rose from deep down in my gut, made its way up my neck, and settled at my temples. Shit, I thought I was pissed before she came, but that was nothing in comparison to what I was feeling at that moment.

"Ricky, step out for a minute," I instructed as I got up from where I was sitting at the conference table and walked toward my desk.

Tomi walked into the office with a smirk on her small pixie face. She looked good, well rested, and happy.

"I can't believe you have the balls to fucking show your face here!" I said through clenched teeth as I stood in front of my desk with my arms folded across my crisp, white button up shirt.

"I'm sorry that it went down like that, Tyron. I really am, but I had to separate Tomi Jordan from all this shit that is going on around you. You've been lying to me and that's not okay," she said calmly.

"You don't do shit like that, Tomi! That shit wasn't right. You owe me more than that! We go way back. We are bigger than that, but you treated me like fucking shit!" I said angrily.

Around the way, everyone always thought me and Tomi was an item. We knew things about each other that no one else knew. I guess people assumed we were a couple because we were always together. No one ever saw me with another girl or her with another man. They had no idea that we'd both figured out a long time ago that she was more into girls than I was and I was more into men than I could ever be into women.

We grew up in Harlem. It wasn't a place where being attracted to the same sex was accepted or ignored. In my hood, you'd get a beat down for gay shit. I even gave a few beat downs for gay shit, so I knew what being on the other end of the stomps from the Timb boots could be like. I vowed that would never happen to me.

I've always been drawn toward beautiful women. I just never felt any attraction or cared to be intimate with one, although I have more than a few times. It's just that men have always done it for me. But, growing up how I grew up, and around the cats I grew up with, having an attraction for dudes was a guaranteed beat down. So, heterosexual I stayed, and so did Tomi. We just let it appear that we were together, did our business way outside of Harlem, and only confided in each other.

It was the music that brought me and Tomi together in the first place. When I first heard her sing, she was sitting on her stoop on 138th and Edgecombe by herself. She was dressed in baggy jeans, Nike Air Force 1's, and a t-shirt. I was hanging out my window in the next building over and sat there listening as she sang song after song, unaware that I was even there. It was an unusually quiet day on our block, so I yelled out my window to her, "Yo, sing that la la la la la song again! You were killin that joint!"

"I didn't even know you was listenin'," she said, and then belted out Minnie Riperton's "Lovin' You." Since she knew she now had an audience, she sang it better than she did the first time. I fell in love with her voice like I'd never heard another person sing before.

I loved the fact that Tomi wasn't shy. She'd sing for anyone at the drop of a dime, because she knew without a shadow of a doubt that she had an amazing gift. She was one of those people that would sing hello AND goodbye to you. She seemed to sing every word that came out of her damn mouth, she sang so damned much. Since she was always singing and I was always making beats, it was only natural for us to come together and make music. We recorded two of her hits in the make shift studio in my bedroom. I had all the equipment and made my closet the recording booth. It was small, and could only fit one person at a time, but she'd go in that room that could barely fit her and the mic stand, close the door, and sing her heart out in pitch darkness.

I knew we would make it big, so from the first day I met Tomi, I began to groom her for the success that I knew was coming our way. I first had to change the way she dressed. She had style, but she needed to learn to be more feminine. Growing up in a house with only her father and four brothers, she was as much of a boy as I was.

Tomi wasn't comfortable unless she was in sneakers or Timberlands and jeans. She also had no idea—nor did me or any of the other cats around the way—how beautiful she was. I gradually got her into fitted jeans and girly tops during our first summer as friends, and from then on, it was over. Tomi realized that not only did she get the unwanted attention from guys, she got the attention she always wanted from the other chicks. She got way more play being a femme than she did looking butch, and that suited her well.

Tomi was talented, fly, and she knew she was going to the top and that's the exact attitude that I wanted her to have. When the music thing took off, everything happened so fast, there was no looking back. She was an overnight sensation.

It was only natural for us to keep the image of us being a couple going. It was the easiest thing for us to do. We didn't have to answer any questions about our love life unless it pertained to us as a couple, and of course, we chose not discuss our private life in public. So the media deemed us "the golden couple" and we ran with it. We kept our private life private and got out to as many events as we could. We made sure the media got plenty of shots of us together as a couple and we did our private thing on the low.

There was no one on this earth that I trusted more than

Tomi. We'd been together most of our lives, which was why what she'd done without forewarning fucked me up so much.

"You are slipping, Ty. Look at what I walked in on. That could have been anybody walking in on you and seeing that."

"No one walks into my office without knockin', Tomi!" I said, raising my voice.

"I did, Tyron." Her calm demeanor was more unnerving to me now than it had ever been before. "Come on. What did you expect me to do, Tyron? There is a lot of stuff going on with you, and I bet I only know a third of it, if that. You lied to me. You weren't straight up about this."

"I didn't lie to you, Tomi! The less you know, the better!"

She walked over to me in high top Maison Margiela denim sneakers, white skinny jeans that side zipped from the ankle almost up to the knee, and a white, loose neck t-shirt that had *"QUIT LOOKING AT ME!"* written in bold letters across the front. From the five four sided diamond and platinum chains that hung around her neck, totaling over eighty carats, that *I* dropped damn near a quarter a mil on for her last birthday, to the platinum and diamond hoop earrings, thick bezeled out band that she wore on the middle finger of her right hand, the multiple diamond bangles, and iced out watch on her wrist, she had on at least a million dollars' worth of jewelry, and was never seen in public without at least a half a mil on.

"Is there a video of you out there, Tyron?" She asked after walking up to me standing directly in my face and staring me dead in my eyes. I couldn't lie to her any more.

Chapter Thirty-five
Simone

"That man is in love with you, Simone. I don't know how you can't see that," my mother said as we exited the freeway only blocks from home. We'd just spent the morning and most of the early afternoon at Deon's house trying to cheer him up. I'd never seen him so down.

"Love?" I laughed. "He isn't in love with me, Mom. Why would you say that? The man is heavily medicated. He just had surgery a few days ago," I countered.

"I can tell by the way he looks at you, Simone. I could tell from the first time I saw you two interact. Trust me, I know what I'm saying." she smiled over at me.

I let her words linger in the air as we made our way up Figueroa.

"We're just friends, Mom. That's all," I reminded her.

"Yeah, for now you are. There is palpable chemistry between you two, Simone. I don't know why both of you are ignoring it," my mother said in a singsong voice that made me laugh.

"Love is the last thing either of us is thinking about right now," I laughed.

"That's when it happens, when you least expect it." She smiled as I pulled up to my building and my phone began to ring simultaneously. It was a 702 area code and I knew that was Vegas.

"Mom, if I pull into the garage, I'm going to drop this call. Do you have your key? I'll be up after I get off of the phone," I asked as I stopped in front of my building, the ringing of my cell spewing loudly through the speakers of my truck, thanks to the great invention of the Bluetooth device.

"Okay, no problem. I need to get to the bathroom!" she said, looking behind us to make sure that Marlo and Ed were in place. Having them with me was probably more comfort for her than for me, although I had gotten used to having them near.

"I'm in the kitchen, honey. Are you hungry?" I heard my mother ask after she heard me enter the house. I couldn't answer her through my sobs. I was so overwhelmed with emotion; I just needed to get to my mother.

"Simone! What's wrong baby?" My mom asked, rushing to me, wrapping her arms around me once I'd walked into the large kitchen area. I couldn't stop crying long enough to get all of the words out of my mouth.

"He..." I cried as my mother pulled me into her arms as tears of worry began to spill down her face.

"Simone, tell me what is wrong with you!" she pleaded.

"He...he..." I cried on her shoulder as all of the pent up emotion and anxiety that I had been holding in since Stacey was murdered rushed out.

"Oh my Lord, Simone, please tell me what is wrong with you!" She cried. "Is someone dead?" She asked, pushing me away from her by holding each of my arms in her hands and looking at me through worry filled teary eyes.

"I'm... sorry... I'm... I'm..." I said between sobs before she pulled me back into her embrace, squeezing me tighter in her arms and rubbing my back, trying to calm me.

"I'm sorry, Mom, I'm sorry... I'm happy!" I was finally able to get out as tears continued to cascade down my cheeks and a smile spread across my face.

"Well, thank you, Jesus! Simone, you had me so worried. Now girl, what is going on?" She asked, sounding relieved as she wiped tears from my face.

"I'm sorry, Mom, I just got so overwhelmed! That was the district attorney from Nevada! She's taking Stacey's murder case to a Grand Jury! She's trying to get Tyron indicted for first degree murder and she wants me and Talise to testify!" I said excitedly, not able to stop myself from dancing in place and waving my hands in the air above my head in celebration.

"Oh thank you, Jesus! That is so awesome, Simone!" She wrapped her arms around me in a tight hug and then kissed both of my cheeks. "Awesome isn't even the word."

Tears still trickled down my face as I stood in front of my mom smiling. "She says she's really sure she will get an indictment or she wouldn't do it! Can you believe it?"

"Yes, I can, honey. Yes I can. God is good! So when is this Grand Jury meeting? Will that man who killed him be there? Simone what do you think he will do when he finds out that you are testifying?" I could tell by the tone of her voice and the look on her face that she was worried.

"No, Mom, don't worry," I said, placing my hand on her

shoulder and squeezing it. "The Grand Jury is meeting in private and was requested by the D.A. The D.A. presents the evidence to the Grand Jury so they can determine whether there is enough evidence to prosecute him. He won't be there. He won't even know!" I said triumphantly. "I have to go to Talise's. I need to see her face when I tell her this!" I said, giving her one last hug.

"Okay, honey. I love you and I'm very, very happy to hear this good news. Kiss Talise and the baby for me."

"Okay, I will. Love you too, Mom," I said before kissing her on the cheek and heading out the door.

Chapter Thirty-six
Tyron

"Yeah, there's a video," I admitted, shaking my head back and forth.

"See? I knew it, Ty. You know I can always tell when you aren't being on the up and up with me. Why didn't you come to me from the beginning, man? I would have helped you try to figure this shit out."

"I thought I could take care of this shit, Tomi. I can't believe it's gotten this out of hand, Yo."

"Tell me what's going on," she said and walked to the small sitting area next to the window and took a seat on the black leather sofa that could seat three people comfortably.

I told her the story, leaving out that Banks was on the video with me. She didn't know about me and Banks, and for some reason, I didn't want her to ever know. I stressed that I had nothing to do with Stacey's death. Me, Curse, and now Banks, no one else needed to know about my involvement in that. That was way too risky. I'd be damned if I was going to spend the rest of my life in the pen over that shit.

"You should have paid homeboy off. You should have done that immediately. There is no choice but to pay that girl and get the video. Put this behind you, Tyron. If she is already saying she will take the two mil then give it to her. Two mil is nothing; what's the hold up? You got it, don't you? If not you know I got you." I didn't want to tell her that my half was only a million because she'd really be looking at me sideways, wondering why I was bitching over chump change.

"Naw, I'm good. You know I could wipe my ass with two million. I just hate giving the bitch anything. Dan just met with her a couple of days ago. He said he'll get the confidentiality shit written up and get it taken care of in the next couple of days."

"What's still bothering you then?" Ever the perceptive Tomi Jordan, she saw through me way too clearly.

"I'm stressing the hell out over this murder investigation. I can't even fucking sleep without having nightmares about 5-0 pulling me out my bed in the early morning and extraditing me to Nevada. Fucked up part about it is, there ain't shit I can do but wait for them to make the first move," I sighed and sat across from her in one of the two black, leather one seater arm chairs.

Changing the subject, I said, "You still could've gave me a heads up, Tomi. I shouldn't have had to find that break-up shit out online. I would've never done no shit like that to you, and you know it."

"I'm sorry, but I knew you would try to talk me out of it, so I didn't tell you. Plus, trust me, it's better this way. If something had went down—and something could still go down, because that situation is not settled—me and my team would have had to take a more aggressive approach. At least this way, we can still be friends publicly, Tyron. You aren't looking at this from the right perspective," she said sincerely.

"It's how you did it that's fucked up, Tomi! Why don't you get that shit?"

"I do get it, Tyron. I really do and I'm sorry. We've been down with each other for way too long. I don't want this to come between us. You're my brother and I love you. You know that, right? Can you forgive me?"

"Yeah, I forgive you. You're my little sis, Yo."

I was the only living child to my still married parents. I was born with an identical twin that died of pneumonia when we were one, so they put all of their energy into me. Both my parents held tenured jobs with the city of New York throughout my childhood, so we did good. I never had to want for anything. I was the spoiled kid on the block. I always had on the hottest new kicks, stayed laced in the flyest and latest designers, and never once had pockets void of money. When all my friends had to hit the block and hustle because they needed to eat, or wanted that new hot shit, I was in my room making beats with the studio equipment my pops bought from a studio that was closing in one of the downtown buildings he inspected.

I was proud of the fact that I never had to get out there and hustle poison to people. I was proud that I never sold a rock of crack or a dime bag of weed in my life, and I was even more proud that I reached the level of success that allowed me to retire my parents to a beautiful new golf course home in Coral Gables, Florida seven years ago.

~ ~ ~ ~ ~ ~

"I need to talk to you about something, Tyron," Tomi said softly.

"What's up? Talk to me."

She hesitated for a minute then spoke, "I'm in love, Tyron!" She exclaimed, her voice showing more emotion than what was normal for Tomi.

"What? Who are you in love with, Tomi?" I was really surprised. Tomi never got emotionally involved with chicks. That just wasn't her.

"Isis!" She said and covered her eyes with her hand then peeked out at me through her middle and ring fingers.

"Isis? As in the rapper and actress Isis? How did that happen?" I laughed. I was starting to get comfortable and relax with Tomi like old times. It felt good being able to talk to her again. The last time we saw each other, it was all bad.

"Yes! I can't believe it either! Well you know I've met her a dozen times before, but she never came at me like that, and you know I'm not checking for no industry chicks. Well, as you know, I had a small part in her new movie, *Tame the Dragon,* and we just seemed to connect this time. It was so crazy, Ty. I've never felt like this before."

"Isis ain't no joke, Tomi. She does her thing," I warned.

"And I'm a joke?" She asked, squinting her eyes and smirking at me.

"You know that's not what I'm saying," I laughed. "She has a rep for lovin' and leavin'. I wouldn't want to see you hurt, sis. That's all."

"I'll be good. I can handle her. Plus, I have her wrapped around my little finger," she said, raising and wiggling the pinky finger on her left hand, causing the diamonds from the dainty rings that spanned up to her knuckle to sparkle and glimmer against the sunlight. I hadn't noticed it before. It was definitely a nice piece. "Cartier, a gift from Isis," she winked as she got up and went to the small mini bar in the far right corner of my office to pour another drink.

"I'll have a whiskey straight up," I said. Tomi stopped dead in her tracks and turned to look at me.

"You're joking, right?" I got up and walked past her to the bar and poured myself a drink as she stood there with her mouth hung open. I took the first shot back, then poured another that I planned to sip on.

"Oh, so you're hanging with the big dogs again?" She laughed, as walked she to me. She poured some in a glass for herself, expertly sniffed the whiskey, and nodded her head in approval.

"Yeah, I needed something to take the edge off, and you know I'm not with no other shit, so drinking it is."

You stopped drinking New Year's Eve 2005," Tomi laughed.

I recalled the night I drank way too many bottles of champagne and mixed it with Tequila and anything else I got my hands on. I was a mess, and wilding out over my ex who had called it quits only the day before. I had been dealing with this cat for over five years, and I was thrown completely off guard when he decided he didn't want to be with me no more. After law school was paid for, after the last payment on his condo cleared, he decided that he didn't want to be a secret, and that he needed a man who could love him openly. Funny how he came to that conclusion after I *made* his ass and set him up real nice with a Stanford Law School education, a million dollar Palo Alto condo, and that damn Audi TT he cried over when I surprised him with it.

"I'm sure you remember that night," she said. "That wasn't a good look at all," we laughed, recalling how embarrassed I was when I found out the next day that I had to be carried out of the back of the club and driven home.

"Back to that Isis situation. You know I support you and I'm happy that you are happy. Just be careful. Don't get caught up like I did," I said seriously.

"You know what, Tyron? I'll never have another public relationship like ours. What we had, that's it. I'm tired of the media in my business and not being able to live my life the way I want to. I'm sick of pretending. This is *my* life! Who I have in my bedroom and spend intimate time with should be of no concern to anyone, yet it is. Look at what you are going through now. Why is it such a bad thing that you were taped having sex with a man? If it were a woman, it would increase your damn net worth! I'm done with the façade, Ty," she sighed.

"So you're just gon' come out and announce to the world that you're a lesbian?" I asked, already knowing her answer.

"You know I can't do that," she sighed, looking at me with sad eyes. "I just want to be free to live how I want to live."

"You are free to live how you want to live, Tomi. It's all a choice, sis. You can take your chances and come out. You can give all of this up and go live privately somewhere. You're financially set for life. Or you can continue to do what you do. Isis has done it for longer than you."

"Yeah, but everyone who knows her knows she's gay," she said, cutting me off. "She just doesn't talk about it. She's a damn chapstick lesbian! She can wear a dress with the best of us."

I couldn't stop the laugh that came from my mouth.

"What in... the fuck... is a chapstick lesbian?" I asked, finally getting the question out, but the laughter didn't stop. Tomi couldn't help it and started laughing too.

"Shut up, Tyron!" She laughed. "A chapstick lesbian is a mix between a femme and a stud. You know, a tomboy, but not butch? Prefers chapstick over lipstick, but would still wear lipstick without losing her identity? Get it?" She laughed.

"Okay, okay, I got it, I guess. That's some funny shit!"

"Whatever! I'm serious though, Ty. I'm sick and tired of pretending."

"Well, you know if you're seen out with Isis, rumors will start flying immediately. The blogs will be hot with that shit! You ready for that?" I asked, looking seriously into her eyes. Tomi didn't know what bad press was. She never had to experience that and I wanted it to stay that way. I wanted to protect her from it, but ultimately, she had to make her own decisions.

"See, the blogs are hot with that blind item shit on you, but what they can't verify, they can't prove. The shit is just a rumor. Now pay homegirl, and make this shit go away, bro. What I'm ready for doesn't even matter right now."

Chapter Thirty-seven
Simone

Testifying in front of the Grand Jury was nerve wrecking. It was one of the hardest things I'd ever done. There was so much riding on their decision that my nerves were frayed. My sanity relied on this indictment. It had to happen. I couldn't wrap my mind around any outcome, aside from him being indicted and then convicted.

Stacey's sister, Joy, was served a subpoena, and she came down from New York to testify. We weren't allowed to listen to each other's statements in front of the Grand Jury, but the purpose of our testimony was to prove that Tyron Marks was indeed having a relationship with Stacey.

Both Talise and I testified, and swore under oath that he was involved with Stacey, and spent an innumerable amount of time with him. We confirmed that Tyron had given Stacey a number of gifts. I was even able to testify that I had spoken to Stacey after he arrived in Vegas and was waiting in the car at the airport for Tyron's driver to return with his luggage.

The three of us weren't in Las Vegas for more than twenty-four hours. We were able to squeeze dinner in before we headed to the airport, and parted ways with Joy as she headed back to the east coast.

"Do you think they are going to indict him?" Talise asked me after we'd gotten settled in our first class seats for the hour long flight back to Burbank.

"The DA seems confident and optimistic. I hope so, Talise. I really need this behind me, and the only way is for him to go to jail.

"Simone, you need to be prepared in case that doesn't happen," she said as I gave her the side eye. "Just hear me out. God forbid they don't indict him, but we don't even know what evidence they have against him. And if they do indict him, there is no guarantee a jury will convict him. You have to protect yourself, Simone!" she said in an intense whisper.

"I can't think like that, Talise. I just can't."

"Well you need to, Simone. I don't want you doing anything stupid if this doesn't turn out our way!"

She let the silence linger between us for a few minutes before she continued.

"What are you going to do with yourself when this is all over, Simone? You've immersed yourself in nothing but getting revenge, and I'm scared you won't have anything to do when all of this is said and done."

"I can't even think about that now, Talise. I just want him to be convicted and to go to jail for what he did to Stacey. He shouldn't be able to get away with this shit," I huffed.

"I know, Simone. I feel the same and want that more than anything too."

"Maybe then I'll be able to move forward. Maybe I'll feel normal again...shit I've never felt normal," I laughed cynically.

"You can find your normal, Simone. It will come," Talise said, taking my hand in hers and holding it. "You've been through so much. We all have. I just pray that when this is over, you can truly be happy and move on with your life."

"I pray the same prayer, Tali. I truly do."

"So what's going on with you and Deon?" Talise finally got around to asking. I was surprised it hadn't come up on the flight in.

"He's cool," I smiled. "I've been with him a lot, especially since he got hurt, you know, trying to help him."

"Mmm hmm. Ms. Darlene told me how that man looks at you," she smiled in turn, making me smile.

"Don't get your hopes up!" I laughed, knowing my friend was already planning my wedding and thinking of baby names for me.

"You must really like him, though. From what I hear, you are always over there. I don't even hear from your butt as much," she laughed, smacking me on the hand she had been holding. "You only call to check on Anastasia," she playfully pouted.

"Oh don't be like that, Tali. You know I love you." I wrapped my arm around her and kissed her on the cheek. "You'll be happy to hear that I do really care about Deon, Talise. He's a breath of fresh air. We are just friends though... really good friends and I trust him," I confessed for the first time.

"Oh my goodness! *You* trust *him?*" She squealed, turning in her seat so she could face me fully. A huge smile was plastered across her face. "That's huge, Simone! You don't trust anyone!" She laughed.

"I know, I know!" I laughed along with her. "It's comforting to be around him, Talise. It's hard to explain it... it just feels so natural. Even when I'm at his house, I don't even have to be in the same room and I feel his energy. It's..." I paused, trying to find the right words, "It's like when I'm around him, I feel like everything is going to be okay," I said in a low tone. "No matter what, I want him in my life and I don't want to mess that up trying to be in a relationship with him, you know? Things are the way they are between us because we *aren't* in a relationship. The thought of changing that is scary!"

"Things are the way they are because you aren't in a *sexual* relationship. You two are getting to know each other and building on a strong foundation without even knowing it. A lot of times, sex clouds things and brings in emotions that should be saved for later in a relationship when the bonds between the two are stronger."

"Yeah, that makes sense. I just want to take care of him. I've never felt this way for a man before. It's like I just want to make sure everything is okay with him and that he is good. I think it's because he is the same with me. Even through this injury, he is still trying to look out for me and make sure that I'm okay."

"Because he cares about you girl, he always has." She smiled. "And you care about him."

"Yeah, I guess I do, huh?" I allowed myself to admit with a laugh.

"Yes you do, and I can't tell you how happy that makes me." She said, reaching over and hugging me tightly.

It felt good to open up to my friend like this. We hadn't had a chance to really talk in the last couple of months, aside from checking in with each other every other day or so. I knew she was genuinely happy for me.

"I just don't want to jump into anything so soon. I don't want to do the rebound thing." I said, taking a glass of champagne from the stewardess.

"Simone, it's been over six months since Carlton. You are way past rebounding, honey. It's time you moved on." She laughed. "It's not like there is any hope for you and Carlton any way! Things happen for a reason. You never know why God brought Deon into your life," she said more seriously. "You have to see it through this time. Ride it out. There may be more bumps, but you need to stay on the ride and see where it takes you."

Chapter Thirty-eight
C. Banks

"**W**HAT?" I yelled into the speaker of the phone that sat on my desk. "Dan, she said she'd take two million. What in the fuck happened? Why is she reneging?" I asked as I paced around the dark wood paneled office in my home.

I couldn't believe this shit. I wondered if this had anything to do with her recent trip to Las Vegas. Something was going on and I needed to know what, to make sure my name wasn't involved in that shit.

"She just said she's changed her mind, Mr. Banks. I tried to convince her to just take the money, but you already know what type of woman we are dealing with." He sighed.

"Yeah, more than anyone, I know what type of woman Simone is. I'll get back to you, Dan," I said and stabbed the button to disconnect the call.

"FUCK!" I yelled.

Before thinking any further, I picked up the phone and placed another call.

"Why are you doing this?" I asked as calmly as I could when the call was answered.

"Who is this?" she asked puzzled.

"I loved you. I did everything in my power to make you happy and one fuck up warrants this?" I asked Simone.

"Carlton, how did you get my number?" she asked exasperatedly.

"Did you ever fucking love me at all, Simone?" I asked as tears fell from my eyes. I needed this shit behind me like I needed air to breathe, food to fucking live! How I got her number didn't mean shit.

"I don't know what you want me to say to you, Carlton." She sighed.

"Why won't you take the money and just give me the video, Simone? Just tell me why you are fucking with me like this. First, you say you want two million, now you won't even sell it... What in the fuck is going on with you? Do you really hate me that much?"

"Are you still there?" I asked after a long moment of silence.

"Yes, I'm here," she said. "How soon can you be in front of my building?" she asked contemplatively.

"I'll be there in less than thirty minutes. I'll call you when I'm outside." I hung up the phone and was out the door and pulling out of my driveway in two minutes flat.

~ ~ ~ ~ ~ ~

"WHAT? Simone, *come* on!" I couldn't believe this ultimatum she was giving me.

"It's the least you can do for me, Carlton! The choice is yours!" she said, standing in front of me in dark blue denim skinny jeans with her arms folded across her simple white V-neck t-shirt. Her hair was pulled up in a messy bun, and for once, I couldn't even think about how pretty she looked because what she was saying was so fucking ugly.

"You'd really do this shit to me, Simone? Really?" I asked as we stood in front of her building, her security sitting in their car at the curb, at the ready.

Fucking Charletta! Why she would tell Simone that Tyron confessed this shit to me was beyond me. This is exactly why I wanted her to stay out of this shit!

"I'll do whatever I have to do to make sure Tyron pays for what he did to Stacey. He didn't deserve that shit, Carlton! No one deserves that shit!"

"I know that, but I didn't have shit to do with his death, Simone! I'm just on the fucking video! If I had known about this from jump, I guarantee you Stacey would be alive today! I don't give a shit if Tyron rots in jail for the rest of his life for doing what he did! He deserves that!"

"Tyron *told* you what happened, Carlton! You know the truth. You can tell the D.A. and it could help send his ass to prison!"

"Do they know about the video, Simone? Did you give them that shit?" I asked in a panic.

"No, I haven't told them about the video nor given it to them, but I will if it comes to that."

"I'm not a fucking snitch, Simone! Aside from that, how can I tell them what dude told me without telling them about the video? Without implicating myself? Have you even thought about that?" From the look on her face, I could tell that she hadn't, so I kept trying to convince her that what she was asking was crazy. "Listen to me, Simone. I'm a convict. I spent eight years in prison for murdering a man with my hands. My fucking bare *hands!* I'm a rapper. If Tyron gets indicted for this, do you know what his defense will do if I come forward and they find out I'm on that video? They *will* try to blame that shit on me, Simone! I'll be his fucking reasonable doubt! They'll say I had reason to kill him too when I didn't even find out about the damn video until way after he was dead! *And* I was in Vegas at the time! Do you see that, Simone? Do you see how this shit could make it worse not better?" I asked.

"Fuck, Carlton!" She huffed as her eyes began to tear. She knew I was right. I could see in her eyes that she understood what I was saying. She may have thought this was a good idea, but it wasn't! "I can't believe this is my life. I can't believe I'm standing here even talking to you about this shit!" She said as tears fell down her cheeks.

"I can't believe it either, Simone. Will you please just sell me the video and get that shit off your hands? Please, Simone. Let me out of this shit! Please!" I begged. I would have gotten on my knees and begged her more if I thought it would have been beneficial.

"I can't sell you the video, Carlton," she said, wiping tears from her face. "Not yet. If Tyron is convicted, it's yours. If not... I'm sorry," she all but whispered before walking back into her building and leaving me standing there with the weight of the world on my shoulders.

Chapter Thirty-nine
Deon

I lifted myself into a sitting position on the therapy table I had been lying on doing prone hang exercises to stretch my knee.

"When can I start jumping exercises?" I asked my physical therapist after we'd wrapped our third session of the week.

"You have at minimum, another couple of months my man. Jumping before the four month mark will only set you back, not pull you forward," Jack said as he packed up his equipment, preparing to leave.

"Well I definitely don't want a setback. I've come too far for that. I'm looking forward to being able to jog in a few weeks, though."

"And the pain should lighten up even more every day, so that's something to look forward to as well."

"Yeah, I'm definitely looking forward to that. I'll walk you out."

I rose from my sitting position and shook the numbness out of my leg before walking out of the room.

"Thanks. Your gait is looking better and better every day. You're damn near walking perfectly," he said proudly.

"Yeah, now it's time to run and jump and get back on the court," I said seriously.

"Patience, Deon. You have to have patience. This will be a long process." He stopped as we got to the front door. "Don't push yourself too hard and set yourself back. We will get you to where you need to be, but an injury like this takes time and a lot of work. I know we can do it." He patted me on my shoulder encouragingly before I let him out the front door. I wouldn't be seeing him again until the beginning of the following week, but I'd be doing some weight training at our team facility in the meantime, to give my knee the rest it needed.

When I walked into the den, I stopped short at the door and watched Simone as she slept peacefully on the large comfortable sofa. She was so beautiful, tenacious, complex, sensitive, and loyal; she was everything I wanted in a woman, I admitted to myself as I stood there watching her.

Over the last couple of months, as I recovered from my surgery, and even before I went into surgery, Simone was by my side. I never even had to ask her; she just stepped up and made herself completely available to me.

Every day that I was with her, I realized more and more that I loved her, that I cared for her more deeply than I ever did when we had an intimate relationship. I wanted her to be mine; I wanted to erase all the worry and drama from her life. I wanted to protect her, to love her and make her happy. I wanted to show her that I could have her back too. I wasn't there when Stacey got killed, but I wanted to make up for that by being there for her from this point forward.

I sat on the floor atop the large area rug and rested my back near the arm of the sofa close to where her head was lying. I extended my knee a few times, wincing through the tightness that was getting better as each day passed. I picked up the remote control and began surfing through the channel guide, but nothing interested me, so I left it on *Almost Famous,* deciding to give the movie a try.

The band was singing some song that I was actually digging called *Fever Dog* and I was deep into the movie by the time I felt Simone stirring behind me no more than forty-five minutes later. When I felt her breath on my neck then her lips kiss my cheek, I turned around to face her.

"Hey," I said, surprised by her show of affection.

"Hey. How long have you been in here?" she asked.

"About an hour. You have a good nap?" I asked, brushing her hair out of her face with my hand.

"Yeah I did, thanks. It's much easier to sleep in the daytime than at night," she smiled. "How was P.T.?"

"Physical Therapy is Physical Therapy. I'm coming along. I can see that now, thankfully. It's going to be a long road though."

"Yeah, but you'll get there," she encouraged, resting her head on her fist.

Looking into her eyes, I could see her vulnerability. By no means did I intend to take advantage of that, but before I could stop myself, I had moved closer and placed my lips on top of hers. Surprisingly, she didn't pull away. She moved in and placed her left hand gently on my face while the other continued to prop her head up. Both of our eyes were open watching each other intently as we kissed like this was our first time. Her lips were so soft and her tongue was like velvet as it rubbed against mine playfully.

"What was that for?" She asked when our lips finally parted.

"I really don't know. I couldn't control myself." I laughed. She leaned in and kissed me much more passionately this time.

"What was that for?" I asked after our lips parted for the second time.

"I couldn't control myself either." She laughed and sat up, folding her legs beneath her as she watched me, unabashed. The snow white yoga pants and spaghetti strapped tank she wore complimented her long and taut body. Her face was without make-up, beautifully toned, and blemish free. Her large diamond studs sparkled against the chocolate hue of her skin as her shoulder length hair lay haphazardly in big, loose, messy curls around her head.

"You are so beautiful, Simone," I said, joining her on the sofa. "Inside and out..." I stopped myself before I spilled the rest. I didn't want to scare her by telling her that I wanted to be with her, that I wanted her in my life, and not just as a friend. I couldn't dare tell Simone that. She'd run from me so fast I'd be questioning if she was ever here in the first place.

"Thank you..." she said before I cut her off by leaning in and kissing her again.

I pulled her onto my lap and wrapped my arms tightly around her waist when she straddled me and looped her arms around my neck, kissing me as fervently as I was kissing her. She took my tongue in her mouth and softly sucked it as I slid my hand under the back of her shirt and caressed her silky smooth skin.

"Am I hurting you?" She whispered as I took her ear in my mouth.

"No. Just keep your weight right where it is on my thighs," I whispered in her ear.

I planted kisses down the side of her neck and lightly licked and kissed my way to the other side of her face. She held her arms loosely over both of my shoulders as her head pitched back and a moan escaped her mouth. She was so damn sexy, I couldn't help that my dick was rock hard in my Nike workout shorts. I knew she felt it when she began a slight wind of her hips that made me feel like I was a damn teenager about to let loose in my pants before anything really got started.

I hadn't felt passion like this in a long time. I wanted her; I wanted all of her. As I nibbled on her ear, I could feel her warm breath on my neck.

"Come on," I whispered in her ear. She lifted off of me, stood, and took my hand as I rose from the couch.

I lead her to my bedroom and brought her into my arms again. I took my time exploring her mouth and enjoying the feel of her lips on mine. I slowly slid her tank up her torso and over her head, only releasing her mouth from mine for the sake of getting the shirt off of her. I unclasped her pretty lace, skin toned strapless bra and let it fall to the floor at the side of my king sized bed.

"Damn, Simone," I moaned as I leaned down and took one of her nipples into my mouth. Her firm C cup breasts fit in my large hands nicely as I gently massaged them and alternated between lapping my tongue across each nipple and taking them into my mouth, suckling as I swirled my tongue over their firmness.

Her breath caught in her throat from the feeling of my warm wet tongue. I kept my mouth clasped to her breast as if I were feeding and lowered myself onto the edge of the bed, needing to take some weight off of my knee that had begun to lightly ache.

As she stood in front of me, nude from the waist up, I planted kisses from her breast down to her navel as she caressed my head, neck and shoulders with her soft hands.

"Deon," she moaned softly as I stroked her bare ass after taking her pants and panties off of her.

"Step back, let me look at you." She took two steps back and stood in front of me, completely nude, aside from the diamond studs and watch she wore. "Damn, Simone. It doesn't get better than you."

I pulled my wife beater over my head then drew her back into my arms, reclining into a lying position with her on top of me. We were skin to skin aside from the workout shorts I had yet to remove. The feel of her breasts and skin against my chest was a feeling I wanted to feel every day, every night. We kissed as I caressed my hands up and down her body, slowly moving them over her ass and snaking my long fingers between her legs where I felt her hot middle. She was drenched, swollen, and ready. The middle finger of my right hand flitted over her clit making her back arch and a moan of pleasure seep from her mouth. I continued to play with her, teasing her as my tongue mimicked the movements of my finger as we continued to kiss.

As my right hand pleasured her clit, I inserted the middle finger of my left hand inside of her opening. She was so turned on, she was dripping wet and moaning with each gentle thrust my finger took inside of her. When I removed my finger, I couldn't help but bring it to my mouth and taste her.

"Mmmm, you taste so good. Bring it to me, Simone," I said, guiding her up my body until her wetness was directly above my mouth. When her beautifully toned legs straddled my face, I deliberately took my time before I touched my tongue to her. I slowly kissed her thighs and squeezed her ass with both of my hands before I drew her middle to my mouth, where I gently sucked on her clit, swirling my tongue over the swollen nub.

The guttural sound of ecstasy that emitted from her mouth excited me to no end. I wanted to consume all of her. An animalistic growl escaped my mouth as I took her breast in my hands and flicked my tongue rapidly as she cried out in pleasure, her body shaking uncontrollably. I locked my arms around her waist, keeping her middle pressed to my mouth as I continued sucking and licking her.

"Oh, Deon! That feels so good!" She moaned, slightly gyrating her hips against my face. I could tell she was about to come again so I increased the speed of my tongue movements and kept her securely over my face. When her body convulsed and went limp above me, I rolled her onto her back and continued to burrow my face between her legs, softly licking all of the wetness that dripped from her middle before gently taking her clit back into my mouth.

Her loud moans of pleasure turned me on even more than I already was. I put my finger inside of her and moved it in and out of her slowly as I softly suckled her, making her cum again. As she thrashed on the bed, I continued pleasuring her. Her hands gripped my head, the sheets, and anything else she could get a hold of. The sound of my name continuously coming from her mouth was like music to my ears.

I continued licking her and easing my finger in and out of her. Her pleasure was my pleasure. *I could do this all night,* I thought as she came yet again, yelling and squeezing my head between her soft thighs.

"Okay, okay," she moaned, but I wasn't done. I flipped her over and lifted her ass so that it was to my face. I bit both ass cheeks and squeezed them before licking my tongue down her ass and finding her clit again.

My knee was starting to pain, but stopping was the last thing on my mind. I wanted all of her; I was cannibalistic, transported, in a zone. Her pleasure pleasured me beyond explanation; it was my only focus. I couldn't stop tasting her. She was like a drug and I just wasn't high enough.

"I want to feel you, Deon. I want you inside of me." Her words jolted me out of my trance and back to reality. *What am I doing?* I thought as I pulled away from her and sat up on the bed. "What's wrong?" she asked, her voice full of passion, heat, and concern.

"We can't do this, Simone," I said, rising from the bed. "You want something to drink?" I asked, heading out of the room.

"No... thanks," she said diffidently before I walked out of the room, leaving her lying on the bed naked and alone. *I can't do that to her. I can't put her at risk like that!* I thought as I walked into the kitchen, feeling lower than I felt when I found out I had this damn disease. How am I supposed to live a normal life with this shit? I can't tell her that I have herpes!

"Fuck!" I said under my breath as I opened the large, stainless steel Viking refrigerator and grabbed a bottle of Gatorade.

I can't tell her this shit. She won't accept me. What woman would? I thought as I paced the length of the large center island, taking small gulps from the cold bottle as I stepped.

"What's wrong, Deon?" I turned around to find Simone leaning against the doorframe in my wife beater, looking so beautifully wounded.

"It's not you Simone, it's me," I said, causing her to roll her eyes.

"Why did you stop?" she asked, staring me in my eyes

like she was hoping to be able to read the truth in them.

"I've decided that I'm not having sex again until I get married." I don't know where that came from, but knew that it would come back to bite me on the ass one day. "Plus, I don't know what's going on with you and that rapper. If you still love him, if you are still dealing with him..." I trailed off deciding to leave it at that before she was able to see through my bull. If I didn't have this... this... *shit,* I'd be inside of her right now.

"I'm gonna go," she said, turning and leaving the kitchen, heading toward my bedroom.

"Simone, wait. Don't leave. I'm sorry. I shouldn't have kissed you." I trailed her as she headed up the stairs, never once looking back. "Simone, stop," I said, grabbing her by the arm once we'd reached the stairway landing. When she turned to me, I could see tears forming in her eyes. I didn't want to hurt her, yet I'd managed to anyway.

"I don't want to hurt you again, Simone. I don't want to get hurt either. I've gotten so used to having you here and having you in my life again; I don't want to lose that," I stated honestly.

"I understand, Deon, but I'm still going to leave."

"No, you aren't leaving."

I grabbed her hand and led her through my room and into my bathroom. I turned on the shower, took off my workout shorts, took the wife beater off of her, and then pulled her into the shower with me. I grabbed a washcloth from the towel rack right outside of the shower, pumped Aveeno onto it from the soap dispenser that was built into the wall, and lathered her body, cleaning her from neck to foot.

"I'm sorry for what I did, Simone. That Byron Boyd stuff.

I don't ever want to hurt you like that again. I'm embarrassed over how I handled that. I won't ever do that again. You've been through enough already. You deserve to be happy. I'm tired of seeing your eyes so damned sad. I don't know what's really going on inside your head, but I can tell it's a whole damn lot," I said as I gently washed her. Tears began to fall from her eyes as I continued to slowly clean her.

"You can talk to me. I won't judge you. You shouldn't keep all that inside anyway. It will only mess you up, Simone. Get that weight off your shoulders, beautiful."

As I rinsed her body free of the soap, Simone continued to cry silent tears as if she were purging herself, releasing. I pulled her into my arms and held her wet, soft body, as close to me as I could get her.

"I won't hurt you, Simone, and I won't let anyone hurt you ever again," I whispered.

After Simone washed me, we got out of the shower and toweled each other dry atop the heated limestone flooring.

"Thank you, Deon," Simone said with a slight smile on her face. Her eyes were slightly red from crying, but I could see a brightness that wasn't there before.

"You're welcome. I don't mind rubbing your body dry. I would do it every day if you'd let me," I laughed, pulling back the covers on the bed.

"That's good to know." She laughed. "but, that wasn't what I was thanking you for, although I do thank you for that. I was thanking you for just being you. I forgot how much I liked being around you. It's different than it was before, somehow better. Do you think it's because we aren't having sex? " She smiled as I slid into the bed, pulling her in with me.

"I think that it has some to do with it," I said, pulling the covers over us. "We've both been through so much in a short time. I think we've matured, experienced things that we hadn't experienced before. I think that plays a part in it too, you know what I mean?" I asked as we lay in bed facing each other. "

"Definitely. You already know I've been through made for T.V. stuff." She laughed.

"Tell me one new thing you've experienced while we were apart."

"I experienced true love," she said sincerely as she looked me in my eyes.

"Wow. Okay, I guess that's good." I laughed, not really knowing how to feel about her answer. "With the rapper?" I had to ask.

"Yes, with *Carlton Banks...*" she said and stopped when I began to laugh. "What are you laughing at, Deon?" The smirk on her face made me laugh even harder.

"I never knew his name!" I said between fits of laughter. "I just knew Carlton and Banks; I didn't know he had the same name as that *Fresh Prince of Bel Air* guy! Hard ass rapper named Carlton Banks! I just keep picturing Carlton from Fresh Prince doing that dance!" I cracked up as she lay there next to me, trying to hold back her laughter that eventually broke forth.

We laughed for at least three minutes before we were able to talk again.

"I have to admit that was funny," she began as she wiped tears of laughter from her face.

After being silent for a few moments she said, "I'm ready to tell you what happened between Carlton and me, but you have to swear on your whole family that you will never tell another living soul."

"Of course I swear. I'd never repeat anything you say to me, whether you preempt it with me swearing or not."

"Okay thanks," she said and paused for what felt like a long time. "Stacey recorded Carlton and Tyron Marks having sex with each other. That's the video I have," she said, catching me completely off guard. To say that I was blown away by her confession would be an understatement. I sat up and asked her to repeat herself.

"Get the fuck out of here!" I said after she confirmed that I'd heard her correctly the first time. "And you saw that shit?" I felt sick to my stomach at the thought of those dudes having sex; I can't imagine how she felt. I have nothing against gay people, I'd just rather not have the visual of two hairy dudes, naked and going at it.

"Yes. Tyron gave him head and then Carlton had sex with him. It's as clear as day on the video," she said with slight indifference.

"They know you have that shit? They'll kill you if they think you will put that out, Simone!" There is no way she could be safe having something like that in her possession.

"That's why Stacey got killed. He had it first, then it ended up in my hands..."

After Simone finished telling me everything that had gone down with the video, Stacey, Tyron Marks possibly being indicted and her relationship with the rapper, I was floored. She was right; she has been through some made for T.V. stuff. I knew I made the right choice hiring security for her. This was way deeper than I thought.

"So that's that story. I have a few others to tell, but I don't want to lay more than that on you tonight. I'm sure that was a doozie." She chuckled. "I'm ready to move on with my life, Deon. I can't keep living like this. It's like I'm allowing my life to be in limbo while I'm waiting for justice, and I know Stacey wouldn't want that. I feel that things are finally moving in the right direction, though. It's been so hard for me to focus on everyday stuff, knowing that that guy is just free and living his life. That's why I lost it at that damn club when I saw him. I'm so embarrassed about that," she said, smiling shyly at me.

"You shouldn't be. I don't blame you for losing it like you did. Plus, all my boys think you're the shit over that," I laughed. *Especially my boy Darryl Withers,* I thought, but I wasn't going to tell her that.

"Oh Lord, they shouldn't!" She laughed. "That was so out of character for me. I'm sure Stacey was somewhere mortified."

"Stacey was somewhere clapping and laughing," I laughed. "This all makes more sense to me now, though," I admitted. "So what about the rapper? I'm sure seeing that video didn't just completely erase the *true love,*" I said, slightly mocking her. *I'll show her what true love is.*

"No, it didn't, but I know that I'm not in love with him like that anymore. It's hard to even think about all the good times I had with him. Every time I think of him, that damn video plays in my head. It's torment, but that's gotten better too. Thankfully, I don't think about him as much." She smiled sadly.

"He doesn't deserve to be in your thoughts, Simone."

"Yeah I know he doesn't," she whispered.

"What do you think about us?" I asked before I was able to stop myself.

"What do you mean? What about us?" The smile on her face confirmed that she knew what I was asking.

"I want to be with you, Simone, but I want to do it right this time. Can I be your boyfriend?" I laughed, trying to make light of my question, although my heart was beating a mile a minute. I was definitely stepping out on a limb here, but I didn't want to have to hide my feelings from her any longer.

"You really want to be my boyfriend?" she asked skeptically.

"Yes I do. Why do you sound so surprised?" I laughed.

"I don't know. Are you sure you're ready for that?"

"I know I'm ready for you, Simone. I've wanted you in my life for a long time. God just took us on a detour for whatever reason, but I don't want to lose you again."

After a long pause, she said the words that made me a very happy man.

"Yes, you can be my boyfriend, as long as I'm your girlfriend, Deon." She smiled and kissed me softly on my lips. "Were you serious about the waiting until marriage thing?"

"Yeah, why not? We've had sex before. We know what we're working with. You think you can do it?" I wasn't sure *I* could, but I knew it was the right thing to do in my situation.

"Okay. I guess I can give it a try," she said, smiling warmly, her eyes twinkling brightly.

"Just know that if we get to that point and I ask you to marry me, we won't be having a long engagement," I said seriously, making us both laugh.

I pulled my woman closer to me and kissed her long and softly, sealing the deal. When our lips parted, she turned so that her back was against my chest and released a long soft sigh. I held her closely until her breathing softened and sleep had taken her. I would never let her go again.

Chapter Forty
Tyron

"License, registration and insurance," the cop said flatly when he walked up to my car window.

"Why did you pull me over?" I questioned the straight laced looking officer as I looked him dead in the eye. *He wasn't going to intimidate me*, I thought as I waited for his reply.

"No right turn on red. You turned right on red. License, registration and insurance," he said more sternly this time. I reached in my pocket and snatched my driver's license out of my wallet while Ricky grabbed the registration and insurance paperwork out of the glove compartment. "You two hold tight." The officer walked back to his cruiser and got inside.

"Mutherfucker!" I huffed. "I'll wipe my ass with that fucking ticket!" I was trying to keep calm, but I knew that I hadn't made an illegal turn.

"Calm down, babe. Don't let this ruin your mood. It's my birthday weekend! That's why we're here... to celebrate. Just remember that, okay?" Ricky patted me on my thigh.

"We'll be at the hotel in no time and I'll make you forget all about this ticket," he said, making me smile.

"What in the fuck is taking him so long?" We'd been sitting for at least twenty minutes and that asshole was still sitting in his damn squad car. Tourists walking the strip stopped to gawk at my car and were taking pictures. I was hoping they couldn't see me through the dark tinted windows.

When I looked in the rearview mirror for what had to be the fiftieth time, two cop cars were pulling up. One parked next to the cruiser behind us and the other pulled in front of us.

"What the fuck is going on?" There were two officers in the cruiser in front of us and one in the other. The two stood on the sidewalk less than ten feet from Ricky in the passenger seat, while the other talked to the officer who'd pulled us over.

A small crowd of curious tourists started to form with the arrival of the two squad cars. "This shit is becoming a spectacle," I said, shaking my head.

"Another car is pulling up!" Ricky said panicking. "Tyron, what's going on?"

"I don't fucking know!" I said under my breath as the black Crown Victoria pulled up with two plain-clothes detectives in it.

When they parked, got out of the car, and I was able to see their faces more clearly, my heart almost stopped beating. I broke out in a cold sweat and my hands began to shake uncontrollably.

"Tyron what's going on?" Ricky asked again, but I couldn't answer him. One of the detectives was knocking on my window. I wanted to take off, but I was blocked in so

I rolled down the window instead.

"Hey, Tyron Marks! Nice car! What is this?" Detective Jenkins asked with fake excitement.

"It's a Bugatti Veyron," I said through clinched teeth. I was so pissed off, but needed to try to control my nerves.

"Oh man! I've never seen one of these before! Too bad I'm going to need you to step out of this pretty little car you have here," he said sarcastically, opening the door for me to get out. "Do you know why we're here, Mr. Marks?" He asked with a smirk on his face.

"I have no fucking clue! Why don't you get on with it and tell me why you're here!"

"You're under arrest for the murder of Stacey Flenoy. Turn around, face the car, and spread'em." In a daze, I did as I was told. The other detective, who had yet to say one word, frisked me roughly before I felt the cold metal of handcuffs clicking into a tightly locked position around my wrists.

"We already questioned your driver, and he sang like a Canary," Detective Jenkins said.

"Yeah whatever!" I replied, knowing that they were lying. Curse would never snitch!

Ricky was out of the car and talking to the two uni-formed cops that had been standing near his side of the car. The crowd had grown larger since I'd exited the vehi-cle. It seemed as if every single one of them were either taking photos or recording this shit. I tried to hide my face as I was shoved into the back of the Crown Victoria, but I'm sure enough pictures and video had been taken before then.

As I was whisked away, I took one last look at Ricky and my million dollar car. I knew I'd be free to be with them both again in no time flat.

Chapter Forty-one
Simone

Loose Lips Sink Ships Exclusive!
Tyron Marks has been arrested in connection with the murder of a GAY man who sources claim he had a HOMOSEXUAL relationship with! This said GAY man was the best friend to Simone Johnson, who is the ex-girlfriend of C. Banks and the current girlfriend of NBA superstar Deon Bradford, AND the woman who busted Tyron Marks' head open at Drai's in Hollywood while partying with some of NBA's elite.

What's really going on you might ask?
Stay clicked in to Loose Lips Sink Ships
Your girl, Lisa Lips

Tyron's arrest was plastered on every blog, news station, and media outlet there was. This was big news, and everyone wanted the inside story. Camera crews had been camped outside of my building for the last week waiting for the chance to hear from me and or take photos.

The previous morning, a paparazzi photographer—hiding behind one of my neighbors' cars in my parking garage—jumped out and snapped shots of my mother and me as we were getting into my truck. Thankfully, Marlo and Ed were there, and strong armed him away from us and out of the secured garage that he had no business being in.

I expected this to happen once Tyron was arrested. He was as high profile as it gets, but I wasn't prepared for their interest in me and my life. I just wanted justice to be served, not to be the focus of attention like I was the one who'd been indicted, like I was the one who's famous.

"I'm sorry. Now they're putting your name in this in connection with me," I began after Deon picked up the phone. I wanted to talk to him before he heard about the latest blog posts.

"Simone, I'm used to this. I don't care what they say about me. I just care about how you're doing," Deon said, cutting me off. "Are you okay?" He asked as tears began to fall down my face.

"No, not really. I feel like a caged animal, a fish in a fish tank being watched every minute of the day," I complained. I had to keep the blinds closed in my home because a photo surfaced on the blogs of me in a wife beater and panties standing in my bedroom, which is on the fifteenth floor, mind you! This was just too much. To say my privacy had been invaded would be an understatement.

"I don't want this, Deon!" I sniffed.

"I know, Mone. I've grown thick skin over the years, dealing with the media, but in the beginning, it was hard. Everything will be okay though. It's a juicy story now, but it will be over soon. They'll move on to the next big story before you know it."

"I hope it's sooner rather than later. No telling how long it will take before this damn trial begins, and when it does, it's probably going to get even crazier. It should be illegal for them to be outside of my building like this!"

"Trust me, Simone, I completely understand."

"I never wanted this, Deon," I said again, venting. "I was uncomfortable having our picture taken at Drai's! I'm a private person. I don't want these people in my business like this!"

"I know. That's one of the things I love about you. Hey, can you get away for a week or two?" He asked as I continued to wipe the tears that continued to spill down my cheeks.

"Yes, I don't see why not," I sighed. "Can *you* get away for that long? What about physical therapy?" Deon's knee was healing better than the doctors could have hoped for. With all the praying everyone was doing, God was definitely listening.

"Yeah, I can. I can train and workout on my own while we're gone. I have it all taken care of. I just want to get you away from this mess and make sure you're good."

"Where are we going?" I asked, feeling better already.

"That's for me to know and for you to find out," he said with a smile in his voice.

"Well, how am I supposed to know what to pack?" I asked with a laugh. My mood was improving rapidly at the thought of getting away from this spectacle for a while.

"Mone, just bring yourself. You don't have to pack a thing if you don't want to."

Chapter Forty-two
C. Banks

"How you holding up, man?" I asked after walking into Tyron's two-story suite at the Skylofts at MGM Grand hotel.

"Happy to be free, B. You want a drink?" He said as we walked down the hall and into the spacious living area with large windows that looked out onto Las Vegas Blvd.

"Yeah, I'll take one." I took a seat on the plush two seater couch and stretched out my legs. "So what's next?" I asked.

"Just gotta ride this shit out. Take this shit to trial. Hide from the media."

"They got a lot of evidence against you?"

"It's a lot of circumstantial shit, from what we know so far, nothing solid. They won't be able to find anyone who can even put me and dude together. My defense team has been on this shit heavy since I got out. I don't know how you survived eight years confined in a shit hole like that."

"You weren't even in the pen. You had it easy where you were. You didn't even spend two weeks. That ain't shit in

County. I'm sure they kept you from general pop, being high profile and shit. "

"General population, seclusion, none of that shit is for me, that's for fucking certain, Yo! I *need* my freedom," he said, handing me a drink and sitting down. "D.A. is trying to get this shit tried and fast, which is a good thing, I guess."

He was much more nervous than he was letting on. I could easily read him. I could see the worry in his eyes, although he was trying to keep up appearances. He was dressed in a charcoal, D Squared cardigan with a white button up shirt underneath, and dark denim jeans. By all outward appearances, it looked like life was good for him.

"What's your defense? You didn't know the cat?" I asked.

He contemplated his answer as he continued to sip his drink. I took back the liquor in my glass in three large swallows then went to the bar to pour another. I brought the Johnny Walker Blue back to where we were sitting and sat it on the glass coffee table.

Tyron filled his glass almost to the rim, sat back and said, "My defense is it wasn't me, it was Curse," he said, looking me in my eyes with no shame.

"What? Curse is taking the rap?" I knew he went hard for Tyron, but I didn't know he was down to do life for the man.

"If I say he did it, there's a chance for reasonable doubt. That's all I got, B. I have to focus on saving myself. He's the one that fucked up anyway! You're not fucking wired, are you?" He said quickly, sitting up in his seat spilling scotch on the expensive rug.

"Get the fuck outta here. I can't believe you'd think some shit like that. I'm not involved in this shit and I don't want to be." I couldn't help but laugh at this guy. "You're fucking paranoid, Ty. You need to reel that shit in man." I laughed.

"Fuck you man, I got reason to be paranoid. I can't believe that bitch still has that video, though. I'm curious to see if that shit will be in evidence once my team gets everything. That's one hell of a fucking motive right there. I wish she would have just sold us the shit. I damn sure don't want that shit included in this fucking trial."

Yeah, me either! I thought. He didn't think twice about throwing Curse under the bus, I knew he'd throw me under that bitch too.

"Naw, she still has that shit. I don't think she'll turn it over. She's probably holding off to see if you'll be convicted. That's how she thinks. She'll release that shit if you get off, though. That's a bet." He had no idea that she'd already confirmed that.

"I *will* beat this case, so we still need to keep trying to get that shit from her, man. You're on that shit too!" He reminded me like I could ever forget.

"I can't do shit else at this point. The media is hot on this case, hovering all over it like flies on shit. All we can do is wait and see how this shit plays out."

"True. I can't even focus on that right now anyway. I'm about to be in the biggest fight of my life. I'll worry about that shit when I beat this case," he said, sounding more sure of himself than I know he felt.

"Yeah, that's your best bet. Listen, Tyron, I actually came out here because I wanted to tell you this face to face, man to man," I said, pausing and taking a drink from my glass. "I want you to buy me out of QP or Sony is willing to buy my share. Either way, I'm out."

"Are you fucking joking, B!" He yelled, jumping out of

his seat, spilling more of the light brown liquid on the white rug. "This court shit hasn't even gotten started and you already want out?"

"I've been wanting out for a while now, Tyron! I have a lot on the line. While you have to deal with this shit, I have my own shit to deal with! This is your mess, Tyron, not mine! The video shit is one thing. This murder shit is another!" I said, getting more pissed off, as I got up and stalked over to him, pointing my finger in his face. I couldn't believe this guy was acting like *I* owed *him* something. "*You* killed that cat, yo! I don't want no part of that shit!" We were standing eye to eye, staring each other down. "You can't fucking convince me that you'd stay if the tables were turned."

I broke eye contact first and sat back down. We both knew I could beat his ass. A staring contest wasn't going to change that.

"Of course I'm taking all of my masters and keeping my percentage in Tomi's and our other artists." There really wasn't anything he could do to stop me. I owned one hundred percent of my masters and fifty percent of all the rest under the QP imprint.

"This is fucked up, Banks. I have enough shit on my plate right now. I can't believe you'd do this shit after Tomi leaving too," he said, pouring another drink and finally sitting back down. "You're not thinking about this shit rationally. You're making hasty decisions. I'm going to beat this shit, Banks!"

"Whether you beat it or not, it's time for us to part ways. I'm not feeling us as a team, as partners, as a business. This ain't my lane. We're headed in two different directions. I gotta look out for me, my family, and my brand first," I said evenly.

"Banks, if you walk out on me, on the whole QP fam like this, I don't have shit else to say to you *ever*! That's my word!"

I gulped down the last of the scotch in my glass and stood.

"Well, then, I guess there's nothing more to say. My attorneys are working out the dissolution papers. They'll be delivered before the week is over. Good luck with everything." I shouted sarcastically over my shoulder before walking out of the hotel suite door.

Chapter Forty-three
Deon

"Less than two weeks?" Simone vented angrily. "How can someone indicted for murder be allowed to bail out? And so damn fast?" She asked indignantly as she paced around the large master suite of my Tamarind Hill villa in Montego Bay, her bare feet flapping against the wide planked, dark hardwood flooring.

"Mone, I know it doesn't seem right, but if he isn't a flight risk, that's usually how it goes down."

I'd sat on the edge of the bed watching her as she spoke on the phone with the D.A., knowing that it couldn't have been good news. I knew that I was right when she hung up the phone and threw it onto the floor.

"I hate him, Deon! *I hate him!*" Tears filled her eyes and fell down her cheeks.

"Come here, Simone." I reached my hand out to her and pulled her onto my lap when she took it. "You have to stay positive, okay? He's out of jail, but you know shit isn't easy for him, and it shouldn't be. That media blitz I got you away from he's feeling that two-fold right now, believe that."

"I hope he's so miserable and embarrassed that he's ashamed to leave the damn confines of his house. I'm glad I'm not out there. I can't take too much more of this! I need this to be over." I wiped the tears from her face, wrapped my arms around her, and hugged her tightly, keeping her in my embrace for a few minutes. "Thank you, Deon. I'm sorry my life is so crazy right now."

"Sometimes life gets really crazy, so you won't be bored when the calm and serenity that's around the corner comes. This will pass, Simone. That's one thing I can guarantee you. You can't let that anger and hate build up in your heart like that, though. That only hurts you, not homeboy...*you!* Stacey wouldn't want that."

"I know. It's just hard. You'd feel the same way if Nichelle's husband hadn't killed himself. *You'd* want to kill him!" She said, wrapping her arms around me and resting her head on my shoulder.

"I wanted to kill him and he was already dead, so trust me, I understand. I was angry for a long time, but the only thing that did was bring me down," I replied, rubbing her bikini clad back.

Simone and I had been in Jamaica for less than a week and it was a much needed getaway for both of us. The two cliff top acres the five bedroom villa sat on overlooking Montego Bay was a place that I knew Simone would enjoy and be able to relax at. No security, no bodyguards; just a huge gated estate that I'd spent no more than a cumulative month in since I bought it over a year ago.

It felt good being away from it all. No one was around, but me, Simone, and the small staff that included the housekeeper, who'd stayed on when I bought the place and came daily. The personal chef that I'd hired the last time I was in town, and the grounds keeper and his wife, who stayed at the estate year round in the small two-bedroom cottage at the back of the property were also there.

"You want me to close the windows?" I asked as chill bumps began to surface on her arms, even though it was close to eighty degrees outside.

The large room barely had any wall space for the many floor to ceiling sliding doors that framed the amazing view of the ocean. They were all open as the breeze blew into the room making the soft white, light linen curtains and sheer fabric on the Mahogany wood, four post canopy bed sway back and forth.

"No, I'm not cold," she said, speaking into my neck, making goose-bumps pop up on my arms as well. "How did you stop?"

"How did I stop what?" I asked, kissing her face as her head continued to rest on my shoulder. *Man I love this woman,* I thought and kissed her again.

"How did you stop being angry? I get so mad sometimes, it hurts! When I think about my friend not being here, how I know he was heartbroken after seeing Tyron and Carlton... what he went through the days before he died. It just makes me so damn angry, Deon. I don't know how to not be angry. I've been pissed off for so long!"

"I was so angry after Nichelle died, I was miserable. I was pissed off at the world..." I paused, trying to decide how much I wanted to tell her. "One day I drove out to Venice beach and was just chilling on the sand, crying like a damn punk," I admitted with a laugh as she lifted her head and looked at me with a smile, her eyes showing clear interest in the story I was telling her. "I didn't care who saw me. It was like I was purging and releasing right there at the ocean. The sun was starting to set and I had been sitting there for at least an hour or two when this damn Pit Bull ran up on me out of nowhere. A really big Pit too, Simone," I laughed, remembering the day clearly.

"The damn dog jumped on me and started licking me before I could get up and run. I just knew I was about to be mauled, but thankfully, the dog was friendly. His owner ran over to get him, apologizing and doing all that stuff that dog owners do when their bad ass dogs get out of hand." We laughed. "It was a woman, an attractive woman who I ended up talking and sitting on that beach with for at least a couple of more hours. To make a long story short, we got into a serious relationship. I introduced her to my family, took her on vacation with us, I really thought I'd end up marrying that woman.

"One morning, while I was at her house asleep, Nichelle came to me in my dreams. She told me that homegirl was hiding something from me. The point of everything I'm trying to say is, when she came to me that morning, she was happy. She looked good; she was smiling. She thanked me for taking care of Tyson. She even mentioned you," I admitted with a sad smile.

"She did? What did she say?" she asked intrigued.

"I'll save that story for another day. The moral of that story is this, what made the anger go away was knowing that she was happy and that she was okay. I'm positive Stacey is okay too. He isn't in heaven holding a grudge, hating Tyron, and being angry every day, so you shouldn't. You're here and able to live life, so you should."

We stared into each other's eyes for a long while,

communicating without words.

"What was she hiding?"

"I'll save that for another day as well."

I don't know how I'll ever be able to look her in her face and tell her that I have herpes, but I knew I had to, and soon.

Chapter Forty-four
Simone

I needed this getaway, I thought as I relaxed poolside in a yellow strapless bikini top and tiny bikini bottoms, letting the sun warm me. It was a beautiful, eighty-degree peaceful day, and I wouldn't have wanted to be anywhere else. We'd spent the last few days on the ocean in a beautiful fifty-foot yacht that coasted around Jamaica, stopping in Port Morant before returning to Montego Bay. It was like a dream. Being on the ocean was just what I needed. I'd forgotten how much I loved it.

"Hey Mone, I'm about to head out," Deon said, taking a seat on the chaise lounge next to me.

"I wish you didn't have to leave," I sighed sitting up. We'd been in Jamaica for over two weeks, and I'd decided that I wasn't ready to go back home, so I wasn't.

"I wish I didn't have to either, but I need to get back to physical therapy, my training schedule, and I have a few meetings that I can't miss. Your fam will be here tomorrow, so you won't be bored." Deon smiled, rising from his chaise lounge and sitting next to me on mine. He'd graciously offered to fly my mother, Mommy and Daddy Miles, as well as Talise, Malachi and baby Anastasia here on the charted plane we'd flown in on, so I wouldn't be alone. I was happy that they were all able to come.

"You look beautiful, much less stressed. This trip was good for you."

"That's an understatement," I laughed, reaching up to kiss his face. "Thanks for flying everyone here. You're so good to me. Why?" I teased.

"Because you deserve it and you're my woman." He pulled me onto his lap, wrapped his arms tightly around my waist, and kissed me lightly on my lips, causing butterflies to flutter in my stomach.

When he pulled away, I kissed him again, letting my lips linger on his. I didn't want to stop; I didn't want him to leave me.

Deon had me feeling things I'd never felt before. I was in love with him and I wasn't the least bit scared, because I knew he loved me too. He hadn't said it yet, but his actions spoke volumes, and that man loves me; I knew it!

"You're coming back soon, right? A week?" He asked, placing small kisses on my shoulder and arm.

"Yes, no more than a week. That's about as long as everyone can stay, anyway. Why, are you going to miss me?" I smiled at the thought. I knew I'd miss him.

"Yeah, I will. Are you going to miss me?"

"As soon as you drive off of this property, I'm going to miss you," I said, kissing the tip of his nose.

"I better head to the airport before I change my mind, and just cancel everything. Million dollar meetings, training, physical therapy, hell, I might just quit the league and stay right here with you forever. Our kids will be Jamaican," he joked.

"Yeah whatever!" I laughed, rising from his lap. "Don't make me call your bluff, Mr. Bradford."

I held his hand as we walked to the front of the house where a car was waiting to take him to the airport.

"I'll call you when I get in. Enjoy yourself, okay?" He hugged me tightly and planted a soft kiss on my lips before getting into the backseat of the black Lincoln Town Car.

I watched it as it pulled off, picked up the newspaper that was on the porch, and took it with me so I could read it as I continued to lounge on the chaise by the pool. I stretched out under the clear blue sky and warm sun, opened the paper, and abruptly sat up when I saw the cover story and photo.

Millionaire Alson Smitey Gunned Down in Cherry Gardens Mass Killing Over the Weekend

Alson Smitey, 41, a native of Kingston, Jamaica, is one of fourteen slain in a brutal forty-eight hour blood bath. Amongst the deceased were two policemen, who were rumored to be on the payroll of Smitey, as well as his wife, mother in-law, and three private security officers. From Cherry Gardens, where Smitey, his wife, his wife's mother, and three bodyguards were slain at the heavily secured Smitey compound, to Denham Town where the two policemen and six others were killed in a shootout that spanned several blocks of Wellington Street. Many families have been left in mourning, trying to understand where this murderous spree stems from.

Tears filled my eyes and poured down my cheeks before

I could finish reading the rest of the news report. Through blinding tears, I speed dialed Talise.

"Al is dead, Talise!" I was barely able to say when she answered the call.

I got up and rushed inside of the house, not knowing what to do with myself.

"What? Simone, try to calm down and tell me what happened!"

"He's dead! Al is dead, Talise!"

"Simone! What happened? Tell me what happened!"

"It's in the paper! I just read it in the paper!"

"What happened to him?" she asked, her voice cracking.

"Someone killed him and his wife... and his wife's mother... a lot of people were killed! I need to get out of here! I can't stay here! I need to leave right now!"

"Where is Deon, Simone? Did he leave already?"

"Yes! I can't think! I don't know what to do! I'm by myself and I don't know what to do! This shit is crazy!" I cried hysterically. I ran into the room, pulled my suitcase out of the closet, and began throwing all of my clothes inside of it.

"Simone, hold on! Don't hang up, okay?"

When she clicked back over, I heard Deon's voice clearly.

"Simone, Simone, wake up babe."

When I opened my eyes and realized that I was lying in bed next to Deon, and it had all been a dream, tears fell from my eyes.

"You okay, Mone?" Deon asked, wiping tears from my cheeks. "It's okay, babe, it was just a dream." He pulled me closer to him and wrapped his arms around me, squeezing me tightly, making me feel protected. Deon was still here; he wasn't gone, my family wasn't coming, and maybe Al wasn't dead. It was only a dream, but I continued to cry because I still had no idea where he had gone, and I had a strong feeling that I never would.

Chapter Forty-five
C. Banks

"So what're you going to do?" Charletta asked as we sat on barstools around the large center island in the kitchen of our home in Alpine, New Jersey.

"I'm not doing shit. I'm not saying shit, and I don't want to talk to no one about that shit. Mums the word for both of us, Char, and I'm serious."

I kept glancing at my MacBook that sat open on the granite countertop, displaying a large photo of Tyron walking out of the courthouse with his attorneys and security surrounding him. The media was all over this like it was some OJ Simpson shit. Being who they thought was the closest person to Tyron, they were itching to hear from me, but I had yet to say one word regarding the shit to anyone aside from Charletta.

Please God, please don't let my name come up in this mess, I prayed for the hundredth time since Tyron's arrest. I didn't want to testify or go anywhere near that courthouse. I wanted to stay as far away from that shit as I could. I'd leave the damn country and come back when this shit was all over, if I could.

"You've changed, Carlton," Charletta said, taking a sip from her wine glass.

"What do you mean I've changed, Char?"

"*She's* changed you."

"Naw, she didn't change me. That video changed me. That shit fucked me up. And having to explain that shit..." I stopped myself before I slipped and said what was really on my mind. I was humiliated that Simone had to know those things about me. That she had to see me on that video was something that I knew would take me a long time to get over.

"Having to explain what shit?"

"Having to explain all this to you," I lied.

"That's not what you meant, Carlton," she said, staring me dead in the eye, not backing down.

"Don't start, Char. I'm not in the mood for this shit. It's over with me and Simone. There's nothing for you to worry about."

She stared at me like she would be able to read my thoughts if she stared long enough. Her eyes were hard and never once wavered. She looked so pretty as she stood there battling her feisty temper. She wanted to say something slick so bad, and it made me laugh.

"Who are you laughing at, Banks?" she asked angrily.

"Don't get mad, Char. Stop it," I continued to laugh as I got up and walked to her. I wrapped my arms around her and squeezed her. "Don't be mad at me."

"If all of this shit wouldn't have gone down, you'd probably still be with that bitch!"

"I would have found my way back to you, Char. Things

happen for a reason no matter how catastrophic. Now please, stop being mad at me." I kissed her and took her plump ass in my hands.

"What are you going to do about that video, Carlton?"

"There ain't shit I *can* do about the video, Charletta. Whatever is going to happen is riding on the verdict in Tyron's murder case. I can't do shit until then. I don't even know what I'm going to do if he gets off and she releases that shit. We just have to wait and see and hope for the best."

Part Two

Seven Months Later

Chapter Forty-six
Tyron

When the heavy iron bars loudly clinked closed, I jolted out of my sleep in a cold sweat. I sat up and was glad that I was in a plush king-sized bed on Yves Delorme bed linens, instead of on a cot in a cell.

You're not going back to jail. You will beat this! You win! You win! I repeated in my head over and over until my heart rate slowed and I felt calmer.

I reclined back onto the bed, resting my head on the plush pillow and wiped the sweat from my brow. Today was the first day of my trial, and I was still having a hard time believing this was my life. I went from being on top of the world to being the defendant in a high profile murder trial in less than a year.

It had taken two weeks to get through the pool of almost one hundred jurors, to finally narrow it down to twenty-four: seven women and five men plus twelve alternates. It was unreal; I needed this shit behind me like I needed money to live.

The day of my arrest, I contacted my attorney, Lem, who immediately headed to Vegas. I was in a fight for my life and needed a legal team who didn't take that lightly. Lem, along with my accountant and business manager, facilitated getting the million dollars that had to go to the court for bail to secure my release.

"Are you okay, honey?" I heard my mother's voice before I noticed her head peeking through the bedroom door.

"Yeah, Ma, I'm okay," I sighed, thankful that I had my mother here with me.

"It's about time to start getting dressed. We have to head to the courthouse in less than a couple of hours. You want me to order your breakfast while you shower?" she asked in her soft voice.

"Yeah, thanks." I pulled myself out of the bed and walked into the bathroom, closing the door behind me. I turned on the shower to hot, stepped in, and let the powerful jets attempt to remove some of the tension from my body.

If it wasn't for my mother, I'd be alone in this shit. I get a call from Tomi almost every day, but I had to distance myself from Ricky since my arrest. I couldn't get caught out there like that, or take any chances at all. My life was on the line here, and I wasn't going to let anything or anyone be in a position to surprise me with some bullshit.

When I got out of jail, I relieved him from his position at QP, gave him a nice severance package, and hoped he understood. I erased him from my life like he never existed, but had hopes that after all this shit was over, I'd be able to get him back, because I did miss him.

~ ~ ~ ~ ~ ~

When we arrived at the courthouse, reporters and cameras were everywhere. I was thankful that cameras weren't allowed in the courtroom, and wished that the same held true for the nosey ass reporters who couldn't be kept out.

I hopped out of the backseat of the black Suburban with my mother following closely behind me. We were immediately surrounded by my four security guys, who quickly rushed us through the crowd and into the courtroom with my attorneys trailing us closely.

"I'm going to keep this short and sweet ladies and gentlemen of the jury and get right down to the meat of why you are here," the D.A. said seriously after the judge had given the jury instructions and gave her the go ahead to begin her opening statement.

Her jet black bob framed her small Asian face perfectly. She was no nonsense. I hated her on sight the first time I saw her. During jury selection she fought tooth and nail for the smallest shit.

"The man you see right here, dressed in his nice expensive suit, is not the man he portrays himself to be. Evidence will prove beyond a reasonable doubt that this man, Tyron Marks, lured Stacey Flenoy to Las Vegas with the intent to murder him," she said, pointing to the large poster sized photo of Stacey with a big ass smile on his face. "Mr. Marks brutally murdered Stacey Flenoy and dumped his body in a shallow ravine because he wanted to keep him quiet!" Her voice was full of disdain and disgust. "The State will prove that Tyron Marks and Stacey Flenoy knew each other and knew each other intimately, while the

Defense will claim that Mr. Marks never *even* knew Stacey! Never saw him before! It's not true, ladies and gentlemen of the jury, and the evidence will prove that. Thank you." She took her seat next to a thin black man in a stiff Brooks Brother's suit who looked to be in his early thirties.

"Ladies and gentlemen, first, thank you for being here. I understand how difficult having to sit on a jury can be and how it can sometimes be disruptive to your everyday lives, so again, I thank you for being here," my attorney, Lori Mathers, said as she got up and stood in front of the jury box. Lem was letting her take the lead and was sitting as my second-chair attorney.

Lori was a tall, regal black woman who looked to be in her early fifties, but was probably in her sixties. She allowed a few strips of gray to streak through her black, short, tapered haircut.

"I'm going to follow suit and keep this short, but not sweet. I'd say simple because there is nothing sweet about this case, ladies and gentlemen of the jury. There's nothing sweet about how this young man was murdered in the prime of his life, nothing sweet about my client, a young man also in the prime of his life, being on trial for his murder! It's sad and definitely heartbreaking, but my client, Tyron Marks, is innocent and the State will not be able to prove otherwise!" She said sincerely. "The State is going to parade witness after witness into this courtroom, but not one, I repeat, not one, will be able to prove to you beyond a reasonable doubt that my client knew Mr. Flenoy, let alone had any type of relationship with him! This so-called *'lure him here to murder him and keep him quiet'* motive is shaky! They will not be able to prove that there was any reason to keep Stacey Flenoy quiet, because my client, Mr. Marks, *did not know the victim*! There is no evidence to substantiate their claims! Don't be bamboozled, don't drink the Kool-Aid!" She said, causing most of the jurors to smile, smirk or chuckle.

"In all seriousness, I can't believe that my client is here. I'll tell you right now, evidence does show that my client's bodyguard, Travis Davis, aka *'Curse;',*" she pronounced Curse like saying it left a bad taste in her mouth, "could be responsible for the murder of Stacey Flenoy, but not my client, Tyron Marks! By God and by jury, *he* should be on trial for this, not the defendant. *He* did not know about the murder of Stacey Flenoy. *He* did not assist, *he* did not instruct," she said, pointing her finger at me. "*He* had no involvement in the death of this young man, and the State will not be able to prove that he did beyond a reasonable doubt. Remember, watch what you drink, ladies and gentlemen of the jury. Thank you." She took her seat next to me and tapped my hand that was resting on top of the wood rectangular table as a few of the jurors smiled in our direction.

"The State may present its case," the judge said in his deep baritone voice, his large frame in the usual black robe sitting high on his bench was imposing. He had to be at least six foot five and two hundred plus pounds of solid mass. I was sure he'd spent years on a football field.

"The State calls its first witness Detective Jenkins to the stand."

Chapter Forty-seven
Deon

Simone was splitting her time between Las Vegas and LA, because she was determined not to miss one day of Stacey's murder trial, although she wasn't allowed in the courtroom until after she testified. She was only in Cali on the weekends if I was in town, otherwise, she'd fly to whatever city I was having a game in to be with me. We'd been together at least five days out of seven since we returned from Jamaica, and when basketball season started, I tried to have her meet me in every city she was willing to travel to. I just wanted her with me. I wanted to see her face at every game she was able to make it to and lay next to her every night that she would allow me to.

Being with Simone was natural. There was no doubt in my mind that she was the woman I wanted to spend the rest of my life with. Whether she'd feel the same after I told her about my "situation" was constantly on my mind, and I planned on telling her once the trial was over. There was just too much going on in her life and I didn't want to add to it.

Somehow, we'd managed to refrain from having sex. Lying next to Simone and having her in my arms nightly and not having sex was harder than all the work it took to get my knee back to working order, but I knew it was the right thing to do.

After running five miles on the treadmill in my gym, I grabbed a bottle of Gatorade out of the small fridge and gulped it down on my way to the bathroom to shower. I had a few hours to spare before I had to get to practice, and I planned to do absolutely nothing until then.

We were close to the end of our season and I couldn't have been happier with how my knee had healed. I felt more powerful and confident than I had before I was injured. I trained harder than I'd ever trained in my life after having surgery and was thankful that it paid off. I was quick on the court and able to handle the ball as well as I had before and knew that we would definitely make the playoffs and possibly get another ring this year.

As soon as I stepped into the shower and began to lather my body with soap, my cell phone rang. Deciding to ignore it, I continued to clean myself enjoying the hot water and powerful showerheads that massaged my sore muscles. When it continued to ring, I quickly rinsed off, grabbed the large towel hanging right outside of the shower, and hopped out. As soon as I grabbed my phone off of the bathroom counter, it rang again. It was my agent, Ron.

"Deon, we have a problem. You need to get over here immediately!" He said as soon as I picked up the phone.

"What's going on, Ron?" I asked, trying not to panic. He had never asked me to his office like this.

"It's not life or death, but it's serious. How soon can you get here?"

"Just got out the shower, I can be there in less than thirty."

"I'll see you when you get here," he said and hung up the phone.

~ ~ ~ ~ ~ ~

"Hey Melissa," I said, greeting my agent's secretary after walking into the office that overlooked the Marina in Marina Del Rey.

"Hey Deon, Ron's waiting for you. Go right in. You want anything to drink?" she asked as she walked me into his office.

"Pour him a shot of Cognac, Melissa," my agent instructed, coming from behind his desk and giving me a hug. He was always very fatherly. He was a trustworthy man and had been my agent since I was drafted out of college. He, his wife and his two sons, who were now in college, were like family to me.

"It's barely two in the afternoon, Ron, kind of early for a drink. Plus, I have practice in a couple of hours." I took a seat on the sofa in the corner of his office anxious to know what was going on.

"Trust me, you'll need the drink," he said as Melissa handed it to me and left the office.

"What's going on, Ron?" I held the half-filled glass of cognac in my hand, but had yet to take a sip. Ron saying that I would need a drink even though he knew I had practice was definitely alarming. I knew this had to be serious.

"Are you familiar with the name, Nadia Sanchez?" He asked, taking a seat across from me and continuing before

I answered. "I hope so, because she just slapped you with a paternity suit."

Chapter Forty-eight
Simone

I was surprised by how calm I was as I walked up to the stand, raised my right hand, and swore to tell the truth, the whole truth, and nothing but the truth, so help me God. I was to be the last witness to testify for the state. A lot was riding on my testimony, because I was the last person to talk to Stacey after he arrived in Vegas and before he was murdered.

I sat down, acutely aware that all eyes were on me. It was an odd feeling, but I'd waited for this moment for a long time.

"State your full name for the record," the clerk instructed.

"Simone Marie Johnson," I replied. I looked at the jury, smiled, and scanned the remainder of the room not once resting my eyes on Tyron.

The courtroom was packed. There wasn't an empty seat in the room. People actually camped out to be one of the first in line to get one of the limited public seats in the courtroom.

"Ms. Johnson, what was your relationship to Stacey Flenoy?" The D.A. Asked.

"Stacey was my best friend," I smiled.

"What type of person was Stacey?" She asked warmly.

I talked about Stacey and what type of person he was, and prayed I did him justice. I didn't want to cry, but talking about him in that way brought back so many memories. I couldn't control the burning in my throat and the tears that began to fall from my eyes when I talked about his humor and his devotion to his friends and family.

She then asked me if I knew who Stacey was in a relationship with when he died. I told her about the first night that Stacey saw Tyron at Guys and Dolls. How we'd catch Tyron staring at him.

"How did they finally meet?"

When I began to recount the story of how Stacey finally hooked up with Tyron when he tricked him into coming to the fake video shoot at his Malibu house, the defense attorney stood.

"The defense objects Your Honor! This is all hearsay. The witness was not there." Her hand was on her hip and the look on her face read *"come on!"*

"Your Honor, I ask that you allow this testimony. We aren't talking about a relationship with any ole Joe Blow, we are talking about a clandestine, homosexual affair with a famous multi-millionaire. It is more likely than not that a person will confide in their best friend!" she pleaded.

"Objection overruled. You may continue, Ms. Johnson." His deep, authoritative voice seemed to reverberate through my body.

With each story that I told of Stacey and Tyron's relationship, the defense attorney objected claiming hearsay and it was overruled, again and again.

I had to have been on the stand for at least two hours when the D.A. asked her final question.

"Was Stacey known to lie?"

"No, not at all. Stacey mastered brutal honesty and tact. He had a way of telling you the truth so gently, there was no way you could be mad at him for it," I smiled.

"Thank you. No further questions," she said sitting down.

"Defense, your witness," the judge said, gesturing to the beautiful older woman in her expertly tailored designer skirt suit.

"Have you ever seen Tyron and Stacey together?"

"No," I answered honestly.

"Have you ever seen any photos of them together?"

"No."

"Ms. Johnson, when you last spoke to Mr. Flenoy, where was he?"

"He was in the car at the airport waiting for Tyron Mark's driver to get his luggage from baggage claim."

"So the last person that you knew him to be with was Mr. Marks' driver, Travis *Curse* Davis?" she said, putting the emphasis on Curse.

"I don't know who is driver was."

"But the last person you knew him to be with was Mr. Marks' driver?"

"Yes."

"No further questions, Your Honor," she said, smiling at the jury.

"Do either of you object to the witness remaining in the courtroom?" The judge asked the State and defense attorneys. "You may step down and remain in the courtroom, if you so choose," the judge instructed after neither side objected.

I did as I was told, and took a seat next to Talise, who was seated next to Stacey's mom, and sister, Joy. I was glad that my part was over, and was looking forward to being in the courtroom while the defense presented their case. Having not been allowed in the courtroom until after my testimony, I hadn't been able to hear any of the D.A.'s case first hand.

"The Defense may call their first witness."

"Your Honor, the Defense calls Abigail Reed to the stand." When the petite blonde walked into the room, I wondered what her testimony could be. I'd never heard of or seen her before in my life.

After she was sworn in, she sat stiffly behind the stand, fidgeting as everyone's attention fell on her.

"Thank you for being here, Mrs. Reed,"

"You're welcome," she squeaked out nervously.

"Mrs. Reed, on August 21st 2010, where were you and who were you with?"

"I was at McCarran International Airport with my husband, Aaron Reed."

"What was the occasion?"

"We were here to see a UFC fight. My husband and I are really huge MMA fans."

"To clarify for the jury, please tell us what UFC and MMA is," she said, smiling at the jury.

"Sure. MMA stands for Mixed Martial Arts and UFC stands for Ultimate Fighting Competition. It's similar to boxing, but infused with martial arts techniques."

"Thank you. While you were at the airport, what did you see?"

"My husband and I were in baggage claim... he actually noticed him first," she began.

"Noticed who first, Mrs. Reed?"

"While we were waiting for our luggage, we noticed a man who we thought was the MMA fighter, Kimbo Slice. That's what caught my husband's attention."

"What did you do next, Mrs. Reed?"

"I grabbed my camera and began snapping pictures of him when a man walked up and started talking to him."

"The Defense would like to show Exhibit A and B to the jury," the defense attorney said, revealing two large photos on an easel. One of a dark skinned man with a baldhead and beard holding a sign that clearly had Stacey's name on it, and the second of that same man and Stacey. "Your Honor, will you inquire of the jury whether everyone can see these photos?" She asked. Once it was confirmed that the jurors could see the photo, she continued.

"Mrs. Reed, can you tell us who's in these photos and what made you come forth with this evidence?"

"When Mr. Marks was arrested and photos of the victim were on the news, I knew I had seen him before, but I couldn't recall where. Then when I saw a photo of Travis Davis, it hit me! I couldn't believe it. The pictures we'd taken when we were at McCarran Airport weren't of the MMA fighter, Kimbo Slice, but of Travis Davis and Stacey Flenoy. That's when I called the district attorney's Office."

"Thank you, Mrs. Reed. No further questions, Your Honor."

"The state has no questions for the witness." Talise and I looked at each other stunned at what had just taken place. That photo could very well be the reasonable doubt that the defense needed to get Tyron off.

Chapter Forty-nine
Tyron

"The Defense calls Maria Parra to the stand," she said as a Latina who looked to be in her early forties walked into the courtroom and took her seat behind the witness stand after being sworn in.

"Thank you for being here, Mrs. Parra. Can you please tell me what you do for a living?"

"I am a housekeeper," she said with a Latin accent.

"On August 21st, 2010, where were you working?"

"At a home on Redbird Drive."

"Tell the ladies and gentleman of the jury what you saw when you were leaving the home."

"I was in my car looking through my purse for my phone before I drove off, and I saw a car pull into the driveway of the house next door to the one I was working."

"Where were you parked?"

"I was parked on the street right outside of the driveway of the house next door. I never park in the driveway of the homes I clean. It's not professional."

"Were you parked on the side of the street where your car was facing the house or away from the house that the car had just pulled up to?"

"I was facing the house."

"Was it daytime or nighttime?"

"It was still light outside. It was right before my kids get out of school. When I left there, I picked them up."

"Tell us what else you saw, Mrs. Parra?"

"I saw a pretty man with long curly hair in a ponytail. *He was so pretty*. He got out of the car and a large dark man with a big beard and no hair on his head was driving the car."

"Who were the men that got out of that car and how do you know who they are?"

"My husband always watches the news. That's all he will watch on the T.V. is the *news!*" The infliction in her voice and the way she rolled her eyes caused the jury to laugh.

"I saw the pretty man who got killed and the man who was with him on the news. I saw the pictures."

"When did you see this news cast?" My attorney asked.

"When Mr. Marks was arrested. I did not know the pretty man was dead until then. When I saw him, I knew his face. I'll never forget his face!"

"Had you ever seen the defendant, Mr. Tyron Marks, before today?"

"Only on the T.V."

"Thank you. No further questions, Your Honor."

"Your witness," the judge said to the district attorney.

"Mrs. Parra, the 'pretty man' you say you saw get out of the car was in deed Stacey Flenoy, correct?"

"Yes. It was him for sure."

"Did he get out of the front seat of the car or the backseat of the car?"

"He got out of the backseat of the car."

"And the dark skinned man that you identified as Travis Davis; what part of the car did he get out of?"

"He was driving the car."

"No further questions, Your Honor."

"The defense calls Tyron Marks to the stand," my attorney, Lori said after the housekeeper had left the stand.

I approached the witness stand, raised my right hand, and was sworn in before taking my seat. I was nervous, but had been well prepared for this moment. There was no way that I wasn't going to testify in my defense.

"Mr. Marks, were you here in Las Vegas during the week of August 21st 2010?"

"Yes I was here."

"Where did you stay while you were here?"

"I had a suite at the Wynn Hotel on the strip."

"The Defense would like to present Exhibit C, receipts from the Wynn Hotel, to the jury."

"Do you own a home on Redbird Drive, Mr. Marks?"

"Yes I do," I answered honestly.

"Why did you stay at a hotel instead of at the home you own?"

"The home I own on Redbird Drive is twenty to thirty minutes from the strip. It was more convenient to stay in a hotel, being that it was down the street from the Grand Garden Arena where my artists were performing."

"Mr. Marks, did you know Stacey Flenoy?"

"No, I didn't know him," I said, looking at the jury of my supposed peers.

"Had you ever met him before?"

"I've never met him before."

"Is it possible that you've met him before?"

"I meet a lot of people in the business that I am in, so it is possible, but I don't recall ever meeting him or having a conversation with him."

"How long has Travis *Curse* Davis been under your employ?"

"Over five years I believe."

"What did he do for you?"

"He was part of my security and he was also my driver."

"Was he your only driver?"

"No. There are multiple drivers that we use."

"During the week in question, where did Travis *Curse* Davis stay?"

"We had a very large entourage of people who work for me, artists and their friends. We had a few dozen rooms at the Wynn so I can't say for sure."

"Did he have access to your home on Redbird Drive?"

"Yes he did."

"How would he have access to the home?"

"There is a hidden key safe on the property that he knows the code to."

"How would he know the code to the key safe on the property?"

"I've actually only stayed in the house once since I bought it in 2009. Curse... Travis Davis spent a lot of time in Vegas, so I let him have full access to the house whenever he was in town."

"That's very generous of you. Why would you allow that?"

"He's been with me for a very long time. I trusted him with everything. If he wanted to stay there, I didn't mind. The house was vacant the majority of the time."

"Aside from you, was Travis *Curse* Davis the only person

who had access to that home?"

"Yes, he was."

"We tender the witness for cross examination by opposing counsel, Your Honor."

Here comes the hard part, I thought as the District Attorney asked her first question.

"Mr. Marks, you say you can't recall ever seeing or meeting the victim, Stacey Flenoy, is that correct?"

"Yes it is."

"So you didn't see him while you were both on that ten plus hour first class flight from Paris, France to Los Angeles?"

Chapter Fifty
Deon

I *wasn't surprised that Nadia had set me up like this.* *It happened all too often, and I was the latest casualty,* I thought as I sat in the conference room at my attorney's office. He'd just told me that the paternity test results were positive, and I was the father of Nadia's baby girl. Nadia and her attorney would be arriving any moment and I wasn't looking forward to seeing her face.

After my agent, Ron, told me about the paternity suit, we contacted an attorney who came highly recommended. He set up the DNA testing for the next morning, so I could get this out of the way before I had to leave to go on the road later that evening.

As soon as I left Ron's office, I called Simone and told her what was going on. She was the only person that I could talk to about this.

"Chances are it's not your baby, Deon," she said after I'd told her about the night Nadia set me up.

"The way she did that shit, Simone... how it all went down, it's a huge possibility that's my baby. She planned that shit to a tee, and I fell right in her trap like a fucking dumb ass!" I was so mad at myself. "She's asking for twenty grand a month in child support!"

"She must be out of her damned mind! She's going for the gusto I see." Simone sounded just as incensed as I was feeling.

"The fact that someone would do this is fucking crazy, Simone! What type of mother could she possibly be, you know what I'm saying?"

"Yeah, I hear you, babe. Unfortunately, there is nothing you can do but wait to find out if that's your child."

The receptionist escorting Nadia and her Gloria Allred lookalike attorney into the room brought me out of my reverie. It had been over a year since I'd seen her last.

"Why would you do something like this? This is a life! A lifetime commitment! We don't even know each other! I don't even know where you live! I don't even know your age! What type of woman are you?" I asked as soon as I saw Nadia's face.

She sat across from me at the long, wood conference table in an expensive looking suit. When she removed her large sunglasses, I could see her red-rimmed eyes. She didn't even look like she had given birth a few months prior.

"I didn't intend to get pregnant, Deon! I swear I didn't!" I would never believe a word that came out of Nadia's mouth. Any woman that could do something like this was trash.

"Then why didn't you tell me you were pregnant? Why wait until months after you had the baby to tell me?"

"I had no way to call you or tell you anything! Plus, I was embarrassed and figured I'd just do it on my own and never tell you, but I couldn't do that! She deserves to know her father!" She said as tears fell from her eyes.

"You're full of shit—" I began before her attorney cut in.

"Mr. Bradford, the baby is here and deserves to be cared for by both parents. Discussing the past will not move you forward," she said softly as if her voice would calm me. *Nothing* could calm the rage that was coursing through my body. I was a dad. I have a child with a woman I don't even know! I never imagined this for myself.

"My client wants twenty thousand a month in child support—"

"I'm not giving you twenty grand a month. You must be out of your damn mind, Nadia!" I said, cutting her attorney off.

"Your daughter deserves to be taken care of properly, Mr. Bradford!"

"If your client can't afford to take care of the child, we'll petition the court for full custody," my attorney bluffed. I couldn't even bring myself to see the child, let alone fight for full custody. I didn't even know her name. "Mr. Bradford is willing to give Ms. Sanchez ten thousand a month and that's it and no more."

"Ten grand?" Fake Allred huffed. "Your client brings in over thirty five million dollars a year! That's almost three million a month, and he wants to give my client a meager ten thousand dollars of that to provide for his *daughter? His own flesh and blood?*" I couldn't believe the audacity of these women.

"If you want to take this to court, let's go! My client is a good guy with a squeaky clean record. When I sit him in front of a judge and he tells of how Ms. Sanchez went about this... this whole getting pregnant scheme, your client may walk away with nothing! I suggest you advise Ms. Sanchez to sleep on this and make the wise decision to accept. You're lucky he's even willing to give you anything," he said, turning his attention to Nadia. The scowl on his face screamed of the disdain he had for her and other women like her. He'd been in plenty of these situations with other high profile clients, which was why I'd chosen him. "I advised him otherwise because I despise women like you, Ms. Sanchez," he concluded, shaking his head at her with a disgusted look on his face.

"It's fine!" Nadia spoke up just when her attorney was opening her mouth to speak. "It's not about the money. I will take what you are offering. I just ask that you please provide medical insurance and pay for extracurricular activities and school when the time comes. I'm not trying to get over on you, Deon. I'm truly sorry all of this happened the way it did," she cried.

Bullshit! I wanted to shout, but instead, I sat there and stared at her. I was having a hard time believing this was really happening. *I'm a dad.*

Chapter Fifty-one
Simone

I shouldn't have been surprised that Tyron got on the stand and perjured himself time and time again.

"I don't recall being on a flight with him," he lied.

"How about staying in the same hotel as the victim, Mr. Marks? You don't recall that either?"

"No, I didn't see him there."

Question after question, the district attorney didn't let up on Tyron as he sat on the witness stand for close to four hours looking as if none of it fazed him.

"Mr. Marks, are you gay?"

"Objection, Your Honor!" Tyron's defense attorney all but shouted as she stood from her seat. "My clients' sexual preference has no bearing on this case! That question is ridiculous!" She huffed.

"It is relevant—"

"Objection sustained. Ask your next question, Counselor," the judge said, cutting the D.A. Off.

"I have no further questions at this time, your Honor."

"Defense, you may redirect if you so choose."

"Mr. Marks, how did you fly to Paris, France?"

"I charted a plane."

"Who all was on that charted flight, Mr. Marks?"

"There were about twenty to thirty of us. I couldn't begin to name everyone, but we all flew out there together."

"Was the plane you chartered packed, Mr. Marks, or was there room for other passengers?"

"There was room. The plane seated sixty passengers comfortably."

"Mr. Marks, was Travis Curse Davis on that chartered flight with you?"

"Yes, he was."

"The Defense would like to present Exhibit G, the flight manifesto showing Stacey Flenoy's commercial flight leaving the same day as Mr. Marks' chartered flight from Los Angeles to Paris, France, to the jury."

"Mr. Marks, why didn't you charter a plane back to the states?"

"It made no sense to do that. Only two of us were heading back at the same time."

"Who were you flying with and sitting next to on your return commercial flight from Paris, France to Los Angeles?"

"I was sitting next to Curse... Travis Davis."

"And I'm correct when saying that in first class, there are only two seats per row?"

"Yes."

"Mr. Marks, the state entered into evidence phone records that show multiple cell phone lines under your business account. It also shows that the victim, Stacey Flenoy's cell phone was paid through your company. Who all has phones under this account?"

"We only have one account for the whole company. Everyone had cell phones that were paid for by the company."

"Did Travis Curse Davis have a cell phone under your business account?"

"Yes he did. Everyone who works for me does."

"Did he have access to change or add phone lines to the account?"

"Yes he did."

"Why?"

"He hired on new security guys and was in charge of providing them with cell phones. Plus, he needed access in case of an emergency. I broke my cell a couple of times and had to send him to pick up another one and get it all set up for me. So he was on the account to handle situations like that."

"The Defense would like to present Exhibit H, which shows that Travis Curse Davis' name was on the Verizon account and had access to add phone lines to Mr. Marks business account. The Defense has no further questions at this time."

~ ~ ~ ~ ~ ~

I sat on the terrace next to the pool in the one story Sky Villa I was staying in at the Palms hotel, with tears pouring from my eyes like the rain was pouring from the sky. I'd been up all night, sitting there looking out at the beautiful view that could still be seen through the streaming rain, feeling completely betrayed and hurt.

When his hand rubbed my shoulder, more tears poured from eyes. I was incapable of stopping them.

"I'm so sorry I didn't tell you sooner, Simone," he said, handing me a glass of wine and sitting next to me.

"It's been over a year, Deon! How could you keep

something like this from me? Reel me in and then tell me some shit like this?" I couldn't even look at him, I was so pissed off. "How can I fucking trust you, Deon?" I asked, wiping the tears that continued to fall from my eyes.

"I was ashamed to tell you! I was scared you wouldn't accept me. I thought it would be better if you got to know me again... I don't fucking know, Simone! I fucked up! I don't blame you if you can't accept me. I'd understand if you never want to see me again, although that would fuck me up!" he said, covering his face with his hands and resting his elbows on his knees. He had flown in late last night so he could spend some time with me before he had to head to San Antonio for their third game of the semi-finals.

"I really don't know what to say, Deon. First the baby, and now this! Every time I love someone..." I began, but decided against finishing that statement. He knew what I had been through so there was no need to say it. I took a sip of my wine and tried to swallow through the large lump in my throat.

"Simone, I love you," he admitted for the first time, making more tears flood down my cheeks. "I didn't get this shit out there being a dog. I loved the woman who gave this to me, and she did it knowingly! I would never do that to you or anyone else. Remember when I told you that Nichelle came to me in my dreams?" He asked, but continued when I didn't respond. "She came to me and told me that Shelly was hiding something from me. When I woke up and she went to walk the dog, I looked around her room, and that's when I found the Valtrax medication and realized that she had been lying to me. I immediately went and got tested, and the results came back negative, so I just went nuts and did me. Then after that Nadia shit, I went to the doctor, and they took blood and tested for everything, and that's when I found out. I was... I am ashamed! But I want you in my life..."

"That's why you wouldn't have sex with me," I realized, cutting him off. Can I have a normal relationship with a man who has herpes? A man who chose not to tell me this shit for over a year?

"No, it's wasn't the only reason. I haven't had an outbreak since the first time when I tested negative... I wanted it to be your choice. I wasn't given a choice! I would never want that for you. Just because I have it doesn't mean you will automatically get it though, Simone,"

"Are you on medication?" I asked.

"No, I'm not and I don't have to be unless I start having outbreaks. Even then, I don't. I take care of myself. I'm a healthy man... I've been given this shit to carry, and it's a hard blow!" I could hear the pain in his voice and could tell that he was crying, but I had yet to look at him, although he was sitting directly next to me.

I couldn't even bring myself to comfort him; I was so angry. How could he do this? How could he wait until I fell in love with him to tell me he has an incurable disease?

"What made you tell me this now? With all the shit that is going on, why tell me now?" I asked, finally looking at him.

"I don't know, Simone. I just couldn't sleep. It's been heavy on my mind and I couldn't keep it from you any longer. There were so many times I wanted to tell you, but I just couldn't bring myself to do it. This shit has been eating me up! It hasn't been easy keeping this from you. I'm really, really sorry, Simone. I can't tell you that enough!" He said, looking at me with sad, pleading eyes.

"I can't do this, Deon. I don't know if I can trust you. You've kept this from me for over a *year* and pretended that you just wanted to wait for marriage to have sex—"

"I did and I do! I didn't lie about that, Simone!" He said, cutting me off. "Having this wasn't the only reason why I wanted to wait. I just wanted to try to do things differently." His tone was begging me to understand.

"I don't trust you right now, Deon. I can't even fucking think!" I huffed, trying to wipe tears from my face as they continued to fall.

"I'll leave if that's what you want. Do you want me to give you some time to think?" he asked. His eyes were so sad that my heart pained looking into them.

"Yes," I said before he got up and left me sitting on the balcony with my thoughts.

Minutes later, I could hear him leaving the suite, taking my heart with him.

Chapter Fifty-two
Deon

I don't know what made me tell Simone about my disease when I knew I'd need to have full concentration to help my team get to the finals, but something just wouldn't allow me to hold it in any longer.

As she slept peacefully, I couldn't join her because my brain wouldn't shut down; telling her was so heavy on my mind. It was like God wouldn't allow me to rest until I came clean with her, so I did.

"Simone, wake up babe. I have something I need to talk to you about," I said, gently nudging her awake.

"What's wrong, Deon?" She asked, sitting up on the bed. "Are you okay?" I could see the worry in her eyes and wondered if she saw the worry and fear in mine. I didn't want to lose her again and wasn't sure if I'd be able to deal with it if I did.

"I don't...I don't know how to tell you this," I began.

"Just tell me, Deon. It's okay," she said, rubbing her hand gently across my face.

"I don't know how," I said honestly as tears began to form in my eyes. How was I going to tell her this? I wanted to change my mind, but knew I'd come too far to turn back now.

"Deon, you're scaring me. Please just tell me!"

I paused for what had to be a long few minutes before I blurted it out.

"Simone, I have herpes."

"What? You just found this out?" she asked after a few beats, her eyes wide with surprise.

"No... I've known for about a year and half now." It took everything in me to continue to stare into her eyes and watch the disgust and anger rise in them.

"You mean to tell me you've known all this time, Deon?" She asked in disbelief as she rose from the bed, her eyes squinted with condemnation. I felt so low, so dirty. I never wanted to see her look at me in that way.

"Yes, I..."

"That's so fucked up!" She hissed, cutting me off before she walked out of the room and slammed the door.

The ringing of the phone jolted me from my thoughts. I looked at the caller ID, hoping to see Simone's picture and number, as I had every time my phone rang since I walked out of Simone's hotel room last night, but it was my mother calling.

"Hey, Mom, how are you?" I asked, trying to put some life in my voice. I sat down on the sofa in front of the floor to ceiling window in my living room as the sun began to rise. I had a plane to catch in a few hours and felt no motivation to even pack a small bag.

"I'm blessed, son. How are you?"

"I'm good. Just trying to stay focused. How is everyone?"

I asked, wanting to get the conversation off of me.

"Everyone is fine. What's going on with you, Deon?

"We play tomorrow. Just trying to get focused."

"Deon, I know when your games are, especially the playoffs," she said sassily before continuing. "Are you sure you're okay?" My mother could always tell when something wasn't right with me. "How is Simone?" she asked.

"I don't know, Mom. Simone isn't talking to me right now," I confessed. "And to be honest with you, I don't know what to do. I messed up. I think I may have lost her for good this time," I sighed. I *needed* to talk to my mother. This was eating me up. I was having a hard time thinking straight and it hadn't even been twenty-four hours since I'd left Simone in Vegas.

"What happened, son? Talk to me," my mother coaxed gently. She had a way that made me feel comfortable telling her anything. I knew she wouldn't judge me and that was all I could ask for.

"I kept something from her, Mom, and I don't know if she will ever forgive me," I began as tears slid down my face.

I told my mother everything, starting with Shelley and ending with my confession to Simone the other night. I omitted everything about Nadia and the baby; I couldn't even bring myself to think about that situation, let alone tell my parents. I still didn't know my daughter's name, nor did I want to see her. I knew that was wrong on so many levels and would be very disappointing to my parents, so I tried to keep it out of my thoughts.

"Oh, Deon, baby," my mother sighed. "We all make mistakes and sometimes make the wrong decisions, but you cannot give up on that girl. You two are meant to be together and you know I've never said that to you before about any other woman. Simone has every right to be hurt, upset, and feel betrayed by what you did. It was wrong. Right now, she is angry and she can't see past that. She can't look at it from your perspective yet, Deon. Have you tried calling her?"

"Yes I have, and she won't answer. I don't know what else to do. I'm so embarrassed and disgusted with myself. I'm ashamed..."

"Well you need to go ahead and get over all of that, Deon," my mother began. "You have been given this to carry, and there really isn't anything you can do about it but deal with it head on. This doesn't make you a bad person or a tainted man! You are still all that you were before, and more! You are a Bradford. No matter what, you remember that! You could have been the type of man to sleep with that girl and never tell her, but you didn't do that! You keep fighting for her, baby. She will come around. I bet you anything."

"I want to believe that you are right, but you don't know Simone, Mom. She doesn't forgive easily. I messed up once before... I don't know if she will ever trust me and let me back in after this."

"I don't need to know Simone, Deon. I know my son and I know that you have a good heart, and that hurting her was never your intention. If she loves you and knows you like I feel she does, she will come around. You just don't give up."

"I don't think I could ever give up on Simone. I can barely think without her."

Chapter Fifty-three
Tyron

"Madame Foreman and ladies and gentlemen of the jury," my attorney began after we'd sat through the state's three hour closing argument. I was happy that this was almost over, but nervous about jury deliberations. "I promise I won't keep you as long as the opposing counsel did. This is a very simple case, in my opinion, and it's riddled with reasonable doubt. First, I'll start by reminding you that out of all of the witnesses the state has paraded into this courtroom to testify for you, not one has *ever* seen my client, Tyron Marks," she said dramatically, pointing at me as I sat next to Lem with a solemn impression on my face, "with the victim, Stacey Flenoy. But, plenty of people have seen the victim with Travis *Curse* Davis! Even the victim's best friend, Simone Johnson, testified in front of you and told you that when she last spoke to Mr. Flenoy, he was with Tyron Marks' *driver* who we know was Travis *Curse* Davis, *not my client!* We have photos that show them together at the airport! We have the housekeeper who had just finished working at the home next door who saw Travis *Curse* Davis and the victim together..." She began before picking apart every piece of the State's case, expertly.

"Please do the right thing and look at the evidence clearly. I'm sorry that Stacey Flenoy lost his life the way he did, but my client is not responsible and should not be convicted of this crime. *Do. The. Right. Thing. Please!* Give my client his life back!" she said passionately, concluding her closing argument no more than an hour later.

I looked behind me to see Tomi and my mother sitting together in the front row. They both gave me an encouraging smile as the Judge gave the jury instructions for their deliberations.

~ ~ ~ ~ ~ ~

"Now all we can do is wait." My mother sighed and patted my shoulders as Tomi made us all drinks. The jury was four hours into their deliberations as we waited in my suite after finishing a late lunch.

"I'm sorry I wasn't able to be here before, Ty. You know I would have if I could have," Tomi said, handing me a glass half filled with whisky.

"I know, Tomi. I'm just glad you are here now. I can't wait for this to be over." I took back the full glass of whisky then sat the empty glass on the coffee table.

"You want more?" My mother asked, taking a sip of her drink.

"Nah, I'll have more when we celebrate my acquittal," I said, hoping that we would be celebrating that, and soon.

"Okay honey," my mother said, sitting next to me on the couch with so much worry in her eyes.

"Everything is going to be okay, Ma. No matter what, you will be taken..."

"Don't you say that!" She said, giving me that look she always gave me when I was younger and said something she didn't like. "I don't want to hear that! You are going to get off Tyron and that is..."

When the ringing of my cell interrupted my mother's rant, we were all silenced. I saw my attorney's name pop up on the caller ID and clicked the talk button. When she told me that the jury had reached a verdict, my stomach dropped. I didn't know if such a short deliberation was a good thing or a bad thing, but was glad that the time had finally come to find out if I'd continue to be a free man or spend the rest of my life behind bars.

Chapter Fifty-four
Simone

I hadn't slept more than a few hours since Deon walked out the door of my suite, and I felt extremely fatigued as we sat in the courtroom waiting to hear the verdict.

I couldn't get Deon off of my mind. I missed him like crazy, but was unable to forgive him for what he'd done. I still loved him, but didn't know how I could ever trust him again. My mind was constantly clouded with these thoughts and I couldn't do what I'd usually do—talk to Talise— because I wasn't comfortable talking about this with anyone. How do I get advice without revealing what he kept from me and without revealing that he has an incurable disease?

The jurors entering the courtroom jolted me from my thoughts. We stood, locked hands, and retook our seats after the last juror sat down in the jury box. By looking at their faces, I couldn't read them at all. Three of the women were wiping tears from their faces as they openly cried, while the other nine jurors held stoic expressions. I didn't know what to think.

Time seemed to stand still when the judge began to speak.

"Mr. Marks, please remain standing and face the jury. Foreperson please stand. Madame Foreperson, has the jury reached a unanimous verdict in this case?" He asked after the woman stood.

"The jury has, Your Honor," she replied.

My hands began to shake and tears spilled down my cheeks. I kept my eyes focused on the jury Foreperson, who had yet to look in our direction. The uncertainty of what was about to happen was overwhelming.

As I sat between my mother and Talise, I squeezed both of their hands tightly as my mom whispered in my ear and reminded me to breathe.

"How say you, Madame Foreperson, how do you find the defendant, Tyron Marks, indictment two thousand and twelve, case two ninety-eight, charging purposeful first degree murder, guilty or not guilty?"

I felt Talise's grip tighten around my hand as the jury foreperson spoke.

"Not guilty." I felt lightheaded, but remembered that he could still be found guilty of the lesser count of second-degree murder. Maybe they couldn't believe that it was planned, but they *had* to believe that he was guilty of the lesser count! *They aren't going to let him get away with this.*

"Say Madame Foreperson that the verdict is not guilty. So say you all ladies and gentlemen?"

"Yes," the other eleven jurors said in unison.

"How say you, Madame Foreperson, as to the lesser charge of purposeful second degree murder, guilty or not guilty?"

I thought the loud cry was coming from my mouth, and

didn't realize that it wasn't until I looked over and saw Mommy Miles and Talise pulling Stacey's mother and sister, Joy, from their seats and guiding them out of the courtroom as their howls filled the room.

I was in a daze as I sat in the pew styled seat with my mother's arms wrapped around me as the judge asked for order in the court repeatedly. Tears spilled down my face and my body shook uncontrollably.

"Breathe, Simone," my mother whispered in my ear over and over as she continued to hold me. She rubbed her hand up and down my arm as she kept me locked in her embrace.

"Say Madame Foreperson," the judge began, "that the verdict is not guilty. So say you all ladies and gentlemen?"

"Yes," the jurors said again as I stared in their direction as the same ladies of the jury cried as they had when they walked into the courtroom.

I couldn't believe this was happening. They let him off! They let him get away with murdering Stacey after deliberating for four damn hours!

As soon as that realization settled uneasily in my stomach, my eyes gravitated toward Tyron. The smile on his face was that of a grateful, wrongfully accused, innocent man.

"I have to get out of here!" I choked out rising from my seat and rushing out of the courtroom with my mother on my heels.

Tears continued to stream down my face as I hurriedly walked away from my mother and through the crowd of spectators and reporters.

"Don't follow me, Mom. I'll be okay. I need to make a call," I said as I stalked down the courthouse hallway.

"Please find Talise and help them. They're probably in

the bathroom," I suggested over my shoulder as I continued down the hallway searching my handbag for my phone.

I pulled the phone from my purse, pressed speed dial number five, and when the call picked up, I was barely able to speak the words.

"Not guilty!" I cried. "He fucking got off!" I said as I pushed my way through the stairwell door at the end of the hallway. Thankful it was empty, I collapsed onto the stairs with a heavy thud as my butt hit the cold metal.

"No way!" he said in disbelief. "Simone, I'm so sorry. How is everyone doing? How is his mom? How are *you*?"

"I'm fucked up right now," I admitted honestly. "I'm in shock. It's time to put what we've been planning in motion."

"Simone, are you sure? Once it's done there's no turning back. This is about to get really real," he said with hesitation in his voice.

"This was the plan, and I'm sticking with it! Are you still with me?"

"Yes, I'm definitely still with you, Simone. I just want you to be sure about this," he sighed.

"I'm more than sure about this! Leak another story to the blogs then I'm releasing the video and exposing his ass! He's going to wish he *was* in prison after I'm done with him!"

Chapter Fifty-five
Deon

"Simone, please call me back." I hung up the phone and threw it on the sofa next to me as I sat in my living room hiding after our upsetting loss to the Spurs.

We were out of the playoffs for the second year in a row, and again, it was my fault. I was usually able to channel everything that was going on in my life, good or bad, and make it work for me on the court, but neither my mind nor my heart was in the game and it seems that energy rubbed off on my teammates. We preformed horribly and I was embarrassed.

I couldn't imagine what Simone was going through and that was all I could think about as I ran up and down the court. I needed to know how she was doing, but she wouldn't talk to me. All I knew was I had to do something to get her back, so I sent her a text.

"You can't ignore me forever," I typed. "I'm sorry that I kept that from you. I need you in my life! I'm messed up right now, Simone." I clicked send and was happy when my phone buzzed with her response no more than one minute later.

"I can't deal with this, Deon. I have too much on my plate! We're both messed up right now and none of this is my fault! How do I trust you?? How do I trust???"

I re-read her message a couple of times, trying to decide on the right response then began typing.

"It's my fault and I made the wrong decision by keeping it from you for so long!! I don't want to be without you, Simone! I'm miserable! I can't think! I can't sleep! What can I do to make this better??? What can I do to regain your trust??? Just tell me what to do and I'll do it!!!"

"You promise??"

"Yes, I promise, Simone. Just tell me and I'll do it!!"

"Give me space! Quit calling me! Don't text me! Leave me ALONE!!"

I couldn't stop the tears that filled my eyes and fell down my face. What could I do but give her what she wanted? I promised.

Chapter Fifty-six
Tyron

My knees damn near buckled when I heard those first two words: not guilty! I tuned out the gasps from the spectators in the courtroom and tried to remain calm.

Okay, not guilty of first-degree murder... will they find me guilty of second? I had a hard time keeping my composure as my attorney, Lori, grabbed my hand to steady me. I could barely hear the second not guilty over the loud cries from behind the prosecutors table.

I'm free! This shit is over! I looked back at my mother and Tomi; tears were spilling down all of our faces. I couldn't help but cry. The relief I felt was indescribable and the weight that was lifted from my shoulders was even heavier than I realized. I hugged Lori and Lem and then grabbed my mother and Tomi in a bear hug.

"I knew it! I knew that God wouldn't take my son... all I have left," my mother cried in my ear as I held her and Tomi tightly as tears poured from my eyes.

"I'm so happy they made the right decision, Ty," Tomi

said, looking up at me. Her small face was bright and her eyes were happy as she looked into mine.

"Hell, I am too. I'm glad this shit is over."

"I bet you are." She smiled. "I'm going to slip out the back. My security is in the hallway. I'll see you back at the hotel." she said and hugged me again, kissing my mother before leaving the courtroom.

"Let's head out and talk to the media," Lori suggested, grabbing her briefcase. The smile on her face was one of triumph. I knew I couldn't have gotten off without her, and told her just that.

"The truth prevailed, Tyron. You should have never been charged in this case. Thankfully, the system worked," she said, patting me on the back as we all walked out of the courtroom no more than thirty minutes after the verdict had been read.

When we reached the front of the courthouse, it was pure mayhem. Reporters and cameras were everywhere shouting questions in my direction as we made our way down the concrete steps, stopping once we'd reached level ground.

"How do you feel, Tyron?" one reporter asked.

"I feel vindicated," I said, adjusting the sunglasses on my face. "Justice was served. I'm just happy to have my life back. I'm ready to put this behind me."

"Do you have anything to say to the family of the victim, Stacey Flenoy?" Another reporter asked.

"I'm sorry for their loss..." I began before Lori stepped up to the mic and began speaking.

"We can't imagine the pain the Flenoy family is feeling right now and pray that they get justice for their son through the arrest and conviction of Travis Curse Davis.

This was a witch-hunt, and justice prevailed. Mr. Marks should have never been charged with this murder. He is an innocent man and the jurors saw that and brought back the correct verdict. That is all," she said, keeping it short and simple.

With the help of my security team, we made our way through the crowd of reporters and onlookers fairly easily. Once we were all safely inside the black suburban and pulling away from the courthouse, I sighed heavily with relief and powered on my phone.

"I'm so happy this is over," my mother was saying as her, Lori and Lem talked.

As I scanned through my text messages, replying to only a few, I was surprised to see one from Curse. I opened the message not knowing what to expect. I hadn't heard from him since before I was arrested and could only imagine that he was feeling some sort of way about me throwing this murder shit all on him.

That's some dirty shit you did, but it will get cleaned up one way or the other. Can't say that I'm glad you got off..." Before I could finish reading his text, I saw a message from Banks flash across the top of the screen. With no intentions of replying to Curse—what was done was done—I clicked on Banks' text, expecting to read a congratulatory message, but instead saw only a link that was pasted into the text. When I clicked the link, my browser opened to Bossip.com. What I read reminded me that this nightmare was hardly fucking over.

Chapter Fifty-seven
C. Banks

"**F**uck, fuck, fuck!" I yelled as I paced around my kitchen after reading the latest blog post and sending the link to Tyron. I was already close to losing it after hearing the not guilty verdict, but seeing that Simone was going through with her plan only added to the intense anxiety that was coursing through my body.

"This shit can't be happening! This can't be happening!" I was talking to myself like a man on the verge of losing his mind. Shit, I *was* on the verge of losing my mind! Thankfully, I was alone and there was no one around to hear me go ape shit.

I had been tuned in to the news all morning, waiting to hear the verdict. From the reports throughout the trial, I knew that it could really go either way. The State's case wasn't as strong as they thought it was and Tyron's defense seemed to pick the shit apart daily.

When the reporters ran out of the courtroom, each trying to get to their cameras to report the verdict, I held my breath, anxious to hear what the jury had decided. My life depended on this verdict, just as Tyron's had, but his freedom would be my demise. As much as I thought I would be, I wasn't prepared when I heard that he was found not guilty.

When my phone rang, I saw that it was Charletta and sent it straight to voicemail. She had been calling me all morning, but I didn't want to talk to her; I didn't want to talk to anyone. I knew my life was over.

Chapter Fifty-eight
Simone

"Simone, you really need to rethink this," Talise said pleadingly, following me into the bedroom of the hotel suite, but I wasn't trying to hear anything she had to say, or anything anyone had to say for that matter. All bets were off.

"Talise, I hear what you're saying, but you already know I'm not going to listen," I said as I began throwing my clothes in my bags, preparing to get the hell out of Vegas. I didn't care to ever see this city again.

"Please, Simone, this isn't going to end right! I can feel it!" She began crying as she sat on the edge of the large bed, watching me through tear filled eyes as I stormed through the room, gathering all of my belongings and tossing them into my suitcase.

"It already hasn't ended right, Talise!" I couldn't even look at her. She was not going to change my mind; no one could change my mind! "Stacey would want this—" I began before she cut me off.

"No he wouldn't! He would want you to go on with your life and to just move on!"

"You don't believe that, Talise! That's bullshit! We talked about this before. I agreed to let the justice system work and it didn't! Tyron was found not guilty, *not* innocent. He did that shit and we know it! I'm not about to let him go back to living his life like this shit never happened!"

"He has to live with this, Simone! He has to answer to God over what he did. That's bigger than anything you could ever do to him!"

"God is all in this, Talise, he sent us Ricky!"

I'll never forget the day that Talise called and told me that she'd received a reference call from QP Records for her old assistant, Ricky, who was trying to get a job there. Of course she gave him a good reference and then called him to see what type of job he was trying to get. By the time he called her back, he had already gotten the job and started working as an executive assistant for Tyron and Carlton. I couldn't believe my luck!

Talise gave me Ricky's number and I took him out to dinner to see if I could get him on my side.

"How close do you expect me to get to Tyron?" He asked.

"As close as two people can get," I replied seriously.

"But I don't think he's gay, Simone," Ricky said as he sat across the table from me at Katsuya sipping on a vodka and tonic. We had an assortment of sushi rolls, sashimi, and saki on the table and we were digging in. I was chewing on a baked crab roll, trying to decide how much information I wanted to give Ricky. I really needed him on my side.

"Tyron is gay, Ricky, trust me," I said, giving him a serious, raised eyebrows look.

"Simone, if you want me to risk messing up this

opportunity, you're going to have to tell me more than that," he said straight up.

I sat chewing on my baked crab roll for a moment as I contemplated how much I wanted to disclose.

"Ricky, what I'm about to tell you cannot be repeated. I repeat, you cannot tell anyone this shit, you hear me?" I asked, finishing off my crab roll before taking back a shot of saki. I could never be sure that he wouldn't repeat what I was about to tell him, but I needed some strong confirmation.

"Simone, I'm not into drama; I don't hang out with drama queens; I do me, plain and simple. You can trust me. If I can help you, I will. If I can't, I'll never repeat what we've talked about to anyone and I hope there will be no hard feelings," he stated sincerely as we stared into each other's eyes both feeling the other out.

"Tyron and Stacey were in an intimate relationship for a while," I finally confessed.

"Shut the front door!" He whisper yelled.

"Yes, they were. They were hanging tough right up until Stacey got killed... I don't want to tell you too much, Ricky. I just need you to trust me and help me out. I'll make it worth your while," I pleaded.

"Simone, like I told you before, you need to tell me everything that's going on. I can't be involved in this if I don't know everything. Even though Stacey and I didn't mess around for long, I really had a thing for him. He was a good guy. You have to trust that whatever you tell me won't go any further."

I sat back and drank another shot of saki, trying to decide whether to tell him everything or just enough. I needed Ricky. I didn't know exactly how yet, but I knew him working that closely with Tyron and Carlton would come in handy. I didn't really have much of a choice if I wanted him on my side, so I leaned in closely and told him about the video and Tyron being responsible for Stacey's murder.

"That son of a bitch! Are you serious, Simone?"

"I wish this shit was a joke, Ricky, I truly do," I sighed.

"So what do you want me to do?"

"I don't even really know yet, but having you working as closely as you do with them will most likely be beneficial at some point. I just don't know when or how." I admitted, taking back another shot of saki as I waited for Ricky to say something. I was hoping he'd agree soon or I was going to be drunk.

"So in the meantime, you want me to just go to work as normal, see how close I can get to Tryon and basically see if he will try to push up on me?"

"Exactly!" I said, wondering if Carlton would try to make a move on Ricky as well. It was definitely a possibility; shit he was gay too! "Just tell me how much you want and I'll give it to you, Ricky. I really need you," I said sincerely, hoping he would help me.

"I can't take your money, Simone. If Tyron did the shit you say he did to Stacey, it will be my pleasure to help you bring that scumbag down."

"Thank you so much, Ricky!" I said excitedly.

"So what's the game plan?" He asked, popping a spicy tuna roll into his mouth.

"Well, you just started working there, so don't do anything differently, just do you. I have a feeling that Tyron will make a move on you. Don't flirt or approach him in that way. Let him make his intentions known."

"So then what do you want me to do after he makes his intentions known?"

"Get as close to him as you are comfortable getting."

"Damn, I can't believe I didn't know he's gay!" he said again. "He's fine as hell!"

"Yeah, he's definitely gay and at one time, I thought he was gorgeous, but he's also dangerous. Watch your back, and whatever you do, don't get caught up in his shit, Ricky. He will throw money at you; he will buy you whatever you want, but he will also turn on you at the drop of dime. Don't ever forget that."

"Don't even worry about that. After the shit you just told me, I'm about to work his ass!" He said, reaching over the table to give me a high five.

Ricky and I spoke at least a couple of times a week since our first meeting. When he called to tell me that Carlton met with a private investigator, I knew it had something to do with me. Then when he told me that detectives had come to their office to talk to Tyron, I felt better, knowing that they were at least putting some pressure on him. When the arrest warrant for Tyron was finally issued, that's when I knew I'd need Ricky the most.

It hadn't been more than thirty-six hours since I'd received the call from the district attorney with the news that the Grand Jury handed down the indictment for first-degree murder against Tyron. I wasn't off the phone with the D.A. for more than a minute before Detective Jenkins called.

"Simone, are you sitting down?" He asked with excitement in his voice.

"Yes I am! I just got off the line with the D.A.! She just told

me!" I squealed as tears ran down my face.

"I just got off the phone with Stacey's mom and sister. The arrest warrant should be processed in a few hours."

"Thank you so much, Detective Jenkins. I really can't thank you enough for working so hard for Stacey."

"I don't like to see anyone get away with murder, especially bastards like him. It's going to be an uphill battle, though. I'm sure he's going to hire the best defense lawyer money can buy. But, the D.A. on this is a firecracker. If anyone can go toe to toe with one of those highfaluting lawyers, I know she can," he said optimistically. "In the meantime, we need to get this guy in cuffs."

"So what's the process? Is someone going to go pick him up?"

"The thing with people of his stature is there is no address on record. License and everything is addressed to an accountant or a lawyer, so we have no way to pick him up unless we catch him out. He had to give an address for his probation, but the man owns so many homes. Once the warrant hits the system, it will most likely get out to the media. Shit like that always seems to leak after a period of a few hours." He huffed. "Then he'll consult with his lawyer, fly here secretly on his private plane, sneak in the station, and turn himself in at midnight and probably be out on bail in less than forty-eight hours."

"What? Are you serious? This is murder!" My heart sank as he spoke those words.

"Yes, it's more likely than not, especially having deep pockets like this guy. Think about it. A million dollar bail is only one hundred thousand if he uses a bondsman. I'm sure that's chump change to him. He could probably pay the one million if he had to. He has no priors. He's pretty much

squeaky clean. He's a high profile guy…"

"Which means he has the means to run," I cut in.

"It also means he doesn't have the face to hide. He's a damned celebrity. It's not easy for someone with his notoriety to go on the lam. The judge will take that into account. Probably have him turn in his passport, but he'll grant bail."

Tears began to spill down my cheeks at this realization.

"Well there's nothing we can do about that, but I want him in cuffs in the back of a damn squad car! He shouldn't be able to just get his affairs in order then turn himself in!"

"Trust me, I'm with you on that, but it's out of my hands. If he lived here, he'd be mine! I'd pick him up personally, but unfortunately he doesn't."

"What if I can get him there?" I asked. I had no idea how I would do that, but I at least wanted the chance to try.

"Get him here and it will be my pleasure to take him into custody and make sure a few people are around to see it."

"Can you keep it from getting out for a few days? Can you give me that?"

"That's about all I'll be able to give you. I'll talk to the D.A. and hold off on processing that warrant to prevent any leaks. Let me know where you're at on things tomorrow."

After hanging up the phone with the Detective, I called Ricky and told him to meet me at my friend, Nicco's, immediately. When he arrived less than an hour later, we hatched the plan to get Tyron to Vegas. I knew having him on my side would come in handy.

The sun was beginning to set when the ringing of my phone jolted me away from my thoughts. It was the call I had been waiting for. No more than an hour had passed since Ricky informed me that they'd made it to Las Vegas Blvd. I called Detective Jenkins to let him know they'd made it to the strip, told him what kind of car they were in and waited for word of his arrest.

"Hello," I answered.

"It's done. Your boy should be getting comfortable in a cell right about now," Ricky said with a smile in his voice.

"Oh my God! We did it! You did it! Thank you so much, Ricky!" I hopped out of my bed and started jumping around, too excited to contain myself. "Are you okay? Where are you?"

"I'm drained, but okay. I just pulled off the strip; they let me keep his Bugatti," Ricky slightly chuckled. "I'm going to get a room and stay for a few nights. Hell, my birthday is tomorrow; I'll be damned if I'm not going to do something to celebrate it. I have a couple of friends out here anyway."

"Good for you. Go pick your friends up in that damn Bugatti and enjoy your birthday!" I laughed. "So tell me, what did he do when he realized he was going to be arrested, Ricky?" The relief I felt knowing that Tyron was sitting in a jail cell where he belonged felt better than I thought it would.

"You should have seen his face! When the detectives pulled up, his whole damned body started trembling. There were so many people standing around taking pictures and video of him being arrested. He was mortified. It will be all over the blogs by morning, trust that."

"Wow, Ricky, seriously, I can't thank you enough."

"The pleasure was all mine. Stacey deserves justice. I hope he gets it."

Chapter Fifty-nine
Deon

"Simone, I'm not leaving until you let me up or come down here and talk to me. I'll stand out here all damn night!" I said, looking into the camera as I stood at the entrance to her building knowing she was watching me. It had been over a month since I last saw her and enough was enough. I'd given her plenty of time to think this shit over and she was either going to forgive me or tell me to my face that she didn't want to be with me anymore. I wasn't letting this ride like I did last time. I wasn't going to just walk away.

I'd been standing there ringing her buzzer for at least five minutes after watching her pull into her garage with the security guys I was still paying for close behind. I'd given her enough time to get inside her place, put her bags down, and take off her shoes.

I pushed her buzzer again, leaving my finger pressed against the button longer than I had the first few times. As the sun began to set, causing the sky to turn a beautiful burnt orange, I pressed her buzzer again when the vibration from my phone averted my attention. I pulled it from my pocket, looked at the caller ID, and saw that it was my agent, Ron.

"Yeah, Ron," I answered.

"I've got some bad news." He sighed wearily.

"What bad news is it now?" I knew that it couldn't be anything wrong with my family because I would have heard from them before hearing from Ron, so I wondered what could be going on now. I knew I hadn't gotten anyone else pregnant.

"It's Nadia Sanchez..."

"What in the hell else could Nadia possibly want from me?" I asked cutting him off. She was already getting what she wanted. Money.

"She's dead, Deon..."

"What? What do you mean she's dead? Where is my daughter?" For the first time since finding out about my daughter, she was all I could think about and I immediately began praying that she was okay.

"She was in a car accident yesterday and passed away a few hours ago."

"My daughter is dead?" My heart began pounding rapidly at the thought.

"No sorry, that's not what I meant. Nadia is dead."

"Nadia is dead? Where is my daughter, Ron? Is she okay?" I asked, cutting in again. I wouldn't be able to live with myself if something had happened to her; to my child whose name I didn't even know, whose face I had never seen nor given a damn about until this moment. I was flooded with the shame I had successfully kept at bay.

"Your daughter is in intensive care. She's at Mattel

Children's Hospital. You need to get there immediately," he began with a heavy sigh then paused. "They don't know if she's going to make it, Deon."

"Where is Mattel Children's Hospital, Ron?" I asked, unable to move. It was as if my limbs were frozen in place.

"Right next to UCLA on Westwood Plaza not far from your place. ICU is on the fourth floor. I'll meet you there," he said before hanging up.

I stood there for another moment in shock before I ran to my truck, hopped in, started the engine and pulled out of the parking space, damn near hitting a car that was passing in the same direction. As I sped down the street toward the freeway, tears filled my eyes. All I could do was pray that my daughter would survive.

Chapter Sixty
Tyron

"*I* want you in my life." I stood in front of Ricky as he sat on the edge of my king sized bed giving me a hard time. After much coaxing, I was able to get him to the Malibu house so I could talk to him face to face.

"Tyron, I've moved on. You can't just cut me off for months and think that when it's convenient for you, you can just jump back into my life," he said calmly. He got up and stood in front of the open French doors that led to the backyard. The tide was beginning to come in and you could hear the waves crashing against the shore clearly. It had been a while since I'd spent the night here and I missed it. I just wanted to have a nice evening and make up for lost time. I wasn't feeling this arguing shit.

"You know the shit I was dealing with, Ricky. Come on man, cut me some slack. I just couldn't focus with that case on my back and I really couldn't have you around."

"Okay," he replied nonchalantly. "I understand that's what you had to do, but I'm not okay with that. I'm a grown man and I'm not with living my life in the dark. We had fun, but that's all it was, fun. Nothing serious and nothing to continue," he said, sounding like he really didn't give a shit.

"So you're saying you just don't give a shit about me, Ricky? Never have?" I asked incredulously, walking to him and standing in front of him daring him to lie and say that shit again. He couldn't even look me in my eyes and repeat that shit.

"Tyron..." He began, then paused like he was trying to filter what he was about to say. "We weren't in a relationship. We were fucking... in secret. That's not how I live my life, so I'd never fall for a man like you."

"You're full of fucking shit! You can't even look me in my eyes and tell me that!" He'd succeeded in pissing me off. I had never been rejected like this and I wasn't about to be rejected now. Especially on some bullshit! I knew he didn't mean this shit he was spouting.

"You knew from the beginning how I had to live my life and you chose to get involved with me. Now you are saying that you could never fall for me? Look me in my eyes and tell me you don't fucking love me! Look me in my eyes and tell me that you don't fucking miss me, Ricky!"

"For you to think that you can let almost a year go by without seeing me and barely speaking to me and just pick right up where we left off is nuts! If you thought I was going to be just sitting around waiting for you, you are sadly mistaken," he said, sounding much more resolved than he had before.

"Look me in my fucking eyes and tell me you don't love me anymore, Ricky. Tell me you don't miss me and I'll let you walk out that door and will never contact you again!" I challenged for a second time.

"I'd be a fool to be in love all by myself, Tyron," he sighed weakly, walking around me and taking a seat back on the bed. His words caused chills to run down my spine. Stacey had said the same thing in this same house. It was the day that I gave him the red Range Rover. I remembered that day clearly as tears began to fill my eyes at the thought of him.

"Yeah, you would be a fool to be in love by yourself, but you are no fool and you're not alone in this shit." I went to him and stood over his slim frame. "I do love you, Ricky, and this time away from you confirmed that shit for me. Stand up," I said firmly. He rose, standing directly in front of me. I wanted him to see the sincerity in my eyes. "I fucking love you man, and I don't want to be without you. Going through this trial shit... almost losing my freedom over something I didn't even do has really made me see shit differently. Don't give up on me, Ricky. Don't leave me like everyone else has."

When tears began to stream down his face, I could no longer hold mine in. I'd never in my life cried like this for a man, but my tears were sincere. The way I felt about this man was sincere.

"I don't know why after all this time, Tyron, but I love you too. I *still* love you." His admission couldn't have made me happier. I knew this was right, and vowed to do right by him no matter what.

Chapter Sixty-one
Simone

As Deon sat in the chair next to the hospital bed holding his daughter's tiny hand, his body was hunched over and his head was bent and resting on the bed as if he were in prayer. As I watched him through the ICU window, tears filled my eyes.

After hearing Deon's side of the conversation between him and Ron, I couldn't stop myself from coming here.

"I'm glad you're here," I heard a man say. I turned around and saw that Ron was standing behind me.

"How is she?" I asked in a low voice as he stood next to me.

"They have her in an induced coma. They performed emergency surgery this morning to reduce the swelling in her brain. Her skull was fractured in the accident," he said, shaking his head as we stood there looking through the window at her tiny frame lying on the bed. Her little head was wrapped in gauze and some type of soft tubing protruded from the top of the wrapping. A breathing tube was in her mouth, as she lay there wrapped in blankets looking so tiny and helpless.

"Is she going to be alright?"

"Time will tell. All we can do is wait, and pray that the swelling in her brain goes down. The next few days are critical."

"How did the accident happen?" I asked, knowing it must have been horrific to cause such damage.

"Someone clipped the back of Nadia's car trying to avoid another accident and her car rolled a few times."

"Where is Nadia's family?" I asked as Deon finally noticed us standing there. He was staring at me through the window like he thought what he was seeing wasn't real.

"I'll let Deon answer that," Ron said as Deon walked out of the hospital room. "I'll give you two some privacy. I'm going to head home. Deon, give me a call if you need me. Otherwise, let's talk in the morning," he said, hugging Deon and kissing me on the forehead before walking down the hall toward the elevators.

"Hey," Deon said as we stood there awkwardly.

"Hi... how are you?"

"I don't know," he replied, never taking his eyes off of mine. "How'd you know?"

"I heard you talking to, Ron... I was listening. I didn't want you to be alone," I admitted.

"Thank you," he said with a slight, sad smile. "This is crazy, huh?"

"Very."

We stood there looking through the window at his daughter for at least a few minutes in a comfortable silence before I spoke.

"What's her name?" I asked.

"Bailey. Bailey Deion Bradford. She's only seven months old," he said, shaking his head. "Did Ron tell you what happened?"

"Yeah he told me. I'm sorry, Deon."

"Yeah, me too. I don't know what I'm going to do if she doesn't make it, Simone. Hell, I don't know what I'm going to do if she does. She doesn't even know me and that's a damn shame," he said, looking at me with tears in his eyes.

"Well, she will get to you know, Deon. All that matters is that you are here now.

"Yeah I know. It's just hard to believe that I acted so silly and missed so much of her life. That's not the man I am, and I'm ashamed of myself," he sighed.

"Have you talked to your parents?"

"No, I haven't talked to anyone. I know I need to call them and I will. They need to know…"

"Where is Nadia's family? Why isn't anyone else here?" I wondered aloud.

"Nadia didn't have any family, Simone. When Bailey leaves here, she's coming home with me."

I was shocked and didn't know what to say, so I said nothing as we stood there in a long silence.

"I'm sorry about what I did, Simone," Deon said, looking down at me, his eyes boring into mine. "I just didn't know how to tell you. I never wanted to see you look at me the way you did that night when I *did* tell you. I *never* wanted to hurt you! I *never* wanted to see that disappointment in your eyes. I know I did the wrong thing, and as we grew closer and time went on, it got harder and harder for me to tell you because I didn't want to lose you. I love you, Simone, and if you let me, I will spend the rest of my life showing you just how much that statement is true. Let *me* show *you* what true love is, Simone. That's what *this* is, *true love!*" He said it so passionately that tears began to fall from my eyes and down my cheeks. "There isn't another man walking this earth that can love you like I do, that *loves* you like *I do,* Simone! Let me mend your heart, baby," Deon said, opening up his arms to me.

I walked into his embrace, wrapped my arms around his waist and held him with all of my might. All of the anger I'd felt toward him instantly dissipated as he pulled me tightly within his arms, kissing the top of my head and the side of my face. *This must be true love because I'd never felt anything like it or heard anything so beautiful.*

Chapter Sixty-two
C. Banks

"You need to get it together, Carlton! You're letting this shit take over your life! You've lost weight. You look a mess! I bet you haven't left this house or that couch in days. You're letting that bitch take your life away and she hasn't even released the damn video yet!" Charletta said loudly, standing over me as I lay sprawled out on the couch in the family room. She was right. I'd been on this couch for days, only getting up to piss. I wouldn't even answer her calls, so I shouldn't have been surprised that she'd hopped on a flight and flew out here to check on me.

"Char, go back to Jersey. I'm good," I said, straining my neck to look around her at the T.V. that she was standing in front of.

"I'm not leaving until you get your ass up off this couch and get your shit together! You fucking gave up?" she asked. "You just rolling over and letting this shit go down without a fight, Carlton?"

"There ain't shit I can do, Charletta!" I yelled, rising from the couch. "What the fuck can I do? She's holding my fate in her hands and all I can do is wait to see how this shit is going to play out!"

"Have you even talked to her to see where her head is at? This ain't even like you. You can't just give up on everything, on *us* like this!" She huffed, tears filling her eyes.

"I don't know what to do, Char!" I said, plopping back down on the couch. "I feel powerless. I don't know what else I can do..."

"You have to do something! You can't just roll over and leave this shit to chance. You need to go see her! You need to offer her more money! You need to do something!" She sat next to me and turned my head so that I was looking at her. "If you don't go see her, I will, and we both know how that turned out last time," she said softly, smiling at me. "Don't give up, Carlton. This shit ain't over til it's over. Call her, go see her, do whatever you have to do and make this shit go away."

Chapter Sixty-three
Deon

After I called my parents and told them that it was urgent and that they needed to get here immediately, they were on the next flight smoking after dropping Tyson off at his best friend's house next door. When my mother and father rushed into the hospital, I was relieved that they were there. They were confused as I ushered them into the private waiting room and explained to them what was going on from the beginning, when I met Nadia, to the end with Bailey laying in the hospital bed fighting for her life.

I never wanted to see the look that my parents gave me. They were very disappointed in me and I could see it clearly in their eyes. I deserved this; hell, I was disappointed in myself and planned to spend the rest of my life making it up to Bailey if God spared her life.

"Take me to my grandbaby, Deon," my mother said wiping tears from her face.

When we walked into the hospital room, my mother rushed to the hospital bed and took Bailey's hand in hers.

"Grammy is here baby. You keep fighting. You stay strong for us," she began before breaking down. I'd never seen my mother cry this way and it brought me to tears right along with her while my father stood at the foot of the bed silently wiping tears from his eyes. "She's just so tiny, Deon. And all banged up."

"I know, but she is getting better each day. The CAT scan results were good this morning. Doesn't look like there is any brain damage. The swelling in her brain has gone down significantly, so the doctors have already started to reduce the coma inducing meds. We're hoping the swelling continues to go down. It's all a waiting game."

"Well she is going to be just fine," my mom began, leaning in and kissing Bailey's face. "I already know that God won't take my first grandbaby, even though I'm just now finding out about her," my mother said, looking at me, disappointment written all over her face.

"I'm sorry, Mom, Dad. I truly am sorry. I can't even begin to express the shame I feel for not being a dad to her all this time."

"You *should* be ashamed, Deon," my father said. "But now isn't the time for all of that. God forgives you and we do too. Just be the man that we raised and be a father to your child from this point on, Deon. How she was conceived and how she got into this world means nothing. She is here now. She is ours, and she is a Bradford!"

Chapter Sixty-four
Tyron

When the alarm chirped as if someone was coming in my house, it woke me out of a deep sleep. I figured it had to be something faulty with the system or maybe I was just hearing shit, but felt the need to check to be sure.

I got up, leaving Ricky lying in bed undisturbed, and walked through the long hallway that displayed my platinum plaques to the front door to check the alarm. Seeing that it was still armed, I walked through the hall past the theatre room and headed up the stairs two at a time to the security room. Once there, I flipped the switch, powering on the six small T.V. monitors that were mounted flush with the wall. I watched Ricky for a few seconds as he slept, then turned my attention to the screen that showed the empty library, then panned to the theatre room, kitchen, living room, family room, the other six bedrooms, then finally the outside perimeter seeing nothing out of the ordinary; all was quiet.

"Damn, I must be hearing shit." I flipped the switch, turning off the monitors and left the room.

Once back in bed with Ricky, he sensed that I was there and scooted in closer to me draping his leg over mine.

"Where did you go?"

"I heard the alarm, but I think I was just..." The sound of a gun cocking made me freeze mid-sentence. Both Ricky and I were quiet for a few seconds before I heard and then felt multiple bullets sear their way through my flesh and into my body. The last thing I remember hearing was Ricky yelling, "No!"

Chapter Sixty-five
Simone

*I*t had been over a week and I still hadn't heard from Ricky. I'd left him several voicemails, but he hadn't returned any of my calls or replied to any of my text messages. I'd been spending most of my time at the hospital with Deon and his parents, keeping vigil by Bailey's bedside, so I hadn't had much time to really think too much into his silence until now. I had a feeling that he was probably back under Tyron's spell, so I moved forward with my plan without him.

After checking my bank account and confirming that the wire had been received, then checking the net to make sure the video had been released, I walked out of the house three million dollars richer and with no regrets. Tyron was finally going to feel my wrath. He may have gotten off legally, but there was no twelve-person jury or no fancy defense attorney to stop this conviction. I wasn't letting him off the hook.

I hopped in my truck, searched through my built-in iPod for Bilal and blasted one of Stacey's favorite songs, *Fast*

Lane, as I pulled out of the circular driveway of the large home with Ed and Marlo close behind.

When the music began to play, the base infused beat produced by Dr. Dre caused goose bumps to appear on my arms and a lump to form in my throat. This song brought back so many memories.

Heyyyyy there it goes again
Different face to the same old tragic end
Who's the blame if he never saw it comin'
Yet he heard the bullet hummin'
And he never thought of runnin'
It's too late for him now layin out on the ground sooo cold, soooo cold

I barely made it out of the driveway and down the street before having to pull over to the side of the road and park. The tears that began to pour from my eyes were blinding my vision. My heart ached as I sat there weeping, not able to prevent the image of Stacey's dead and cold body lying on the side of the road as Bilal's operatic voice spewed from my speakers.

I don't know how long I sat there crying, but by the time I got myself together enough to pull away from the curb and head back down the hilly street, *Soul Sista* was playing and tears continued to slide down my face. When I headed east on Sunset Blvd., the music stopped and the ringing of my cell blasted loudly through the speakers.

"You did it... how does it feel, Simone? Does this make you happy now? An eye for an eye, right?" he said admonishingly after I answered.

"I feel fine!" I replied, trying to hide the fact that I was crying. "An eye for an eye would mean he'd be dead, not just humiliated," I was surprised at how fast the video had gotten out and back to him.

"Simone, you are playing with fire! Is Ed and Marlo with you?" He asked, sounding alarmed.

"I couldn't shake them if I wanted to, Deon! Why do you sound so mad and surprised? I told you I was going to do this and that no one could change my mind!" Deon had tried to talk me out of releasing the video more than Talise had, but I wasn't trying to hear anything he had to say, just as I wasn't trying to hear anything Talise or anyone else had to say. With the not guilty verdict, my mind had been made up. I was releasing the video. Only death could have stopped me.

"When are you going to move on with your life, Simone?" he asked, not answering my question. "When are you going to leave this shit in your past and start living your life like Stacey would want you to do? Like we all want you to do, Simone?"

"Now, Deon!" I cried openly, unable to keep my voice from shaking. "I'm done! It's done! It's over now, okay?" I said, feeling the truth in those words lift the heavy burden that had been weighing me down for far too long.

"It's not over now, Simone. It's only beginning! Do you think they're just going to let you get away with this?" he asked, consternation thick in his voice. "Simone, meet me at my house now. Come straight here." There was silence on the line for a few beats before his voiced boomed through my speakers causing me to jump, "Do you hear me?" he asked, raising his voice at me like he had never done before.

"Yes. I'll be there in ten minutes." I clicked the off button on my steering wheel and Bilal's voice commenced the singing of *Soul Sista* as I headed south on Beverly Glen toward Wilshire Blvd.

Chapter Sixty-six
C. Banks

It was fucking strange that I hadn't heard from Tyron. The video was blowing up the net and was being talked about on almost every damn TV channel, and he hadn't called me once, flipping out like I knew he would... and should be! I'd never seen anything like this. The attention this shit was getting was on some O.J. Simpson shit for real. There were debates on *Headline News* with gay rights activists asking if this would be such a huge media sensation if it had been a man and woman caught on video having sex instead of two men. They thought not and I did too.

My phone had been ringing off the hook all morning and every time it did, I expected it to be Tyron, but none of the calls were. Something wasn't right. I could feel it in my gut. When my phone rang for what seemed like the hundredth time, I looked at the caller ID and immediately answered the call.

"Yo, have you heard from Tryon?" I asked.

"What in the fuck is going on, Banks?" Tomi asked. "I can't believe this shit! I thought he paid that bitch!"

"She reneged. Have you talked to Tryon, Tomi?" I asked again.

"No, I haven't heard from him in almost a week. I've been calling his phone all morning since this shit started. The media is camped outside the Ritz and the Malibu house..."

"I know, I've been watching," I said, cutting her off. "I noticed two of his cars at the Malibu house. Ricky's shit is parked out there too. Something ain't right, Tomi. I know me and dude been on the outs, but he would've called me."

"This shit is unreal, Banks! Who do you think that is on that video with him?"

I'd been sitting outside of Simone's building for less than an hour when I finally got the text from Marlo that they would be pulling up in five minutes. Having Marlo on Rob Maynard's payroll, therefore on my payroll, was priceless. He filled me in on everything that was going on with her, which was how I always knew where she was, what she was doing and who she was doing it with. She had no clue that I had infiltrated her security.

This was my last ditch effort, and I prayed she would listen and take my offer. I got out of my car and stood on the sidewalk so she could see me when she pulled up. She parked in front of her building when she saw me, got out of the car and didn't say a word as she walked up to me with Marlo and Ed and on her heels.

"Frisk him," she said to Marlo and Ed as they walked over to me.

"Are you serious, Simone? You still think I'd harm you?" I asked her, shaking my head in disbelief. I knew I looked a mess because this shit she was doing with the video was

taking me to the brink of insanity, but I could never hurt her. I'd already come to that conclusion and knew what had to be done if she released that video.

I spread my arms and allowed Ed to frisk me. When she was satisfied, she sent them back to the car and asked me what I wanted.

"So what happens now, Simone?"

"You know what happens now, Carlton. You already know; that's why you're here," she sighed. I could easily tell that she no longer cared about me from the look in her eyes. I knew at that moment that what we had was over and prayed that she would at least hear me out.

"I have one final proposition for you, Simone, will you hear me out?"

"There is nothing you can say to me that will change my mind, Carlton. I'm releasing that video."

"I know I can't change your mind about that and I know you don't give a shit about me, but if you release that video..." I stopped, trying to swallow the lump in my throat unsuccessfully. "If you release that video, you'll be responsible for leaving my kids fatherless, for leaving my mother without a son, her only child!" I finished with tears in my eyes that I refused to let fall.

"What? What are you saying, Carlton?" The look in her eyes told me that she knew exactly what I was saying.

"I can't live with that shit out there, Simone. It's not worth it. I can't see the look in my mother's eyes. I can't look at my kids, knowing they will be teased about that shit forever. It will be everywhere. I wouldn't be able to hide from that and I can't live with that, Simone. I know it's some punk shit, but I'd rather be dead," I admitted calmly. I had already made up my mind and knew that I wouldn't hesi-

tate to put the barrel of my nine-millimeter Beretta to my head and pull the trigger when the time came. I was resolved to end my life before I was humiliated in front of the world.

"That's really fucked up…"

"It's all fucked up, Simone. All this shit is fucked up, but would you really be willing to put me out there like this if that motherfucker hadn't killed Stacey? I know I hurt you! I know that shit fucked you up more than it fucked me up, knowing you saw it and know this shit about me! I can't change it… if I could, I'd give everything I have to change that shit. I truly would. I'm fucked up knowing I can never have you again. It fucks me up just seeing the look in your eyes when you look at me. It fucks me up knowing you are with that ball player cat and moving on, but I do want you to be happy, Simone! You deserve that shit… you always have and I always tried to make you happy and bring you happiness, but I turned your world upside down with this shit, I know it!" The tears that streamed down her face gave me my opening. "I don't think Tyron should get off again, you're right about that. What he did was fucked up and I know that, Simone. I'll give you three million dollars if you give me the video. I will release that shit for you, just let me blur myself out of it, Simone! Please!"

And with the video editing software on my Mac, I was able to do just that. I even lightened my skin tone making it look as if the person on the video with Tyron had light skin. There wasn't one mention of me being involved in this shit. I finally had my life back.

Chapter Sixty-seven
Deon

"This is never going to end, is it?" I asked as soon as Simone walked into my home. I had been impatiently waiting for her to get there since I had gotten off the phone with her.

"It was something I had to do, Deon. I've always told you that!" She huffed, sitting her handbag on the sofa and taking a seat next to it, placing her elbows on her knees and her face in her hands.

"What makes you think that those dudes won't come at you over this, Simone? Why can't you see the danger you're putting yourself in?" It was clear as day to me and I couldn't understand why it wasn't to her.

"Who knows what Tryon will try to do?" She began removing her hands from her face, rising from her seat and standing in front of me. "I really don't care, Deon! People need to know who he is! He sat in court and lied and denied that he even knew Stacey! He really got off easy, not having to spend the rest of his life in prison. This is justice for Stacey and I don't expect you to understand that..."

"What about C. Banks, Simone?" I asked, raising my voice, trying to get through to her even though it was already too late; the video had been released.

"I talked to Carlton, Deon! *He* leaked the video, I didn't..."

"What do you mean? Why would he put the video out, Simone? He's on that shit!"

"Have you even seen the video, Deon?"

"Hell no, and I don't' want to see that shit, Simone!"

"He was waiting outside of my house when I got home from the hospital a couple of days ago..."

"Why didn't you tell me?"

"I was going to tell you, Deon, but we haven't had any time alone. We've been in the hospital with your parents and there just wasn't an appropriate time. He offered to buy the video from me. He said *he'd* release it if I allowed him to blur himself out of it so he could protect his family, so I did. I don't regret it, Deon. I think I would have if I would've released it and people found out about him. His mother and kids don't deserve that. I'm not even sure he deserved that. I hated him for so long, for what he did to me, but I also love him for all of the things he did for me. He found my mother for me; I could never repay that! He showed me that I could really love someone. He opened me up and brought down walls that I thought were impenetrable! Carlton walked into my life at a time when I really needed someone like him. I *know* Carlton loved me... I can't hate him anymore, it was driving me crazy!" she said, trying to make me understand, not realizing that I already did. "He gave me a way out. I wanted Tyron to pay. I made Carlton pay enough with the threat of that damn video being released looming over his head for over a year. He gave me three million..."

"He gave you three million dollars, Simone?" I asked, cutting her off.

"Yes, but I don't want any of it! I'm giving one million to his mom so she can retire and one million to his sister so she can stop working as hard as she does and maybe start her fashion line like she's always wanted to do. I'm using the rest to start an LGBT outreach center in Stacey's name so kids can have a professional resource. A place to go for support so these kids can learn to accept who they are and not be ashamed of their sexuality! Maybe if Tyron had some place to go, he wouldn't be so fucked up, hiding who he really is! Hell, Carlton too! This 'down low' shit needs to stop!"

"That down low shit will probably never stop, Simone, but what you're going to do is great. I'll help you in any way that I can. I'm proud of you and I know Stacey is proud of you as well."

Chapter Sixty-eight
Simone

When the police entered Tyron's Malibu home seven days after the video had been released and found Tyron's and Ricky's decomposed bodies in bed together, the media went into a frenzy. Rumors of a double suicide was all over the news and blogs, but when the Medical Examiner confirmed that they had both died from multiple gunshot wounds and had been dead for at least five days before the bodies were found, the suicide theory died quickly.

Everyone was speculating as to the motive behind the double murder, and the news that they were found in bed together was as salacious as the video. The media attention was at a fever pitch, and it was nowhere near dying down. It wasn't more than two weeks after Tyron and Ricky were murdered, when Curse's body was discovered in the trunk of his car in one of the parking garages near the Los Angeles International Airport. He'd been dead for over two weeks before he was discovered with multiple gunshot wounds to the head.

I'd been interrogated numerous times and continued to tell them that I had nothing to do with these murders and knew absolutely nothing about them. Although I couldn't say that I was sad that Tyron and Curse were killed, I did feel bad that Ricky got caught up in this, and would always wonder if he'd still be alive had I not recruited him to get close to Tyron.

Before Curse's body was found, I would have bet everything I had that he was responsible for killing Tyron and Ricky. Tyron blamed Stacey's murder on him and I was sure that he didn't want to spend the rest of his life in prison, just as Tyron hadn't, but now I was as clueless as everyone else.

Once the detectives were able to confirm that I was at the hospital with Deon, his parents and countless nurses and doctors when the murders occurred, I was finally cleared and taken off the suspect list, and they focused their attention elsewhere.

I immediately hopped a flight to New York to surprise Stacey's mom and sister with the money. To see their faces when I handed them each certified checks for the staggering amount was something I'd never forget. I felt Stacey's presence all around me and knew that he was finally resting in peace.

From New York, I flew to Montego Bay, not wanting to see L.A. anytime soon. I was still in a bit of a haze, not knowing how to feel, now that the video had been released and Tyron wasn't alive to deal with the consequences. He would never see it. He would never feel the embarrassment or the humiliation of his secret life being exposed to the world like I was hoping. I doubted he was resting in peace though; how could he be after killing Stacey the way he did?

On my third day at the villa, I was finally winding down and able to fully relax as I lay on the living room sofa reading *The Midnight Hour* by Brenda Jackson. I could easily hear the waves crashing against the cliff below and the breeze that billowed through the open window was perfectly cool.

I was deep into the story when the doorbell rang. I could hear the housekeeper, Greta, making her way to the door as I turned the page and delved into the next chapter.

"Simone, someone ear ta see ya," Greta called out from the front door.

"Okay, I'll be right there, Greta." I finished the short paragraph, placed the bookmark between the pages and then sat the book on the coffee table before getting up and walking to the front of the house. "I got it Greta, thank you," I said.

When I got to the door, tears filled my eyes when I saw who was there; the friend I thought I'd never see again was standing within arm's reach with a big smile on his face.

"Aye gal, you gwon let me in or jist stand der wit ya mouf open?" Al laughed.

I rushed into his arms, giving him a big hug before I released him and punched him in the shoulder.

"Aye what's dat fa?" He laughed again.

"That's for leaving me and not telling me where you were going or contacting me... and to make sure I'm not dreaming!" I laughed. I couldn't believe that my friend was standing in front of me. After he deeded the building my salon was in to me and then disappeared without another word, I was certain he was dead. "I thought you were dead, Al!" I hugged him again and then pulled him into the house. "I can't believe you are really here! Where have you been?

Are you okay? How did you know where to find me?" Questions tumbled out of my mouth one after the other.

"Whoa whoa whoa. One question ata time, Monie," he laughed again. I didn't know whether to laugh with him or punch him again; I was so happy to see him.

"I'm sorry, I'm still in shock. Okay, I'll start with, how are you?" I said, sitting down next to him on the sofa I had been lying on. I pulled my feet onto the couch and turned so I would be facing him fully.

"I'm good dahlin! Eryting jes fine wit me. I'm happy ta see ya, Monie," he said, patting me on my knee.

"I'm happy to see you too! Where have you been? How did you know I was here?"

"I been ear an der, ya know me had to get away from da states, but eryting is good nah."

"How did you know I was here?" I asked again.

"You tink you can come ear and me not know it? Me always know where ya are. Me knew when ya was ear last time wit ya boifrin," he teased.

"Well why didn't you come see me then?" I asked, swatting him on the arm and remembering the horrible nightmare I had when I was here last. Seeing his face would have really eased my mind.

"Ya wa nevah alone, Simone. Me doan wanna make ya boifrin jealis..."

"Oh whatever! You could have come; Deon isn't the jealous type!" I laughed, cutting him off.

Al stayed with me for the rest of the day, leaving late into the night. We ate lunch and later dinner as we sat and caught up with each other. It was just like old times.

After hugging and saying goodbye to Al, I stood outside his car door after he had gotten in. He started the car and rolled down the window. "Ya make sure ya call me. Me come back an see ya before ya leave ear?"

"Okay, I will," I said, smiling before turning and walking back to the front door.

"Aye, Simone," Al called out to me. When I turned back around and he was sure that he had my attention, he told me something I could never forget or tell another soul. "Me took care ah dem fah ya. Da batty boy, him driver... him boifrin jus so happen ta be der. Casualties ah war. Jes so ya know," he said and backed out of the driveway as I stood there staring after him with my mouth hung open in disbelief. *I wished he would have just kept that shit to himself,* I thought as I walked back into the house knowing I inadvertently had Ricky's blood on my hands.

Epilogue

One Year Later

The genuine happiness Simone felt at this moment made her realize that she had never truly been happy before.

When Sade's sultry voice gave her the cue, she began her walk down the aisle as *Couldn't Love You More* spewed crisply from the speakers.

> I couldn't love you more
> If time was running out
> Couldn't love you more
> Oh right now baby

Simone continued slowly down the aisle toward Deon, willing herself not to cry to the beautiful music and the sight of him waiting for her to reach him. Neither of them could believe that this day had finally come and that in less than an hour, they would be husband and wife.

> If everyone in the world
> Could give me what I wanted
> I wouldn't want for more than I have
> I couldn't love you more if I tried

The Jamaican sun was beginning to set and the ocean breeze was the perfect temperature for her strapless, fitted, pale yellow, satin and lace floor length gown that covered her bare feet. Her hair was pulled back into a tight chignon, held together with beautiful diamond, floral headpins that were borrowed from Deon's mother.

Simone looked to the left front row and smiled at her mother, feeling so thankful to have her in her life. Darlene beamed with happiness as she wiped tears from her face, giving Simone an encouraging smile. The sight of her beautiful daughter taking this huge step couldn't have made her more proud. She knew that Simone allowing her to be a part of her life was the greatest blessing from God. Simone then looked to the Miles' who sat next to her mother and grinned as Mr. Miles gave her a wink and Mrs. Miles blew her a kiss. She then looked at Talise, who was the only woman standing next to the altar as her maid of honor. Tears were in her eyes and a beautiful smile was spread across her face as Simone made her way to Deon as Darryl Withers stood to the right of him as his best man.

It's taking forever for her to reach me, Deon thought, when Bailey jumped off of Deon's mother's lap and ran to him, calling out for her daddy. She wrapped her little hands around his leg and said, "Up daddy!" Waiving his mother off, Deon lifted Bailey into his arms with a laugh and together they watched Simone continue toward them, finally reaching the altar as the music faded. Bailey wrapped her arms around Simone's neck, wanting to be held by the woman she called mommy. Simone took her into her arms and kissed her face, making Bailey giggle.

"Go sit down with Grammy, okay Bailey?" Deon lifted Bailey from Simone's arms, planted a kiss on her chubby cheek, and put her down, watching her as she ran back to his parents.

Refocusing his attention on his soon to be wife, he took Simone's hands in his, told her that she looked beautiful, and couldn't stop himself from planting a kiss on her lips.

"Hey, hey, hey, I haven't said you may kiss your bride yet, Deon," The pastor teased, causing everyone to chuckle. "I'll hurry and get started so you can officially kiss your bride," he smiled. "We are gathered here today to unite this beautiful couple in holy matrimony. First, let us thank God for this union that is about to occur here today between Deon Jushon Bradford and Simone Marie Johnson. For, without our heavenly father, we know that their paths would have never crossed and we thank you for that, Lord. We thank you for blessing this couple with a love that has truly been ordained by you, and because of that, this love will continue to grow, day after day, week after week, month after month, and year after year.

"Marriage is one of the greatest, as well as one of the most challenging things we will ever do in life, but how great and how challenging is truly up to the both of you. No ceremony can create your marriage union. Only the two of you can do that—through love, understanding, patience, perseverance, communication, love, communication, love, communication..." he said repeatedly with a smile on his face, making everyone laugh again. "What this ceremony *can* do is witness and confirm the decision that the two of you have made to become life partners and to stand together through thick and thin. And now for your vows. Deon, you may begin."

"From the first time I laid eyes on you, Simone, something inside of me shifted," Deon began, holding tightly to Simone's hands and looking intently into her eyes. He was doing his best to keep his emotions in check, but the overwhelming love that he felt for her had him awestruck. He never knew that he could love someone this completely. "I didn't know what it was at first, but every time I saw you, I was pulled toward you. There was something that kept me moving in your direction. I had no power over it; it was much bigger than me. Now, after everything that we have been through, for us to be standing here today, you taking me as your husband, me taking you as my wife, my best friend, my partner and the woman I promise to love forever, I know what that shift and that pull was. It was God telling me that you are the woman that I was born to be with. The woman that I was created for. I'm here on this earth for you, and you for me, and I will do everything in my power to live up to this birth right, this blessing, *this* honor.

"I promise to always put you first and uplift you. To keep this glow in your eyes and this smile on your face will be my number one priority. If I succeed in that, I know all will be right in my world. I vow to always honor you, to *always* respect you, to always listen and be *honest* with you. I vow to challenge you and accept challenges from you. Above all, I vow to love you in mind, body and spirit until the day that I die. I couldn't love you more, Simone," Deon concluded, lifting Simone's hands to his mouth and placing kisses on them as the tears she tried in vain to hold in, dripped from her eyes.

"Deon, no man has ever loved me as purely and unconditionally as you have. And I have never loved a man as I love you, purely and unconditionally. At first, I didn't think I deserved someone as good as you. I didn't think I deserved to be loved the way you love me. I pushed you away so many times, but God always brought you back to me and I am eternally grateful," Simone said as more tears streamed down her face at the honesty of the words that were coming from her mouth. Deon squeezed her hands in his, encouraging her to continue as he stared into her eyes, feeling grateful to be standing there exchanging vows with the woman he has loved for so long. "*I know without a doubt that I deserve you!*" The passion and sincerity in her voice sent chills through Deon's entire body. "Some spend their whole lives searching for their soul mate and I am thankful that I am one of the lucky ones, because my soul mate, my *one* true love, is standing right here in front of me. I respect you, I honor you and I promise that I always will. I vow to uplift you, to be there for you through sickness and in health. I vow to always stand by your side, no matter what obstacles come our way. I will walk to the end of this earth for you, Deon. I couldn't love *you* more," Simone concluded as Deon released her hands and wiped tears from his eyes before taking her hands in his again.

After Deon and Simone recited their vows, the ceremony progressed rather quickly. They placed rings on each other's fingers, were pronounced husband and wife, and Deon was told that he could officially kiss his bride, and he did. For the first time as husband and wife, they kissed like they weren't standing in front of a hundred of their closest friends and family members.

An expansive white tent was constructed on the large grassy yard in the back of Deon's Montego Bay villa. As they waited at the entrance of the tent for the DJ to announce them, Deon proudly held Simone in his arms and kissed her glowing face. He loved to see this sparkle in her eyes and knew that she was now truly happy.

"I have a surprise for you," Deon said as he pulled her closer to him.

"What is it?" Simone asked excitedly, reaching up and planting a long, soft, sensual kiss on Deon's full lips.

"It wouldn't be a surprise if I told you," he laughed as the DJ's voice boomed out of the tent.

"And now, I present to you, for the first time, Mr. and Mrs. Deon Bradford!"

Deon and Simone walked into the tent holding hands, smiling, and waving at their friends and family as they made their way to the middle of the dance floor for their first dance. When John Legend's "So High" spewed from the speakers, Deon took Simone in his arms, pulled her close to him, and whispered in her ear. "I dedicate this song to you. Every single word of this song is exactly how I feel about you. I love you, Simone," he said as they commenced a slow sway to the beautiful piano chords. When Simone heard the soft humming that opened the song and a voice say over the mic, "Congratulations Deon and Simone. I wish you an eternity of happiness." She looked to the stage and saw John Legend sitting behind the piano. Before the shock of having him singing live at her wedding could even register, he began the first verse.

Baby since the day you came into my life
You made me realize that we were born to fly
You showed me every day new possibilities
You proved my fantasy of what love could really be
Let's go, to a place only lovers go
To a spot that we've never known
To the top of the clouds we're floating away
Oh this feel so crazy, oh this love is blazing
Baby we're so high, walking on cloud 9

Deon knew that John Legend was one of Simone's favorites; there wasn't a price he wouldn't have paid to get him there. His voice sounded exactly like the record, and just by looking at Simone, he could easily tell that she was mesmerized by it. No one could wipe the smile off of her face or erase the sheer pride that Deon felt, knowing that he was going to spend the rest of his life with this woman; spend the rest of his life doing everything in his power to make her happy.

"I love you, Deon. Today you've made me happier than I ever thought I could be," Simone grinned as he spun her around showing off his smooth dance skills.

"It's only just begun. You haven't seen nothing yet, Mrs. Bradford."

~ ~ ~ ~ ~ ~

After getting settled on the sofa of the private jet, Deon pulled Simone onto of his lap.

"This has been an amazing year. I got you, a daughter, *and* a championship ring!" Deon smiled.

"You deserve all of that and more. I love you, baby," Simone said planting light, soft kisses on his lips.

"I love you more, Mrs. Bradford," Deon said, wrapping his arms around her waist. "Damn, you're my wife!" he said in awe. He took her warm, soft tongue into his mouth and pulled her closer to him.

The fact that they would be flying for the next fifteen hours before landing at Nadi International Airport in Fiji didn't bother either of them. The Gulfstream G650 private jet was the epitome of luxury and opulence; it had everything one could need. After the ball, they'd had at their wedding reception—dancing, drinking and eating until well after 1 a.m., prior to leaving their guests to change into something more comfortable before heading to the airport to make their 3 a.m. chartered flight. They both knew that the majority of their time on the aircraft would be spent in the comfort of the bedroom. They couldn't wait to explore each other's bodies now that they were husband and wife. Their decision to wait until marriage before having sex again had proven difficult for both of them.

When the stewardess knocked twice on the door before walking into the main cabin, Simone released her mouth from Deon's and smiled at the pretty older woman as she wrapped her arms tighter around Deon's neck. The stewardess carried a tray that held a silver ice bucket with a bottle of champagne resting inside of it, two champagne flutes, and a platter of sliced kiwi and strawberries.

"Don't you newlyweds stop for me. Just pretend I'm not here," she teased with a wink.

She sat the tray on the polished wood table across from them and began pouring champagne into the glasses. "Here you are Mr. and Mrs. Bradford." She sat the crystal flutes, the platter of fruit and the bucket that held the champagne on the table and picked up the silver tray before moving toward the cabin door to make her exit. "Just ring me if you need anything. I'll leave you two alone." Before she could get out of the cabin and close the door, Simone's lips were back on Deon's. Neither of them gave a second thought to the champagne or the fruit.

Deon rose with Simone still in his arms and carried her to the back of the jet where the large bedroom and king sized bed beckoned. He gently laid her on the luxurious bedding and lowered himself on top of her, knowing that she could already feel the hardness in his pants. He was ready for her, and had been since she'd come back into his life. They were both burning with desire and were intent on connecting in a way that only a man and woman who understood and loved each other as much as they did could.

Deon slowly unfastened the small round buttons that held the silk Maxi dress Simone wore together. He pulled each spaghetti strap over her shoulders before sliding the dress from underneath her and letting it drop to the floor. His breath caught at the sight of what had been hidden beneath the pretty dress. He took a moment to savor the woman that lay before him in the strapless, lace, aqua blue negligee. He'd never seen anything or anyone more beautiful.

"*Damn*! You are all mine. All mine, Simone, forever."

As he pulled his shirt over his head, dropping it to the floor alongside her dress, he began having second thoughts.

He wondered if she was afraid to have unprotected sex with him for fear of being infected as he had been. He didn't currently have an outbreak and hadn't since that first time many years ago, but there were risks; there would always be risks and he needed to know that she was okay taking that risk. He'd brought condoms just in case, but even those weren't fool proof.

"Simone, are you okay with doing this?" Deon asked as he stood over her, shirtless with his linen, drawstring pants hanging low on his hips, accentuating his chiseled stomach. His body looked as if it were sculpted by the Gods. Everything about him turned Simone on.

"Am I okay with what, Deon?" she asked, sitting upright on the bed confused by his question.

"I brought condoms..." he began before Simone cut him off.

"Deon, come here," she said lowly, patting the bed with the palm of her hand. "I agreed to marry you knowing the risks that would be involved when we are intimate," she began after he'd taken a seat next to her. "The time we were apart after you told me was spent doing a lot of research, soul searching and praying. Chances are I can get it, and chances are that I may not get it, but you know what, Deon?" Simone asked, scooting in closer to him, gently taking his face into the palms of her hands. "I can't imagine my life without you. So if contracting this disease is the worst burden I am faced with throughout our marriage, I'm still a lucky woman." She straddled him and wrapped her arms around his neck. Staring into his eyes, she said, "I *want* all of you. I want to *feel* all of you. Flesh to flesh. I don't want *anything* between us." Deon was speechless as he continued to stare into Simone's eyes.

His wife was truly amazing, he thought as he wrapped his arms tighter around her waist, pulling her closer to him so that their faces were mere inches apart.

"I love you so much, Simone. I hope you never get tired of hearing me say that because I will never stop telling you how much I love you." Simone could feel Deon's breath on her face from his whispered words.

"I love you more."

"Impossible," Deon countered, placing his lips on hers, kissing her with so much fervor and passion Simone shivered from the sensation of his tongue exploring her mouth and teasingly caressing the roof it.

Deon lifted Simone from his lap and placed her flat on the bed, positioning himself on top of her. His large hands slid up the outer parts of her long, soft legs, causing goose bumps to surface from his gentle touch. Simone wrapped her legs around him, feeling his erection through the thin fabric of the lingerie she wore and the linen pants and boxer briefs that covered him. Grinding her hips into his, she sucked on his tongue as Deon cupped her breasts in his hands, rubbing the palm of them back and forth over her stiff nipples, causing a moan of pleasure to release from Simone's mouth. He lowered the lacy fabric that covered her breasts, freeing them so he could have a better vantage point. Immediately lapping his tongue across her hardened nipples, he alternated between the two; taking his time sucking one while teasing the other with his thumb and middle finger, making Simone even hotter and anxious than she had been only moments ago.

Raking her fingers up and down his muscled back, her breath caught when she felt his hand moving up her inner thigh. The anticipation of the pleasure that was sure to come when his hand reached its destination made Simone huskily call out Deon's name. When his hand softly touched her middle, her back arched involuntarily from the sensation. He caressed her slowly over the thin fabric of the negligee, feeling the extreme wetness seeping through and onto his fingers. He brought them to her breasts and covered each nipple with her juices before slowly licking it off. Simone thought she would come purely from the sight and feel of what he was now doing to her.

"Mmmm, baby. I will never get enough of you," Deon said gruffly as he lifted himself from atop Simone.

He stood at the edge of the bed, removing his pants as Simone lay before him watching him with a smile on her face. With only his black, silk boxer briefs containing his hardness, Simone extended her leg and ran the ball of her foot from his chest down to his large dick and began massaging it through the silk fabric. Placing her other leg on his chest, Deon took hold of it and brought her foot to his mouth. He softly kissed and licked the ball of her foot, causing her to giggle from the tickle as she continued to rub him with her other foot. He then kissed each toe before taking the biggest into his mouth, running his tongue over and around it slowly as he softly sucked on it.

"You are driving me crazy, Deon!" Simone whispered hoarsely.

"I'm just getting started, Simone."

Deon placed her feet back on the bed, positioned them so that her knees were bent and spread apart, and leaned in and ran his tongue down her inner thigh, stopping just before reaching the spot that he knew eagerly awaited his touch. He slowly licked the lace between her thighs and reveled at how drenched she was. He knew that once he removed the sexy piece of clothing that covered her, she'd be oozing with a wetness that he couldn't wait to sink his thickness into.

He slid the material to the side, exposing all of her, and took her clitoris into his mouth, savoring her flavor. Sucking on it softly, he swept his tongue back and forth, circling her pulsing button ravenously. Simone's moans were the best melody he'd ever heard, he thought as he continued licking, sucking, stimulating and worshiping her.

Simone gasped with pleasure when Deon inserted a finger inside of her and began slowly moving it in and out of her wetness as he kept his mouth clasped on her clitoris licking and sucking it simultaneously. The intense euphoria that snaked its way from the bottoms of Simone's feet and slowly up her body made her spasm uncontrollably with ecstasy as a low yell escaped her mouth.

"Oh yes, Deon! Oh my goodness..." Simone's words caught in her throat as she desperately clutched Deon's head with her hands.

She rolled her hips, wanting to feel his finger deep inside of her as a second orgasm engulfed her. It was truly like nothing she'd ever felt. Her body continued to quiver when Deon rose from between her legs and removed their remaining undergarments. Simone sat up and took his thickness in her hand. She stroked it, enamored with its smooth, long hardness. Every inch of Deon was flawless and the perfect size. She took him into her mouth salivating from the taste of him. She loved the feel of his skin on her tongue, caressing her lips as she brought him in and out of her mouth, doing her best to take in all of him without gagging.

"Oh, Simone, just like that, baby, yes, just like that,"

Deon sighed, holding Simone's head gently as it bobbed back and forth, making his large dick disappear into her mouth and reappear again. "I need to be inside of you right now, Simone. I can't wait any longer... right now!" He repeated, guiding her back and positioning himself between her legs.

"I can't wait to feel you inside of me, Deon," Simone whispered, wrapping her arms around his neck and pulling him in for a kiss.

Their tongues dueled for a few beats before she felt him slowly entering her, his hardness probing further and further until he was completely immersed inside of her. Sighs released from them simultaneously, but their mouths stayed connected as their bodies moved together as one.

"You feel so good, baby. You're so damn wet and hot. *Shit*, Simone!"

Deon cupped her breast in his hand and continued to immerse himself inside of her moving slowly and methodically, doing his best to keep his composure. He had to concentrate so he wouldn't come until he was ready. It had been a while for him, and Simone's tight, velvety softness was saturating his dick and driving him over the edge.

The feeling of Deon inside of her, caressing her from within was making Simone hunger for more and more of him. She could feel her juices on the bedding beneath them as she gyrated her hips, meeting him stroke for stroke, clenching his hardness every time Deon slid inside of her. With their bodies joined in the most intimate way possible, their hot, sweat moistened skin meshed together as he lay atop her, careful not to put too much of his weight on her. Running his tongue across her ear lobe, taking it into his mouth and nibbling it, he could feel the shiver coursing its way through her body. When Simone clutched him inside of her and clasped her legs tightly around him, her body convulsed with spasms of pure bliss as Deon increased his speed, releasing in her only moments later.

As they knew they would, Simone and Deon spent the rest of the flight in bed making love, and the majority of their honeymoon exploring each other's bodies. They couldn't get enough of each other and wouldn't anytime soon.

~ ~ ~ ~ ~ ~

C. Banks threw the *People* magazine to the polished hard wood, got up and stood at the floor to ceiling windows in his office. The cover photo of Simone looking so beautiful in her yellow wedding gown standing next to Deon Bradford was more than he could bear.

"She's married," he whispered, looking out at the city lights of Hollywood. "She fucking married that cat!" He said again in disbelief.

"Huh? Who're you talking to, Carlton?" Charletta asked walking into his office right in time for them to make their 7 p.m. dinner reservations.

He tried to swallow the lump that had formed in his throat and gather his composure before turning to face Charletta. She would know that something was seriously bothering him. It was like she could read his mind, and the last thing he wanted her to know was how much he still loved Simone. He figured he always would, since almost two years had passed since he'd last been with her, yet there wasn't a day that went by that he didn't think of her. The price he was paying for sleeping with Tyron was huge. It cost him the woman who really made his life complete. Simone made everything seem right in C. Banks' life, and after all of this time, he was still trying to figure out how to live life without her.

"Just talking to myself. You ready?" He asked, finally facing her. He didn't know that she had already noticed the *People* magazine on the floor and had discreetly lifted it to see if it was the issue she thought it was. She'd seen the cover photo earlier that day and wondered how Carlton would feel once he saw it. He claimed that he no longer loved Simone, that he no longer desired her, but the way he was acting right now proved otherwise.

"Yes, I'm ready." Charletta was trying her best not to let C. Banks see the tears that had formed in her eyes.

The realization that the man she loved with all her heart was still in love with another woman was a pill that was getting harder and harder for her to swallow. She couldn't understand why he still loved Simone. *What does she have that I don't have?* She wanted to ask him that every time he got that faraway look in his eyes, but she knew he would continue to deny that his love for Simone remained. C. Banks would never admit to still loving the woman he was going to divorce Charletta for. The woman who almost ruined their lives with that video. Yes, he would never admit that, and Charletta wouldn't bring it up either. Now that Simone's last name was Bradford, she felt a sense of relief, knowing that she was now married... taken by a man that seemed to really love her. All Charletta could do was hope that one day Carlton would love her as much as he loved Simone, and she hoped that day would come soon. She wasn't sure how much longer she could allow Simone to hold her husband's heart.

~ ~ ~ ~ ~ ~

When Bailey ran up to Simone and jumped onto her lap, Simone wrapped her in her arms, squeezed her tightly, and planted kisses all over her chubby face.

"Get down, mommy," Bailey laughed, wiggling out of Simone's grasp and running off with Anastasia.

The July sun was shining bright, and it was a warm eighty-five degrees as Simone and Talise sat under the large awning in the backyard of Simone's and Deon's Calabasas home while Anastasia and Bailey played on the large, wooden jungle gym. Simone's mother was keeping a close eye on the two as she sat in the sand, watching the girls play.

"I love seeing you with her, Simone," Talise smiled, taking a sip of ice tea. She was so overjoyed by the obvious changes that had taken place in Simone's life. She'd been so worried about her best friend after Tyron's acquittal. She thanked God that chapter of their lives was over and was even more thankful that Simone had moved on with her life and had a wonderful man who loved her like she deserved to be loved.

"I can't believe how much I love that little girl, Talise. I really can't imagine my life without her." Simone smiled, looking at Bailey as she slid down the slide, landing in Darlene's arms.

"Now you know how I feel!" Talise laughed.

"Yes I do," Simone laughed, looking at the girls playing in the sand.

"I'm really looking forward to the opening of the outreach center next month. This place is going to help so many teens."

"I am too, Talise. We found the best director and staff.

It's amazing how it's all come together. Stacey would be so happy," Simone smiled.

"Stacey *is* so happy," Talise countered as Deon and Malachi walked out of the large French doors of the massive house.

"We're about to head out," Deon said, leaning over and placing a long, soft kiss on Simone's lips as Malachi stood behind Talise rubbing her shoulders affectionately.

"Have fun at the boring baseball game," Simone teased. The last thing Talise and Simone wanted to do was go to a baseball game.

"It's the Dodgers and the Yankees! You two don't know what you're about to miss!" Malachi laughed.

"Yes we do! A long boring baseball game, as Simone said," Talise chuckled as Bailey and Anastasia ran over.

"You want to go to the baseball game with your daddies, baby girls?" Deon jokingly asked Bailey and Anastasia, picking them up and spinning them around, making them giggle loudly before placing them back on their feet. They all laughed at the girls as they wobbled around dizzily.

"You guys aren't planning to watch the game if you're taking those two," Simone laughed, taking a sip of her lemonade.

She loved to see Deon interact with the girls. He was such a wonderful father and Godfather, that the thought of bringing another child into their fold warmed her heart, but neither of them were in a rush for Simone to get pregnant. They were enjoying Bailey immensely and had easily adjusted to being parents of one.

"Mom, mom!" Bailey squealed when Darlene walked over to the bunch, her face beaming with the love she felt for her first and only grand baby.

"I'll take them in and get some food in these little munchkins," Darlene said, taking hold of the little girl's hands after Deon planted a big kiss on her cheek.

"Thanks mom, mom," Deon smiled. He had taken to calling Darlene Bailey's version of grand mom and every time he did, it tickled Darlene so. She thanked God multiple times a day for Simone, her new son and grandbaby *and* for her new life. After the death of Dean, the man she'd spent so many loving years with, she never imagined that life could feel this complete.

"We better get going if we plan to make opening pitch," Malachi said, leaning in and kissing Talise on the neck.

"Have fun guys. Remember our dinner reservations are for seven this evening," Simone reminded.

"Yeah, and if you guys aren't back on time you'll be meeting us there," Talise joked. "We'll be good and hungry come seven."

"We'll be back on time, Mrs. Edmonds," Deon laughed as he and Malachi left the two best friends by themselves. This would be the first chance they had to catch up since Simone and Deon's return from Fiji.

"How does it feel to be a married woman, Mrs. Bradford?" Talise asked with a smile on her face.

"Girl, I can't imagine *not* being that man's wife."

"Well if you would've listened to me and Stacey a long time ago, you two could be on your second or third anniversary," Talise joked. "I'm just kidding. I know things happen in God's time, not ours."

"Exactly," Simone laughed. "Plus, we probably wouldn't have Bailey had Deon and I stayed together. I can't imagine not having her in my life."

"I can't imagine it either, Simone. You've adjusted to

being a mom much faster than I thought you would." They laughed.

"Hell, much faster than I thought I would too!" They giggled, enjoying the time they were spending with each other. "You know, Talise," Simone began, her face now serious. "Having Bailey in my life really makes it hard to understand how Marie treated me the way she did. When my dad took me from my mom, I was only a couple of months old. I've only had Bailey since she was eight months and I love that little girl so much. Marie had me all that time. She watched me grow up, and just couldn't love me," Simone said, smiling sadly.

"Like Marie explained, Simone, she wasn't capable of loving anyone. She didn't even love herself."

"I know, Talise. I'm not angry anymore and I forgave her, it's just something I think about from time to time. It's just sad... I'll never be a mom like her."

"You've already proven that, Simone, and I'm so proud of how far you've come and how much you've grown. It's been a long, hard road for you and I'm so glad you made it through all of that!" Talise's eyes began to tear as she looked across the table at her friend. "I really am, Simone. There were times when... I didn't know how all of this was going to end for you."

"I know, Talise, and I'm so sorry for putting you through so much drama. I don't know what I'd do if I didn't have you in my life," Simone said, reaching across the table to grab Talise's hand. "Thank you for always being here for me..." Simone paused, not wanting to shed one tear; she'd cried enough for one lifetime. "Since we were kids you have been here for me, and I'm *so* grateful! You were my friend and loved me no matter how crazy I was or how crazy I acted. Sometimes it's hard to believe that not too long ago I tried to kill myself. I was so ready to just give it all up, not knowing that something as beautiful as this was in my future. I thought I wanted my life to end after Stacey and Carlton and all that crap, but I really just wanted the pain to end... you know what the craziest thing is, Talise?" Simone asked rhetorically after a few beats. "I'd go through all of it again, now that I know that this is the outcome. That the way I was living before wasn't the way my life was supposed to be. *This* is my destiny, *this* is life!

Author's Note

Thank you all for your support!

Please be sure to leave a review &/or contact me with feedback. I love hearing from you all!

Be on the lookout for my next novel The Great Pretender starring Tomi Jordan, c. Banks & Charletta!

Shakara

Made in the USA
San Bernardino, CA
28 November 2013